The Guardians

Meleana Smith

ISBN 10: 0615804438
ISBN 13: 9780615804439
Library of Congress Control Number: 2013920936
CreateSpace Independent Publishing Platform
North Charleston, South Carolina

To my family, Scott, and Jason,
For their love and support that helped me through this
To my friends,
Meg, Amber, and Heather
And in memory of Jessie B.,
For the inspiration that was given to me

I

Just Another Morning

"It's another beautiful day…," the radio blared.

"Followed by a crash," I said with a smile, as the alarm clock hit the floor. I snuggled back into the warm down comforter, letting it engulf me. Then I heard the all-too-familiar sound of my doorknob being turned and the door opening slowly. A smile crept across my face, which I tried to hide under the corner of my blanket. It was Nan, and she knew how to get any teenager out of bed. I listened as she carefully stepped across my room toward the window to open the curtains. I braced myself for the light to hit my eyelids.

"Miss Serina, I know you are awake. You'll be late for school," Nan said trying to hide her Spanish accent.

Nan is short for Nanny, and that is what I have always called her since I was little. I never thought any less of her, and at times I loved her more than my own mother. I slowly lifted my head and sat up in bed. Nan came over and pushed my long black hair out of my face.

"Nan, what if I told you that I did not feel good?" I asked, trying to avoid going to school for the day. It was Friday, and that meant having to wear the cheerleading uniform and putting my hair up. I sighed, thinking of all the things I needed to do. Maybe if I used the excuse that I didn't feel good I would be able to stay home from all of it.

"Then I tell your father you not feel good," Nan said with a smile. Nan always played the daddy card. She knew that I would have no choice but to give in when it came to my dad. He was never mean to me, just stern, and he was usually away on business. However, if Nan had to call my dad while he was away, then I knew that he would just ground me for something.

"Serina," came the all-too-sweet voice of my mother, dancing into the room like some bad *Leave It to Beaver* show. "Steven will be here soon to pick you up. You need to get ready."

"Mom," I said, like I had this brilliant idea that the world just could not wait to hear. I quickly shot up from my bed. "I have this, I don't know, crazy idea. Why don't I drive myself to school? That way, if I'm late, then Steven won't be."

My mother's eyes shifted from those of the sweet *Leave It to Beaver* mom to those of the don't-mess- with-me-before-I-have-had-my-coffee mom. "Why do you have to start with me this early in the morning?" she asked, leaning against the frame of my bedroom door.

"Mom, I'm not starting with you. I just don't see why he has to come pick me up, when I am more than capable of starting my own car and driving it to school."

"Because your dad wants your car in the shop, to get it painted the color that you want for your birthday. Steven's mother is going to drive my car while I drive your car to the shop to drop it off," she said with an evil grin. "Besides, any girl in your school would kill to be given a ride to school by Steven."

"Why did you tell me that?" I yelled back. "Why do you have to ruin everything my dad does for me?"

"Because you would have sat here for an hour arguing with me until I just let you take the car, instead of getting dressed and ready for school," she snapped back. "Nan, is the coffee ready?" she asked in a tired voice.

"Yes, Mrs. Kartone," Nan answered quickly. "I also have breakfast ready."

"Then Serina should get ready for school before Steven and his mother show up," my mother said, as she turned and went down the hall to the staircase.

Tears welled up in my eyes as Nan put her arm around me. "I never asked for this type of life, so why is she so determined to make me live the life that she wants?" I asked, as the tears seemed to flow more quickly.

Nan lifted my head with her hand and gently wiped my tears. "We want more for our children than we have. That, and your mom, she is…what is that word?" I looked at her with a half grin. She knew exactly what word it was, and she wanted me to say it. "There is that smile. Go get ready, and I will be waiting downstairs for you," Nan said. She kissed me on my forehead and then closed the door to my bedroom.

I looked around my bedroom and saw the pictures of my so-called friends. In all of them we were smiling and laughing and making stupid faces. I picked up the picture next to my bed. It was one of the four of us when we went to Florida for spring break. I wondered if they were really my friends, or if they just acted like it since we were all born into the same class of people. You know, the people that make you sick, like the girl who cries because she can't make up her mind about a silver Mercedes or a red one. I hate to say it, but welcome to my life.

I looked at the clock on the floor and tried to read it upside down. "Seven forty-five," I read out loud. I went into my bathroom to get ready. For the first fight of the day, it was not a very long one, but I had to make up time before Prince Charming, as my mother describes him, and his mother showed up.

II

A Perfect World

It was Friday, and I knew that meant putting on my uniform. I quickly curled my hair and put it into a ponytail. I looked at the purple ribbon with a gold stripe down the middle and sighed as I tied it in a bow at the top of my ponytail. I put my makeup on and carried my makeup case to my bed. I opened my walk-in closet door to find the purple-and-gold uniform lying on the center island. I put it on and then examined myself in the mirror. I always wondered why my mother thought I looked so cute in this cheerleading outfit. I guessed it was because of the stupid bow in my hair. It made me look like I was five instead of seventeen.

"Miss Serina?" Nan said as she peeked into my room.

I walked out of the closet, bouncing up and down, and asked, "Do I look like a peppy cheerleader?" I let my hair bounce around with a smile on my face.

Nan smiled. "No, you look like a peppy cheerleader who will be late if she not get downstairs for breakfast."

I looked at the clock on the floor; it was 8:10. I quickly stuffed my makeup bag in my backpack and followed Nan downstairs. Nan pushed open the door to the kitchen and I walked in, toward the table where my mother, Steven, and Mrs. Brockway sat.

"There is my beautiful daughter," my mother said in her all-too-sweet voice, as she sipped her coffee and smiled at me. I quickly returned the smile, knowing that if I didn't, it would throw off the balance of the perfect morning for my mother.

I smiled at Steven as he pulled out my chair. "Good morning, Mrs. Brockway," I said in the most caring voice I could. Deep inside, I wanted them to be at their own house and leave me in peace.

Steven kissed my cheek before he sat down next to me. I forced a smile as I looked at him and said, "Good morning, football star." It always made Steven start talking about himself when you mentioned football. That way, I did not have to say anything until we left for school.

"I hate to brag," Steven said in his deep voice, "but I do look handsome in the new uniform." He started to laugh, and my mother and his mother quickly joined him. That was when I started to tune them out.

The perfect magazine picture of the nice well-to-do people all sitting around the breakfast nook having a good time before they sent their children off to school. The mother with the perfect blonde hair and blue eyes and the body of a trophy wife sitting next to her perfect son, who was handsome with his short light brown hair and blue eyes. Then there was my mother, with her long dark hair and emerald green eyes and tanned skin.

"Serina!" my mother said sharply, invading my thoughts.

"Yes, Mom." I answered her as I was coming out of my daze.

"Steven was asking you something, and I think that it is very rude of you not to be listening," she said, looking toward Steven with a smile.

"I'm sorry, Steven. I was thinking about…how fun the football game is going to be tonight," I said, hoping that he would go off on another one of his tangents.

"You see, that is why she is the captain of the cheerleading squad!" he exclaimed. "She has so much school spirit that she thinks about it day and night!" I gave Steven a half smile and wondered if he could really hear himself speak if he would speak at all. That thought made me smile bigger and look interested. "Well, as I was saying," Steven began as he grabbed my hand, "the winter ball is coming up at the club and I was wondering if you would like to be my date." I felt the eyes of my mother and his mother watching my every move. I knew the answer I was supposed to give to him. A wonderful, "I'm -so lucky- that -you -asked- me and- not- anyone- else- who- would- jump- to- have- you- ask- them" yes. The real answer I wanted to say was no, I don't want to go with you or anybody else. I don't want to go at all. I don't want to go to the boutique shop with my mom to pick out a dress and have her dress me like one of her dolls. NO! NO! NO! was what I wanted to scream.

"You two need to go or you will be late to school," Nan said, interrupting the awkward moment as she poured more coffee into my mother's cup and gave me a smile. *Nan, I thought, you are a gift from God! You always seem to know how to get me out of these sticky situations.*

"Nan is right," I said. "We will discuss it in the car," I said, as I threw my book bag over my shoulder and walked swiftly over to my mother. "Have a good day," I said, as I kissed my mom on the cheek and then kissed Mrs. Brockway on the cheek. I walked over to Nan and whispered in her ear, "Thank you." She smiled as Steven opened the front door for me and then shut it.

"Serina?" Steven said in a low voice. "Are you in a bad mood?" I quickly felt the ping of guilt with that question. Why does he say things like that? It was not his fault that he followed the same rules his parents did or that his parents taught him how to act. Maybe it was about the fight that I had with my mother this morning. I was taking it out on everyone, and everyone who was in my path became a victim. I turned around to face him.

"Steven, I'm sorry...it's just that my mom and I got into this fight and—"

"It's OK," he said. He hugged me and kissed me on the forehead. I looked at his strong arms and the muscles seemed to tighten around me to let me know that I was safe. It made me think about when my dad hugged me. Steven then opened the door to his Jaguar and waited for me to get in. As I sat I felt the cold leather seat under my legs and it gave me goose bumps. Steven shut the door and walked to other side of the car. I grabbed my seat belt, only to see the two sets of eyes peering out the kitchen window. Steven started the car and looked at me. "Ready for the day?" he asked.

"I'm ready," I said, as I leaned over and kissed him on the cheek. I knew they would not have missed that, and now they had something to talk about when they dropped off my car and went to lunch, or to the gym, or to wherever. *Yep, by the end of the day, Steven and I will be going to the dance together and then we will be married and then we will have children and all will be well.* In their perfect world.

III

Who Has Spirit?

The ride to school was definitely different. I was used to listening to the radio with no one to talk to. Just me time. Time to think about the day and time to get ready to be someone I was just not comfortable being. We rounded the corner to see the red building with windows that lined each wall of our school. The billboard read: GO LIONS! FEED THE SPARTANS TO THE LIONS!

The Spartans are our biggest rivals. I never quite understood why, but the legend goes that a long time ago our school was playing the Spartans on their homecoming night. The Lions beat the Spartans that night and later the football team decided to pay a visit to Spartan territory. Let's just say that the dummy that was covered in fake blood and lying on the school steps with a huge lion standing over it as it looked like it had a great meal was just not the greatest thing to see in the morning. Needless to say, no one confessed to the crime so the whole football team was punished by having to spend one afternoon cleaning our school. Yep, our school, not the school they vandalized. So began the rivalry.

"Are you going to stay in my car for the day?" Steven asked as he looked down at me. He extended his hand toward me. I gracefully took it as I stepped out of the car. I quickly took a deep breath, closed my eyes and exhaled with a smile. I knew what was coming next.

"Serina!" Holly screamed from two cars down. Holly was the one in our group that everyone loved. She was outgoing, smart, and funny. She was wearing her uniform and her long brown hair swayed backed and forth as she ran toward us.

"Here comes your team," Steven whispered into my ear. He was right. Holly could cheer all by herself and the crowd would go nuts. It still bothered me to know that I beat her out when trying to make cheer captain. I would have thought she would have made cheer captain over any of us.

"Hey, Serina," Holly said as she hugged me. She saw Steven behind me and a smile crept across her face. "So, Serina, was Steven nice enough to give you a ride to school?" she asked.

"Where is the rest of the team?" Steven asked as he put his hands around my waist. Holly smiled as she looked at me. I quickly elbowed Steven and took Holly by the arm to walk into the school. I went straight to my locker, opened it, and took a look in the mirror that was hanging on the door. Suddenly the door opened wider and there stood Mandi, Anna, and Holly.

"So tell us," Mandi said with a smirk. "How was your ride to school?" She tried to hide the laugh that was building up behind her question. Mandi of all people should have known how I felt. She was my best friend, and I considered her the friend that only comes along in a lifetime. I told her everything. She was just torturing me this morning.

"Tell you what?" I asked, trying to avoid the conversation altogether. The thought of kissing Steven in front of our moms popped into my head. This would only encourage the perfect-world syndrome. *Great!* I thought. *Having to deal with it at home is bad, but having to deal with it at school is worse.*

"You know," Anna said, trying to pry more into what everyone was talking about. "Holly said that—"

"Well, they looked like they were together in the parking lot," Holly jumped in. "I mean, the ride to school and his arms around her waist. They just looked so cute together." She smiled at me.

"You guys do look good together." Anna smiled. I shot her a look that could have pierced anyone's soul. She took notice and slowly backed away.

"Oh, come on, Serina, you know it is bound to happen sooner or later," Mandi said, her soft brown eyes staring at me. I hated it when she did that. It made me feel like she was peering into my soul. Mandi was the one in our group that always knew the answers and seemed to keep us together. She was our glue that kept us grounded.

She was right about my future, though. The captain of the cheer squad usually ends up with the captain of the football team. There was that perfect-world syndrome again and me stuck in the middle of it. Now, most people would probably love to be given the chance to live like I have, with everything given to me, but all I wanted was a normal life. One without all the hype. I watched as many of my classmates walked by me and I wondered if any of them got into a fight that morning with their mom about the color of their car, or if they just got into a fight about how they have to get a part-time job after school to pay for a car they want. I just wanted to know the feeling of going home after school to a mom who was tired from actually doing something rather than just out wasting the day and a dad that came home and sat down on the couch with a cold beer in hand and watched the news.

"There she goes, into her own little world again," said Heath as he hugged Holly. Holly kissed him on the cheek and smiled.

"Yeah, she does that when we start talking about things that she would rather ignore when the whole school saw it happen," Mandi chimed in.

"First," I said in a contradicting voice, "I am not ignoring you guys, I heard everything you said. And second, the whole school did not see anything in the parking lot when nothing happened."

"Who is she trying to convince, us or herself?" Adam asked Anna as he took her book bag from her, throwing it over his shoulder.

It was Mandi who answered him. "She tries to ignore the things that everyone else sees, to hide from the world who she really is."

I rolled my eyes as I looked at Mandi. If she was going to start with me this early in the morning, I was going to make her work for it. She was going to answer the question that we all have known and were too afraid to ask. I turned to her with a small smile and asked, "Who am I, Mandi?"

Mandi gave me that half smile. "You are part of the group that most girls want to be in and most guys want to date. Deal with it," she answered with confidence and a laugh.

This made my blood boil. People always thought that just because our parents had money and the house and the cars that our lives should be perfect, and they weren't. The truth was that I felt alone and I really didn't fit into this life. Something about me was different from the others. I had always felt this way and my friends were the only ones that made me feel as if in some small way I actually belonged. They were my safe haven. I took a look around at my friends as they smiled at me, awaiting the response they knew was coming. It was as if they were waiting on me to do something, but what? As if they were protecting me, but from what?

"There she goes again, into her little world," Heath laughed.

I gave him a deadly stare. They wanted an answer. I had an answer for them. "The only reason most girls want to be in this group is because—" I stopped myself and looked at my friends. I knew the words that would come out would end up hurting them, and although I was unsure just how I became friends with them in the first place, the fact remained that I really did not know anything outside my social circle. "We have such a good friendship and that is hard to find. Now, most guys want to date me because—"

"Because you have a nice car, and they know that once they are with you they are set for life," Matthew said as he grabbed Mandi's hand. "I got you something, Mandi," Matthew said with a large smile on his face as he handed her a white and red rose. Mandi blushed as she took it from him and kissed him.

"What is this for?" she asked as she smelled it.

"Well, let's just say that I was thinking about you and I wanted to get you something." His crystal-blue eyes sparkled as he tried to contain his smile. Matthew, the hopeless romantic of the group of guys. He was always surprising Mandi with something.

Suddenly the crowd in the hallway shifted and started to head toward the courtyard.

"What's going on?" Holly asked, noticing the same thing.

The boys stood there and smiled and then started to holler with the crowd. Mandi looked at me and said, "Grab your pom-poms." We all headed toward the courtyard and out the door as we pushed through the massive crowd of our classmates. When we got outside, the sun was refreshing and warm, but the autumn breeze was cool. The crowd started to shift to a different direction. I looked behind me to see if any of the teachers were around. I noticed some of the guys had painted letters on their stomachs as they took off their shirts and some of the girls had the lion on their cheeks. It was a sea of students that was getting bigger, and some of them had just arrived at school and saw the crowd walking and decided to join it. A hand grabbed mine and pulled me toward the outer sea of students.

"I didn't know there were that many students," Holly said, watching as the crowd around us seemed to grow bigger and bigger.

"Well, it looks like we are headed toward the stadium," Adam said, out of breath from screaming with the crowd.

"Steven just texted me and said that we are to meet him on the field," Matthew said with a little more control.

We started to walk toward the side entrance to the field when I noticed the goal posts had the familiar Spartan dummy hung over them. *It must be that the principal is allowing us to have the pep rally early*, I thought. When we finally reached the edge of the field the guys ran to Steven, knocking into him and laughing and hollering. I looked over to see the stands filling with students, and the teachers standing and walking, trying to usher them into the stands. The students were excited and some were yelling and some just seemed to sit there. The usual groups sat together and talked as they were all waiting to see what was going to happen next. In the distance you could hear the bell ring, letting us know that it was time for our first class. I was excited because I didn't like my first class anyway. We were going to start dissecting frogs today and I wanted to skip it. In a split second I was being hoisted into the air and put on Steven's shoulder.

"Put me down," I said with laughter in my voice, but before I knew it, Steven was headed toward the stand in the middle of the field. I saw the rest of the football team and the rest of the cheerleading squad all standing in a group, the guys all laughing and doing what guys do. The principal looked at the football team and started giving directions to us. Mandi and I had to stand at the two front corners of the stage as the rest of the team stood at each step, with Holly on the field in the middle. The football team all stood on the stage as the principal took the mic.

"Good morning," came a booming voice through the mic, and the crowd of students started clapping and going wild. "Now, let's settle down. Tonight is the big game…," the principal began.

I started to look around the field. It was meant to look like a massacre on the field. There were Spartans lying everywhere and Lions hovered over them. Of course, there was no fake blood on anything because it might ruin the stadium, and the principal was very proud of the new stadium that our parents had bought.

"So this is the important things the boys had to do last night," I whispered to Anna.

"To try and remake a killing ground. I suppose so," she said, not turning around.

I looked out toward the crowd as the banners flew, and the students seemed very enthused about the upcoming game.

"You know what's really making them smile?" I asked. "It's not the game at this point. It's that we're missing our first class."

"Serina," Anna said in a low voice, "you need to smile." I looked out into the crowd and saw our cheer coach, Mr. Semp. He was a regular-size guy with a keen sense of fashion. He was standing at the gate, staring at me, with his arms crossed in front of him and a look like he could kill me. I could hear him in my head saying, *I don't know what you are doing right now, but it's wrong and you need to fix it.* I quickly straightened up and put a smile on my face. Mr. Semp seemed to approve, as he gave the squad two thumbs up. "He is such a perfectionist," Anna said. We both tried to contain our laughter as the principal introduced the football coach.

The squad started yelling and jumping as the coach made his way to the mic. The football coach was a younger guy than the rest of the teachers at the school and he seemed to understand the students better. He always had his short brown hair combed back and wore nice tight shirts that fit his well-toned body. *This is what Steven will look like when he gets to his age*, I thought as the coach introduced his team. The rally lasted for an hour before the principal finally took the mic again.

"Well, we have a lot to look forward to for tonight's game, and who can work on a day like this with all this excitement. Now, I promised all the parents that I would keep you guys here until at least ten and it is now...ten o' one. Go home and get ready for the game tonight!"

The stadium erupted with cheers and students poured out of the stadium as if there was a fire. The squad was cheering and the football team was celebrating as students ran out of the stadium. I watched as my group of friends made their way toward one another and I walked toward them.

"What shall we do with the day off?" Holly asked in her cheering voice.

Mandi smiled at her. "Don't know," she said in her own cheering voice. "Holly, stop it. Save the cheering for the game. It's too early to do this, and what school do you know lets its students out because of a football game?"

"Our school!" Adam said with a smile. "It's because this school cares about school spirit and it has never had someone drop out. So we reap the benefits."

"Or it might be because they used today as a teacher workday," Anna said, smiling. The group turned and looked at her. "What?" she asked. "Helping out in the office, I hear everything."

"Again, the question remains…what shall we do for the day?" Holly asked.

I thought for a moment and just wanted to head home. I searched for my keys and then remembered that Steven had driven me here. "Well," I started, "I'd like to go to my house for a minute and—"

"Then it's off to Serina's house!" Holly yelled.

"We have to be back at school at three to start getting ready for the game," Steven said.

We walked through the field, pushing by the students to get to the parking lot. Steven gently placed his arm around me as we pushed through the crowd of people. Mandi looked over and grinned at me. At this point, I was kind of happy to have Steven helping me through the crowd. Before I knew it, I was sitting in the silver Jaguar watching as the cat that seemed to want to leap off the car led the way.

"I don't remember the weatherman calling for rain," Steven said, puzzled.

I watched as a little drop hit the windshield. "It's not sup-posed to rain," I said. "It's supposed to be sunny for the rest of the day, but then again, the weatherman has been wrong before."

Before I could finish my sentence the rain came pouring down. I watched as it streamed down the window and how dark it became. It was as if the black clouds had appeared out of nowhere. In fact, I didn't remember seeing a cloud in the sky since that morning. We pulled up to my house and all scrambled to get through the door. We were all laughing and almost fell into the foyer.

"Shh!" Adam said in a whisper. "Do you hear that?"

A silence fell over the group as we heard sniffling and whining. It sounded like my mom.

I walked over to the family room, slowly opened the door and stuck my head in. "Mom," I asked quietly. "Are you OK?"

"Serina," she said through her sniffles as she quickly wiped her tears away. She put her cell phone on the table next to the couch and got up to meet me.

"Mom, what's wrong?" I asked as I slowly pushed the door closed behind me.

"Nothing is wrong, honey," she said as she forced a smile. "Is Steven with you?" she asked, as her eyes became a little brighter at the thought.

"Yeah, the whole group is here," I answered her. "Why are you—"

"The whole group?" she asked with a smile. "Oh, that's right, tonight is the big game,, she said with a giggle, as she left the room to entertain my friends.

I was leaving the room when I heard the faint ring of my mom's cell phone. I walked toward the table and saw the phone light up. I picked up the phone to see that she had received a text message. *It must be one of her friends*, I thought. I clicked on the message to see a name I didn't recognize. "Who is Brad?" I asked quietly, reading the name. I opened the message to see who my mom was talking to. It read:

I found you. It didn't take as long as the last time. You have to tell her; you have kept it from her long enough and she is almost eighteen, it's time for her to take responsibility. I've been looking for the both of you for years and you need to stop running with her! I will find you and I will tell her myself if you haven't!

I felt my heart drop. Questions flooded my mind. Who was Brad, and was he talking about me? Was the father that I had known and loved not my father at all? My heart sank further into my stomach and I could feel the tears start to well up in my eyes. Had my mom lied to me my whole life? Did she lie to Dad all this time? Or maybe my dad knew.

"Serina, honey," Nan said as she looked at me with caring eyes. "Is everything OK?" she asked as she slowly made her way toward me.

Without taking my eyes from the phone, I asked, "Nan, who is Brad?"

Nan hesitated, and then answered, "I don't know."

I could tell that she was lying from the way her voice shook as she answered me. My blood felt hot from anger and I wanted to scream at her, but I knew it was not her fault. "Please, Nan," I pleaded, "tell me who Brad is, 'cause I know that you are not telling me the truth." I still did not take my eyes off the message, and read it over and over again. I started to go through the rest of the messages, hoping to find any others he might have sent. I found none.

"Serina," Nan said lovingly, "you need to ask your mother. I have not heard that name for years. I will tell your mother that you need to speak with her." She let herself out of the room and shut the door. I turned to look at the fireplace with our family portrait that hung over it. All of us were smiling and looked like the perfect family. The family that should have a dog posed in the middle of us. The family that would have been found on the front cover of one of those family magazines. I heard the door open; my mother walked toward me as I turned around, and she snatched her phone from me.

"What are you doing?" she asked in anger. "Going through my phone!" she screamed. "I don't go through your phone and I expect the same respect from you!" she scolded.

I looked at her with hateful eyes. "What are you keeping from me?" I screamed, as I tried to hold back the tears that were fighting to be released.

"I don't know what you are talking about!" she screamed back. "Nothing that you should have any worry about."

"I read the message and—"

"A message that was not for your eyes! It was on my phone and it has nothing to do with you," she shot back.

"Really?" I asked. "So I guess you're turning eighteen and you should be telling yourself something. Who is Brad? Does Dad know about Brad?" I accused. My mother looked at me as tears filled her eyes.

"It's not your concern!" my mother answered. "Do you want this whole life ripped from you? Do you want to lose everything?" she asked.

Before I could answer, Steven came in and asked, "Serina, is everything OK?" All my friends were at the door by now, and Mandi pushed her way through the crowd. She quickly walked over to me and took my hand. I wanted to pull back because my mom was going to answer my questions. What did she mean when she asked me if I wanted this life ripped away from me? That I would lose everything? She was going to answer a lot. Mandi led me to the outdoor patio and I just started crying. She rubbed my back as my warm tears soaked her uniform. The rain had stopped and I felt the warm sun through my uniform. Mandi shifted and I felt someone else grab my weary body. I looked up to peer into Steven's crystal-blue eyes. They seemed so concerned and so full of love. I quickly grabbed him and started to cry harder. His strong arms embraced me as I allowed him to pull me closer. He slowly started walking me to his car. He opened the door and I fell into the passenger seat. I looked through the windshield and met my mother's eyes. She had been crying as well. I never heard Steven get in the car or start it up. My mother's eyes and mine never left each other as she stared at me through the kitchen window. It was then that I noticed the dark clouds forming again.

"It looks like rain again," Steven said, finally breaking the silence.

I looked at him and forced a smile. He gently stroked my face with the side of his hand. I looked at Steven with caring eyes, knowing in the back of my mind that we would never be what he wanted us to be in this lifetime. I had to find out what my mother was hiding from me. I felt around my feet for my purse and fumbled through the contents. I finally found what I was looking for. I quickly dialed the number and a strong, deep voice made me feel safe again.

"Hello, princess."

"Daddy," I said in a weak voice. "We need to talk," I said, as my voice threatened to give out on me.

I V

I'm Coming Home

Hearing his voice made me miss him even more. He had left on a business trip two weeks ago and would not be returning for another week. He was in the computer business and I was not sure exactly what he did. All I knew was that when he was home he never talked about his work, and even if you asked him, he would say, "I had a good day."

"Daddy, do you know who Brad is?" I asked with my voice shaking. I wasn't going to beat around the bush with this. I was going to go straight to the problem. By his answer I would know if he knew anything at all.

"Is he your boyfriend?" he answered lightheartedly. "'Cause you know, I always thought that you and Steven…"

This shocked me. He really didn't know.

"No, he was on Mom's cell phone, text messaging her today," I blurted out without thinking. Steven looked over at me, his eyes wide with curiosity.

The phone went silent, and instantly I regretted the words that had come out of my mouth. Thoughts of how I could have said it better, or even brought it up better, swarmed through my head. Then the unexpected thought of my parents getting a divorce, and the perfect family that I had known all my life being torn apart, and it was all my fault! This was what my mom meant when she asked me if I wanted my life ripped from me. That I was going to lose everything. I don't know what I would do if my dad left. He was my protector and gave me hope for each day. I heard my father sigh.

Finally my father spoke. "Princess," he said calmly, "what did the message say?"

I thought for a moment. Should I tell him the truth? Or should I try and make something up? As much as I complained about how perfect my life was, I would never know what to do if it was torn from me. Would I have to leave my friends? Would I have to choose between my mom and dad? Where would my mom go? She had never had a job in her life. How would she take it if she knew that I told her secret? It was my dad's right to know. I mean, another man was texting my mom, and it was not her hairdresser or her aerobics instructor reminding her of her appointment. This was all her fault.

"Princess," my dad's voice boomed through the phone, "WHAT DID THE MESSAGE SAY?"

I had never heard my dad raise his voice, let alone scream at me. It snapped me back to the reality of what I had just started.

"It said," I started in a whisper afraid of what I had just started. I couldn't take it back now. I closed my eyes as tears started to run down my face. I didn't want my father to be mad or leave me. I wanted to continue to be his princess.

"Princess, I'm sorry I yelled at you. You just need to let me know what the message said. I need to know so that I can explain the situation to you," he said, trying to make me feel better. "I can't understand you when you whisper, honey, so you have to talk to me."

"It said that he found us and it didn't take as long as it did the last time and that she was turning eighteen and she has to take responsibility and…" The words fumbled out of my mouth and sounded like a mess. "Daddy, is he talking about me? You are my dad, right? Tell me I imagined everything I read."

The phone went silent again. "Princess, the big game is tonight, right?" he asked, as if the conversation had never happened.

"Daddy!" I blurted out. Had he not heard a word I said? Was he in shock, too? Maybe he knew and it didn't surprise him.

"I'm coming home tonight," he said. "I will be there to see you cheer. Don't worry about Brad. He is an old family friend. Tell your mom I'm bringing friends home. Let Nan know that we need the two spare bedrooms made up for company and a big breakfast for tomorrow. I will see you tonight. I love you." And with that, the phone went silent. I looked at my phone to see that it was on the home screen.

"Serina, is everything going to be OK?" Steven asked. I looked over to see all my friends on the other side of the window. Adam opened the door as I unhooked my seat belt and got out. Steven got out and grabbed my hand. I leaned on him as we walked toward the mall.

"My dad is coming to the game tonight," I said to break the silence. My friends stopped in their tracks.

Adam gulped and asked, "He is coming home tonight?"

"Yep, and he said he was bringing some friends home," I answered as I watched the mall get closer. I saw the bright lights that shone out and I watched as the children played on the little mechanical riding toys with smiles on their faces. I sighed, wishing that it was me on that ride with no cares and no worries at this moment.

"You are staying at my house tonight," Mandi said sharply.

I glanced over at Mandi, her eyes full of worry and sorrow. I let her words sink in as it suddenly hit me. She thought that my mom might be having an affair and things were going to get ugly. The fighting and yelling that could happen. Did she really think that my father would hurt my mother? No! He wouldn't hurt her. He never once drew his hand in a threatening manner.

"He would never hurt my mom," I snapped.

"We all know who he is and what he does," Matthew snapped back. "You will never outlive the name you were given, and the fact is, our parents know who your father is and what he does."

This statement enraged me. I had heard it all. The reason my father was gone all the time was because he was away on business—unethical business. Sure, police showed up every so often accusing him of stealing something or something ended up missing. To my knowledge, it was all stuff that had to do with the past, and some of it was stuff that no one in his or her right mind would steal. I mean rocks and paintings. Still, he would never hurt my mother.

"It's all rumors!" I shouted back. I could feel the blood in my veins start to warm up again as I felt the cool breeze push my ponytail.

"Of course not," Holly stated. "No one will ever say anything against your father."

"If they did, they would not be here to keep the rumor going," Anna said with a scared look on her face.

I looked at Anna, shocked. Was she really suggesting that in order to keep my mother quiet my father would go to the extreme of killing her? This was turning out to be absurd.

"Oh, please," I said, looking at Anna. "Your dad is like my dad's best friend, so are you saying that your dad is in on it, too?"

All my friends put their heads down, knowing I had beaten them at their own game. All of us were tied to the same life in one way or the other. All our parents were friends and hung out together, with summer cookouts and pool parties. All their dads went out of town just like mine and their moms never worked. We had everything given to us, and although none of us admitted it, we knew what it was like to have Officer Friendly come up to us at least twice a week, asking if we knew when our dad was coming home or if everything was good at home.

Steven swung me around, then put his strong hands around me and said, "Let's just enjoy the day off, 'cause in about two hours we are going to have to get back to the school."

All my friends shrugged as if the topic had never come up as we walked toward the food court of the mall. Steven brought over a pizza and we dug into it, and then we walked around the mall. We stopped at our usually spots—the game store for the boys and the bath store for the girls. We even ended up talking the boys into walking around the department store with us, in which Holly and Anna found shoes they just could not live without.

I took a good look at my friends as they smiled and laughed, not caring about the world around them. It made me feel better not to think about the situation that happened before, although I knew I would have to face it tonight when my father returned home. I shook my head, trying to run from the thought that had entered it. I didn't want to deal with it right now. I wanted to just enjoy the shopping spree that was happening at the time. It was not until Steven reminded us that we needed to get back to school before we were late that I noticed the time.

I leaned into the cool leather seat of the Jag and watched as the beautiful day around me was flying by. I sighed, knowing that not a word of the situation was mentioned, and for those two hours I felt as if nothing was wrong, and the only thing I was thinking about was the game that was happening tonight.

V

The Homecoming

The stadium lights were blinding as we got the banner out for the football team. I was happier tonight than I had felt in a long time. The sky was clear and the moon filled the sky with a lucent white light. The crowd was shuffling into the stands and the ambulance sat at the other end of the football stadium. I could hear the Spartan cheerleaders as they tried to be heard over the crowd.

"Don't they know that they are about to be slaughtered?" Anna asked as she flipped her ponytail.

"They won't be happy for long," Holly said, and she started to do backflips down the field. The crowd went wild. They started to holler and shout.

"Lions, Lions, Lions!" Holly shouted. The crowd returned the chant. The crowd was then stomping their feet on the concrete floor as some of the girls waved their purple-and-gold pom-poms in the air.

I heard the door to the locker room open and shouted for Holly to get back to the line.

"Welcome to the most anticipated game of the year," the voice on the loudspeaker announced. "The old tale of the

Spartans versus the Lions!" The crowd erupted with cheers from both sides.

"I see your dad," Mandi said, as she nodded her head toward the stands. I looked over my shoulder to see my mom and dad sitting, and then my dad saw me. He waved and blew me a kiss as I waved back at him. I could see why my mom fell in love with him. He was a very handsome guy. He had short brown hair and brown eyes. He was medium built, but very strong. His eyes had always given me comfort and made me feel as if the world could not hurt me—not by guns, not by fire. Nothing could touch me when my dad was around. Just then, I heard the announcer say, "Let those Lions out of their dens!" I turned just in time to grab a piece of the banner as the football team burst through it.

The squad ran over to the sidelines to start cheering the game on. We cheered for what seemed like all night. The mascots ran after each other throughout the game. For the first time in a long time I was actually having fun with what I was doing, and Mr. Semp seemed to notice it as well. He came up to me and said, "You need to cheer like this all the time."

I smiled and kept my eyes on my mom and dad. Maybe it was because they were both there and I felt whole again. My mom looked like she had been crying again, and my dad just kept his arm around her and kissed her on her forehead every so often. At the fourth quarter my mom seemed to spring to life and her smile was one that I had not seen in a long time. She put her arm through my dad's and they looked at each other. He pointed at me and they both smiled and kissed. The game ended and we won. Thirty-six to fourteen was the final score. We watched as the crowd started to leave.

My dad met me at the gate as I ran to him and threw my arms around him.

"I missed you," he said as he hugged me.

"I wish she was that excited to see me," Steven said as he laughed.

My dad looked at him and said, "You will earn it one day." Steven stuck his hand out toward my dad and they shook hands. "Good game," my father said.

"He'll be drafted to a good team," Mr. Brockway said as he walked toward my dad. "You are home early," Mr. Brockway said as he shook my dad's hand.

"I have to take care of my home before my work can be done," my father answered him with a smile as he looked over lovingly at my mother.

"Understandable," Mr. Brockway said, as he nodded his head in agreement.

"You know what happens when the king is away," my father said, laughing. "You can't leave the queen alone with the princess too long before they start fighting."

"I understand. My queen fights with my prince when I am gone for a while, too. What are you going to do?" he asked as he shrugged his shoulders. "Party at your house?" Mr. Brockway said to my dad.

"Of course. Steven, tell the football team to come over and bring their swimsuits. I'll call Nan and tell her to turn on the lights to the indoor pool," my father said with a smile. "Should I order pizza?"

"I'll order pizza since you opened your house," Mr. Brockway said.

"Are you going to ride with me?" Steven looked at me.

"Well, my dad just came home and I wanted to go home with my parents," I answered softly.

"Go with Steven, princess. Enjoy the night. I will see you when you get to the house," he said as he kissed me on the forehead. He put his arm out and my mother grabbed it as they turned and walked away. She put her head on his shoulder and I knew that everything was OK as I watched them walk into the night. I watched until I lost them in the sea of people that were leaving. Everything seemed to be back to normal. I smiled as Steven walked me to his car.

VI

Dreams

That night we filled up on pizza and soda. We took a swim in the pool and the parents sat around telling about their high school days and how their children were following in their footsteps. The air was filled with laughter and happiness. I looked around for the visitors that my father told me he was bringing home and saw none. I knew everyone there.

"Daddy," I started. "Where are the friends that you said you were bringing? I was sure that I was going to meet them." I smiled.

My dad smiled. "They are asleep, but you will see them in the morning."

"Probably jet-lagged." Mr. Brockway chuckled. "Are you sure we aren't making too much noise? I mean, the pool room does echo."

My father waved his hand. "I'm sure they're fine. If we were too loud one of them would have come down," he laughed.

"How many of them are there?" I asked curiously. Did he bring a family? Maybe they had kids my age. "Who are they, Dad?"

"Well," my dad started.

"They're longtime family friends," my mother interrupted him. "You probably don't remember them, but we'll make sure you meet them tomorrow. Tonight, go celebrate with your friends," she encouraged.

I looked over at the pool where Holly and Anna had joined a volleyball game in the pool. The team loved it when my father opened the house to them and let them play. I looked around for Mandi. I spotted her sitting on the side of the pool with her legs in the water, watching the game. I slowly made my way over to her and sat down, putting my legs in the pool.

"Penny for your thoughts," I said, half laughing.

Mandi looked at me and smiled. "Something feels different. Like I should know more, or at least be doing something right now. It's a weird feeling." Mandi shook her head and smiled. "Sorry, spaced out there for a moment."

I laughed. "It's all right. You know I space out from time to time."

Mandi looked over to me. I noticed her eyes seemed to sparkle more, yet she seemed more confused. I could tell she was thinking about something, but what?

"Mandi, you're starting to scare me. What's wrong?"

"Something is different. Serina...did you ever feel like... like..." Mandi looked at me as if I had an answer.

I shook my head slowly. "Like...what?" I smiled.

Mandi shrugged. "Like there is more to us than we know. Look at us...were we meant to do something else?"

I let the thought swirl around in my head. Do what? Make a difference somewhere? Do something more than what our parents do now? The thought made me feel as if something was missing. Like I should be doing something right now. "What should we be doing?" I asked Mandi.

"Like joining in the fun?" Matthew said as he splashed us.

"Hey!" Mandi laughed as she splashed him back.

"Hey there, beautiful," Steven said as he walked toward me. "Don't you want to join in the fun?" he smirked.

I felt a cold chill run down my spine at that instant. I watched him carefully as I felt my body tense up. I suddenly felt uncomfortable around him. I quickly stood up and smiled. Steven gazed up at me in confusion. "Have to catch me first." I giggled, hoping that would appease him for a moment. I quickly went back toward my dad as I heard Steven get out of the pool.

What was going on? It did feel weird. I felt like Steven was a threat. I shook the idea out of my head, only to have it return. I watched as my dad got closer, and I could still hear Steven laughing as he made his way toward me. I felt my heart start to race as if I was scared. I stopped in front of my dad as he looked up at me.

"Are you all right, princess?" he asked as Steven put his arms around my waist.

"Caught you." I could feel his smile. "Time to play," he said as he picked me up. I felt my body being lifted and turned toward the pool. I saw Holly and Anna laughing and knew that Steven would never hurt me, but I didn't feel safe at this moment.

"Now, be careful with her, honey," I heard Mrs. Brockway say behind me.

"Put me down!" I shrieked. "Steven…don't you dare!" I felt my body being dropped and felt the water. I quickly pushed myself to the surface.

"Are you all right?" Anna asked with concern.

"I'm fine." I smiled and then turned to Steven, who smiled at me. I quickly splashed him with water. "That wasn't funny."

"Sure it was, beautiful." He smiled down at me and then did a perfect dive into the pool. He quickly surfaced and shook the water from his head. "You're a good swimmer. Besides, we're here to have fun."

Holly looked at me with understanding. "He won't hurt you, I promise." She smiled, as if she knew that I had felt unsafe.

I glanced back at Mandi, who was slowly walking toward me with Matthew by her side. She knelt down by the pool. "I'm going to go home and rest. I think I may just be tired." She sighed.

"Aww…Mandi!" Anna exclaimed. "Don't go. Tomorrow is Saturday and we can sleep in. Stay and have fun with us."

Matthew shook his head. "It's no good. She's tired and ready to go home. Maybe we'll see you guys tomorrow?" he said.

"Yeah!" Steven shouted. "We can all meet for brunch at the club."

"Sounds like a plan." Matthew smiled as he put his arm around Mandi and they said their good-byes.

It was midnight when the last person left the house. I slowly walked up the stairs as the conversation with Mandi started to run through my mind again. I walked past the first guest room quietly and tried to listen. I heard nothing. I started to approach the next room when the feeling of some-thing missing took over. I stopped and stood next to the door. I listened and heard nothing. I looked around and saw no one. I gently and quietly grabbed the doorknob. My heart started to beat faster as I slowly turned it. Something behind this door was suddenly making me feel nervous. I felt the knob stop as if it was stuck. I pushed harder, only to find that the knob wouldn't move. Maybe they had it locked. I slowly let the knob go as it rested in place.

All of a sudden I felt feelings of love and loneliness. I watched as I lost control of my hand and it moved to the door. I closed my eyes and felt a feeling I had never felt before. I stepped back and looked at my hand on the door, wanting to push on it to see if it would open. Another feeling of love hit me, and a picture of me in a wedding dress appeared. I quickly shook my head as I felt a hand on my shoulder. I looked to the side to see my dad smiling at me.

"What are you doing?" he asked.

I pulled my hand away from the door. "Nothing. Who's in there?" I asked.

"Some of our guests." He smiled. "I'm pretty sure they're asleep, though. I'll introduce them in the morning, I promise," he assured me, and walked me to my room.

I went into my room and shut the door. I quickly undressed and sat down in front of my vanity. I brushed my wet hair and braided it. I stood up, and as I walked to my bed, my heart leapt in my chest. I felt happy and content. I stopped and looked around. I looked at myself in the mirror and noticed that my eyes looked brighter. My heart leapt again. I was excited about something and didn't know what. Then I noticed someone behind me. I turned around to see my dad smiling.

"You're so pretty," he said. I smiled back at him and gave him a hug. He walked me over to my bed and I lay down. "Did you have a good time, princess?" he asked, as he pulled the covers over me.

"You do know that I am about to turn eighteen," I said through a smile.

"Oh, so now you are too old for your dad to tell you good night?" he smiled.

"Never!" I shouted.

My father's eyes shifted from those of the loving father to those of the lecturer. "You do know that you shouldn't go through your mom's phone," he said, as he lowered his head and his dark eyes stared at me.

"I didn't mean to," I said with a half smile, trying to warm his heart so he would not yell again.

"Princess," he said, "we will talk in the morning, and please come down dressed because I have friends over."

"OK. Good night, Daddy," I said as he turned out my light. I dug deep down into my bed, wrapping my blanket tightly around me.

"Good night," he said as he shut my door.

I lay in my bed, closed my eyes and dropped off to sleep.

The next thing I knew, I was looking into the night, hearing a crowd yelling and shouting. The smell of burning wood filled my lungs. I heard a little girl crying out for her mom over the screaming crowd. I quickly looked around to see nothing but trees. Where was I, and why did I wake up here? I was just at my house. I was dreaming…had to be dreaming.

"Mommy! I want my mommy!" I heard the little girl yell through her soft sobs.

I walked out of the woods to find a crowd in a circle, and in the middle of the circle was a woman who looked scared tied to a long wooden pole. I walked slowly toward the crowd of people dressed in colonial dresses and hats, which reminded me of pilgrims at Thanksgiving. The wind blew and I felt the rush of heat as pieces of amber rushed passed me. I heard a woman screaming through her sobs as I looked up in horror. There she was, dressed in a long black dress with long black hair that covered some of her face. I watched as the flames licked the bottom of her dress and she screamed in agony. I walked closer, trying to find the little girl that was screaming. The smell of fire and flesh filled my nose as I scanned the crowd, trying to find the scared little girl.

"Mommy!" she screamed. I looked up to see that fire had engulfed the bottom half of the woman's legs.

"Brad!" the woman screamed. "Get her out of here, NOW!"

My head jerked up. Brad? The name that was on my mom's cell phone. I looked up to take a closer look at the woman in the middle of the burning wood. To my horror it was my mother. I frantically started making my way toward her to see if I could find the little girl. My heart raced as I pushed people out of my way. Hot tears streamed down my face as I fought the crowd to get to my mother, and I noticed that the screams of my mother had stopped. I looked up to see her head down, with her long black hair hanging down so that I couldn't see her face. My legs gave out from underneath me as I hit the hard earth. My fingers wrapped around some grass as I pulled it up and threw it at the person in front of me. He didn't seem to notice as I cried. I felt my blood get warm again and I looked at my hands to see a blue light that surrounded them. I felt an electric charge as I slowly rose to my feet again. What was happening to me? My long black hair flowed out as if the wind was blowing hard, although there was hardly any wind at all. I felt the anger start to engulf me as I seemed to rise above the bloodthirsty crowd. I looked to my left to see a dark shadow running into the woods with a little girl in tears. I screamed as the electricity within me flowed to my fingertips and formed an electric blue ball launched at the figure. The figure fell as the little girl screamed for her mother. I felt myself lower to the ground and I started to run toward the little girl. When I reached her, I wiped her hair out of her face and stared into my own little eyes.

———⟋⟍———

I screamed as I sat up in my bed and a light blinded me. My dad had grabbed me, stroking my head as I put my face into his pajamas. "It's OK, honey. Everything is going to be all right." He tried to comfort me.

My mother rushed to my other side. "I'm here," she cooed, as she wrapped her arms around my shaking body to try and comfort me. "It was all a dream, a very bad dream. You're safe now."

"It's time," my father said in a whisper. "He is almost here, and it's just going to get worse before it gets better."

My mother grabbed me as she kissed my forehead. "Sleep, my child," she said, as she lay me back down and my eyes felt heavy. I don't remember much more of that night, but I do know that when I finally did wake up the next morning, I heard many voices I did not recognize.

VII

The Santiagos

I looked over at my nightstand, only to remember that I had knocked off my alarm clock yesterday. I rolled over to look on the floor. I picked up the soft blue clock and saw that it was nine thirty. I let my head hit my pillow again. I decided that it was time for me to get up and meet my father's friends. My feet responded first as they pushed the covers off me. I stretched and swung my body into action. I walked to my bathroom and stared at myself in the mirror. My long black hair was still in the braid that I made last night. I slowly took it out and unbraided my hair. I turned the water on to my shower and got in, I just let the warm water fall on my face. It felt good. That's when I noticed the water at the bottom of the tub turn brown. I looked at my hands. They had dirt stuck to them. I quickly scrubbed them while the images of my dream flooded my head. The burnt smell started to fill my nose again. I could feel the panic start to overwhelm me. I put my hands over my face and I closed my eyes and screamed, "STOP! STOP IT! GO AWAY!" The sound of the shower filled my ears and the smell of shampoo and soap surrounded me. I let my hands slide down my face and looked around. I quickly finished and got out of the shower. I was curling my hair when I heard a soft knock at my door.

"Are you OK?" Nan asked. I opened the door to see the short-statured woman staring at me.

"I'm OK," I said with a smile. "I had a bad dream last night and it's still haunting me this morning."

"Your mom and dad are waiting for you down the stairs," Nan informed me.

"I'm coming," I said. I finished my hair and walked over to my bed to see that she had already laid out my favorite outfit.

"Thank you, Nan," I said as she shut the door. I loved my dark blue jeans with the baby blue shirt with spaghetti straps. Across the front was a crown and it had *Princess* under it. My dad got it for me on one of his business trips. I put my sneakers on and ran downstairs.

"We're in here!" my dad yelled from the dining room. I walked through the double doors and saw my dad at the head of the table. To his left sat my mom, her smile not as big as yesterday. On my dad's right there sat a man that looked about the same age as my father. His short brown hair was neatly combed, and by the look of his hands he was a laborer. They weren't smooth like my dad's. Sitting next to him was a guy that sat with his arms folded. He looked very familiar to me. It was as if I had met him before. His tight black shirt hugged the tops of his arms. My heart leapt, which shocked me. My dad watched me and smiled. "Everything all right, princess?" he asked. I shook my head and smiled. My mother studied me, her eyes wide, and a glimpse of hope could be seen in the guy's eyes. A small smile crept across his face. The girl that sat next to him watched him and then looked at me, and a small smile formed on her face. The girl looked to be his sister. She was a thin girl with limp light brown hair.

My dad rose to his feet and said proudly, "Princess, this is Mr. Santiago."

"Hi," I said, as I walked toward my seat next to my mother. "Nice to meet you, Mr. Santiago."

"This is his son, James, and his daughter, Alexis," my father continued.

"It's nice to meet you," I said with a smile. The smell of bacon, sausage, and pancakes filled the room. I quickly scanned the table to find my strawberries that Nan always had for me. Just like she was reading my mind, Nan came in and put my plate in front of me. She handed me a latte and quickly left the room.

"Is that all you feed your princess, Dave?" Mr. Santiago looked at my father.

"That's all she'll eat in the morning," my father said with a smile. "She never was a big breakfast eater."

"It's what keeps her fit," my mother said with a snobbish grin as she rubbed my arm.

I took a sip of my latte and almost choked when James said in a rough voice, "She looks too thin from when I last saw her."

The comment struck me. When he last saw me? I didn't remember meeting him before. Thoughts ran through my head as I was trying to see if I could place him. The only people I could remember were my friends. I grew up with them and hung out with them. I knew that they didn't go to my school because they just got here. I had to know how he knew me or where he had seen me before.

"I'm sorry, have we met before?" I asked as I picked up my strawberry.

Alexis elbowed him and said, "Your mother and our mother were good friends a while ago. You probably didn't remember once you moved to this beautiful place."

I looked over at my father and mother and smiled. "You must have me confused with someone else. We've always lived here."

James rolled his eyes as he stood up. "Mr. Kartone, I'm sorry, I can't do this. I'm going to the back porch."

I quickly stood up against my will. "I'm sorry. Was it something I said?" I asked, as I watched James quickly go through the kitchen door. My father motioned for me to sit down and I slowly sat down.

"Please excuse my son," Mr. Santiago said to my father.

"It's not his fault," my father said as he shot my mother a look.

The room was a filled with an uneasy feeling. The tension seemed to build, and before it got to its breaking point I decided to say something that I would soon regret.

"So, Mr. Santiago, if you don't mind me asking, is your first name Brad?" I asked, as I sipped my latte and leaned back in my chair. I heard all forks hit the plates and I smiled inside. If this was my mother's fault, like my dad implied, then I was going to get my answers this morning.

"Serina Starr Kartone!" my mother snapped.

Mr. Santiago raised his hand with a smile. "No, my first name is Joshua. Do I look like a Brad?" he asked.

The question caught me off guard. "No, I was just asking," I said. "Is Mrs. Santiago here?" I asked.

Alexis lifted her head from the waffle she was enjoying and her eyes filled with tears. At that moment I knew that what had just come out was going to land me in more trouble. "James is right I can't do this either!" Alexis screamed, as she threw her fork on the table and stomped out of the room. I got up to apologize when Mr. Santiago motioned for me to sit. I slowly sat back down.

Mr. Santiago began, "Dave, I'm sorry—"

"No, it's to be expected with the thought of their mother, God rest her soul," my father said solemnly.

At that moment I felt like the biggest loser in the room. I was the weakest link and I knew that I needed to apologize. I got up and quickly started toward the back of the house. I ignored the parents that tried to get me to stay in the room. The only thing I knew was that I needed to apologize. I felt like a jerk that was just trying to be mean, although I didn't know. I wasn't supposed to know, was I? I didn't remember these people, yet they all seemed to know me.

As I approached the back door I saw James holding Alexis. I stepped outside quietly. "Alexis," I said, my voice cracking. "I'm sorry. I didn't mean to…"

James turned to me with a stern look on his face that turned soft in an instant.

"You don't really remember, do you?" he asked.

I put my head down to look at the wooden deck. "No," I said under my breath. I felt like I should remember somehow and was not sure. He came over to me and put his hand on my shoulder. A pounding started in my head and I felt my legs go out. Before I knew it, James had his strong arms around me, holding me up. He helped me over to the bench that was attached to the deck. I sat down and looked up at him. He had his arms crossed and a smug look on his face.

"Is the headache gone yet?" he asked with a smirk.

"How'd you know—"

"I know a lot of things about you," he interrupted me. "You are the one that has to remember," he said in his rough voice. He then turned to Alexis and opened the door for her. Before he went into the house, he turned to me and said, "Pay attention to your dreams, they are the keys to your past."

I sat on the bench as the pounding stopped and Steven walked out. "Are you all right? I mean, who does he think he is, touching you like that?"

I shook my head and looked at Steven. "What are you doing here?" I asked, still trying to recover from my headache.

"I wanted to see if you wanted to join us for lunch at the club, and maybe go shopping?" That usually worked for me, but I was not done with my newfound friends. James had a lot of explaining to do, and so did my parents. How did he know about my headache? And for that matter, what did he mean that my dreams were the keys to my past? I took Steven's hand and walked inside. Everyone was in the living room talking. James looked up with a face of disgust as he stood up. Mr. Santiago stood up and motioned for him to sit down. My mother looked up to see what was happening and her face lit up.

"Are you and Steven going somewhere?" she asked in that all-too-cheery voice, noticing that I was holding Steven's hand. "Maybe the two of you can show Alexis and James around. They will have all their stuff moved into the house next to us in just a couple of days."

The pounding in my head started again and I hit the hard wooden floor with my knees. Steven touched me and the pounding got worse. I put my hand up and said in a low voice, "Don't." He grabbed my arm, and I turned to him and said a little louder, "Don't touch me." I sat on the floor rubbing my eyes with the palms of my hands.

"Princess," my dad said as he rushed to my side. "Are you OK?" he asked as he tried to pick me up off the floor.

James came to his side and my dad moved. James got close to my ear and whispered, "Shake it off."

I tilted my head to the side as my hair blocked my view of his face. I drew in two huge, deep breaths and said with my teeth clenched, "You don't know what's wrong!"

I could feel his smile as he whispered, "I told you. I know more about you than you know about yourself. Stop making a scene and get up." And with that, he got up and casually walked back to his seat.

The pounding started to subside and I was able to get to my feet again. I flipped my hair back, looked at Steven with loving eyes, and asked in the sweetest voice I could muster, "Can you get me some Tylenol?"

Steven looked at me, a little confused. "Sure," he said, as he helped me to the seat my dad had been sitting in.

When Steven left the room, my mother shot James a dirty look. "What are you doing?" she asked with hatred in her voice.

"Something the rest of you are afraid of!" James stood up and said.

Mr. Santiago stood up in front of James, pushed him back in his seat, and tried to threaten, "If you ever do that again in front of someone—"

"What?" James shot back. "You can't do anything. Mom isn't here."

Mr. Santiago dropped his head. It was tiny Alexis that surprised us all.

"Stop it!" she yelled as the room got quiet.

My dad took control of the room. "Princess, I think that Steven should go and maybe we'll all go out on the boat."

"That's a great idea!" Alexis chimed in. "I've always wanted to go on a boat."

And with that, Alexis ran toward the door, almost knocking down Steven, who had a glass of water and Tylenol in hand. Steven handed me the water and Tylenol. I quickly grabbed it and swallowed the pills.

"Thank you," I said as I touched his hand.

"Steven," my father said, "we are going to go on a boat ride with our friends and princess, and will be back later."

"OK," Steven said with disappointment in his voice.

I quickly stood up, grabbed Steven's arm, and said, "I will walk you to the door," as I looked over my shoulder. James's eyes looked as if they had flames behind them. I didn't know why I felt I had to show off in front of him. Besides, what did it matter? He had just gotten here.

"I'll see you later, then?" Steven said with a smile as he kissed my forehead.

"Yep, tell everyone, party tonight!" And with that, I shut the door and saw James standing by the living room double doors.

He better keep his hands off, I heard him say as I walked past him. I quickly turned to face him.

"What did you say?" I challenged, as I stood on my toes to reach his eye level.

James put his hands up in defense. "I didn't say a word."

"Princess, I think we should get your hearing checked, 'cause no one said anything," my dad said as he came up behind James. My dad headed up the stairs.

My eyes met James's eyes. "I know what you said, and it's none of your business," I said through clenched teeth.

"Whatever you say, princess," he said with a smile.

I walked up the stairs and turned to look. He was watching me; it made me feel weird. *He is cute and all, but who does he think he is? I don't know*, I thought, *this could be fun*. He was definitely different from the rest of these guys around here. He could also answer a lot of my questions. This could be a good boat ride after all.

VIII

The Test

My mom and dad walked arm in arm as we walked down the pier. Mr. Santiago walked close to James and I walked and talked with Alexis. "I take it that your brother doesn't like me very much," I said, hoping that it would spark a conversation.

Alexis rolled her eyes and then smiled. "You have to get to know him better." I watched as the wind blew her hair in her face and wondered how much about me she knew.

"So tell me," I started, "are you guys really moving here?"

"Yep," she said with a smile. "Your dad came over two weeks ago and started talking to my dad. The next thing we knew, we had a moving crew at our house and my dad was having our school records sent here. We weren't supposed to be leaving until the end of the month, but your dad insisted that we go."

"Yeah, my dad has a way of doing that," I said with a half smile. "So, did my dad stay with you guys while he was on his business trip?"

"What business trip?" Alexis asked, giving me a puzzled look. "He called my dad two months ago and arranged to stay with us and talk with us. He said that he had not seen us in a long time and was trying to find us before next weekend." She turned to me like she had a brilliant idea. "Your birthday is next weekend, isn't it?"

"Yeah, I will be eighteen," I said with a smile. "How'd you know?"

"That's perfect... that's why we're here," she said, like everything was coming together. She leaned in closer to me, but I had a hard time hearing her over the waves that hit the pier and the wind. "It's our turn," she said with a smile. "Is that your parents' boat?" she asked in amazement, ignoring my puzzled look.

I turned to see the white thirty-foot boat that rocked back and forth in its slip. It did look pretty in the light as the brass railing glowed from the sun. "Yep, that's it," I said.

"You could probably live on that thing," Alexis said, admiring it from the pier.

"You can have really good parties on it," I said with a snicker.

"If I find that you have been on the boat with your friends without my knowledge, Serina," my father said. The sound of my actual name coming from his mouth shocked me. He never calls me by my name unless he is introducing me to someone or I am in really deep trouble. I went up to him, opposite my mom, grabbed his arm, and looked up to him with the biggest smile I could manage.

"Daddy," I said in the voice of my mother, "I would never be on this boat without you knowing it." My dad's eyebrows arched as his eyes turned a dark brown. I released his arm and stepped back. "I swear, Daddy, I was never on this boat without you knowing it," I pleaded.

"OK, princess, keep it that way." Good, he called me princess. At least I knew that battle was over.

My dad walked over to James, who seemed to be admiring the boat as well. "Have you ever driven a boat before, James?" he asked.

Without taking his eyes off the boat, he answered, "I have never been on a boat, let alone driven one, sir."

My dad shuffled in his pants pocket and pulled out the keys. He quickly grabbed James's hand and set the keys in it. "Princess, go with James and show him how to start her up." James, realizing what had just happened, quickly tried to hand the keys back to my dad.

"Sir, I'm not sure that is a good idea," he said, his voice shaking as he tried to hand the keys to the boat back to my dad.

My dad put his hands up and said, "Princess has been taught, and I am sure she will be able to show you." When I put my hand out to take the keys, my dad grabbed my hand and stood between James and me. "James keeps the key, you just show him how to start it," he said. "We don't pull out or move, just start it."

"Can I go?" Alexis asked, excited, as she clasped her hands together and looked up at my dad. "I can help start the boat."

"I'm going to teach you how to get things ready before they can start the boat," my dad said as he put his arm around her neck. "Gosh, it's great to all be back together," my dad said with a smile.

"We're all one happy family," my mother said sarcastically. I could see her rolling her eyes behind her sunglasses.

"Come on," I instructed as I grabbed James's arm, pulling him toward the boat. As we climbed up the stairs to the wheel room I noticed that James was mumbling something. I decided to ignore it, because if he wasn't man enough to say it to where I could hear it, then he was…just not a man. The thought made me giggle a little.

"I'll tell you when we get to the room," he said, as he reached the top and put the key in to open the door. "Ladies first," he said as he extended his arm. I passed by him with a puzzled look. Could he hear me? Did I speak out loud? No. I'm sure that was my thoughts.

I walked in and immediately went to the windows. I heard him fumbling with the keys. "Don't do anything yet," I said, as I tried to open the second window.

"Why? Will the boat blow up if I put the key in?" he laughed.

"No, you can't just start it up," I said. "You have to wait until my dad says everything is OK. So, tell me what your problem is with me," I asked sharply.

"I don't have a problem with you. I have a problem with the situation," he answered, as he tightened his fist and looked out the window.

"What situation?" I snapped back.

"This," he said as he lowered his head. "Why can't it be the way it used to be?" He slowly lifted his head and his hazel eyes gazed into mine. I could feel sorrow in the room. The tension had left and his hand was now resting on the windowsill. I could feel a cool breeze blow in through the open windows. My heart felt heavy with sadness as I felt him grab my left hand. I watched as he put it up between us and studied it. I wanted to pull it back and ask him what in the world was wrong with him. He touched my ring finger as if he remembered something. His touch was soft and magical; it was like something had surrounded me and was guarding me. He put my hand down and brushed past me. I put my hand back up and noticed a tan line at the end of it, as if a ring had sat there. I shook my head in disbelief, and like that, the tan line disappeared.

"What did you do?" I turned to ask him.

"Remembering a happier time," he responded. "A time you will soon remember, if…I am that lucky."

"What happened that I can't remember?" I asked as I stomped toward him. That was it! I couldn't take it anymore. Enough of the half sentences and riddles! I had had enough and he was going to answer. "Was I in an accident? Did I get hit in the head and have amnesia?" I demanded.

His soft hazel eyes turned to look at me. "You could say something like that." He began to go by me again and I grabbed his arm in anger.

"Oh no, not this time!" I screamed. "You will tell me."

"Hey, guys!" Alexis screamed from the deck. "Your dad says it's OK to start it."

James walked over to the wheel and I talked him through each step of starting the boat. He turned the key and we both listened as the engine roared beneath us. My dad opened the door behind us as Mr. Santiago followed him.

"Princess, why don't you go help your mother and Alexis get some lunch ready while we teach James a little about how to drive this thing."

I shot James a look and headed down to the cabin. I walked into the cabin as Alexis was sipping on a bottled water.

"Do you want one, honey?" my mother asked me.

"Please," I responded.

My mother handed me the bottled water and I opened it and took a big gulp. My mother got a bottle of wine out of the chiller and poured herself a glass as I sat next to Alexis. It was quiet in the cabin as my mother gulped her glass of wine and then poured herself another. The bottle fell over as we felt the boat jerk. I got up quickly, grabbing napkins, and rushed toward my mom, when I noticed the liquid suspended over the floor. I watched in amazement as the wine drew itself back into the bottle as if someone had hit the rewind button on a movie. The bottle sat back up and the cork replaced itself. I shook my head in disbelief.

"Alexis?" I looked over to her.

"Isn't that cool? No mess to clean up," she said happily, as if she knew what I was going to ask.

My mom turned around and took a step toward me. I quickly took a step back and looked at my mother with concern. "How did you do that?" I asked. She gave me a look of concern that sent a cold chill down my back. I was starting to feel afraid and trapped. My mother took another step toward me, and without hesitation I started to run toward the stairs to the deck. The door swung open and James stood there. I was trapped between a witch of a mother and a mad man. I could feel my heart start to beat faster. As James took a step down and I backed away, I turned to see that my mother was still heading toward me, and a rush of panic overwhelmed me. My heartbeat felt like it was off the charts and my breaths were hard and short. I quickly bent my knees and tucked my chin into my chest as I put my hands over my head.

"LEAVE ME ALONE!" I screamed. I heard several crashes as I stood up and looked around me. James was lying on his stomach on the deck and my mother was over by the sink. This was the perfect opportunity to get out. I stepped onto the deck as James pushed his knees under him to get up.

I felt someone grab me around my waist as I tried to pull away. "LET ME GO!" I screamed. I felt the grip let go and I started to run toward the other side of the boat to the bedroom.

"James, stop her, before she hurts herself or one of us!" I heard someone shout as I rounded the corner. I pulled on the knob and felt it jerk back, not allowing me to go inside. I felt the warm tears start to go down my face. I jerked it again and again. "I will break you open!" I screamed, as if it were able to answer me. I heard James's heavy footsteps getting closer to me and I scanned around to find something to protect myself with. Out of the corner of my eye I saw the little red box that held the flare gun in it. I quickly opened it and loaded the gun. I turned with gun drawn and James standing in front of me. James quickly put his hands up as he stepped back.

"Hey," he said, out of breath. "Put the gun down," he pleaded with me.

Now I was in control and no one was taking that away from me. I quickly looked around and saw nothing but water. There were no other boats around, no one to come get me off this crazy ride. *How did we already leave the harbor?* I wondered. *Was I down in the cabin for that long?* It didn't matter; all I knew was that I wanted to be somewhere else, anywhere but here. My dad and Mr. Santiago rounded the corner behind James. They both quickly put their hands in the air. I felt the cool breeze hit my back and flip my hair around my face.

"Princess," my dad said quietly, "put the gun down, please. You can hurt someone."

I felt the tears roll down my face again. I quickly brushed my hair back with my right hand, my left still on the trigger of the gun.

"James, take the gun from her," my dad said under his breath.

"I can't…her grip on the trigger is strong and I can't get hold of it," James whispered back with his hands still in the air.

I felt the boat rock over the waves and I started to feel weak. *My adrenaline is coming to a halt*, I thought. *No, it can't! Not now! How am I going to defend myself against these people? These people who can suspend liquid in the air and give me headaches. What else can they do to me?* I was not going to let them win. My mom and Alexis came behind my dad and Mr. Santiago.

"Serina!" my mother shouted. "What in the world do you think you are doing?"

"It's OK, Mrs. Kartone," James said with a smile as he lowered his hands.

"Put your hands back up!" I shouted, squeezing the trigger. The gun started to shake in my hands and my arms were starting to feel the strain of holding the gun out like that.

"OK," he said, slowly lifting his hands. "I have something for you and it's in my pocket. Can I get it out?"

"You have nothing that I could possibly want," I snapped back.

"I have a necklace that belongs to you," he said, as he brought his left arm down and stuck his hand in his jean pocket. He pulled out a necklace with a heart on it. He bent down and slid the necklace toward me. I looked down to see it stop at my foot. The gun still pointed toward the group, I bent down to pick it up. It had the infinity symbol engraved around the chain and a heart at the end of it. I wrapped the chain around my fingers until the heart rested in the palm of my hand. It was engraved with two capital *S*'s that intertwined into each other. I turned the heart over to see the words *I will always watch over you* engraved into it. "Open it," he encouraged.

I took the locket between my fingers and pushed it open. I looked at the picture and immediately threw the necklace back at him. He caught it in midair. "What is this?" I asked between sobs. "How can that be?" It was then that I noticed my legs were trying to give out and my arms had started to drop. I jerked my arms back up to keep them from dropping too far down. I couldn't stand any longer and I dropped to my knees, with my head down and my hair in my face. The tears ran down my face like rain. I felt someone slowly take the gun out of my hands and pull me toward him.

"It's OK, princess, Daddy's got you," I heard him say as he rubbed my back. I put my arms around him and dug my face in his shirt.

"Daddy, Mom's a witch." My voice was muffled from his shirt.

"I'm not sure that I would call her that, but maybe…" He laughed. He lifted my head and brushed my hair out of my face. His brown eyes studied my face for a while and then he helped me to my feet. "Why don't you tell me what your mother did to scare you like that, princess?"

"What do you mean, what I did?" my mother snapped. "What about what James has done?"

"I didn't do anything," James insisted, his rough voice getting louder.

I listened as they started to fight back and forth.

"Enough!" my father shouted. "Princess, why don't you and I go into the cabin and get something to drink and wash up." I shook my head no and started to push back. "OK, we won't go back there," my dad said.

James walked over to me and put his hand on my shoulder. "I'm sorry," he said, as he laid the necklace in my hand and walked away.

I opened it again to see the picture of him and me, and started to run after him.

"Wait!" I yelled.

James stopped, not turning around.

"What is this?" I demanded. "When was this picture taken? Do you stalk me?"

James turned to give me a wary look. "That picture was taken a long time ago," he answered. He turned back around and with his back to me, he lifted his head toward the sky as if searching for answers.

"But…it looks like a recent picture. Do you have a computer?" I was searching for some kind of explanation for this picture of the two of us.

"What does that have to do with anything?" he asked as he rubbed his arm. "Do you even realize how much you hurt me and your mother!" he said as he turned to face me.

"I never touched you!" I screamed back, as I looked at the space between us. I watched as the waves behind him seemed to be going away from the boat and how it sparkled as the sun hit it.

"Don't you get it yet?" he laughed. "You don't have to touch anyone to hurt them," he said, shaking his head. His stare then turned cold and I watched as his hazel eyes started to turn brown. He extended his strong arm and said, "It's your fault she's like this. Fix it!" He pointed toward my mom.

I turned to see my mom push her sunglasses over her eyes. "I can't, not this time. This time, she has to remember on her own." Her smile was cold and unfriendly. James started to walk toward my mom as I watched her extend her arm and felt a gust of wind blow by me. I turned to see James slide back with his arms crossed in front of his face. "You're not as strong without her," my mother laughed. "You need her help. Would you like me to help her remember?" My mother's smile sent a chill down my spine and I felt that the next thing that was going to happen was not going to be nice. "Let's see if she remembers now."

The wind seemed to be stronger and I noticed as dark clouds started to form. The waves crashed against the boat and splashed up onto the deck. I quickly grabbed the railing to keep my balance. I shut my eyes, hoping it would go away, when a scene flashed in my mind. I watched as Alexis started to walk toward me, keeping her hands on the railing to stay steady. A wave hit the boat and she slid under the rail into the water. I quickly opened my eyes to see Alexis grabbing the railing. "Alexis!" I yelled. "Stay there, I'll come to you." I watched as my dad and Mr. Santiago were holding on to the back of the boat and I turned to see where James was.

"Keep your hands on the railing!" James yelled, trying to be heard over the wind and water.

"Alexis!" I yelled. "You have to help her!"

James looked at me with concern in his eyes. He knew something was going to happen.

"What did you see?" he asked, trying to keep his balance as his body seemed to sway with the ocean that surrounded us. Behind him I could see the dark clouds that loomed overhead, and the sound of thunder rolled in the distance.

"She's going to get hurt!" I screamed over the wind as my hair lashed around my face. "You have to help her. If you don't, she'll go over the side of the boat!"

He looked at me, realizing something. "You help her," he said calmly.

"What?" I shook my head, not believing the words I had just heard. This was his sister, someone I just met, and he wanted me to help her. How did he expect me to do that?

"You help her," he repeated, as if he were hearing my thoughts.

"She's your sister and she needs your help!" I pleaded with him.

"No," he said calmly. "She needs your help," he encouraged. "I can only do so much, but you...you are stronger than you think. You can do so much more than you think you can."

I turned to see Alexis still watching us as she gripped the railing. What was I supposed to do? Her eyes were filled with worry and I watched as she mouthed, *Help me*. It was then I felt my body push itself away from the railing and stand up. I started to put one foot in front of the other and walked toward Alexis with no trouble. She had one arm extended toward me as I looked to her side and saw the wave getting ready to hit the boat. I watched as my right arm extended and my hand went up. I watched as the wave seemed to hit an invisible wall and fell back into the ocean. I felt someone grab my hand and turned to see James.

"Make the storm stop," he instructed. I gave him a puzzled look and watched him smile. He knew that I had no idea of what to do. "Remember when we first got on the boat. The clear skies, the calm water. See it and it will be true."

I instantly closed my eyes and envisioned a calm day with the water still and the sun out. I felt the warmth of the sun on my face as I opened my eyes. I watched as my dad and Mr. Santiago got on their feet. My mother was standing by Alexis helping her up. Alexis started to run toward me.

"You did it!" she screamed as she hugged me. "I knew you could do it! All you had to do was remember how."

I felt the energy drain from my body; as it went limp James grabbed me. I looked up at his hazel eyes, which became more of a blue. "I'm tired," I said hoarsely. And with that, I shut my eyes and fell asleep.

—⚏—

James picked up my body and went toward my dad.

"We can put her in the bedroom," my dad instructed. James followed him to the back of the boat, toward the bedroom.

"Do you think she'll remember?" Alexis asked, almost jumping with joy from all the excitement. "I mean, look… the sun is out and the ocean is calm. She did that. She remembered, right?"

James looked down on me. "She still looks like an angel when she is asleep," he said, as he lay my body on the bed and pulled the blankets over me. He put the necklace in my hand and closed my fingers around the heart. "This should help her to have good dreams," he said as he kissed my forehead.

"You do know that we have a lot of explaining to do," my dad said as he turned to my mom. "You have so much more to teach her and tell her of all the time she has missed."

"I know, but for right now let's let her sleep, and think of a way to break it to her easily. She has missed over hundreds of years of her life," my mom said softly as she closed the door.

IX

The Wedding

I could still hear them as the door shut. I didn't even have the energy to shift onto my side as I just drifted off into my dreams.

I heard a lot of noise coming from outside my door. I quickly got up and noticed that I was not on the boat, but in a room much like my sitting room at home. The only thing missing was the family portrait. The curtains were a different color and the furniture was definitely different, but it still looked like the same room. I lifted myself off the couch and walked slowly toward the door. The voices were getting louder as I opened it. I watched as people were swarming around in a frantic frenzy. I saw chefs move in one door and out another. It looked as if they were preparing a feast. Then I watched as a woman with short blonde hair and wearing a nice blue suit open the double doors to the front of the house and started giving directions to the men standing in front of her.

"You're late!" she screamed at them. "The flowers were supposed to be here an hour ago! Take them to the back gazebo and arrange them like we planned. Then I need you to take the other set of flowers and arrange them in the front of the house for when they leave. And for goodness' sake, please don't forget to put some flowers at each table." I watched as she closed one door and moved to close the other. Her jaw dropped and she rushed out the door. "These are not the flowers we ordered!" she screamed. "They're the wrong color!" I watched as a man approached her from behind, putting his hand gently on her back and whispering something in her ear. She turned to him and smiled. "OK, put them up," she ordered. She then walked to the back of the house.

I walked around to see all the excitement and watched as people went in and out of the house quickly. I walked out to the back porch to see the chairs that lined the backyard and the flowers that surrounded the area. I saw the gazebo that had a chandelier hanging in the middle of it. *Must be someone's wedding day*, I thought. The smell of flowers and food filled the air, the sound of music flowed through the wind, and then I heard the deadliest scream come from an upstairs room. I ran inside and up to my room. I quickly scanned the room to see it littered with tux suit bags and shoes. Some of the flowers were lying on the floor and no one was there. I watched as some people ran past the room and into my parents' room. I quickly followed the crowd. As I pushed my way through the crowd, no one seemed to flinch. It was like I wasn't there. I finally got to what the crowd was looking at; it was a woman in her wedding dress with my mother standing over her.

"What have you done?" I heard that rough voice scream. I turned to see James going over to the woman, cradling her in his arms. He gently pushed her hair back, and with tears in his eyes he looked up at my mother. "Why now? Why today, of all days? Why today?" he screamed in anger.

"It's not time," my mother answered coldly. "I'm not ready yet." She folded her arms across her chest. "It's best if you leave."

James glared up at my mother. "You selfish…" James kissed the woman's forehead and then lay her back down. He got up with his head down and walked out the door. Alexis and Mr. Santiago walked out behind James, never turning around. I walked over to the girl and looked at her.

It was me.

I gasped. I sat up in bed to stare into the darkness. I looked at the clock and it read seven thirty. *Was I asleep for that long?* I thought. I felt something in my hand. I felt around for the light and found the switch. My arms still felt weak and stiff as I lifted the golden necklace to my face. I examined it more closely. The infinity symbol etched into the chain glistened from the light and the heart just dangled as it spun around. I took hold of the heart and ran my finger down the double *S*'s that were etched into the locket. The double *S*'s were interlocked and engraved in beautiful calligraphy writing. I didn't want to open it again, but my curiosity got the best of me. I opened the locket to see the picture of James and me. We were staring at each other and looked like there was nothing that could tear us apart. Our smiles seemed to brighten the room. That's when I was overwhelmed with a feeling I had never felt before. I could feel a tingling sensation that moved up my arms. I took a deep breath and closed my eyes.

"It will pass." I quickly opened my eyes to see my mother standing at the door. "How do you feel?" she asked.

"OK," I said wearily. "Are we going back home soon?"

"After we talk," my mother answered as she sat on the corner of the bed.

"What's going on, Mom? What is happening to me?" I asked, fighting back the tears.

My mom didn't move. She just watched me in disbelief. She got up off the bed and moved to the small circular window.

"You're special. You have many…different talents," she said, her voice dropping to a whisper.

"What do you mean?" I asked as I wiped my eyes.

"You have to explain it to her, honey. It's not fair what you have done, not only to her, but to James as well," my dad said in a stern voice. "Tell her about the house, the day you came back into her life and took it away from her," he said, as his face turned a shade of red from anger.

All these accusations being thrown around the room. The day she came back into my life. She'd never left my side as far as I could remember. I watched as my mother continued to stare out the window. She was stalling for time and I knew it. If she wasn't going to tell me, then I knew someone who might.

"No, don't tell me, 'cause I know someone who will," I said as I tried to get out of the bed. I pushed my legs over the bed and fell to the floor with a hard thud.

"You're still weak from earlier," my mother said with laughter in her voice.

My dad came toward me as I put my hand up. "I'll do it myself," I said as I pushed my hair to the side. I grabbed the side of the bed and lifted myself up. I felt my legs burn, refusing to let me move another inch. I fought the feeling of tiredness and the aches that I had throughout my body to reach the door.

"Do you need help?" I recognized the voice right away and looked up into James's loving eyes.

"Please," I said, and he bent down and picked me up. He carried me out of the room and placed me on the bench at the back of the boat.

"You lose a lot of energy when you don't use it for a while," he explained.

"Use what?" I asked, the events of what happened earlier still going through my head. *How did I do that? More importantly, what did I do?*

"She still won't tell you?" he asked staring in front of him as he clenched his fist in anger.

"No, but I have a feeling that you might," I said. The night air felt good blowing through my hair as I pulled it up into a bun. I leaned toward him, anxious to hear how he might explain the events that happened earlier.

"Well, where should I start?" he asked with a smile.

"Well...you could start by explaining this picture," I said as I held up the locket.

"Too far into the future," he answered. "Let's start at the beginning."

"OK," I said, feeling the air lighten between the two of us. It was as if we were starting off on the right foot, like we were getting another chance to introduce ourselves to each other.

"Well, tell me about the dreams you've been having," James said with a small smile.

"Don't you know? 'Cause earlier you seemed to know that I was having dreams," I answered with a smirk.

"All right," he said, chuckling.

I watched as his smile grew larger, and I couldn't help but smile along with him. I put my arm around his. "So tell me about us," I pried again.

He lifted my face up to his and said, "It's too much into the future."

His hazel eyes were as blue as the water around us. *I could get lost in his eyes*, I thought.

"You used to get lost in my eyes," he said, answering my thought.

"How'd you…?" I asked, quickly removing my arm from around his and sitting back. *How did he do that? How could he hear my thoughts?*

"It's how we are," he said. "It's who we are and what we do."

"Who are we?" I asked.

"You're a guardian," my mother answered from the side of me. I watched as she stood in front of me with a look of concern in her eyes.

"A what?" I asked.

"A guardian," she repeated. "We make sure that people live the lives they were meant to live. Our most well-known identity is guardian angels. We do what is right and fight battles that need to be fought. However, you and James are different."

"What do you mean, different?" I asked.

My mother sat down next to me and her eyes filled with tears. "We were young and didn't quite understand the conse-quences of what and who we were," she started. "All I have done is try and protect you from it, honey," my mom said as the tears started to flow.

"We better get down in the cabin," James said as he picked me up.

"Why?" I asked.

"It's going to rain," he answered as a drop hit my head.

I looked up into the sky that was once clear, with no clouds, as it suddenly filled with clouds and rain started to fall. How was that possible? The weatherman said that it would be sunny all weekend long, with no chance of rain. Where was this coming from?

James smiled at me. "That too you will learn with time," he said, and he walked toward the front of the boat to the cabin.

X

My Past

James sat me on the bench in the cabin. Alexis sat across from me and Mr. Santiago stood near one of the windows. My mother, followed by my dad, came down the stairs in the cabin.

"I called in and said we are dropping anchor and will be spending the night out here," my dad said. "I feel it's going to be a long night."

"Do you want a bottle of water?" Alexis asked me as she smiled.

"Don't do that to her, Alexis, that's how this whole mess started," Mr. Santiago snapped.

"It's OK, but yes, I do need that bottle of water," I said. I watched as Alexis got up and walked over to the small refrigerator. I looked at her with a puzzled look on my face as she handed me the bottle.

"What? Were you expecting me to move it with my mind?" Alexis laughed.

I blushed, not knowing the answer. Maybe I was, with all that had happened today. "Maybe." I smiled at her and shrugged my shoulders.

"Alexis is not one of us," James explained.

"How can that be?" I asked. "She is your sister. If the two of you are related, it would only make sense that she would be able to do what we do."

"My mother married her father—"

"Hi." Mr. Santiago waved his hand at me and laughed. "I am Alexis's father by blood, and James is my son by marriage."

"The two of us were here before they got married, Alexis was ten when my mother met her dad and twelve when they got married," James explained. I looked at James with a quiz-zical look. I didn't quite understand; the puzzle pieces didn't quite fit. James smiled as he said, "It will all make sense soon." I listened as the rain seemed to hit the boat harder outside. My mother grabbed another tissue. I watched as my father took my mother into his arms and stroked her back, whispering something into her ear. She shook her head and wiped her eyes. She then walked over to James as he stood up. "Not a chance. The last time I lost her. Not this time!"

My dad grabbed a chair, set it in front of me, and ushered my mom into the seat. "Everyone happy?" he asked. "James, sit beside her," he growled.

My mother grabbed my hand and started her story:

"My mother didn't tell me what I was until the day I met Christina. Christina is James's mother. We grew up together and became friends quickly, and that's when I noticed strange things happening. Like the day we were walking in the woods and ran into a bear cub. Christina touched it as the mother came out from behind a bush. I watched as Christina put an invisible wall between her and the mother. I ran toward the house with Christina yelling at me to stop, and that's when I noticed the bear in front of me. My mother showed up behind the bear as it stood up in front of me. I heard my mother yell at it to get down and I watched in amazement as it obeyed. My mother started petting the bear and then told it to go, and I watched as it went back into the woods. I was fearful like you are now and I ran toward the house, with Christina running behind me. Little did we know that someone else was watching. The townspeople came to my house that night, grabbed my mother and Christina's mother, and dragged them into town. They were put on trial for being witches and sentenced to death."

"Wait!" I interrupted. "A witch? How old do you think you are?" I asked with a smirk. "I mean, come on, when we go shopping together people think we're sisters, not mother and daughter." It was true my mother never seemed to age. She never had a wrinkle and she never had a gray hair in her head.

"Princess, let your mother finish," my father said as he sat on my other side.

"Christina took me to her house where our fathers were sitting at a table, talking. My father hugged me and told me that we had to go. We saw my mother for the last time that night, and the four of us moved to another town. As I grew older, Christina helped me to understand what was happening to me and how to hide our talents from others. Our favorite thing to do was to sit in the field in the beginning of spring and touch the flowers to make them bloom. At the age of seventeen I met a handsome stable hand. We talked every day and my father seemed to approve, Christina met a rich governor's son. On my eighteenth birthday, I watched as a strange man came to my house and talked to my dad. The man looked at me and told my dad that I looked like my mother. He then asked if I enjoyed being who I was and if I would like to continue my mother's legacy. I didn't quite understand, but I told him that my mother was a kind person and I would try to be as good as she was. I watched as my father nodded in agreement and the man left. That summer Christina and I married the men we had met. I became a nurse and Christina became a mother. You were so cute when you were born, James. Anyway, the next winter was a hard one and Christina came over to my house with James. She began to tell me that James was not her husband's child. She told me that her husband was never at home and was always at work, and she had met a man with talents much different from ours. She went on to say that the same man that visited us on my eighteenth birthday had visited her and told her that light and dark cannot mix. I didn't know how to help her. James was a product of something new and different. He had both light and dark talents. I promised Christina that nothing would happen to her son. The next spring I found out I was pregnant. Your father was so excited. You were born that winter with a blanket of snow covering the ground. When I held your little body in my arms it was the happiest day of my life. I named you after my mother. I thought that you would one day be as kind as she was, and I knew that you would follow in her footsteps. That night, your father and I talked about how one day he would die and his wife and daughter would go on without him. I told him that all we would have to do was grow old together and that I would soon pass the responsibility to you. I mean, you were half human and half guardian, you could only do so much. Some years passed and you and James became good friends. Christina and I watched as the two of you played so well together. Then one night I noticed something different about your father. He was holding you while you slept. I looked into his eyes, which seemed soulless. I put you in your bed and went back to your father and asked him what had happened. He told me that he had made a deal with this guy to be able to live like us. He wouldn't ever have to leave us—that we would be together forever. That's when our front door was kicked in and some men grabbed me, accusing me of being a witch. They said that one of the other nurses watched as I helped a wounded solider, and with my touch his gun wound closed and he started breathing again. I was found guilty on our front lawn and taken into town. You must have heard the noise and—"

"Watched as they burned you," I said, remembering my dream. "So the guy that grabbed me is my father."

"Yes," my mother said with more confidence.

"But, I saw you die in my dreams," I said.

"So did the townspeople," my mother went on. "I was sent back to watch over you because I never explained things to you, and James was moved to another town. I caught up to you and your father five years later and I noticed that you had adapted to what he was. I went back to see the man that had visited me on my birthday. He told me that because I was not around for five years that you had both light and dark talents as well, and you were becoming stronger than me. I asked him how I could prevent this from happening to you so that you could just live a normal life. He told me that I had to keep you away from your father and that on your eighteenth birthday he would visit you. So I did what any mother would do, and that was to take you back and start slipping through time. I kept you at an age that I could handle until I met someone who was worthy of being a father figure. I finally met that man decades later. He has been your father for so many years now, and we moved out here to keep you away from your real father. I knew that as soon as I met the man I would spend the rest of my life with, you would start aging again, and now your eighteenth birthday is coming up. I was hoping that when that man asked you, you would look at him with a crazy look and be spared the life that I was forced to live. You would be able to live a normal life. And it was almost that way, until your father found our number two months ago. The only way I knew to protect you was to get James back to you."

"Again!" James corrected her. "Back to her again."

"Yes, again," my mother continued. "So your dad," she said, pointing to my dad, "went on a manhunt, and with the help of the Internet and wireless electronics, found him and convinced him to come here."

The room was quiet for a while as we looked at each other. I picked up my bottle of water, taking a long, hard gulp, and could feel my strength returning. I waited for someone to crack a smile or start laughing, but nothing came. This was why I felt out of place, because I was. I was not like my friends, I was very different, and now I knew why. My family was not what I thought, and I was not what I thought.

"You have a choice," my mother said. "We can pretend this never happened," she went on in a promising voice as she grabbed my hand.

"Or she can learn about how to control it and help me," James said as he pushed my mother's hand down.

"Or I can ask, how old am I really, then? I mean, if what you are telling me is true, then I'm older than eighteen and I would have already talked to this man," I said, looking around the room for an answer.

It was Mr. Santiago that answered me. "Honey, you are well past the age of eighteen."

"Honey," my mom said, "if you choose not to see this, then we don't have to worry. You can marry Steven and be happy, and nothing like this will ever happen again. James will be able to handle this by himself, and you can live a normal life."

The room went quiet as everyone looked at my mother in disbelief that she had said something like that.

I grabbed James's hand and asked, "How old are you?"

He looked at me and asked, "Does it matter, as long as I found you?"

His eyes never left mine. I could feel my cheeks start to get warm and I quickly turned my head. My mom grabbed my hand and looked at me.

"Honey, you don't want to live this life. It's not a life, it's a pain," she said, as if trying to get me to back down.

"No!" I yelled, standing up. "It's about this perfect life that you want me to have with Steven! Mom, I like Steven as a friend and nothing else. He's a self-centered football jock who thinks that everyone should bow down to him! We will never be!"

The room went silent as James grabbed my hand and walked me upstairs. The rain had stopped and the water around us looked like a mirror. I watched as the stars above us twinkled.

"It's pretty, isn't it?" James asked.

"Yeah. So tell me, the dream I had about my mother ruining our wedding… was it real? Did it really happen? Or was it just a dream?"

"That was the very last time I saw you, about twenty years ago. Then your mother showed up and took your memory from you so that you couldn't remember me or anything that happened because she wanted her little girl back and wanted her to have a normal life. Not the type of life I would be able to give you," he said with his head down.

"Well, maybe I would be interested in learning who I really am and why I feel the way I do when I'm around you," I said, as I approached him and grabbed his hand. He tried to hide his smile and grabbed me by my waist. His touch sent shivers down my body. His touch was much different from Steven's. When Steven touched me it was like I was his property, but when James touched me it felt very different. He didn't have to like me or love me, he just did. I could feel his pulse echo mine as he gently touched my face.

"Will you teach me?" I asked as I closed my eyes. I felt his soft lips touch my forehead.

"Is it what you want?" he asked me. "Are you sure?" He kissed my cheek, then his eyes met mine.

"Yes, I want to remember all this and help you. Help me to remember, 'cause this feeling that is running through my body is—"

"Is something we had a long time ago and still remains between us," he said.

I put my hands on his chest to put little distance between us. "Did we…?"

James threw his head back and laughed. "No, you're still as pure as the day you were born…well, pure in that way."

"She'll stay that pure until she finds someone suitable," my father said from our side. "The two of you look good together again," he said with a smile. "In fact, I haven't seen my princess smile like that at anyone but me. Princess, your mother and I are tired and ready to go to bed, so I will put the cot out in the room. I do expect you to be in soon," my father warned as my mother followed behind him.

"You don't know what you are doing," my mother whispered as she went past us.

"Don't worry," I smiled at James. "She means well. She is my mother, after all. The cabin can be rearranged to have beds in it," I said as I looked at James.

"Princess, bedtime," my dad called from around the corner.

"I'll see you in the morning," I said. I could feel him watching me as I turned the corner, but I looked over my shoulder and he wasn't there. I stepped back around the corner; there was no way he walked to the cabin that fast. I turned back around as my heart sank. Then I felt my back hit the wall of the boat and took a deep breath. I felt his body heat and his strong spirit as he passionately kissed me. I closed my eyes and felt a surge of energy run through my body as his strong hands gently held my head.

"I've waited over twenty years to kiss you again, and by the way, you can open your eyes," he said as he walked back to the cabin.

"Princess," my dad said as he rounded the corner, "are you coming to bed?"

I shook my head and walked to the bedroom. I lay my head on the pillow, and as I closed my eyes, I knew that tonight was going to be a restful one. I could still feel his pulse in rhythm with mine, and it put me to sleep to know that although he was not there with me, he was.

XI

Disappearing Act

I woke up that morning earlier than anyone, or so I thought, and stepped out onto the deck. The sun made the water sparkle like little diamonds in the waves around us. I could hear Alexis and Mr. Santiago talking and I started walking toward the front of the boat. "Good morning," I said, walking up behind them. Alexis turned around to face me; Mr. Santiago still faced the water.

"Good morning," Alexis said, throwing her arms around me.

"What are you guys doing?" I asked, peering over the boat to see what they were looking at.

"My dad and I swore we saw this huge fish that went under the boat, so we were waiting for it to come back around," Alexis said as she peered over the boat again.

"What kind of fish do you think it was?" I asked, turning my head toward Mr. Santiago.

"Not sure when you just see a dark outline," he answered, not taking his eyes off the water.

"My dad has some fishing poles in the cabin. Do you want me to go get them?" I asked. "I can also turn on the fishing monitor thingy that my dad uses sometimes."

"Can we fish here?" Alexis asked, jumping up and down.

"Sure, just don't tell my mom she has to clean it or anything." I laughed.

"Princess, I'll get the poles," my dad said from behind me. "Good morning." I turned to see my dad walking toward us. My mother must have still been asleep because she was not following my dad around.

"Morning, Dad," I said as I walked down to the cabin with him. I hadn't seen James and figured he was still asleep. Maybe I could sneak a peek at him before he woke up. I wondered if he was one of those guys that just slept in his boxers, or maybe a guy who wore boxers with one of those tight shirts to bed. My dad opened the cabin door slowly, looked around and then walked in.

"He must be up," my dad said, "'cause he's not in here." He opened the thin closet door. He handed me four poles and grabbed the tackle box. My heart sank a little. I mean, if he was up, why didn't he say anything to me? I knew he knew I was looking for him. I reached the deck and started to walk toward Mr. Santiago and Alexis when I heard him.

"Just boxers," he whispered into my ear, as he grabbed the poles and walked toward his dad. "Morning, Mr. Kartone," he said as he caught up with my dad. I laughed as I ran toward him and he handed the poles to his dad.

"You have to be faster than that," he laughed. I looked up to see him sitting on the top of the cabin.

"Cool, I love this game," Alexis trilled.

"How did you do that?" I asked, shielding my eyes from the sun to look at him.

"How'd I do what?" he asked from behind me.

"That disappearing thingy," I said, trying not to laugh as I turned around.

"Disappearing thingy?" he said from behind me again. He had done it to me again. I looked into the space of nothing.

"OK, you're starting to get on my nerves with that!" I said, as I crossed my arms and glanced over at Alexis. I could tell that she was trying to hold back the laughter that was building up inside her.

"OK, turn all the way around. I promise not to move," he said. I turned to face him; he had a playful look on his face as he tried to contain the laugh that was forcing its way out.

"So, are you going to teach me how to do that?" I asked with my arms still crossed.

"OK," he said as he grabbed my hands. "Close your eyes."

I looked at him like, *No way*.

"Please close your eyes," he pleaded. I closed my eyes and the sounds around me became louder. I listened and could hear each ripple of the water hitting the boat and the whistle of the wind rushing by me. "Now, think of someplace on the boat that you would like to be." I instantly thought of the cabin. "Open your eyes," he instructed.

I opened them to see the table in front of me and him at my side. "Did I do that? I didn't even feel myself move."

"It's actually a defense mechanism," he said. "It helps get us out of danger's way. Sometimes it works and sometimes it doesn't." He went on to explain, "You see, if it doesn't work, then you have to understand that what is about to happen to you was meant to happen. If it does work, then you go on doing what you were doing."

"Can I move through time?" I asked with my eyes wide, like a child learning.

"That is a whole other thing I will teach you later, but for right now, let's just move in small spaces. I don't want to lose you again," he said as his face got a more serious look on it. "Do you want to try it on your own?"

"I'm a little nervous. I mean, what if I put myself somewhere I can't get out of?"

"The trick is to clear your mind and visualize where you want to be. I'll be waiting on the deck," he said as he disappeared.

I stood in the cabin looking around the room. *I must be crazy to think that I can do this*, I thought. I started to walk toward the cabin door when Alexis abruptly opened it.

"James said you're trying to cheat," she said, laughing. "You can do it. He said just believe in yourself. And by the way, I'm supposed to stay here until you do it." She stood between me and the door with her arms crossed and a wide smile on her face.

I took a step back and decided to amuse them; I closed my eyes and saw the deck where he would be waiting for me.

"Was it that hard to do?" James asked.

I opened my eyes to see James, my dad, and Mr. Santiago all staring at me as Alexis came running from the cabin.

"She did it!" Alexis said excitedly.

I looked around to see the deck and the beautiful clear blue sky. "Can I do it with my eyes open?" I asked James.

"Not really, 'cause you have to focus on where you are going and actually see it in your mind," he explained.

"I'm getting hungry," Alexis said, peering over the boat into the water. "Do we catch our breakfast this morning?"

"Alexis, honey," my mother interrupted. "We don't eat fish for breakfast. If you are hungry, then I suggest we head back to the club and have some breakfast," my mom said. "And Serina, honey, don't do that when we get back to shore."

"Your mom's right," James said. "Everything we can do, we can't do around people 'cause it's dangerous. If someone sees you do it, they can tell someone else, who tells someone else, and before you know it, everyone is looking for you. Not to mention if the government got hold of you."

"Are there any more of us?" I asked, not wanting to lose sight of him. He was very handsome as the light shone down on him. His eyes the crystal blue and me lost in them.

"Sure, but not too many choose the path to continue, and some don't even know. In fact, the last time I checked, besides your mom, I was the only one left here in the United States who chose to continue this. And now I won't be alone if you choose to follow this path with me," he said, as he grabbed my waist and pulled me closer to him. *I could stay in this spot with him for the rest of my life and be happy*, I thought. He made me feel like we were the only ones around for miles and nothing could tear us apart.

Alexis, James, and I sat on the deck as we watched the pier come in sight. James sat with his arm around me as we pulled up. We talked and he explained more of who I was and how it affected life around us. There was so much more that I needed to learn, but he told me that it would come in time, when I started to remember things. I told him that I hoped I could remember soon. Alexis reminded us that we had five days before I was visited by this mysterious man on my birthday, and to my surprise, no one seemed to ask his name—or maybe he just never told anyone. When we arrived at the dock, James helped my dad and Mr. Santiago tie the boat down. I helped Alexis off the boat while my mother locked everything up. We walked into the bright autumn-colored dining hall, where we were seated immediately.

"It helps to call in," my mother said casually.

James pulled a chair out for me and I gracefully sat down next to him. Nothing could ruin this perfect morning for me. I had never felt so happy, so alive, so content…

"Good morning, beautiful," a voice said behind me. I didn't have to even turn around to know that Steven was there. The sound of his voice made me cold and uneasy. He put his hand on my shoulder and kissed me on the cheek. "What a surprise to see you here," he said in his deep voice.

"Good morning, Steven," my father said. "Are your parents here?"

"Yeah, Dad is doing laps in the pool and Mom is in the sauna, then we're supposed to go out on the boat for a fishing trip," Steven answered him with a smile.

"Have you eaten breakfast?" my mother asked in her most cheerful voice.

"Not yet. I was coming down here to wait for them and grab a bite to eat," he replied.

I could feel the anger coming from my left and turned to face James. He was acting like he was reading the menu, although I could see in his eyes that he was listening to everything that was going on around him. I decided to say something before my mother caused any more trouble.

"So you're picking something up and then meeting them at the boat?" I asked as I looked up at Steven.

"Yep, and I was pleasantly surprised to see you here," he answered quickly. "I tried calling you last night, but only got your voice mail. Then Matthew said he heard something about your dad calling and you guys staying out on the water for the night."

"Mr. Kartone decided to entertain our guests on the water," my mother said with a huff. "If your parents aren't here yet, why don't you join us, Steven?" my mother said, and called for a waiter to bring another chair.

"I would hate to intrude," Steven objected.

"You're not intruding, you're like family. Why don't you sit next to Serina?" my mother insisted. The waiter brought another chair and set it to my right. I looked over to my mother, who just sat there and smiled.

What are you doing? I mouthed to her from across the table. She pretended not to see me and continued with conversation.

"So, I see they have the ballroom almost ready for the winter ball this Friday," she said as she looked at me.

I could have died right there. I put the menu up to my face. I already knew what I was going to order. The menu hardly changes except for around the holidays, when it has festive names for plates that were already on it.

"Dad, there are no prices on this menu." Alexis tried to whisper so no one could hear her.

"You know what my dad always says, if you have to ask the price then you can't afford it," Steven said. He laughed, and my mother quickly followed with her fake laugh.

I elbowed Steven in his side. "We have guests here," I said through clenched teeth.

"What? I was just joking," he said as he put his arm around me. I quickly leaned toward the table to avoid his touch.

My dad made the situation right. "You see, Alexis, they don't put the prices on so that the ambulance won't show up here, just at your house when they send you the bill."

"Really?" she asked innocently.

"No, my dad is just joking," I said. "The price list is at the house. The people here think it's tacky to put prices on their menu, and besides, it's all charged to the account they use when you become a member here."

"The usual, Mr. Kartone?" the waiter asked as he poured my father a cup of coffee.

"Yes, please," my father answered.

"And for your guests?" the waiter asked as he acknowledged the Santiagos.

"Breakfast is on me. Let them order to their hearts' content," he answered.

"Miss Kartone, your latte," another waiter said as he placed a cup in front of me.

"Thank you." I was hoping that maybe I had made someone here mad enough at me to slip something in my drink so that I could escape this madness. I had a man on my left that was perfect in my eyes; he asked me how I was and treated me like a person and not some trophy. And then I had the jock on my right who thought of me as nothing more than a trophy. I took a sip and closed my eyes as the warm liquid slid down my throat.

"Not here," James said in a whisper as he put his hand on my leg. I opened my eyes and looked at him. He smiled at me.

"So, Serina, you never did answer my question," Steven said, as he shot James a look of displeasure.

"And that question would be?" I turned to Steven.

"What are you wearing to the winter ball, and when am I picking you up?" he asked.

I choked on my latte as I jumped up. Both James and Steven got up as well. I looked down to see that some of my latte had spilled on my shirt. "Excuse me, I'll be right back," I said, and walked quickly to the bathroom. I opened the door and saw that no one was in there. I grabbed a towel, put some water on it, and started wiping the stain off my shirt. The stain was not going to come out, although it looked a little better. Then I heard the door open; it was Alexis.

"I have a spare T-shirt in my book bag," she said. She handed me a white T-shirt that had a rhinestone heart in the middle of it.

"Thank you," I said, as I took it and went into one of the stalls.

"Is your mother always like this?" she asked.

"Worse, sometimes," I said as I pushed my head through the top of the shirt. I flung my hair out of the shirt and quickly went to the mirror. I pushed my hair back and pulled it up into a ponytail as Alexis watched me.

"Here, I'll put your shirt in my book bag," she said, and she took my shirt and shoved it in.

"Let's go before anything else can happen," I said as I opened the door.

Alexis just stood there. "Please don't hurt him again," she pleaded, as her eyes began to fill with tears.

"What?" I asked. I stepped back into the bathroom and let the door shut behind me.

"When your dad came, it took him two weeks to talk James into coming back because James knew your mother didn't want you to know about him. James knew that once he saw you again it would hurt more if you..." Her eyes started to fill with tears. I quickly grabbed another towel and handed it to her.

"Look, I want to remember. I want to know your brother more, and if that means defying my mother, then that's what I'll do! Your brother makes me feel…whole." Saying that word made me realize that was the difference between Steven and James. James made me feel like I was a whole person, not two people working to become one. We were one already. "Come on," I said as I grabbed Alexis's hand. This was one battle my mother was going to lose. I had five days before I turned eighteen and legal enough to make my own decisions. I was going to start today.

Alexis and I walked back to the table as I watched as both James and Steven reached for my chair.

"Sorry about that," I said as I sat down.

"Are you all right, princess?" my dad asked.

"I'm fine, just went down the wrong pipe," I said. The food was already at the table and my fruit bowl sat in front of me. I picked up my fork and shoved half a strawberry into my mouth.

"Good morning, Dave," I heard Mr. Brockway say.

"Good morning," my dad answered as he stood up to shake his hand. "I'd like you to meet my friends: Joseph Santiago, his daughter, Alexis, and this fine young man is his son, James."

"We need him on the football team," Mr. Brockway said, standing back to admire James. "A good strong boy like you could have probably save my son's butt from being tackled this season. Do you play?" he asked.

"No, sir," James said, as he stood up and shook his hand.

"A good grip there, too," Mr. Brockway said. "So, you guys will be our new neighbors."

"Yes, sir," James answered. "We will have all our stuff here tomorrow afternoon."

"It's too bad you guys didn't move here sooner, you would have been able to play. But I think we have only one more game and then it's off to the finals," he said with a smile. "Oh, well, maybe we can talk you into joining the wrestling team. I would like to see the faces of the boys who will come up to you," he said with a laugh.

"Oh, honey, stop bothering him," I heard Mrs. Brockway say. "Let them finish their breakfast."

"It's OK," my mother said in a cheerful voice.

"Well, I hope my boy was on his best behavior," Mr. Brockway said as he ruffled Steven's hair.

"He's an angel," my mother answered him with a disgusting smile on her face. It made me wonder why she would go through all the trouble she did to try and fit in, when the fact remained that she always fit in.

"Well, Serina needs to let him know what color her dress for the winter ball is so his tux can match," Mrs. Brockway said. Listening to this was like listening to fingernails on a chalkboard. It made my blood run cold.

"I don't have a dress yet," I said, not taking my eyes off my half-eaten bowl.

"Well, I think that we girls should go shopping," my mother said. "It is this Friday." She let her voice go up an octave.

"Hey, I have an idea…why don't we let the boys go fishing and we'll take the girls shopping for dresses!" Mrs. Brockway said, trying hard to hide her excitement at the thought of dressing us up like dolls.

"Well, we were going to fish early this morning and we got hungry, so we came back," my father started. I instantly shot my dad a look. He looked at me and said, "What, princess?"

"Sounds like a plan," Mr. Santiago said. "I like to fish! Would you like to go with them, Alexis?" he asked.

"Yeah, Alexis, we'll have so much fun," I said with a smile.

Alexis looked up at me. "I've never been to a ball before, and besides, I don't have a date."

"It's OK," I said with a smile as I put my hand on Steven's shoulder. "They're new here, so why don't we do this…Steven, you take Alexis, and James can be my date," I said, smiling at James. The group went silent and my mother looked defeated. If she could have choked me at that moment she would have. I smiled, knowing that I had won her little battle. Yes, one point for me.

"Actually, that's not a bad idea," Mrs. Brockway said. "I mean, how better to make a first impression than to be seen with two of the most popular kids at school."

"It's settled, then." I smiled. "I'll be waiting outside," I said. I stood up and walked out, not turning back to see the shocked looks on the parents' faces.

"I'm going with her," Alexis said as she walked out behind me.

"Me too," James joined in.

"Serina…wait!" Alexis shouted as she tried to catch up with me.

"Stop!" James yelled behind me.

My feet felt like two cement blocks. I almost lost my balance as my body came to a halt.

"Did you do that?" I asked, as I turned my body to face James. It was as if my feet didn't want to move and I was stuck in place.

"What was that back there?" he demanded, ignoring the question I had asked. I shot him a look and he grinned. "They won't move until you tell me what's going on."

"Look, I don't want to go, let alone with Steven!" I answered. "Besides, with the two of you there, maybe we won't have to stay too long. Come on, don't you want to go with me? I mean, it would be a shame to lose me again," I said, as I took my index finger and slid it up his chest. I felt the weight of my feet start to feel normal again.

"If he does anything to my sister!" he said as his eyes turned a dark brown.

"He won't touch her as long as we're there," I assured him, as I took his face in my hands and kissed him. I felt him slip his hands around my waist and pull me closer to him.

"Um, guys, we have company," Alexis said. I turned to see Steven headed in our direction, and mad was not even the word to describe the way he looked. "Serina, your boyfriend is coming and he looks upset!"

"HE IS NOT MY BOYFRIEND!" I yelled. I looked over James's shoulder to see Steven stomping his way toward me. I knew this look. This was the look I despised. This was the difference between James and Steven. Steven looked at me as if I was nothing more than an object and James had taken it from him.

James looked behind him and then slowly turned to me. "OK, now he looks pissed. I think he heard you say that."

"James, now would be a good time to teach her something else," Alexis said. Her voice shook a little. "Maybe like calming him down, or making him go in another direction. James…do something."

James turned to look again. "I can't, he's too close now," he sighed. "We're going to have to just play this one out. Hopefully, we can talk our way out of this situation.

Remember, Serina, let's keep our anger under control. Don't lose it."

In that instant I felt James's arms releasing my waist as he stepped back. I saw Steven looking down at me. "I will deal with you later!" he said as he pushed me to the side. I fell to the ground, heard a snap, and felt a searing pain go up my leg. I screamed.

"Serina!" Alexis screamed, and she bent down beside me. "Go get someone to help!" she screamed.

Steven, stopping only for a moment, looked down at me in horror. The sound of the snap was loud enough for everyone to hear. Not knowing what to do, Steven ran back toward the club in a hurry. James watched as he entered the club and then calmly knelt down beside me. I sat there whining as the pain got worse and I could feel it start to throb.

"Where does it hurt?" James asked as he gently touched my leg.

"STOP! IT HURTS!" I yelled. "DON'T TOUCH ME!" I felt it start to swell up, and more pain shot through my leg as if it had been stabbed. I felt the tears start to form behind my eyes and I began to panic. *Maybe I broke it*, I thought.

"It's your ankle," he said calmly, as he put his hand on the throbbing part of my body.

"I SAID, DON'T TOUCH!" I yelled again, as another wave of pain hit me. He grabbed my ankle in his hand and squeezed it. I screamed in pain and then punched him in his arm.

"That hurt…a little," James said. He laughed and got up.

"I am going to hurt you!" I said, as I got up and walked toward him. "What were you thinking? My ankle is probably broken and you're squeezing it, you jerk!"

"How bad does your ankle hurt?" James said. He smiled, trying to hold back the laughter that was aching to come out.

"It hurts a lot and…I'm standing with no pain," I said, realizing why James was laughing at me. I looked over at Alexis, who also started to giggle a little when she realized that I was all right. "You're really starting to get on my nerves with things like this. So, let me guess, you healed my ankle, right?"

"She can be taught," he said. "I'm just glad that Steven went in to get your parents. Otherwise, I wouldn't have been able to do that. He is a jerk, though. I ought to—"

"But you can't!" Alexis quickly intervened. "Remember, the two of you can only do so much, and don't you even think about it, James! I don't want you ending up on the wrong side. Please," she pleaded.

James smiled at her. "Don't worry. I wouldn't. I just wish that sometimes people would think before they act on their first feeling. It's what gets us in trouble."

"So how do we explain this to our parents?" I asked, still putting my weight on my ankle in amazement. A few minutes ago I would have never dreamed of standing on it, and now it was as if nothing had happened at all. I had to admit it was pretty cool.

"It's not our parents we have to worry about, it's his parents and him," James corrected me.

"Just make something up." Alexis shrugged. "It's not like we haven't told a story or two in the past."

James glanced over at Alexis. "First of all, they're not stories, they're just not complete, and second, she twisted her ankle when Steven pushed her. The snap we heard came from the branch she stepped on."

"What branch?" I asked, looking around the ground.

James looked behind me and pointed at the thin twig that appeared there. "That one." He smiled as he slowly walked toward it and stepped on it, breaking it in two.

I laughed and shook my head. "Should I get back down on the ground and hold my ankle?"

James smiled and crossed his arms. "No! Drama queen." James quickly looked behind him, as we all did, when we heard the door to the club burst open and the parents following Steven out. "Here comes the cavalry," James said.

My dad was the first one to come to my rescue. "Princess, what happened?" he asked as he pulled me close to him. He examined me from head to toe and then looked up at me. "Where did you get hurt?"

"I'm OK. James and Alexis helped me up. I think I just twisted my ankle," I said, looking at James as his eyes turned worried again. He stood beside me as he looked at my dad. I watched my dad smile and then nod his head toward Steven. James shook his head slightly and showed my dad my ankle.

"No, I heard a snap!" Steven jumped in.

"We all did," Alexis stated. "She stepped on a twig when she fell back. Besides, if you hadn't pushed her, none of this would have happened!" she yelled.

"Steven! You pushed Serina," his father scolded as he made his way toward Steven.

"No, I moved her out of the way," Steven replied.

That's when the chaos of Steven trying to explain himself and his father watching him with hawk eyes to make one wrong move began. I moved closer to James as my dad watched and shook his head in disappointment.

"You know, maybe we should go fishing later," my dad said, interrupting the disagreement among everyone.

"No, 'cause I want to take the girls shopping," my mother whined. "Besides, Serina said she was all right and it sounds to me as if it was all a misunderstanding. Nothing to worry about. The dance is Friday, and Serina needs to try on a dress and we need to find one for Alexis."

"Then take the girls shopping and we men will go home and relax," my dad sighed.

"No, Dave, I would like you and your friends to join me and Steven, please. It's the least I can do," Mr. Brockway said as he shot Steven a dirty look.

"Joseph, what do you say?" my dad said, turning toward Mr. Santiago.

"Kids will be kids," he said. "I say we try and start back on the right foot." Mr. Santiago shrugged.

"All right, then!" my dad exclaimed with his hands cupped together. "Princess and Alexis, you have fun picking out dresses and we'll have fun fishing."

I turned to James. "Be careful," I said, my voice low.

"It's you I'm worried about, being alone with your mother," he said, looking toward my mother as she smiled at him. "I don't trust her yet."

"Serina." I felt someone grab me from behind. "I'll see you later," Steven said as he kissed my forehead. He never took his eyes off James.

"Steven," I started as I rolled my eyes.

"Come on, Serina," my mother instructed. I walked with Alexis, following my mom and Mrs. Brockway.

I looked over my shoulder to see that James was walking with my dad and talking to him. I wondered what they could be talking about. Hopefully it was about what happened and it would be the truth, not what Steven probably told everyone.

The ride to the boutique shop was a boring one. My mom and Mrs. Brockway talked and laughed all the way. The first conversation consisted of what the ballroom would look like and how many pictures they should get of us.

"Mom, it's not prom," I said. I rolled my eyes and watched as we passed cars on the highway. It felt as if it were going to be a long ride, although we weren't far from the usual boutique.

"Speaking of prom…has Steven asked you yet?" my mother asked, glowing.

"No, and what if he wants to take someone else?" I said. "Besides, Steven could ask any girl and I'm sure she would love to go with him. I mean, I'm not the only girl who goes to that school."

"Serina, honey, he will ask you soon. You do know that he would like to be able to call you his girlfriend," Mrs. Brockway said with a smile. "The two of you look so cute together, and I can honestly say that out of your circle of friends, you are so well mannered and so very pretty."

"I value our friendship too much," I said, hoping that would stop the conversation.

To my surprise, it did, and the rest of the ride was very peaceful and quiet. My mother and Mrs. Brockway would say a word or two, but for the most part it was very relaxing. I looked over at Alexis as she stared out the window and watched as the traffic went by her. She looked a little nervous and not so comfortable with her surroundings. I started to feel bad for putting her in the middle of this. It wasn't as if she had asked for this type of punishment. She had just come here, and already she was going shopping for a dress for the winter ball and being pushed to have a date with someone she hardly knew.

"Alexis," I said very quietly.

Alexis slowly turned to face me. "Hmm," was all she said.

"I'm sorry for dragging you into this. You know, if you don't want to go or do this, I can always let my mom know. You don't have to go if you don't want to," I said, starting to feel even worse about what I had just done.

Alexis shrugged. "It's all right, Serina," she said, as she turned to look out the car window again.

The car turned and I noticed we were headed down the exit ramp. We passed a couple of streets and then made a left. I watched as the trees started to surround us. The boutique was a small shop in the middle of nowhere, but housed such nice dresses. It was like a diamond in the rough, which was what my mother always called it. We pulled into the small parking lot as my mother's eyes lit up with excitement. "We're here!" my mother exclaimed.

Alexis looked at me. "Thanks a lot!" Alexis looked worried and uncomfortable. I watched as she opened the door and then just sat there. I could tell she was anxious and had no idea what to do or say. I felt bad for her, and it was partially my fault that she was dragged along with us in the first place. I say partially because her dad agreed with the idea.

"You're welcome!" I said with a smile, then I opened the door and got out. Alexis followed me as my mother and Mrs. Brockway behind us with their chatter of how we would love it and how exciting it was to go shopping for dresses.

"You know, Alexis," Mrs. Brockway smiled at her, "I've always wanted to go dress shopping. I have a son and never got to shop for dresses except with Serina and her mother. If you would like, I could help you," she said in a caring voice.

Alexis pushed her hair behind her ear and nodded her head. "Sure," she said in a small voice, looking at the ground.

I opened the door to the boutique. "Good morning, ladies," a tall thin lady greeted us at the door.

"She looks like the wicked witch with those long fingers," Alexis said with a laugh.

We walked into the small boutique full of beautiful dresses and Alexis looked around the shop in amazement. My mother put her hand on Alexis's shoulder and said, "The shop is open, honey, go and find any dress you like." The look in Alexis's eyes was like that of a child in a candy store as she ran to the first rack of dresses.

"I remember when you used to be like that," my mother whispered into my ear. She followed Alexis and Mrs. Brockway to start showing her some dresses. I slowly made my way to the small rack and started shifting through some of the dresses, trying to figure out what dress to wear to this winter ball.

"Serina," the old woman said behind me. "Your dress is already in the dressing room," she informed me, as she ushered me to the back of the store. "The dress is in here. Come out when you are done." She pulled the door shut. I looked at the back wall to see a blue dress with sparkling snowflakes that lined the skirt. I quickly undressed and stepped into it. As I stood in front of the mirror, I thought, *What a beautiful dress*. I looked at the off-the-shoulder straps that accented my arms and loved the way the skirt flowed out. I actually felt like a princess, and to know that I was going with James made my heart skip a beat. I wondered what he and my dad were doing with Steven and his dad.

XII

The Catch

"OK, boys!" Mr. Brockway said as he tugged on his line. "Get the net, we have a live one here."

Steven grabbed the net as he shot James a dirty look. "Let me show you how a real man catches a fish."

"I'll show you how a real man catches a fish!" James said under his breath. He walked over to his dad and my dad as they smiled at him.

"Here, take my pole son," my dad said as he handed James the pole. James took the pole as he watched Mr. Brockway and Steven pull up an unusual-looking fish.

"Good work, son!" Mr. Brockway said as he patted Steven on the back. "Not sure what this fella is doing out here this time of year."

"What type of fish is it?" Mr. Santiago asked, looking at it.

"It's a cobia," Mr. Brockway smiled. "They like warmer waters and are usually found in Florida. This guy must have taken a wrong turn and just happened upon my son's line," he laughed.

James rolled his eyes and stared out into the water. He closed his eyes and concentrated on the task at hand as he let his energy run through the pole. He felt a jerk on the line, and then another. James opened his eyes slowly as he quickly tugged the line, and then felt it start to fight. He knew he had something.

"Hold on to it!" Mr. Kartone yelled. The group quickly made their way toward James and my dad, watching the line in the water.

James's muscles in his arms strained as he held on to the pole. "It's bowing the pole!" James said as he pulled up on it.

"It will hold her," my dad said.

Mr. Brockway and Steven were now on the side of the boat. James grunted as a fin broke the top of the water.

"What type of fin is that?" Steven asked, pointing to the water and trying to be heard over the excitement in the boat.

"Not sure," James said. He pulled the line again and saw that something else had broken the surface of the water. James tried to see what it was. It looked like the thin twig that Serina had stepped on. James smiled at the thought.

"It's a swordfish!" my dad said excitedly as he pointed toward the water. "Look, that's the tip of its nose!" All the men moved closer to see a piece of the thin sword break through the water again.

"Steven, move everything out of the back of the boat, now!" Mr. Brockway commanded.

Steven walked slowly to the back of the boat to move the cooler and fishing line that were lying on the deck.

"James, move him to the back of the boat," Mr. Brockway instructed.

My dad and Mr. Santiago helped James move to the back of the boat.

"This fish is going to get away!" James yelled, trying to get hold of the mighty fish that was fighting for its life. "I don't think it wants to give up."

"No, just tire him out." My dad smiled. "Besides, what fish do you know that wants to be caught? They just give you a fight until they get tired." My dad laughed, and the rest of the group joined in on the amusement.

"Look!" Mr. Brockway yelled as he pointed toward the water. They all watched as the majestic fish jumped out of the water and slammed the top of it with a hard thud as it fought the line.

"Reel him in, he's starting to get tired," Mr. Santiago encouraged.

James tugged on the line again as his muscles ached from the fight. "He's starting to tire me out," James said as he kept walking to the back of the boat.

"Get the holding tank ready, Steven, 'cause we are taking this fish home!" Mr. Brockway shouted proudly, not taking his eyes off the water.

"Where is the hook?" my dad asked.

"It's hanging on the side by the tank," Mr. Brockway said, pointing to the tank, still watching the fish that James had been fighting for what seemed like a lifetime.

"I'll get it," my dad said, running to the side of the holding tank.

The boat was full of energy as they watched James fight with this fish for a good forty-five minutes. Finally, the fish gave in and James reeled it to the back of the boat. Mr. Brockway grabbed the fish with the hook as my dad and Mr. Santiago grabbed the front part of the fish. They put the fish in the holding tank and Mr. Brockway tried to measure it.

"What's the grand total?" Mr. Santiago asked proudly as he slapped James on the back.

"He is twelve feet!" Mr. Brockway exclaimed, and they all congratulated James on the wonderful catch.

"That's how a real man fishes," James said. He smiled and laughed as the rest of them joined him. Steven shot him a dirty look as he stomped back into the cabin.

They reached the pier and Alexis ran up to the boat. "I want to see the fish!" she exclaimed.

"Hold on, honey, Mr. Brockway has to get someone to help us get it out of the holding tank," Mr. Santiago said.

I ran up to my dad. "So, you guys finally caught a big one?" I asked, laughing. "I guess that means the fish stories you tell tonight will actually be true."

"No, James caught the big one," my dad said as James walked off the boat. "He fought it well and has earned the right to brag." My dad smiled. "He gets to tell all the fish stories he wants tonight."

"Mr. Kartone." My dad looked over to see Alexis standing beside him, pouting. "I want to see the fish, but no one will take me to see it."

"OK, I'll take you to see the fish," my dad said as he took Alexis's arm.

"So you caught the fish?" I asked as James approached me.

"Yeah," he said with a smile. "It gave me a run for my money. I had to fight it for forty-five minutes before it finally gave in." A crowd had started to form because news of a swordfish being caught was spreading through the club like wildfire. Men were coming up to Mr. Brockway wanting to see it, and waiting for help to arrive to get it out, weigh it, and get an accurate measurement of the fish. "Want to go see it?" James asked as he held out his arm.

"I would love to," I said, as I took it and followed him to the holding tank. As we approached the boat I saw the crowd that had started to gather. A couple of guys ran past us to join in the festivities. James took my hand and helped me up on the boat as Mr. Santiago and Mr. Brockway laughed. I saw my dad looking down at the small holding tank where the fish lay. Alexis was looking over the side and then looked at me.

"It's sad," she said with a frown. "It's a pretty fish and now it's dead. It's very big." I looked behind her to see the long fish lying in the tank, its big snout in the form of a sword and its eye staring up at me. I agreed with Alexis; it was a pretty fish and I felt sorry for it.

"I didn't hurt it," James said, looking at me sympathetically.

I glanced over at him. "Really?" I rolled my eyes. "You caught it with a hook in its mouth and you didn't hurt it?" James shrugged as our dads pushed us out of the way, and some guys helped them get the fish out and carried it to the pier. I watched as they pulled it up by the tail and it hung.

"So you're the one that caught it." A tall man came up to James.

"Yes, sir." James smiled. "She put up a good fight for a while."

The man congratulated him on his catch and went to join the others while they weighed it. We all watched as it was weighed in at a hundred pounds.

"So, what are you going to do with her?" Mr. Brockway asked James. James shrugged.

"Well, he could have it cut up and we could have sword-fish for dinner tonight." My dad smiled.

"We could have it mounted." Mr. Santiago smiled. "His first fish, and he caught a beauty."

James smiled over at me. "I did catch a beauty." I knew instantly that he wasn't speaking of the fish that was hanging.

Steven walked by me with a scowl on his face. "Beginner's luck," he mumbled under his breath. "Bet he can't do it again."

"If he wanted to, I know he could." Alexis laughed over by me. Steven shot her a dirty look and walked back to the club. We watched as the fish was taken away and the crowd started to disperse.

After all was said and done with the fish, I watched as James walked over to my dad and started talking with him. I watched as they both laughed and my dad motioned for me to join them. My heart skipped a beat as I walked closer to James. "Princess, James wants to see the stables and where we keep our horses," my dad said. I gave my dad a puzzled look.

"He wants to see the horses?" I asked.

"Yes, princess, he wants to see the horses," my dad answered. "Take him to the stables and go for a ride."

"Does Alexis want to go?" I asked, turning to see if she was around.

"No, we'll catch up to you two later," my dad said as he joined the others.

"Why do you want to see horses?" I asked James as we pushed through the crowd and off the pier. He shrugged his shoulders.

"I'll tell you later," James said. We continued walking until we reached the path for the stables. "It's pretty out this way," he said, admiring the trees and the walkway we followed.

"Yeah, you should see it in the spring when the flowers are blooming," I said. "So tell me, how old are you again?"

James laughed. "Older than you." He watched a bird fly from the nearby trees.

The rest of the way to the stables was quiet except for the occasional bird chirping and the way the leaves crunched as we walked through them. Soon, a long wooden building came in sight. A beautiful black steel fence surrounded the area where the horses were let out to graze. There were two horses in the yard, one brown and one white with small brown spots, grazing on the grass. I looked over at James, whose eyes became a soft blue as he looked on with excitement. We walked over to the front of the stables as James looked at the archway.

"That is really nice, the picture that is etched into the wood," he said as he stopped to admire at it. It was a picture of a horse draped with a blanket that had a family crest on it, kind of like the ones you would find in medieval times.

I walked over to my stable. "James, this is Starr," I said as I stroked her head. "This is my horse."

"I guess you called her Starr because of the star-shaped marking in the middle of her forehead." James smiled as he petted the horse.

"Is it that obvious?" I asked as I turned to face him. "She is all white except for this brown star shape here."

"Does your mom and dad have horses?" he asked.

"My dad has a horse that he keeps behind those doors," I said. "I've never seen him, but when I was little my dad said the horse was stubborn and to never go near the door 'cause he could hurt me."

"So you've never even seen the horse?" he asked with a grin. James started walking toward the door at the end of the stable. The horse behind the door started to whinny and kick.

I grabbed James by the arm. "What do you think you're doing? My dad said the horse is dangerous and you shouldn't go near it." James looked at me and grinned as he took my hand and started toward the door again. I watched as we got closer and the hinges of the door threatened to come off. The horse behind the big door neighed louder, and the horses around the stable started to rear up as if they were as scared as I was. James took my hand from around his arm. He went up to the door and unlatched it. He opened the door to the stable as the horse whinnied louder. A black horse reared up as the door opened. James calmly reached up with his hand.

"It's me, old friend," he said quietly. I watched as the horse came down and shook itself. James opened the gate and went into the stable. He stroked the horse gently. "I've missed you." He looked down at its front leg and rubbed his hand over the scar that was there. "That was a nasty battle and you still have the wound to prove you were there."

I walked closer to the stable and looked at the pure-black horse. "She's a fine horse," I said admiringly.

"He's a fine horse," he corrected me. "His name is Midnight and he has been my horse for years. I have an idea! Let's take the horses out for fresh air."

"OK!" I said, as I walked over to Starr to get her ready to go out.

James was already out and waiting with Midnight when I brought Starr out. "So my dad was just keeping your horse here?" I asked.

"Your dad has watched over many of the things and persons I had to leave behind," he said as he mounted Midnight. "Is there a trail where no one goes?" he asked.

"Yeah, but we can get hurt going on them," I said.

"I won't let anything happen to you. Trust me!" he said as his eyes became bluer.

"OK," I said. I led the way to a trail that led to an open field. Once we were out on the trail, I realized that I had forgotten how much I missed riding Starr. It looked as if Midnight had missed James just as much as James had missed Midnight. It took us about an hour before we hit a clearing and James looked around.

"This is the perfect place," James said as he dismounted Midnight. James walked over to help me down from Starr.

"Want to see something cool?" he asked, almost childlike, as if he were going to show off a brand-new toy.

"Sure!" I said, as I grabbed Starr's bridle to tie her to a tree.

"Just leave her," he said. "She'll stay where she is."

I dropped the leather straps and walked over to Midnight. James was stroking him as I started to smell something burning. I looked down to see all four of his hooves burn a blue blaze as the horse reared up in front of James. Midnight let out a loud neigh as his eyes got wide and turned a fiery red. I fell backward as his coat turned so black that it looked like midnight blue. The horse then ran in circles as if he were being held back from something he wanted. He started running in circles around James as if to taunt him to play. Every so often the horse would stop and then run in the other direction. James started laughing. "Get it out of your system," he said. I watched in amazement as the horse bucked and kicked at the air. The horse stopped and looked at me. He then looked back at James. "I'll get her," he said as he walked toward me. "Come on," he said as he grabbed my hand to help me up. We walked over to Starr, then James took the bridle out of her mouth and took her saddle off.

"What are you doing?" I asked.

"Come here," he said. "See the star in the middle of her forehead?"

"Yeah, so what?" I asked.

He took my hand and placed it over the star on her forehead. "Close your eyes and listen to what I say."

"Are you going to teach me another trick?" I asked with a smile.

"Yes, except this time we won't have to keep doing it. Once the horse remembers, then it will remember every time you come to see her and she knows that it's safe," he explained.

I closed my eyes as I listened for his voice. His voice never came but images flashed before my eyes. I watched as I saw Starr, or what I thought was Starr. She was pure white, with golden hooves and streaks of gold through her mane and tail. The star on her forehead was gold, with a horn that stuck out from the middle of it, and her eyes were pure blue like island water. She was a beautiful white unicorn. I watched as light shined down on her and the gold throughout her mane and tail reflected it. She was absolutely breathtaking. "Open your eyes," I heard James say. I looked to see her playing with Midnight. She was just as I saw her when my eyes were closed. The two seemed to play like brother and sister. It was like they had been apart for so long that they had a lot of catching up to do.

"What happened to them?" I asked.

"We use them sometimes in battle," he went on to say.

"What battles? How did Midnight get the scar on his leg?" I asked, hoping he would give me the answer.

"All these questions will be answered in time," James said, satisfied. "You see, the more I tell you, the more danger I put you in."

"Why would knowledge of my past put me in danger?" I demanded.

He looked into my eyes with concern. "You see, the more you remember, the more they start recognizing what and who you are, and the less time you give me to teach you. Everything has a time and place, and we still have a long road ahead of us."

I listened as the horses played. James sat under a tree and I sat down beside him. I lay my head on his chest and listened to his heartbeat as we watched the horses play. A tear fell down my cheek as I tried to remember who I was and what this life was meant to be. James lifted my head with his hand and brushed away my tear. "It will come in time...don't rush it," he said as he kissed me on the forehead. We watched as the sky started to turn a soft pink and the horses looked like they had settled down a bit. Midnight walked over to James, nudging him, as Starr followed. I watched as the horses returned to their appearance the first time we saw them at the stable. Midnight's eyes turned brown as his coat turned to a regular black and his hooves went out. I saw Starr turn back to a dull white and her star turned back to brown.

"OK," James said, laughing. "We'll go."

We saddled up the horses and started back toward the stable. We were almost done putting the horses up when we heard Alexis shouting.

"Come on, guys, we're going home 'cause we have to get ready for school tomorrow!"

James grabbed my hand as we walked out of the stable toward the car. Tomorrow was a new day for my new beginning. Maybe the perfect-life syndrome was gone. I still had five days until my birthday to figure it out and to set my own destiny.

XIII

Daddy Dearest

We arrived home to a ham dinner that Nan prepared for us. Nan's smile seemed a little larger than usual as she saw James and me walking together. After an exciting dinner of fish tales and horseback riding I felt exhausted. I told my parents and Mr. Santiago good night as Alexis, James, and I walked upstairs to our bedrooms.

"I'm so excited about going to a new school!" Alexis exclaimed. "I get to make new friends and have new teachers…and the two of you are ignoring me like you used to!"

James stopped staring at me to look over to his sister and put his arm around her. "I haven't seen her in years and I see you every day," he said with a smile, putting her in a headlock. I chuckled as we made it to the top of the stairs. "And what are you laughing at?" he asked, turning to me.

"Nothing," I said, putting my hands up and feeling my back hit the wall.

"Good night," he said as he kissed my cheek.

"Good night," I said as I opened my door.

I turned to watch him and Alexis walk down the hall as they shoved each other back and forth. I shut the door and sighed. I had never had such a good weekend. It started out rough and there was still things that I needed to understand, but it ended on such a good note. I knew that I would sleep well tonight.

I leaned over and turned my alarm on. Nan must have been in my room because the clock was right on my night-stand. I could feel the cold sheets as I slipped under my comforter. Tomorrow would be a good day. I could just feel it. I slipped off to sleep thinking of the weekend I just had and of James.

—⟋⟍—

Suddenly I heard many voices. I opened my eyes to a dark room. I waited for my eyes to adjust to the dark. I looked around to see that it was not my room. It was a small room with green wallpaper. I saw a dresser with a large mirror that was attached to the back of it. I watched myself as I got up out of bed and looked in the mirror. My hair was being held in a low ponytail by a ribbon and I felt the ruffles on my long white nightgown. I heard the noise again as I looked around the room to find a housecoat. I found a shawl instead, and quickly draped it over me and opened the door. I saw the glow of the light coming from downstairs as I cautiously walked down the hall. When I reached the top of the stairs I felt a chill run through my body. My mouth started to ache as I took my first step down the stairs. *I need a heater*, I thought, *it is cold in here.* The voices started to get louder and the light brighter as I reached the bottom of the stairs. The light was coming from my right as I saw it escaping beneath the double doors to another room. I tiptoed over to them and put my ear up to see if I could hear the conversation.

"She's turned into a beautiful young woman," I heard a man's voice say.

"She has, and every day she looks more and more like her mother," another man's voice said.

I listened as their voices got lower and I could not hear the rest of their conversation. Suddenly I heard them both roar with laughter, and then nothing. The door opened and I tumbled in. I heard them both laugh as I looked up to see one of them standing over me. He was a man in his thirties with light brown hair and fair skin. His hair was pulled back into a ponytail; his eyes seemed untrustworthy as he held his hand out for me to take.

"Honey, you're supposed to be asleep," he said as he helped me to my feet. I stood back from him and he came closer. "What's wrong, honey? Tell your dad. Did you have a bad dream?"

"Dad?" I said. *No, you're not the dad I know*, I thought.

"Brad, she looks like she might be cold," the other man said from his chair.

Brad…the thought of my mother's cell phone popped into my head. I studied his face for a moment. This was Brad, the man that had taken me the night they burned my mother. This was my biological father. Why did he look so different? He looked cold and lifeless.

"Here, honey," he said as he wrapped me in a blanket. "You are cold."

"It's cold in here," I finally said weakly, trying not to make a scene. I didn't want to interrupt what was happening. I wanted to play along to keep up with my memory. *This will help me to see what I have missed and memories I have lost.*

"I think she is adapting to you," the other man said. Brad looked over to him and then quickly turned to me. He put his hands up to my face and I leaned away from his touch.

"Serina, honey, let me see something," he said. He pushed my face toward him. I felt him lift the side of my top lip and let it go. "Open for me." I looked at him, puzzled. "Serina, open your mouth," he commanded. I didn't like his tone. My dad would never speak to me like that. I slowly opened my mouth and he looked in. "I think she is adapting to me, and she must be hungry," Brad said.

I quickly scanned the room for a mirror. I had to know what he saw. I found a mirror hanging above the fireplace and quickly went over to it. I looked in the mirror to see nothing but the room. I looked behind me to see the two still sitting there, watching me in amusement. I looked back at the mirror and saw nothing. I rubbed my eyes and looked one more time. I put my hand up to the mirror and touched it. Still the mirror reflected nothing. I felt a sweep of panic run through me.

"Honey, you can't have a reflection when you are in this state," Brad said. "Vampires have no reflection."

I looked down at my hands and turned them over. They were colorless. It was as if I had no tanned skin. A vampire… they were legends. They didn't exist. They were stories made up by people in the earlier years. I couldn't be that. "How can that be? I saw myself upstairs," I said.

"You weren't hungry upstairs," Brad said.

"I'm getting a little hungry," the other man said as he got up. "I'll get us something to eat." He walked out the door.

"Honey, is everything OK?" Brad asked me.

I shook my head and followed Brad out of the room. I moved my tongue to feel the two fangs that were now there. *No way!* I thought. They did feel like fangs. This wasn't happening. Vampires were legends, not truth. I continued to walk with Brad down a flight of stairs, then we came to a room that was dark and smelled of death.

"NO, PLEASE DON'T!" I heard a woman yell. I looked over to see a young woman about the same age as me shackled to a wall. Tears streamed down her face as the man approached her. "I changed my mind," she pleaded. "Please let me go." She sobbed as the man calmed her down. He was speaking to her and stroking her long brown hair when he put his face near her neck. She tried to cry out for help, but all that came out was a gurgle and her body went lifeless.

"Honey, come here." I looked to see Brad standing at a pillar. I walked toward him, afraid of what he was going to show me. He was pointing to a young man that was asleep. The man looked to be in his twenties.

"I put him to sleep 'cause I know how much you hate the fight," Brad said. "Do you remember what I taught you?" he asked. He put his hand on my back, urging me toward the man. I shook my head no and tried to back up, but his strength was stronger than mine. He grabbed my hand and pulled me down to my knees. I watched as the young man breathed, not knowing his fate. Brad moved the man's head to expose his neck, then took his finger and stroked it in a straight line on the man's neck. "You have to bite there. It's a main vein and less painful to them," Brad explained. I got up to run, but Brad grabbed me. "Honey, you have to feed or you won't be able to go out tomorrow. I know that you are adapting to me, but without feeding you won't be able to stand the light. Then you will be like me, I miss the sunlight. Take a deep breath, Serina, and you'll be OK."

I took a deep breath and smelled something sweet, like candy. I breathed in again to make sure I hadn't mistaken the smell for something else. The smell got stronger. I then heard a thumping noise in my head. It took me a minute to realize that the noise was the young man's heartbeat. I bent down toward him and the sweet smell filled my nose again. Something in my heart was telling me this was all wrong, but something else was telling me that I needed to do what I was told. *He is your real father.* I shook my head.

"Didn't your dad ever tell you not to play with your food?" the man standing behind me said. I got to my feet and walked back toward the door.

"Serina! Come here!" Brad instructed.

I turned to face him. "He's a human being, not some animal!" I said as tears started to run down my face.

"Humans are animals!" the other man said. I didn't like the way he looked as he approached me. "It's kind of like eating a raw steak." He laughed. His laughter sent chills down my spine and I wished James was here. He would have told them to leave me alone. I then heard another deadly scream.

"*Ella est muerta*! Senor Kartone!"

I opened my eyes to find that I was dreaming. As I lay in bed, I touched my tongue to my teeth to find that they were normal. I thought I had a cut in my mouth because of the taste of blood.

"Serina *est muerta*!" I heard Nan yelling as I sat up in bed.

"Nan!" I yelled. "What is wrong?"

James ran into my room and I watched as his eyes got wide. "Serina, are you hurt?"

"No. Why do you ask?" I said. As I looked down, I saw the blood on my comforter and all over my hands. I let out a scream as James rushed to the side of my bed. "Wha…wha… help…help!"

"Shh!" James said. He examined my bed and lifted the covers. "You don't seem to be cut," he said.

My mother came running in, with my father right behind her.

"Mom!" I said, starting to cry.

She held me close to her stroking my head. "Shh! It's OK. It was all a bad dream," she said as she gently let me go.

I looked down again to see that the blood was gone. The taste in my mouth was gone, too.

"He's here," James said as he crossed his arms.

My father went to the window and looked out the curtain. James joined him, and I could tell that he was searching for something.

"He can't come out in sunlight, dear," my mother said. "But that doesn't stop him from coming out at night. Besides, he knows that James is here and he won't be able to come around unless he is with someone else."

James looked at me. "I will make sure that nothing happens to you, do you understand me, Serina?" I nodded my head in agreement.

"Do you still want to go to school?" my mother asked. "You can stay home and relax. I think you're still shaken up from this and it might be good to stay here."

I looked at her. "I want to take a shower, and then I will get ready for school," I said.

"That's right, show him that you aren't scared," James said. "They feed off fear."

"OK, everyone out! I want to take a shower," I insisted.

If what James said was true, then I was going to let him know that I was stronger than that. I was not going to let him scare me, and I was going to go to school as if nothing was wrong. Then James and I were going to have a talk on the way to school. He knew who and what Brad was and he was going to tell me. I quickly took a shower and started to pack my stuff for school. I ran downstairs to see everyone at the bottom looking at me.

"I'm fine, really," I tried to reassure them.

"Princess, your car's in the shop until the end of the week. Why don't you take my car?" my dad asked, handing me the keys.

"You mean, you trust me to take your car?" I said with a smile. He smiled back at me. I looked down to see the keys to the Range Rover. "Dad!" I whined. "I hate driving this thing!"

"Then I'm sure James won't mind driving it," my dad said, taking the keys out of my hands and placing them into James's.

"He doesn't know his way to school," I said as I took the keys back. "I'll drive it."

I walked outside, followed by James and Alexis. I stood for a moment wondering why the taste of blood had come back. I searched my purse for gum and quickly popped a piece into my mouth.

"I hate sitting this high," I said as James climbed into the backseat. Alexis sat up front with me. I adjusted the rearview mirror and asked James, "Why did I wake up like that?"

"I thought we weren't going to talk about it," he answered, staring out the window, as if he was blaming me for the dream I had.

"First, I said that I wasn't going to allow them to make me afraid. Second, why do you act like you're mad?" I snapped back.

"Alexis, let me sit up front," James said, and Alexis got out. James slammed the door as Alexis climbed into the back and put her seat belt on.

"Here they go again." Alexis sighed, rolling her eyes as she slouched into the backseat and started to stare out the window.

"Drive!" James commanded.

"I'll go when I'm ready," I said, staring at him.

"I don't want to be late," Alexis said softly.

I watched as she sat back there with her eyes pointed to the floor, as if she was a little girl in trouble. I put the car in drive and started toward school. A few minutes had passed and James finally spoke.

"Serina, it's very important that we make good choices. Everything that happens to us is because of the choices we make. If we decide to make a bad choice it could harm us. For example, you woke up with blood on you because you made a bad choice."

"What do you mean, I made a bad choice?" I snapped back. "You weren't in my dream! How can you tell me I made a bad choice?" I argued.

"So, tell me about your dream," James said.

I told him everything that happened and the choice I made to walk away from it. He looked at me, puzzled. "So, did I make a bad choice?" I asked softly as I parked the car.

"No. Brad was mad because you made the right choice," James said as he held my hand. "I'm sorry I didn't believe you."

"It's OK. I'm still new at this and you worry. So, tell me why our choices are so important."

"It's because we're both half good and half evil. If we make good choices, then our good side takes over, and—

"If we make bad choices we may turn evil," I said, finishing his sentence.

"Yes, and that's not what we're supposed to be. We are guardians and we help people, not harm them."

"I understand," I said as Holly tapped on my window.

"Morning, Serina!" she said, all too cheery in the morning. I opened the door and hugged her.

"Morning, Holly," I said, excited to see one of my normal friends again. After this weekend I needed a little normalcy in my life. I needed to get away from the storms and the disappearing act. James and Alexis joined me on the other side of the car.

"Hi. I'm Holly," she said as she held out her hand.

"Hi. I'm James, and this is my sister, Alexis," James said as he shook her hand.

"They're new here and are moving in next door to me today," I said with a smile as James took my hand.

Holly noticed all too quickly and her eyes got wide. "Where's Steven?" she asked, her eyes never leaving my hand, which was intertwined with James's.

"Not sure. I haven't seen him since yesterday," I replied.

"Did you hear that someone caught a swordfish yesterday?" Holly said with a big smile on her face. "I heard it weighed a hundred pounds! Cool, huh? Had to be someone very strong to bring up a fish that big."

"Yeah, it was James," I said proudly, looking at him and waiting for Holly's reaction. This was going to be classic. I wondered to myself what Holly was thinking right now and smiled a little.

"It was you?" Holly asked, surprised. "You caught the swordfish? What are you going to do with it?"

"Yes," James replied, laughing. "I'm not too sure. I think my dad was getting it cut up and then he wanted to mount it on the wall in the house. Mom would not have stood for it, but I guess he can do it now."

"Cool!" Holly said, turning her attention to Alexis. "So, Alexis, do you cheer?" Holly asked, taking Alexis by the arm and heading toward the school.

"No, but I would like to learn," Alexis said as her eyes brightened that someone was talking to her. I felt bad spending so much time with James and not getting to know her. James and I followed Alexis and Holly into the school, where the principal met us near the front door.

"Your dad called, Serina, and said you were bringing two new students with you," he said as he looked over James and Alexis.

"Hi. I'm Alexis Santiago, and this is my brother, James," Alexis said, with Holly still by her side and seeming a little more confident than she was when we first left for school.

"Nice to meet you, Alexis," the principal said. "And James, I see you have met our cheer captain." He looked at the two of us holding hands and smiled.

James let go of my hand and held it out to the principal. "Yes, sir," he said as he shook hands.

"Alexis, do you cheer?" the principal asked.

"No, sir, but I would like to," she replied. Holly's eyes seemed to get a little brighter at the thought of helping out someone who was new.

"Well, tryouts for the basketball season are next week… I'm sure Serina can find room on the team," the principal went on to say.

"Sure we can," I said with a smile. The truth was, we were one short for the routine and everyone that had tried out for the football season was no good. We could teach Alexis with no problem.

"Well, I do have your schedules ready. The truth is that I have been expecting you guys since Friday," he said as he handed them to James and Alexis. "If you need help, then Serina and Holly can help. Nice to meet you both. Oh, and James—"

"Yes, sir," James said, taking his eyes off his schedule to look at the principal.

"Holding hands is appropriate, but nothing past that," the principal warned with a slight smile.

"Yes, sir. I mean, no, sir. I mean, I understand, sir," James said, fumbling through the words.

I grabbed his hand and we went to my locker, laughing. I looked at James's schedule, noticing it mirrored mine. "You are something else." I smiled at him. James shrugged and smiled back at me. "It sure is funny that we have all our classes together. Not that having a cute guy in all my classes is a bad thing."

"Talking about me so early in the morning?" Steven said, as he opened my locker door wider.

I turned to face Steven. "Well then, maybe I should rephrase my words. It's nice to have a strong, handsome man in my classes like"—I turned to James—"James in all my classes."

"Starting trouble already this morning?" Matthew said as he grabbed Steven by the shoulder.

"He's a nobody! The only reason he's here is because he is the son of one of your father's friend!" Steven snapped back.

"Serina," Mandi said, coming between Steven and me. "Who are your friends?" she asked with a little worry in her eyes. For a split second, Mandi almost seemed as if she recognized them.

"I'm Alexis, and this is my brother, James," Alexis answered her.

I could tell that the memory was lost and Mandi smiled. "Do you have any more brothers, Alexis?" she asked.

"No. Why?" Alexis asked, a little confused at the question.

"Oh no, Mandi!" Matthew said, letting go of Steven and grabbing Mandi as he laughed. "I wouldn't know what to do if I lost you to someone else."

"I would never dream of it." Mandi laughed as she grabbed Matthew's hand.

"Where is Anna and Adam?" Holly asked.

"Skipping school at her parents' cabin. They'll be back tomorrow." Mandi rolled her eyes. "One of these days they're going to get caught."

Matthew chuckled. "You know Adam…once he gets something in his head he doesn't let it go. He goes full force into it, without thinking of the consequences."

"Alexis, we have the same first class so you can sit with me, and I think you're in the same class as Mandi for your second class," Holly said, looking over at Alexis's schedule.

"I'll show her where to go," Mandi said. "I'll meet you at the end of the first bell and show you where you'll go from there. Spanish is such fun." She groaned.

"Students…class time," the principal said as he walked past us. "Serina, Holly, I expect you two to show our new students around."

"Can do," Holly said, excited, as she grabbed Alexis by the arm. Alexis didn't seem to mind; she had met her first new friend.

"Come on, let's get to class," I said, grabbing James's hand, leaving Steven behind.

Alexis joined us in the last class of the day. It was fun to have them both in the same class because he would make faces at her and she would just shoot him dirty looks. It was comical to watch them. I started to play with my pen. I really wanted my pen to have purple ink so that I could draw some flowers and stuff on the paper. *I guess I could draw black flowers*, I thought. I put the pen on the paper and started to draw the center and noticed the ink was orange. I stopped and looked closely at the ink in the pen. It was black, but the circle that was on my paper was orange. I started to draw the petals and the ink was purple. I picked up the pen again and saw that the ink hadn't changed color. I elbowed James and pointed to the paper. He looked at me with a puzzled look.

"Wait, watch," I said in a whisper. I drew another petal and the ink was purple. "Look, the ink in my pen is black," I said softly. James took his finger, put it on my drawing and drew a heart. I watched as it changed and the colors mixed together.

"Serina," the teacher said. "Is there anything that you and James would like to share with the rest of the class? Maybe like the answer to the question I just asked?"

Suddenly I heard James say in my head. *It's the Alamo.* James looked at me with an expression that said, *Answer her.*

"The Alamo?" I tried to sound confident.

"Very good, Serina. I guess you two were listening," she said, surprised. She was really hoping to catch us not paying attention. I took notes during the rest of the class and suddenly heard the bell ring. I got up quickly and grabbed my books as the teacher reminded us of the homework that was due next class.

I grabbed James by the arm. "How did you do that?" I asked.

"Do what?" he asked. "The color-changing pen, or when you heard me in your head?"

"Both," I answered. "How was I able to change the ink, and how did I hear you?"

"The pen," he smiled, "is a small trick. We use it to hide words as well. When you heard me…" He looked as if he was searching for the right words. "We're connected in so many ways. You just have to learn how to do it," he said with a smile as he grabbed my book bag.

We walked to the Range Rover, joking and laughing. James stopped in his tracks and looked toward the car. I looked up to see Steven leaning on it.

"I'll take care of this," I said, starting my way toward the car.

James grabbed my arm. "Watch your anger and keep it under control," he said calmly.

As I walked toward the car, Steven pushed himself off it and started to walk toward me.

"What are you doing?" I asked, trying to keep my composure.

"Waiting for you. Wondering what happened this weekend and when I lost you to him," he said. I could feel the anger in Steven's voice.

"Steven…we were never meant to be." I spoke quietly. "I mean, even before he came around we weren't together.

Everyone just assumed we were. I value our friendship so much, Steven. I mean, what if we were together and then got into a fight and never spoke to each other again? Today we can fight and tomorrow you will still be my friend."

Steven laughed. "Are you kidding me, Serina? I have heard you say that same exact line to every guy that wanted your number or wanted to talk to you, and now you are telling me this. So, I guess James is your new play toy for the week?"

"What? Do you really think that I'm that shallow?" I snapped back.

"Serina. Look at us, look at who we are! We were meant to be together. You and me. So go ahead and have your fun, but I guarantee that by next week you'll be saying that same speech to him and you and I will be back together," he said. He walked away from me and toward James. I turned to watch James heading toward Steven and saw Steven rolling something in his hand. I looked closer to find out what it was. I then watched as Steven slipped his fingers into it and realized what it was.

I started to feel an anger that I could not control. It started to consume me, and before I knew it, it had taken hold of me. Dark clouds started to form in the sky as the wind started to blow. "James. Watch out!" I yelled. "Steven! What are you doing?" I asked, starting to run toward him to stop him.

James watched as Serina's hair turned so black that it looked blue, and then he noticed her eyes. The loving brown eyes he was used to seeing were now black as night. He watched as the dark clouds started to consume the once beautiful blue sky. He knew he had to stop this before it started. He quickly ran past Steven, who tried to hit him and missed. He grabbed Serina by her arms.

"Stop this," he said quietly. "Don't do this here and now. Make the right choice. We're guardians, not demons! Control your anger, don't let it control you. Please, Serina, I don't want to have to hurt you, my love." He watched as the clouds started to turn gray and felt a drop of rain. He then watched as her hair turned back to a regular black and the black in her eyes start to drain down to reveal her beautiful brown eyes again. He then felt her weight against his arms as her head fell back. He grabbed the keys out of her pocket and set her in the front seat. He knew his battle wasn't over. There was still Steven.

XIV

Who Won?

I awoke in the family room lying on the couch with a blanket covering me. My head started to pound. I grabbed it, hoping that it would stop.

"It won't go away for a while, and no Tylenol will take it away. It has to take its course. Or you could stop being evil," James said, as he put an ice pack on his head, lay back, and shut his eyes.

"Oh my gawd! What happened to you?" I asked, trying to get up. Another sharp pain hit my head and I quickly lay back down.

"I just sat here and waited for you to wake up to show you what your friend Steven did. I knew he was going to hit me. I just didn't want him to hit you and I didn't want you to get angry. However, you did, and this time you made the wrong choice and almost got us in trouble," he said. He got up and grabbed my face. "Don't you understand that once you use your power of evil you let it consume you and then the balance is thrown off! Let me spell it out for you: WE ARE GUARDIANS, NOT DEMONS!"

"I don't understand. Why are you comparing us to demons?" I asked as I lay my head back down. "Please don't yell, either. You're just making my headache worse."

"It's the only way to describe them for you to understand, honey." My mother came into the room and touched James's head, and his scar faded away. She then touched my head and my headache slowly faded away.

"Are they called demons?" I asked. "I mean the things you protect people from?" I felt better and slowly sat up, waiting for the pain to hit again. Nothing. I felt relieved to get rid of that pain and waited for my mother to explain it all to me.

"No, they are called many things, but it's the only way to describe them for you to comprehend. Your dad is one because he does harm to people, not guard them. Your biological dad, that is. He did harm to you when you were a child and that's why you are half guardian and half evil," she explained.

"So, he turned me into a vampire when I was little?" I sat there and thought about what I had just said. I shook my head. "No, he tried to," I said, still trying to figure out exactly what had happened in my dream.

"No, you were still young and learning how to use your powers, but he could not teach you good ways, only evil ways, because of the path he chose. Your powers then adapted to him. When I finally found you, you had already adapted half-way and the human side of you disappeared. I took you and tried to teach you good ways, but his influence had already settled, so I tried to make up for time as much as I could. When you are around James you seem to be able to keep the evil side under control. It's because James has found a balance and now you have to. He has to teach you how to balance it out. I can't because I don't have evil in me. I'm completely guardian."

I looked at her with a sarcastic look on my face. "Mom, you can be evil," I said with a smile.

"No, honey. When you think that I'm being evil it's because I'm guarding you and didn't want you to follow in my footsteps. I wanted you to be able to live a normal life, but I see the way James looks at you and you at him. I now know that when you do make your choice I will be able to finish my work here. That you will be safe and he will teach you things that I cannot. He will guard over you."

"I'll show her and guard over her," James said as he sat next to me. "Why didn't you let me do it the first time?" he asked, watching my mother and waiting for an answer that he had searched for so long ago.

"Because I wanted to feel like a mother. I wanted to watch my little girl grow up and I didn't want her to feel like I left her again," she said as she started to cry.

I slowly got up and hugged my mom. "I love you, Mom, and I will never feel like you left me. I don't remember you leaving the first time." I giggled.

"You don't understand, honey. When guardians decide to finally pass on this trait to their children, we finally live as if we were human. We age and get called back. We are only here to accomplish a task, and when that task is done we go back home."

I didn't quite understand. Home was here. "Where is home, Mom?" I asked, like a child listening to a story.

My mom smiled. "It's a wonderful place. There is no sadness, no hurt, and no dark." I watched as my mom's eyes turned soft and her smile brightened the room. For the first time I could tell that she was at peace.

I was still at a loss. "Where is it? Can I go there? Can we visit it?" I asked.

My mom turned to me. "When the time is right you'll be able to see it." She turned to James. "When the time is right I will still watch over the two of you, so please take care of her. Please don't let anything happen to my princess. I'm entrusting the most precious person in my life to your hands, and if anything happens to her…let's just say my wrath will put me back here." She turned back to me. "You know, honey, you still have a couple of days before he meets with you."

"Is it easier to live like I have been, or the path I might choose?" I asked, hoping to gain some insight into what my future might look like.

My mom smiled. "It's not my choice, it's yours. You have to make that decision on your own."

"But that doesn't answer my question," I argued back. "I want to know about the challenges I'd face and the things I'd see if I decide to become a guardian."

"What your mom is trying to explain is that you are starting to feel the effects of being a guardian, so it's your decision whether or not to continue it," James explained.

"What happens if I choose not to continue, what happens then?" I asked. James stood up and I could see the hurt behind his eyes. My mother looked shocked. "I mean, do you still have to be a guardian, Mom?" I didn't feel like I was asking the right questions and tried to feel for what was in my future.

"Honey, I will always be a guardian. It will just be that I will continue my work here. If you choose to become a guardian, then I will continue my work from home."

"What is it that you do, exactly?" I asked. "I mean, can you describe a typical day?"

"Well, I don't go to the gym to work out and drink cappuccino all day long until you come home." She started to laugh. "I travel to where I am needed. I either help or accept the fact that it was meant to happen. If I cannot guard people, then they have made their choice and will have to live with the consequences of their decision."

"What happens if the person changes his or her mind?" I asked.

"Humans are funny in that way. They change their mind like they change clothes. But, if they do decide to change their mind, then the hold on them is loosened and I will be able to help, but only so far, because they would still have some choices of their own to make."

"So you are an angel," I said, like I had put all the puzzle pieces together.

"You could say something like that. There is just one big difference between an angel and me." My mother giggled.

My eyes widened with curiosity. "What is it?" I watched as my mom's smile got bigger.

"That is one thing you will have to figure out. I can't tell you 'cause it could sway you one way or the other. When he comes to talk with you on Saturday, then you have to give him your answer, and he has to know that it comes from you and not from what anyone has told you."

"After I give him my answer, will you tell me then?" I asked, disappointed.

"No, because then you will know the answer." She smiled at me.

"Well…if James has already made his decision, then he knows the answer, too, right? So James," I said with a smile. I turned to see him staring out the window.

"He's out there. I can smell him," James said, as he stared intently out the window. He didn't move an inch, and if I hadn't known better I could have sworn he was holding his breath. He looked as if he was ready for someone or something to attack.

"He's been out there since she woke up." My mother sighed.

"Who's out there, and how can you smell someone from outside?" I asked, turning to my mother as I got up.

My mother took my hand and led me to the window. "Do you see anything?" she asked as she pointed outside. I looked in the direction she was pointing and saw nothing but the rosebush by the gate. I had never noticed until tonight how big our front yard was, not until I had to look for something. I kept searching the yard, hoping that whatever was out there would move or breathe or make some type of movement to catch my eye.

"I don't see anything, Mom," I said, still searching the yard, trying very hard to see what my mother and James were watching.

"It looks like he brought friends," James said, his voice rougher than usual.

"No, they're here 'cause they know the time is near. They won't be able to touch her until she makes her decision. So they'll come and wait," she said as her eyes darted around the yard.

I wanted to see what they were seeing. I looked out the window again and squinted my eyes. Still nothing was there.

"Well, I'm not afraid of a rosebush," I said as I walked toward the door. I walked into the foyer and saw that my mom and James followed me. I put my hand on the doorknob of the front door and opened it. James took a step toward me and my mother held him back. I watched as James's eyes turned to a dark brown. I stepped outside onto the porch. I looked at the rosebush by the gate and then looked around. It was a quiet night; every so often I would hear a cricket chirping. I stepped down the stairs and started to walk toward the rosebush.

"Where are you going?" James asked as he stared into the yard. I could tell by his voice he was a little nervous about what was out there.

I turned to him and smiled. "A big man, you are. You're scared of a little rosebush. Look around you, there is nothing out here. Except crickets, ooh," I said, trying to sound like a ghost and then laughing. I kept walking toward the bush. I turned to see my mother watching me beside James on the porch. The rosebush was only steps away and still nothing. I bent down beside the rosebush to find one loose rose. I bent the stem and broke it off. "Call the camera crew, we have a story for you tonight. Girl walks all the way to rosebush and picks rose in her own front yard—at night. Story at eleven." It was then that I felt a chill run down my spine. I turned around. There was nothing there. I looked down at my arms to see goose bumps flowing up each of them.

"Something wrong?" James asked from the porch. "Did the cricket jump on you?"

I shot him a snobby look. "No!" I said as I started walking back to the house. I could feel a brush of cold air go past me as the trees started to sway. I looked over at the big oak tree beside the driveway and watched as it cast its shadow in front me. I stopped at the edge of the shadow and noticed it get darker. The chill ran down my spine again.

"Do you think she sees it?" James asked my mother.

"No," she said calmly. "OK, honey, you've proved your point. Now hurry up and get back in the house before you catch a cold. I'm pretty sure James doesn't want to take a sick person to the winter ball."

I looked up to see my mother waving me in. I started to walk faster and almost jogged up the stairs. "Look, I picked a rose for you, Mom," I said. "See, nothing to it. There is absolutely nothing out there to get you." I turned and walked into the house, swinging my arms in triumph. James closed the front door and smiled.

"Don't you two have school tomorrow?" my mother asked. "'Cause it is getting awfully late."

"Where is everyone?" I asked. "I haven't seen Dad, Alexis, or Mr. Santiago."

"They went to see a movie," my mother answered. "They should be back soon."

"Oh." The thought finally struck me. "By the way, James, who won?" I asked, smiling.

"What?" He sounded puzzled.

"The fight?" I asked.

James smiled. "Well, when the principal saw Steven hit me, he called for the security guards to come and get him."

"You know, it's funny that I don't remember seeing the principal around the parking lot." I smiled, already knowing the answer.

James shrugged. "He came from somewhere," he laughed.

I turned and started up the stairs, then noticed that James wasn't following me. I turned to see him still standing with my mom, watching me. "Well, aren't you going to bed?" I asked.

"I promised to help your mom clean up a mess…" He paused and turned to my mother, as if he was searching for an answer.

"I made out in the garage before your father comes home," my mother finished. "I just need help taking care of some things. He'll be up in a minute. Go, get some rest, and I'll see you in the morning. I love you, Serina."

"All right " I shrugged. "Love you too, Mom. Good night…and stay clear of rosebushes," I said as I turned and continued up the stairs.

"She really has no idea," James said to my mother.

"No, and she won't understand until Saturday. So, are you ready to help me clean up the mess she made outside with her little fiasco?" my mother asked calmly.

James sighed. "Yep, I guess we'll be cleaning up after her until Saturday, huh?"

"Yep, and then the two of you can clean up your messes together, and I'll get a little vacation," my mother said, closing the front door behind her.

XV

Four-Letter Word

"It's going to be a cold one today..." I opened my eyes and hit the off button on my alarm clock. I awoke this morning feeling sluggish and as if I could sleep for another two or three hours. I rolled over and slowly shut my eyes, knowing that I would regret it as sleep almost found me again.

"Miss Serina. You awake?" Nan asked, peeking into my room.

I rolled over and smiled at Nan. "Good morning, Nan," I answered her groggily.

"Breakfast is ready downstairs," she said, and left the door to my room slightly open.

I stretched and yawned as I sat up in bed. "I'll be right down." For the first time in a couple of days I was able to sleep through the night. I wondered what made last night different. It seemed that James and my mother had seen something last night and it freaked them out. I was sure that I was going to have bad dreams, but I slept through the whole night. Nothing got me and my mom got a rose out of it. I jumped in the shower, then quickly curled my hair and walked downstairs.

"Well, I guess you guys get to sleep in your own new house tonight." I heard my dad laugh as I entered the dining room. I looked at the spread that Nan had made as she filled my dad's cup full of coffee.

"My room is bigger than my old one," Alexis said, excited. "Dad even said that this weekend we could paint it. I'm not sure how I want it done, but I know I want a huge bed like Serina's," she smiled.

Mr. Santiago shook his head. "Well, we never have lived in a house this big before, but I don't think Alexis will have a hard time adjusting to that."

I sat down still with the look of sleep on my face. "Did you have another bad dream?" James asked as he cut into his waffle.

"No. In fact, I slept very well," I said, and sipped my latte. Nan put my fruit bowl down. "Actually, Nan, can I have a bagel with cream cheese?"

"Sure, Serina. I'll go get one," Nan said as she left the dining room.

"Serina, honey, is everything OK?" my mother asked.

As she rubbed my back, I felt my muscles relax, and tried to fight the feeling of sleep. I just couldn't shake it this morning.

"Yeah, I think I slept too much yesterday," I said. Nan set the bagel down in front me. "Thank you, Nan," I said, smiling at her. That's when the thought hit me. Was Nan one of them, too? Maybe she knew some of the answers. "Nan, how long have you known my mother?"

The room froze around me. Nan stopped in her tracks and gave me a quizzical look. "Why do you ask?"

I yawned. "It's because when…" My head hit the table as I fell asleep again.

"It's because yesterday is catching up with her," James said as he looked at her mother.

My mother looked over at James. "Well, are you going to help her? After all, Saturday I will be on vacation."

"News flash—I'm afraid of rosebushes," James said, laughing as my mother laughed with him. James got up and walked toward me. "Her energy level is really low." He put his hand on my back and closed his eyes. I could start to feel the energy flow through my body as I lifted my head.

"What happened?" I asked, pulling my head from the table as the room around me giggled. I felt my head and noticed that the top of the bagel was stuck there. I quickly picked it off and looked over at James.

"The rosebush got you," James said as he sat back down.

"Very funny, but really, what happened?" I asked, still feeling a little groggy. What was happening to me? Why did I feel like I could sleep for a hundred years and be fine with that?

"The energy that you used yesterday drained you. Remember, evil takes more energy than good," my mother said. "Think of it like an adrenaline rush, you have it for as long as you need it and then you crash."

"Oh," I said, finally understanding. "Using good energy doesn't make me tired, but using evil energy does. Makes sense."

"We're going to be late!" Alexis jumped up from the table. "I promised Holly I would meet her in the gym this morning."

"Why are you meeting Holly?" I asked, taking a sip from my latte, hoping that the caffeine would soon kick in and I would feel alive again.

"'Cause she is going to help me learn the routine," Alexis said. "I want to be the best that you have at the tryouts. I want to know without a shadow of a doubt that I'm going to make the team." She quickly looked at the clock on the wall and her eyes got wide again. "We're going to be late!"

"Calm down. We'll get there in time," I assured her. I slowly sipped my latte and got up. I felt as if I used all my energy getting out of the chair.

"I'll drive!" James said. He grabbed the Range Rover keys and rushed out the door. Alexis followed him out as I lagged behind.

"Have a good day, guys!" the parents yelled as the door slammed.

—∞—

"Do you think they heard us?" my dad asked.

"Nope, it's just like old times," Mr. Santiago replied. "I miss Christina."

"We all miss her," my mother said. "I will be seeing her soon."

My dad looked over and grabbed my mother's hand. "I love you, and you did a good job with Serina."

"We did a good job. Now it will be their turn to pick up where we left off. I love you, honey, and please never forget it." My mother smiled lovingly at him.

—∞—

We arrived at school and Alexis jumped out of the car to see Holly waving her in through the gym door. "See you guys later," she said as she slammed the door, running toward the school.

"We have forty-five minutes till school starts," James said as we sat in the car. "You do know that I don't expect to get that speech in a week."

I unbuckled my seat belt and thought about what he said. "What speech?" I asked with a grin. James looked over at me with a pleading in his eyes and sorrow. "You know you won't get that speech in a week." I leaned over and kissed him. A feeling like no other went through my body and I shivered.

"What's wrong?" he asked.

"I just had a shiver," I said, blushing.

He grabbed my face and kissed me again. I could feel a rush of energy flow through my body, and then he said, "I love you, Serina."

"What?" I said, sitting back down in my seat.

"I love you," he repeated.

I didn't know what to say. I sat there as many other words went through my head. Was it too soon? What did he want me to say? The four-letter word popped up too soon. "Who taught you that it was a four-letter word?" he asked with smile.

"Will you stop that? Or at least teach me how to do it," I said, frustrated. He could hear everything I said without me saying it. I smiled and closed my eyes. *Teach me to do that*, I thought.

"It's not that hard. Just focus on someone and listen. We were meant to hear people so we can help them," he explained.

I opened my eyes and watched as a girl walked in front of our car. *I wish my mom would get rid of her boyfriend. I hate the way he looks at me.* She smiled as if nothing was wrong when she noticed me watching her. I smiled back.

I looked at James. "Did you hear that?" I asked. "I heard her!" Then the thought occurred to me. She was nervous and afraid. She felt unsafe in her own home.

"Yeah, she said the same thing yesterday in class," he said as he watched her walk toward the building.

"She's in our class? Which one?" I asked as I watched her, too. She didn't seem to meet anyone at the school and looked like someone who kept to herself. She seemed unhappy and very scared.

James laughed. "You really do live in your own little world, don't you?"

"I just never noticed her," I shrugged.

"She was the one that was in the hospital a couple of weeks ago, but no one knew and no one visited her," James went on to say.

"Why was she in the hospital?" I asked.

"She overdosed on sleeping pills because her mom's boy-friend went into her room that night. He didn't touch her, he just stared at her, but it's just a matter of time," he explained.

"How do we help her?" I asked, looking at James. I wanted to help her. I wanted her to know that if she needed help that we could help her. It almost seemed as if the girl had no friends of her own and I felt bad for her.

"She has to ask for help. Then it depends on who she asks," he said, looking at me.

"I don't understand. I thought you said that they don't know who we are."

"They don't, but again, choices have to be made and they have to ask. If they ask us, then we will hear them. If not, then we won't hear them," he said, as he got out and walked to my side of the car. He opened my door and I got out. "There are a couple of rules I have to tell you. Rule one: now that you heard her you can't ask her if everything is OK. You have to act as if nothing is wrong. If you sway her in any way she could be lost."

"I don't understand. How do I act as if nothing is wrong? That I know nothing," I asked as we walked toward the school.

James smiled at me. "The same way you didn't notice her in your class. The way you've been acting before you heard her. You had no idea who she was and what she had been going through until now." His words hurt me deeply. I hadn't noticed her or even given her a glance, and how shallow was I for worrying about my birthday present and how my life was when she couldn't even sleep at night for fear of her mom's boyfriend. James stopped me at the front of the school and smiled at me. "You know…it's not easy to know that something is wrong and not be able to do anything about it. You have to give it time. Believe me when I tell you that not all people want our help, but we hear them anyway, because there is always a small glimmer of hope that they will ask for our help."

I looked up at James with sad eyes. "Does rule two make it easier than rule one?"

"I will let you know when you get to rule two," he said. He grabbed my hand and walked me into school. *I have the prettiest girl hanging on my arm, and although she loved me before, she can't tell me she loves me now*, I heard him say in his mind.

"Give me time. I will remember our love," I said as I looked up at him with a smile.

"Now I kind of wish I would have taught you that trick last," he said with a smile as we walked through the front doors.

All day I thought of the girl I had seen that morning. It made me worry about what was happening to other people. I tried it throughout the day and heard nothing.

James and I were sitting in the last class when we saw Alexis come in with a huge smile. We both watched as we saw her say good-bye to someone and then dreamily sat down at her seat. I looked over at James and he gave me a puzzled look.

I tapped on Alexis's back. "So tell me the story," I said.

"What story?" she asked, blushing.

I had to think quickly to make sure she didn't catch on. "What you and Holly were talking about."

"I wasn't talking to Holly," she said as she turned back around.

The bell rang and history class began. I watched as the minute hand finally made its way around to two thirty. James and I got up as Alexis slowly gathered her things.

"Is Holly going to teach you some more of the routine after class?" I asked.

"No, I'm waiting for someone," Alexis said trying to sneak a peek at the door for whoever she was waiting for.

"The person who walked you to class?" I asked, not caring if she knew I was prying into her little secret that everyone had noticed.

"Yep," she replied with a huge grin.

"Alexis, are you ready?" The familiar voice rang in the classroom like a bad omen. I looked at the door where Steven leaned against the door frame.

"Yes," she said as he walked over toward her and grabbed her book bag. I felt heat come from James as he watched Steven pick up Alexis's book bag.

"Hey, sorry about yesterday. I was too busy thinking of myself, and then I noticed your sister," he said, holding out his hand.

James shook it and pulled Steven closer to him. "If you touch my sister or hurt her, I will hurt you," he said with clenched teeth.

Steven put his hands up. "I understand. If I had a sister who was as pretty as Alexis, I wouldn't want just anyone being around her or trying to date her." He smiled and leaned in closer to James. "Remember that I'm not just anyone."

James balled his hands into fists and Alexis noticed.

"James! Please don't," Alexis said. She slipped her arm around Steven's and they walked out.

"James," I said quietly, "are you OK?"

I watched as James closed his eyes and took several deep breaths. He then tossed his head from side to side and picked up my book bag. "I'll be fine. I just lost my cool and had to regain it."

Mandi met us in the hallway. "I'm a little late," she said, as she watched Alexis and Steven walk down the hallway.

"You mean Alexis and Steven?" I asked. "When did that happen?"

"This morning. Holly and Alexis were in the gym working on the routine when Steven walked in. He started talking with Alexis and from there it was all she wrote. You do know why he's doing this."

"To get back at me for yesterday." I scowled.

"Yep, and what better way to do it than to go after his sister," Mandi said. "We have to stop it before he hurts her."

"James!" Alexis yelled from down the hall. "Steven is giving me a ride home. Toodles."

"Oh, yeah," Mandi said.

"She has been hanging around Holly too much already." I rolled my eyes. I ran toward Alexis. "Alexis…Alexis, wait a minute," I said, catching up to the two of them.

She turned around. "Yes?" The look she gave me was like that of the rest of my friends when they didn't want to be bothered.

"Does your dad know that he is taking you home?" I asked. "I mean, he kind of expects you to come home with James and me."

She shot me a look. "Is this because I'm with him? Is it not enough that you have my brother's attention? You have to have Steven's attention, too?" she snapped back.

"Alexis!" Mandi shouted from behind me. Mandi grabbed Alexis by the arm and I followed them. "Listen to me and listen good. Serina has done nothing but be your friend, and between the two of us we will decide who makes the cheer squad, so I would watch how you talk to her."

"So, are you saying that just because she's the cheer captain I can't have Steven show any interest in me?" she snapped back. "She doesn't want Steven, she wants my brother."

"This has nothing to do with you and Steven, but when she suggests something, I would do it. And remember: she introduced you to us, and even if you are with Steven, it does not mean that we will choose your side over hers. She was here before you and she will be here after you."

The statement must have hit Alexis like a ton of bricks, because her eyes calmed down and she looked at me. "Do you want to use my phone to call your dad?" I asked as I held out my phone. She took the phone and dialed the number. I looked over at Mandi, whose arms were crossed. "Thanks for backing me up, Mandi," I said.

"That's what friends are for," she said.

Mandi kept a close eye on Alexis, who seemed to be nervously talking with her dad. She looked as if she could start crying at any moment. She slowly walked toward us with the phone extended to me.

"My dad wants to talk to you," Alexis said as she handed me the phone.

"Hello?" I said, afraid of what I might hear from the other end.

"Serina?" Mr. Santiago said. "Is she being serious? She wants to ride home with Steven? When did this happen?"

"This morning, I guess," I replied. "We're all a little shocked at this." I smiled, trying to keep the conversation light.

I heard Mr. Santiago huff as the awkward silence took over. I looked at James and smiled, but his face beamed with anger as Matthew approached him, trying to keep him calm. Finally, Mr. Santiago spoke again. "Serina, she is old enough to make her own decisions. What is James doing?" he asked.

I turned to see James talking with Matthew. "He's talking to Matthew, and Steven is at the other end of the hall."

Alexis looked at me with her big brown eyes as if to say, *Please*.

"Mr. Santiago, why don't we do this? Alexis can ride home with Steven, and James and I will follow to make sure she gets home OK," I said, hoping the compromise would work.

"OK, but he is not to come into this house," Mr. Santiago said sternly. "Oh, and Serina, let Alexis know that I want to talk to her when she gets home."

"OK, bye, Mr. Santiago," I said, hitting the end button on my phone. I turned to Alexis. "OK, Alexis, stay here while I go and get James. Mandi, can you stay here with her?"

"Sure can," Mandi answered, not taking her eyes off Alexis.

I walked back over to James and Matthew. "He is a piece of work," Matthew snarled.

I shot Matthew a look. "He's your best friend. Tell us what he's really up to," I accused.

Matthew looked back down the hall. "I wouldn't use the term *best friend* anymore. He's being very secretive and not like himself. It's like he's turned into a whole different person overnight. So, to answer your question, I'm not sure what he's up to, but I think that getting you back is part of his plan."

"James, give me the keys," I said, holding out my hand.

James found the keys in his pocket. "Why?"

"Because we are following them to your house," I said, as we all started walking back toward Mandi and Alexis.

"Do you want us to follow you guys?" Matthew asked.

"No, it's OK. I'll call you later, Mandi," I said as I kissed her on the cheek.

"OK," Mandi said.

"Come on. Let's go," I said.

James and I watched Alexis walk ahead of us toward Steven. We followed Steven and Alexis to her new home. We pulled up as Mr. Santiago waited outside on the porch. I parked the Range Rover at my house and walked with James over to his new house. Steven was coming out of the driveway as Mr. Santiago and Alexis were going inside.

"I'll see you later?" I asked James.

James looked at me. "Yeah, we just have to work this thing out," he said. He kissed me and then went inside.

I walked back to my house and saw that my mother and father were in the foyer waiting for me.

"Mr. Santiago is upset," my father said with his arms crossed.

"I know," I answered him, and quickly regretted the words that came out. I shook my head. "I mean, I didn't know, I swear," I pleaded.

"It's not your fault, princess, but your mother and I are going out to dinner. Would you like to join us?" he asked.

"Sure. Let's go." I sighed. A nice quiet dinner with my mom and dad was what I needed now to get away from all this drama.

We sat at the dinner table as the low lighting of the club set a peaceful atmosphere. I listened to the slow music in the background as I looked over the menu. I let my mind wander to the girl again. I could see her clearly in my mind, her long limp brown hair and her sad eyes. I wondered where she was eating and what she was doing tonight. Maybe she had friends that I just didn't see. Maybe she would be able to eat in peace surrounded by good friends. I sighed and my mother took notice. Her eyes stared at me with concern.

"Serina…honey…is something bothering you?" she asked. I sat there quietly, wondering if she already knew. If she could do the same thing James taught me today.

"Princess," my dad said, and I felt his hand grab mine. "You look worried. If it's about Alexis or Steven, I'm sure everything will be worked out."

I shook my head. "It's not about them at all." I sighed. "It's about a girl I saw today at school. I was able to hear her, and I'm not too sure if she was asking for help. And if she was, how do I help her?" I watched my mother as her eyes became wide.

"You heard her?" my mother asked as the waiter poured her some more water. I nodded my head. "Did James hear her, too?" she asked.

"He said that he heard her yesterday, but we have to act as if we know nothing. Mom, I don't understand. I don't understand how we can continue our everyday actions as if nothing is wrong, when it's clear that something is wrong." I quickly took a sip of my water. "I mean, what do I do? I want to help her...I don't want her to feel alone and scared. I don't want her to feel so bad," I said as tears started to form.

"Excuse me," said a tall thin man in a very sophisticated voice. "Are you ready to order?"

My dad looked at us and then answered him. "I think we'll go with our usual tonight. I would like a steak, medium well, with asparagus. My wife would like the fish. What is in season right now?"

My mom waved her hand and interrupted my dad. "No, a nice salad with grilled chicken will be good, and for the dressing I would like raspberry vinaigrette."

"Me too. I would like a salad with grilled chicken and the same dressing." After I spoke up, the waiter smiled and quickly left to put our order in.

My mother looked at me with sadness in her eyes. "Serina, honey...this is not the easiest thing to do, but patience is a virtue. The one thing you have to remember is that everyone has a choice, and whether that choice is to ask for help from us or from someone else, it's their choice. We can only do what we can."

"What your mother is trying to say"—my father rolled his eyes—"is that she knows it's not easy, and as much as you would like to let this girl know that you're there for her, you can't. Remember that it's not you that's there for her...it's your boss. You only carry out his orders. If you haven't heard anything from him, then you must know that it's not time for you to help."

I gave my father a puzzled look. "My boss?" I asked. "Who is my boss, and how do I get hold of him? I didn't know I was working."

My mother smiled. "You know your boss. He's my boss, too, and I had to learn just like you do, that you have to wait to hear him. You have to listen and be ready when it's time."

I watched as the waiter casually made his way over to our table and set the food down in front of us. I slowly picked up my fork and took a bite of my salad. I wanted to know if the girl was all right. I wanted to know that everything would turn out for the best.

XVI

The First Battle

I walked downstairs to find my parents in the breakfast nook. "Good morning, princess," my dad said from behind the newspaper.

"Morning, Daddy," I replied, and sat down to eat my fruit.

"Honey, did you know Cynthia?" my mother asked casually as she sipped her morning coffee.

"No...can't say that I know a Cynthia. Why?" I asked, eating a piece of strawberry.

My mother folded her paper and pushed it toward me. I looked down and started to read:

Local Girl Kills

Police reached a house on Pretty Lake Lane to find that a girl, whose name is being withheld at this time, stabbed her mother's boyfriend six times before she turned on her mother. She then stabbed her mother four times before calling the police. When the police arrived, they found the girl sitting in a chair with a knife over her wrists, covered in blood from head to toe. After hours of negotiating the girl finally handed over the knife to authorities and was taken to the juvenile detention center where she will be given a psychiatric evaluation. Police are asking for anyone with any information to please come forward.

I put the paper down and looked at my mother. "The article does not give a name. How do you know her name is Cynthia?"

"Because she asked for help yesterday," my mother said, sipping her coffee again.

"Why didn't you help her?" I asked as tears started to well up in my eyes.

"I did, and that's why she gave the knife to the authorities," my mother said as she watched me.

"Before that! How could you let her kill her mom and her mom's boyfriend before you helped her?" I accused.

"Because, honey, she didn't ask for my help before that. She chose to let her anger consume her and then asked for help from someone else," she answered.

"Good morning, Mr. and Mrs. Kartone," I heard James say. He walked in and sat down next to me.

"Good morning, James." My mother looked up.

James looked at me and then looked at the article. "Oh, Serina, it's not anybody's fault," he said as he hugged me. "Your mother did the best she could before Cynthia could hurt anyone else or herself."

I looked up at James and the thought struck my heart. "That was the girl we saw yesterday in the parking lot, wasn't it?" James nodded his head. "You could have helped her yesterday. Why didn't you, before she did this?"

My mother sat down next to me. "Honey, once we hear them it's not up to us who they decide to ask for help. Evil will always be there 'cause that's what they do. We as guardians are always there, we never leave them, but you have to remember that it's their choice who to listen to."

I pulled away from my mother in anger. "You knew… didn't you?" I accused her. I watched as my mother stared at me with sadness. "She did this before I even told you last night!" I felt the warm tears start to glide down my cheeks. "You let me tell you how I felt and everything and you didn't say a word! Why? Why didn't you tell me?"

James turned to me. "Because you haven't made your choice yet. You haven't decided to follow in your mom's footsteps yet."

"If I had?" I asked. "If I had, would it have made a difference? Would I have known? Would I have heard our boss, as my father puts it?"

James looked over toward my parents and sat down next to me. "Yes, you would have heard him. He would have told you and you would have known," he said, trying to comfort me.

"Did you know?" I asked, trying to contain the tears of sadness that were building up inside me.

James hugged me. "I knew sometime yesterday afternoon. I also knew that your mother was the one that was called out to the scene. I was to stay with you yesterday. I didn't say anything because again, we all have choices, and your feelings to help someone are so strong that this could have made the difference in whether or not you take your mother's place."

I looked up at James. "That's a good thing, right? I mean, I want to help others and protect them. This could have been something that I could have helped prevent."

James smiled at me and shook his head. "No," he said quietly. "We don't take on that role. We have to sit and wait until the order is given and then we take action. Something you will learn here soon. It is a good thing that you want to help and be there for people, but you have to make this choice, not because of something you saw or because you think that you can make a difference, but because you want to. Do you understand?"

I shrugged my shoulders. The comment my mother made about us always being there, how could that be? "How can we always be there? I mean, there are only two of you guys… right?" I asked, wiping the tears away.

My mother looked at me with loving eyes. "Yes, but we help where help is needed. You'll know when your help is needed."

"I have to leave school early today and I think that you should come with me," James said.

My mother looked over, grabbed a note out of her pocket and handed it to me. "Yeah, she will go with you."

"Where is Alexis?" I asked James, noticing that she wasn't with him.

"Holly picked her up this morning so they could practice, and she is riding home with Holly," he said.

"Good. Steven is starting to cross grounds he shouldn't, kind of like his father," my dad said, never putting the paper down.

"OK, you two, off to school," my mother said as she rushed us out the door.

"What was all that about?" James asked.

I shrugged as James opened the door for me. "I can't wait to get my car back," I said as James started the car.

The article was the talk of the school that morning as people watched the police cars in front of the building. The police talked with her teachers and guidance counselor. They even drew a line in front of her locker so no one would touch it. I watched as the other students would whisper when they saw some of the teachers walk by and how some of them would just point and laugh. Finally, the principal made an announcement.

"Students, we had a tragedy happen with one of our students yesterday, and because of the investigation we need to send you home. All parents have been notified, and if anyone feels that they need to speak to with one of us, please don't hesitate. We will be in touch with you if school is to resume at the regular time tomorrow. Please be careful and have a good day."

I watched as the rest of the students slowly gathered their things. James looked at me and said nothing. The atmosphere in the school had changed. It was quiet in the hallways and no one was celebrating. I watched as many of the students called someone on their cell phones. There was one girl that seemed to stand out among them all. She was a plain girl with short red hair, standing at the end of the hallway near the exit. She stood there and kept looking back like she had forgotten something as other students passed by her. I watched as I heard her small voice inside my head.

Should I go and talk with them? I didn't know she would really do it. She told me that she was going to skip class to take care of something at home. If I keep standing here, then they will know that I know something. I have to go.

I turned to see that James wasn't behind me. I quickly scanned the hallway to see where he might have gone. Was that her asking for help, and if it was, what do I do? I turned to see if the girl had left and saw James walking beside her with his hand on her shoulder. He motioned for me to come over. I walked quickly up to him.

Listen, if you speak out loud she will hear you. All you need to do is watch, I heard him say in my mind.

It's going to be OK, Pam. All you have to do is tell them the truth, James said as he stroked her back.

I must be crazy, talking to myself in my head, Pam thought. *Still, don't leave me, I'm scared.*

I won't leave, but you have to tell someone, James said. I watched in amazement as we walked her to the principal's office.

The office was quiet as we walked in; I saw some ladies walking with paperwork and some talking quietly on the phone. I watched as a lady in her thirties noticed Pam at the counter.

"Can I help you?" she asked.

Pam looked at her like she was unable to speak. *I can't do this. I want to go home*, I heard her say in her head.

I haven't left you, and you can do this. Just tell her that you need to talk with the principal, James said.

Tell her to hurry up, you have more important things to do with all this paperwork and then having to find the papers on Cynthia. She's just wasting your time, I heard a raspy voice say. I looked to see a small ugly creature hanging on the back of the lady. I watched as it poked the lady in her head with its pointed fingernail. The lady rubbed the side of her head.

"Honey, look, I'm starting to get a headache with all this stuff I have to do—"

"I need to talk with the principal," Pam said softly.

What did she say? the creature asked as it poked the lady again. The lady rubbed the side of her head again as she closed her eyes in pain.

"Honey, I'm sorry, I didn't hear you," she said, still rubbing her head. She opened her eyes and huffed impatiently. Her eyes looked weary.

"I need to talk with the principal," Pam said, louder, her eyes fixed on the counter in front of her.

He's too busy to talk to anyone, with the cops in his office and the teachers all having to deal with some girl whose mother was an alcoholic and we all knew it. What happened was bound to happen sooner or later, the creature said as its smile bared ridged, yellow teeth.

"The principal is busy," the woman snapped. "You can go talk with a counselor if you would like, or you can wait there in the seat until he is finished."

Serina, I heard James say in my head. I turned to face him. *I need you to put your hands on her shoulders and not let go. Don't say anything, either.* I nodded as I took James's place behind the girl. The creature watched him as he disappeared.

She's going to go home and nothing will be done, the creature said as it stared at me with its yellow catlike eyes. *You're not strong enough to handle someone even as little as I am. Let her go and we can all go home safely.* My grip on her shoulder tightened as I watched her rub her shoulders. *Look, you hurt even the one that you're trying to help. Are you sure you're supposed to be here?* it said, laughing.

Be ready. She is going to run toward the principal and you can't let her go, I heard James say.

I looked around to see where he was and saw nothing. The door to the principal's office opened, and Pam ran toward the principal, threw her arms around him, and started to cry. The creature noticed that I no longer had my hands on her and decided to take a leap. I ran toward Pam, reaching her first. I felt the creature's nails tear the flesh down my back. James quickly put his hand over my mouth as we both watched the creature jump to the principal.

Ask her what she wants, the creature instructed.

"What's wrong?" the principal asked, looking at Pam. He bent down so that he could look her in the eye. I watched as the creature made its way onto his face so that it was also at eye level with Pam.

*Nothing is wrong,*the creature said, looking at Pam. *I made a mistake, there is nothing that I needed. Then walk away, 'cause it's your fault this happened. You could have stopped it and didn't. What kind of person are you, anyway? You're a nobody, a nothing, and that's what you'll be for the rest of your life. Cynthia was too afraid to end it, but you're not, and that's what you should do—go home and end it. Do the world a favor and end your life.* I watched as foam ran down its mouth with each word it spoke.

I've had enough! I heard James in my mind. James stood between the creature and Pam. I watched as the creature stood up on its hind legs and blinked its eyes. It turned its head to look up at James. *Serina, I need you to push Pam into the principal's office and sit her down in the chair. Don't say anything, just move her.* I moved Pam around the principal and into a chair that was in front of his desk. I watched as the creature watched me move her, and James followed me. The principal closed the door and sat down. The creature bent down and started walking on its hands and feet like a lizard, across the desk toward Pam.

Do you see the two policemen there? They're going to take you away just like they took Cynthia. You'll be an embarrassment to your family! To your mom and dad! You have a little brother and sister, and what do you think this will do to them? The creature seemed to be getting madder with each word it spoke.

You'll be a hero, Pam. 'Cause only a coward would run and not tell the truth! James slammed his hands on the desk. I watched as the creature backed up.

"You see, I talked with Cynthia yesterday…" With my hands on Pam's shoulders, I listened as she told her story. She cried and James told her it was OK. I watched the creature as it slowly faded away with each word Pam said, until it was gone. When she finally finished the two officers thanked her. One of the ladies in the office had called her parents to come to the school. The principal had them come in and she told the story the second time. Her mom cried as she hugged Pam and her dad told her how proud of her he was. I watched as her younger brother and sister grabbed her hand, asking her many questions. The two police officers thanked her parents and gave her brother and sister a sucker they had in their pockets.

James grabbed my hand. *You can let go now*, I heard him say. I looked down at my hands still on her shoulders. I lifted them, James took one in his hand, and we walked out of the office. I turned to watch Pam and her family walk out the front door as the afternoon light shined through the windows.

"Ouch!" I said, as I felt James touch the scratches on my back.

James laughed. "Got your first battle wound, huh?"

"Serina, James, what are you two still doing here?" the principal asked.

"I forgot my math book," James replied. "Is she going to be OK?" he asked, nodding toward Pam.

"Yeah, she did the right thing," the principal said.

I felt James put his hand on my back and felt a warm feeling in my wounds. I knew that he had healed them.

"Well, it's five fifteen and you guys need to get home," the principal said.

"Have a good night," I called back to him. "Why did you ask him that? Did they not see us?"

"No. When we work, no one sees us, and that's why it's important to ask sometimes," James said as he smiled. "Just to make sure they didn't. We work under cover."

My phone started to ring. "Hello? Hi, Mom, you'll never guess what I saw today. Yeah, he's with me. OK, we'll meet you guys at the restaurant." I ended the call and said, "She already knows." I beamed at James with excitement, feeling that in some small way I helped today.

James smiled as he opened my door. "You did good today. You have a lot to learn, but you did good today." He kissed me and shut my door. He was right, this did feel good. It made me feel good to know that I had helped in some way.

XVII

Dinner

We arrived at the Italian restaurant my parents loved so much to see their car parked in front. James opened the door and we walked in. The place was dimly lit and the colors of red, white, and green were all over the place.

"Fancy place," James said.

"It's the paintings and the piano player that make it look that way." I giggled, still really happy about the events that happened today. There was nothing that was going to take away this sense of accomplishment.

"Miss. Kartone, your parents are in the back," the hostess said as she walked ahead of us. James looked at the paintings on the wall as we passed the piano player.

"Serina!" my mother said as we rounded the corner. She got up from the table and hugged me. "Hi, James. So, she did well?" she asked as she hugged him.

"She did well," James said as he pulled out a chair for me.

"So, princess, tell us what happened," my dad said, smiling.

"Oh, let's order first, and then she can tell us," my mother insisted.

"So, does she remember anything yet?" Alexis snapped from behind a menu.

"Alexis, I'm sorry about yesterday, and about—" I stopped when I noticed Mr. Santiago across the table, shaking his head very slightly and pressing his finger to his lips.

"About Steven?" Alexis snapped back as she set the menu down. "Well, if you must know, you have ruined my life for the second time. Steven won't be taking me to the dance and now I have to find another date. All thanks to you and my stepbrother." I watched James's eyes. Alexis's comment hurt him deeply. I had never heard her call him a stepbrother until now. Up to this point he'd been her brother and nothing less.

"Alexis!" Mr. Santiago cut in. "That's enough. We are going to enjoy dinner."

"No, we're not. We're here to celebrate Serina and her doing something she was supposed to be doing by now, except her mother butted back into her life, erased her memory, and I watched my mother die because her mother wasn't ready to go yet!" After she took a deep breath, Alexis said, "That's right, Serina, your life isn't perfect. It was never perfect. Everything you see is a lie. The day you were to become my brother's wife, your mother came and stopped it. Why, you ask? Because she didn't think that my brother could protect you, and that he would tell you exactly who and what you were."

"That's enough, Alexis!" James said through clenched teeth, trying to control his anger.

"Oh no it's not! James, we lost your mother that day because her mom was a selfish, know-it-all…" Tears started to run down Alexis's face. "James, I miss her, and I've been forced to live this life with you because Mom said you would watch over me until the time was right. She was the only mother I knew because my mother died after she gave birth to me. I never knew my mother, but I knew yours, and she treated me like I was her daughter. Has that time come, James? Am I able to go on now?" Alexis asked with tears streaming down her face.

"No," James said quietly. "The time is not right yet."

Alexis put her face in her hands and sobbed. She then got up and ran toward the front. I watched as everyone just sat there. I looked at them and then got up to see where she had gone.

"Excuse me," I said to the hostess. "Did you see a girl run past here, and where did she go?"

"She went to the side of the building," she answered.

"Thank you," I said as I walked out. I saw smoke coming from one side of the building. Maybe someone saw where she went. I turned the corner to see Alexis smoking a cigarette.

"Yeah, so what?" she asked. It was her eyes that gave her away. She was definitely older than she looked.

"Nothing," I said. "Well, you're the only one that will probably tell me the whole story, so why don't you go ahead and do it."

"'Cause it doesn't work that way! Have you not learned anything?" she asked, leaning against the wall.

"Then tell me about you," I said, hoping to turn the conversation to something light, which hopefully would let Alexis vent to me.

Alexis turned to face me. "What?"

"Tell me about you. Why are you so angry? What did I do that made your life horrible?" I asked as tears started to well up in my eyes.

"It's not completely you. Look, when I was born my mother died. The doctors told my dad that I wouldn't make it past the age of three. He spent two years looking for a cure and nobody had one. Then he met James's mother and fell in love. He told her about me and she came in and healed me. He was thrilled. We lived next door to you for years. The two of you were never without each other. We all grew up together, went to prom together, and then you guys fell in love," she said. She paused to take a drag off her cigarette. "The day that the two of you were to be married you noticed some strange things happening to you. You see, what James and his mother did not realize was that your mother had already started to erase some of your memory." I listened as anger started to build up inside me. I took a deep breath and exhaled. *Keep the bad side under control*, I thought. I listened more to what Alexis was saying. "James told you that he would tell you about it on your honeymoon. On your wedding day, your mother came in and saw you in the wedding dress. I'm not sure what she said to you, or even what she did, but your mom saw that she erased your memory and told James that she was not ready yet. She was going to be a mom and had to make things right. James was not strong enough to overpower her yet, so he did the best thing he could and that was to walk away. That night we left and stayed at a hotel, James in dismay and Mom trying to make him understand. I can't remember exactly what happened, but I recall my mom screaming and then blood. The next day we watched as my mom lay in a hospital bed. She told James that she wanted him to speak to someone. This man came in as my father and I watched him talk to James and Mom. When the man left, my mom touched me and told me that James would watch over me until I was ready." Alexis held out her hand to show me a birthmark on her finger.

"What's that?" I asked, examining the birthmark.

"Not sure, but it's why I'm still here. Mom kissed me there before she died that day. You'd think after all these years I would have figured it out. I don't have powers like you guys, but something is holding me back from going on and James is supposedly watching over me." She threw the cigarette down and smashed it with her foot.

"Alexis, I'm sorry for all you've been through. It's just that Steven..." I sighed, looking toward the sky for answers, or at least some kind of explanation that would be good enough for Alexis about Steven.

"It's no good. I know. I just felt that in some small way I was hurting you, and for that I am sorry. But for as much as you and I have grown up together, there will be fights," Alexis said, finally cracking a smile.

"Look, if you ever need to talk again you can always call me. And I am truly sorry about everything that has happened. Can we start over?" I asked.

"Sure," she said as she hugged me. I pulled back and saw that her eyes were young again as she smiled.

"I was just wondering if you two were going to eat sometime tonight," James said from around the corner.

Alexis shot him a dirty look and then smiled. "Why? Are you guys waiting on us?"

"Yes," he answered with a smirk.

"Then I think Serina and I have to talk about some more things. Besides, I don't think you'll starve," she said, chuckling.

We started walking back toward the restaurant. "Thank you for listening, Serina."

"Anytime, Alexis," I reassured her.

"Sometime tonight we are going to eat," James said as he ran past us. Alexis ran behind him and he shut the door, holding it closed so she couldn't get in. I watched as she laughed, trying to pull the door open. He finally opened it and held it to let me in. We arrived at the table to see the food was already there.

"Everything all right?" my mother asked.

"Water under the bridge, right, Alexis?" I asked.

"Yes, Serina, it's water under the bridge. We move on tonight to make a better tomorrow."

XVIII

Meet Mark

The next day we rode to school together and Mandi met us in the parking lot. "Did you hear?" she asked. "Some girl named Pam helped the police yesterday find out that Cynthia was raped by her mom's boyfriend and she lost it. I mean, she still has to probably stay in juvie, but at least they know what happened. That is so gross. I could not imagine what that would be like."

"Yeah, it's a sad thing," I said, as James came up behind me and grabbed my waist.

"You know, I always thought that you and Steven belonged together, but now that I see you with James, it just looks perfect." Mandi smiled.

"Well, thank you, Mandi," I said with a smile, and for the first time actually feeling like this was perfect. I didn't feel as if James was doing this for show or for that perfect-world syndrome. No, this felt right. This felt like he really loved me deep in his heart. I took a deep breath as Mandi turned to Alexis with excitement in her eyes.

"Oh, Alexis, I found you a date for the winter ball tomorrow," Mandi said with a smile.

"Now you're in trouble. I mean, when Mandi starts playing cupid, it could turn dangerous." I laughed.

"Don't listen to her!" Mandi said as she threw me a dirty look. "His name is Mark and—"

"Wait a minute…Mark? You mean Mark from the baseball team? That Mark?" I asked.

"Yes, that Mark," Mandi said, rolling her eyes. Her smile stretched across her face in a very gratifying way.

"Oh, Alexis, he is hot," I said, smiling at James, who just rolled his eyes.

"His dad is a police officer and we got Mark into the winter ball," Mandi said.

"What do you mean, got him into the winter ball?" Alexis asked.

"Well, the winter ball is by invitation only, but thanks to me, I was able to get him in," Mandi announced proudly.

"Then how come we were invited?" Alexis asked with a confused look on her face.

"Because you moved into the right neighborhood," Holly said as she grabbed Alexis's arm. "We have to practice. You only have today and tomorrow. Tryouts are on Monday."

"He's going to pick you up Friday at seven at Serina's house!" Mandi yelled as Holly and Alexis went into the gym.

"Where's Steven?" I asked.

"Let's just say that when my dad and your dad visited his dad, they decided to move. In fact, the moving truck should be in front of his house right now," Mandi said, with her eyes looking devilish.

"His dad got reassigned by the same company all our dads work for," Matthew said as he put a rose in front of Mandi's face.

"Well, thank you," Mandi said as she turned around to face Matthew. "I love seeing you in the morning."

"Speaking of seeing people, where have Anna and Adam been hiding?" I asked.

"Didn't you hear?" Matthew exclaimed as Mandi lay her head on his chest. "They got detention for skipping school on Monday and Tuesday."

"What does Mr. Semp say? We need Anna for the routine," I blurted out.

"He says that Anna has to serve the detention, and she has to sit out for the first two games," Mandi said. "That's why we have to get Alexis on the team, 'cause she is about the same size as Anna. When Anna is allowed to cheer again, then we can bench someone else and put Alexis in her place," Mandi explained.

"Yeah, but then we have to find someone else to flip." I gasped with fear, already knowing the answer and not wanting to be tossed in the air. "No, Anna is just going to have to talk Mr. Semp into allowing her to cheer."

Mandi looked at me with a deadly stare. "I have been thrown in the air while you got to sit and watch."

"I know, but we need two people for this routine," I argued back. "We would have to get two people trained."

"She knows that," Matthew said with a smile. "That's why you should be in there practicing with them. That way, you only have to train one."

"No, I'm the captain and I do get a choice in the matter," I argued.

"That's not what Mr. Semp said," Mandi sang to me.

"Well, I know that I'm not ending up in detention with Anna and Adam 'cause the first bell is going to ring in about ten minutes," Matthew said as he started walking toward the school.

"We'll discuss this later," I told Mandi as we followed Matthew.

The day went by so slowly as I daydreamed while looking out the windows of the school. Each class seemed to last three hours; finally it was lunchtime. We all sat at the same table in the cafeteria. Alexis was still trying to see if she could guess who her mystery date was.

"So, are you driving us to the dance, Serina?" Alexis asked while looking around the cafeteria.

"First off, it's not a dance, it's a ball. And secondly, no, the limo will be picking us up," I said.

"Are we going together?" Alexis tried again. "I mean, we're all riding in the same limo…right?"

"I can't take this anymore," Matthew said, as he got up from the table with his drink still in his hand.

"What's wrong?" James asked through his smile. I could tell he was thoroughly enjoying the torture we were putting his sister through.

"The torture these girls are putting Alexis through," Matthew said, as if he could read my mind, too. I smiled behind my half-eaten sandwich.

"I think it's funny," James said as Alexis threw a chip at him. James moved slightly as it hit him in the chest. He laughed and dusted it off onto his tray.

"Come on, James. I'm going to introduce him to you," Matthew said, looking around the cafeteria. He started to walk to the exit of the cafeteria.

"All right!" James said as he followed Matthew.

"Can I go?" Alexis asked, getting up.

"No!" they both answered at the same time, laughing.

Alexis stood up to watch them as they walked out of the cafeteria. We started laughing at her. "This is not fun," Alexis said, sitting down to pout.

"Think of it as sorority rush," Holly said.

James and Matthew walked back into the cafeteria still laughing. "He seems nice," James said.

"So what does he look like? Does he look like my type?" Alexis was asking James rapidly.

James thought about it for a minute. Then he fluttered his eyelashes and said in his best girl voice, "He is soooo hot."

The table burst out laughing. Alexis got up and bumped into someone. "Sorry, I didn't mean to do that," she said as she looked up.

"It's OK," the guy said with a nice smile. "So you're Alexis."

"Yes, and you are?" Alexis looked at him, a little annoyed.

"I'm Mark," he said with a smile. "It's nice to meet you."

"Close your mouth, Alexis. We know he's hot, but you don't have to stare at him like that," Mandi said, laughing.

Alexis blushed. "Sorry. Yes, I am Alexis," she answered, without taking her eyes off him.

I watched as she seemed to be in a dream state, very similar to the state I was in when around James—the state that we were the only two in the room. It was so nice to see Alexis smile like that. It brightened her eyes and her face.

"So, I'll be at Serina's at seven?" he asked, still watching her, yet watching the group in front of him as well.

"Yeah, I'll be there," Alexis answered.

"Would you like me to walk you to your next class?" he asked. "We can talk then, so they won't pick on you."

"Sure!" she said, and he picked up her book bag. We watched as they left the cafeteria together. I had to admit, Mandi did a good job introducing the two of them.

"Am I good or what?" Mandi asked, smiling.

"Or what is right," I said, as Mandi threw a grape at me. The bell rang and we went to our next class.

By the end of the day I was ready to leave. I wanted to go home and talk with James and my mother about the things that had happened yesterday. We didn't get a chance to talk at dinner since Alexis had to get some things off her chest. I wanted to know what the creature was and where it came from. I sat next to James in the last class of the day. I kept watch of the door to see Alexis. She finally came in with that dreamy look on her face again.

I waited for her to take her seat in front of me. The wait was killing me. I wanted to know what she thought and how things went. "So?" I asked.

"You're right, he is hot!" she blurted out in excitement. "I can't wait until tomorrow night."

I looked over at James, but he was concentrating on something else at the moment. "What are you looking at?" I asked. He pointed at the door. The teacher was talking with someone I could not see. She had a look of concern on her face. "What's going on?" I asked him.

"I can't hear them," he said, looking at me.

"Then read their minds," I said with a smile.

"Can't. We can only do that if something is seriously wrong," he said. "But, for some odd reason, I think something is wrong and I just can't hear it."

The teacher turned and walked toward me. "Someone is in the office for you," she said as she handed me a hall pass.

I walked down the hallway to the office wondering who in the world would be looking for me. If it was my parents they would have just texted me on my phone. I quickly took my phone out and saw there were no missed calls or text messages. I reached the office and opened the door. I saw Mrs. Brockway standing there.

"Hi, Serina," she said with a half smile.

"Hi, Mrs. Brockway." I wondered if she had asked to see me. She was probably going to tell me how much she would miss me and how much she loved me. I looked at her to go on.

"Serina," another voice said.

I turned and almost knocked into a man behind me. "Yes," I said as I stared up into his dark—almost too dark—brown eyes.

"Your father sent me here to drop off a message," he said as he handed me an envelope.

"Why didn't he text me?" I asked.

"Have a good day," he said, then turned and left the office.

I ran to catch up with him, but when I opened the door he was gone. I ran toward the front of the school and there was nothing. I looked at the envelope and turned it over. I saw a wax marking on the back and noticed it was a crown. *Who goes through the trouble of putting a wax seal on envelopes anymore?* I thought. Before I could open it, a hand grabbed the letter from me. I looked up to see Alexis with the a pass.

"James sent me to find you," she said, as she took the envelope and looked at it. "That's cool. I haven't seen those in years. A wax seal. Someone important?" She laughed.

"Can I have it back?" I asked, trying to swipe it from her.

"No, he said he wants it," Alexis said.

"It was given to me. He's not going to read it before I do," I argued. "Look, I'll hold on to it and after class we'll all read it together."

"Then I'll hold on to it until after class," Alexis said. She turned and walked back to class and I followed her. The teacher noticed us as we quickly took our seats. I watched the clock and waited for the end of class.

When the bell finally rang, I got up and tapped Alexis on the shoulder. "Can I have it back, please?" I asked, holding my hand out.

"She doesn't have it," James said as he ushered me to the door.

We all walked to the car and got in. James sat behind the wheel and I looked at him staring at the envelope. "Will you please let me open it?" I pleaded.

"No, your mother needs to open it," he said, backing out of the parking space. The ride home was quiet as I sulked because James would not let me have the letter. When we arrived at my house I noticed both my parents standing in the driveway. My mother ran to the car and opened my door.

"Are you all right? He didn't hurt you, did he?" she asked.

"Who? Dad, why didn't you send me a text message?" I asked.

"What are you talking about, princess?" he asked.

My mother grabbed my arms and turned me to face her. "Who came to see you today?"

"I don't know. It was a young man with brown hair and brown eyes. He said that my dad sent him to drop something off," I said, trying to get out of my mother's death grip.

James handed her the letter and she looked at it for a moment. She turned it over to see the wax crown on the back. She shook her head.

"He always dreamed of being noble blood. Nothing has changed." She broke the seal, took out the letter and stared at it. "He's smarter than I gave him credit for." James took the letter and looked at it. He then handed me the letter. I looked at the blank piece of paper. I looked at my mother, puzzled. "Serina, you need to learn that anything we do, we must focus our energy on it."

I stared at the paper and watched as gold letters started to appear across it. I read the letter:

Dearest Serina,

If you are reading this, then your mother has taught you well. If it wasn't your mother, then thank James for me. How I have missed you since that day your mother took you from me. I want to let you know that I am here and would like very much to see you. I can meet you tonight somewhere. Just name the place and I will be there.

Love,

Dad

I finished reading it and turned to my mother.

"I guess I have some explaining to do," she said.

"No, I already know. I had a dream about him and I think he's a monster. He's not a guardian, and he made his choice a long time ago. He made the wrong choice," I said as I balled up the paper and threw it away. I went to my dad and hugged him. "You're my dad and I love you. I've made my own choice." My dad put his arm around me and we walked into the house.

"She understands some, but not all," James said.

"Yeah, she doesn't know that she is going to have to face him one day," my mother sighed. "But tonight we are going to get you a tux for the ball tomorrow."

"I hate dressing up!" James sighed.

XIX

Answers

That night my mom stayed with Alexis and me as we tried on our dresses, making any alteration she thought needed to be made, while Dad and Mr. Santiago went out to find James a tux. Alexis went first, so I sat on my bed looking through a magazine, figuring out what style I wanted my hair. The thought of my birthday popped into my head, and the fact remained that I still hadn't made a decision to follow in Mom's footsteps or to just go on with my life as if nothing had happened. The fact remained that I was falling for James, and although we were not really officially "boyfriend and girlfriend," we seemed to act the part. In fact, during the past week my life had changed in so many ways—from watching my mom not make a mess when wine was spilled, to meeting James, to fighting creatures I had never seen before, to being able to disappear and reappear somewhere else. Then I received a letter from a father I never knew. The whole thing seemed like a huge mess and no one was explaining it to me!

"Serina, if you have questions, why don't you ask?" my mom said, as she stood back and studied Alexis.

Great, now my mother was doing the same thing James did, and it was starting to get on my nerves.

"I don't know where to begin," I said, trying to act as if nothing was wrong while I flipped the page of the magazine slowly.

"The first thing that pops in your head," she said, fixing the bottom of Alexis's dress.

"I understand that no one could see us or that creature the other day. But, what was that thing?" I asked.

"Well, from what James told me it was a nuisance. Alexis, walk around a little and tell me if you still feel like you're going to trip over the dress," my mother instructed.

I watched as Alexis walked very carefully around my room and twirled. "I know it's a nuisance, but doesn't it have a name? And what does it do?" I asked curiously.

"That's what we call them. They are nuisances. They have very little power. The only thing they can do is to persuade someone to do something. The thing about nuisances is they are very well equipped to persuade someone to feel things like headaches and little pains. They also make people feel bad about themselves, to the point of no return sometimes. They tell them they are fat, ugly, and no one loves them. Things like that," she explained, never taking her eyes off Alexis and her dress.

"But, this thing told me that I wasn't strong enough, even for it," I said, lying flat on the bed and staring up at the ceiling.

"Did you believe it?" my mother asked with concern in her voice, taking her eyes off Alexis for the first time and looking at me.

"Well, I am new to this whole thing," I said as I sat up. "I think it knew who I was, but I didn't know what it was and what it could do."

"Alexis, honey, there are some new shoes for you and Serina in the foyer. Can you go get them and bring them back up?" my mother asked.

Alexis's eyes lit up. "You bought us shoes for the ball tomorrow?" she asked as she headed downstairs.

"Alexis," my mother called after her, "don't run in the dress!" My mother sat down beside me and put her arm around me. "Honey, listen to me. If you decide to continue this, then you have to learn to show no fear. Believe it or not, it was a small challenge, and not only can they sense fear, they can smell it, too. They will use whatever power they have to get you to back down. The trick is to know that good always conquers evil. Sometimes good loses a battle, but it is because that outcome was supposed to happen. So, no matter how big or small something is, never fear it!" she explained.

"But it hurt me!" I argued. "It scratched me all the way down my back, and James had to cover my mouth to keep me from screaming, which I still don't understand."

"OK. For one, whenever we fight something it does not mean we won't get hurt. Just know that we can heal ourselves. Just because we're guardians doesn't mean we won't feel pain. It feeds off pain. Another thing is that if you had screamed, she would have heard you, and it can turn that against you."

"So, whenever I get hurt, I can't grunt or anything? I mean, it's only natural to do that," I said, looking at her with a puzzled look.

"Well, at first you'll grunt and show pain, but as you grow into your powers you'll stop doing it," she explained. "Honey, if you do decide to go on, I know that you will do fine. You're strong and I know you'll make me proud," she said as she hugged me. She made me feel better not only about the situation, but also about myself.

"So how do I look?" Alexis said with her dress and shoes on.

"You look like a princess," my mom said. "Your turn, Serina."

"I'm going to look through the book to find a hairstyle," Alexis said, trying to contain her excitement.

I put my dress on and stood in front of my mom as she smiled. She knelt down to look at the bottom of the dress. "Actually, I think your dress is perfect. Put the shoes on and they'll raise you enough so you won't trip on it," she said.

"I love the small snowflake imprints on the dress," Alexis said admiringly.

I put the shoes on my feet and stood in front of my mother. "Remember, you guys are to sign into your homerooms and then I'll be there to pick you both up. We will go and get our nails done, makeup done, and hair done," my mother instructed.

"I can't wait!" Alexis screeched.

XX

I'd Be Honored

I was cozy under my comforter as I shifted my head on the pillow. It was so warm and comfortable that I had turned my alarm off to give me a few extra minutes. Since I had taken my shower last night, I figured I'd just put my hair up in a ponytail when my mom took Alexis and me out today. I started to drift back to sleep when my door swung open and Alexis jumped on my bed.

"Serina! Get up! I want to get this day to start now!" she screeched as I squeezed my eyes tighter. "Serina," she whined.

"OK, I'm up," I said sleepily.

"I am so excited!" It's my very first ball. I've never been to a ball!" she exclaimed like a little girl. I got out of bed and walked toward my bathroom as Alexis went on about the ball. I couldn't blame her; the first time I got to go I was excited. I finished my morning routine and started downstairs as Alexis followed, still taking about what we were to do today.

"Good morning, sunshine," my mother said in her cheery voice. She went over and hugged Alexis. "Are you ready for today?" she asked.

"Ready!" Alexis said through her smile.

I sat down at the table and put my head down.

"Morning to you, too," James said. I looked up without lifting my head.

"Did your sister get you up, too?" I asked as I yawned.

"Yep, she's been up since six," he replied.

I looked at the clock on the wall. It was eight. "I guess we should get to school," I said as I got up.

"See you girls later," my mother called after us.

I handed James the keys to the car.

"It's your birthday tomorrow," James informed me.

"Yep," I said, as I lay my head against the passenger side window and shut my eyes. I heard Alexis start giggling.

"It's such a beautiful morning," James said. "I think we could use some fresh air."

I felt my window start to go down. I quickly lifted my head as James and Alexis burst out laughing.

"OK, you two! I'm up and aware!" I said, trying to conceal my laughter. "That was not funny. What if my hair got stuck in the window or something?"

"Your hair is in a ponytail, safely secured behind your head," Alexis said, trying to sound serious but bursting out with more laughter. We arrived at school and was greeted by no one. "Where are Holly and Mandi?" Alexis asked.

"Probably going with their mothers to the same place we're going," I replied. We walked into the school to see that it looked almost empty. Many of the usual groups were missing people. I walked over to my locker and opened it.

"Serina, I thought you and your mom would be out," I heard Anna say.

"What are you doing here?" I asked. "I thought you would be out with Mandi and Holly."

"My mom is punishing me for skipping school with Adam. So, I hear you have a new guy since Steven left. I heard he was HOT!" She looked at me eagerly, waiting for a response.

"What's his name?" I asked her, smiling, knowing that she had spoken with Holly. Holly probably had given her every detail there was to know. I tried to conceal my amusement at the thought.

"Joe or Jean or something like that," she said, waving her hand in the air and waiting for me to correct her. If she was trying to conceal the fact that she knew nothing, she was not doing a good job of it.

"It's James, and you must be Anna," James said as he leaned up against the lockers.

Anna turned around to face James. "Wow, you are HOT!" she said as she studied him, and then turned to me and smiled.

"OK, I might have not cared if it was Steven, but James is—" I quickly stopped. He was a friend, I thought. No, he was more than a friend. He was someone who was teaching me what I was supposed to be. That was it.

"Is what?" Alexis asked as she came up behind me, interrupting my thought.

James looked at me and smiled. "I'm what?" he asked, joining in the fun with Anna and Alexis.

"You're my date tonight," I said as I shut my locker door. "Where's Adam?" I quickly asked Anna, trying to turn the attention from me to something else.

"He's in the gym," she said as she rolled her eyes. "Are you going to the ball tonight?"

"Yeah, my mom is picking up Alexis and me from school after homeroom," I answered her, as James took my book bag and threw it over his shoulder.

"Alexis is who?" Anna asked. She turned toward her and pointed. "You're Alexis, and you are…" She left the sentence hanging.

"James's sister. Are you going?" I asked.

"Yeah, but my mom is waiting until the end of the day," she said with a huff. "She is so mean sometimes."

"Are you grounded?" I asked.

"Yeah, not allowed to have the keys to the cabin until the summertime. So I guess no parties on the weekends," she said gloomily.

The first bell rang, I grabbed James's hand, and we started walking to our class. It was going to be a long day. James and I sat down as the teacher started taking roll.

So what am I? I heard him ask in my head.

I turned to face him. He was staring at the front of the class as if he was listening.

Not sure. What are you? I asked with a smile.

You never finished your sentence, I heard him again.

I thought you were so good at finishing my sentences that you could finish that one, I thought.

"I want you to finish that sentence," he smiled.

"Well, given your age and how long you supposedly have been around, I thought you might be a gentleman about it," I answered him.

Out of the corner of my eye, I could see James look at me and smile. I watched as he took out a piece of paper and started writing. I watched as he folded the paper and slid it toward me. I opened it and read:

My dearest lady, it would be an honor if we would become a couple. To be able to know that I could have a bona fide princess to call my own. Would you do me that honor?

The words on the paper shocked me. I was expecting something short and simple. Nothing like this. I felt my face start to turn red and I felt my mouth widen from the smile. Then, the teacher came up behind me and took the note. In an instant my heart flutters turned into hard thumps. She opened the note and looked at it. She then put it down in front of me and walked toward the front of the class. I looked at the paper and saw his class notes slowly fade into the words that were there before. At the end it said, "Nervous?" I smiled as I started to write.

Don't write. I can't change your handwriting, James said in my head.

You have to teach me how to do that. I would be honored to be known as your princess, I replied.

So does that make US official? he asked.

I nodded my head and felt something tickling my neck. I put my hand up to get whatever it was and felt a chain. I looked down to see the necklace hanging around my neck. I didn't pay much attention to class that morning as I played with the pendant. I felt happy and like I had butterflies in my stomach. I now looked forward to the ball and to my birthday. At first it seemed to be happening too fast, but I was also changing. I was starting to notice things differently. I started to see the world as something new that I had never seen before. Well, not like this; the colors were brighter and the air was lighter. It was as if I was seeing the world as someone else. The bell rang sharply, interrupting my thoughts, and I jumped from hearing it.

"Daydreaming?" James asked me.

"You could say that," I said as we walked to homeroom.

"Serina," my homeroom teacher said, catching me in the hallway.

"Yes?" I answered, still feeling so overwhelmingly happy and watching James walk beside me. I hadn't even noticed that we had already made it to my homeroom. It was as if I was floating down the hall.

"I see you and am marking you here, and this is your pass to go to the office," he said, handing me the note.

"Well, I thought she would have at least waited until my next class," I said as I looked down at the hall pass.

"I have to get to homeroom so I'm not marked absent," James said. "I'll see you later?"

"With my dress and all made up," I said, smiling.

"You're beautiful just the way you are," he said.

"Come on, Serina, your mom is waiting for us," Alexis said.

She grabbed my arm and started down the hallway with me. I just shrugged my shoulders, leaving James behind.

Alexis and I went into the office and saw my mother speaking with one of the secretaries and laughing. As Alexis walked up to her, my mother noticed her, put her arm around Alexis and smiled. "These balls are such a great thing for the kids. They get pampered and everything for the day." The secretary smiled as she handed my mom our excused notes as we walked out of the office.

"Mom," I said, "why did we even show up for school?" I laughed. "I mean, we sat through first bell and didn't even make it to homeroom. I could have slept a little longer."

My mother turned to me with a smile. "Serina, honey, sometimes it's good to get up, even when you don't want to do something, and then be able to play. Remember that in all things, do what's important first."

Alexis giggled as we made our way to the car, and my mother drove us to the spa where we would get our hair, makeup, and nails done.

XXI

The Winter Ball

I sat in the car and watched Alexis beam with joy as she held out her hands in front of her to admire her manicured nails. She was pampered today and loved every minute of it. Her hair was in an updo, with curls cascading down her back. Her makeup accented her emerald green eyes. She would look beautiful in her white and gold dress. She looked like a Barbie doll all made up.

"What time is it?" Alexis asked, not taking her eyes off her nails.

"It's six," my mom replied.

"Mark said he would meet us at seven," Alexis proudly replied.

"Mark...the guy on the baseball team, the pitcher?" my mother asked.

"Yeah, Mandi worked her magic," I said, giggling.

My mother looked over at me with a smile. "Leave it to Mandi to play cupid. I think she should get a job doing that, she would be good at it." My mom pulled up to see the Range Rover parked, and Mr. Santiago and Dad standing in the driveway laughing.

"Dad!" Alexis jumped out of the car. "How do I look?" she said as she showed him her nails and hair, and fluttered her eyelashes.

"You look beautiful!" he said, hugging her. "You look just like your mother."

"Where is James?" my mother asked. The two men started laughing.

"Well," my dad said, "I think he's in there fighting with his tux."

"Why aren't you guys helping him?" she scolded. "Girls, go get dressed and I will help him. Where is he?"

"He's in your kitchen," Mr. Santiago replied, still smiling.

"You two are still like little children! Men, they never grow up," my mother said, as she gently put her hands on our backs and guided us toward the house.

I went into the house and opened the kitchen door. I saw James sitting at the table looking defeated. I walked over to him. "You know, for as old as you are, you'd think that you would know how to get dressed in one of these penguin suits," I said. "Here, let me help you."

James looked up at me. "You look beautiful," he said, as he stood up and handed me his tie.

"Thank you," I said as I took it and wrapped it around his collar. I started to hum a tune as I put it on. I watched as my fingers expertly slip the wide end of the tie through the center and I tightened it.

"Where did you learn that?" he asked.

I kept humming until I finished the tie and then straightened it. "I learned it from watching my mom when she helped my father with his ties. It's called a windsor knot." I grabbed his cuff links and started to straighten his sleeves.

"Serina, honey, you need to get dressed. I'll finish here," my mom said as she grabbed the sleeve I was working on.

"OK," I said as I walked toward the door. I could feel him watching me over my mom's shoulder.

"She is a beautiful girl," my mother said.

"Yes, she is," James said. "Has she talked to you about her birthday?"

"No, but you are going to have to guide her and keep her safe. Tomorrow they'll all know and, depending on what she says, will determine her fate," my mother answered with nervousness in her voice.

I walked into my room to see that my closet door was shut. I gently knocked on it. "Alexis, are you in there?" I asked.

"Yeah, but I'm having trouble," she said, opening the door and stepping out with a defeated look on her face.

"You look fine," I said. Alexis turned around and I noticed the back of her dress wasn't zipped up. "Oh, that's not trouble. I'll help you zip it."

"You know, living with two men for so long, I've learned to do many things on my own," Alexis replied. "But I've never really had to put one of these things on. I mean, I never had one that needed to be zipped up in the back."

"Where were your friends?" I asked. "I mean, you never played dress up where you had to help each other out or anything?"

"Didn't make too many. I tried not to get too attached to anyone 'cause I knew that we would just move somewhere else. So how do I look?" she asked, as she twirled around for me to see.

"You look beautiful." I smiled as I remember the first time I went to the winter ball. I was just as excited as Alexis was now. I felt as if I was a princess for the day, and I imagined that was how she was feeling right now.

"Well, I'm going downstairs." Alexis turned to leave.

I ran to the door and leaned against it. "No. As your friend I'm going to teach you something." Alexis looked at me weirdly. "You make them wait. They expect it and it makes your entrance even grander," I said with a smile.

Alexis smiled at the sound of this new concept. "How long do we wait?"

"Nan will come and get us. Here, put some perfume on and sit. I have to get dressed," I said.

Alexis sat there with a smile. I walked into my closet and looked at my dress. It was really pretty. The snowflakes made the dress seem like the perfect winter picture. I put it on and walked out. "Alexis, can you zip me?"

"Sure," she replied, as she jumped up and ran over toward me. She quickly found the zipper and zipped it up. "You look so pretty."

"Thanks," I said. I picked up my perfume and dug through my jewelry box. "Here, I think these should go with your dress," I said, as I handed Alexis my diamond necklace and earrings.

Alexis slowly walked over and took them. She stared at them for a while and then looked at me with tears in her eyes. "You don't mind?" she asked.

"Nope, I'm going to wear my pendant and the snowflake earrings my mom got me," I answered. I turned around and saw the tears starting to form in her little eyes. "Alexis! Don't cry, your makeup will run." I smiled as I got a tissue and gently wiped her face.

"Serina," Alexis said softly, "for as long as we've been here, I have never felt so pretty and so accepted as I do right now." She sniffled. "I mean…I feel as if I actually belong."

I hugged Alexis. "You've always belonged, you just never noticed it before," I said as I looked over at our reflection in the mirror.

There was a soft knock on the door and Nan poked her head in. "Miss Serina and Miss Alexis, you look so beautiful. The boys, they are downstairs and ready," she said.

"OK. We'll be down in just a minute," I said as I finished latching Alexis's necklace. We put our earrings on and headed out the door.

"Now get ready, 'cause our parents will be taking pictures and everything else," I said as we rounded the corner to the top of the stairs.

I watched as my parents and Mr. Santiago stood there talking with Mark's parents. Alexis moved and I grabbed her by the arm. "Wait until someone notices you and then walk," I said in a whisper.

"Why?" she asked.

"'Cause it's a game I play with my mother," I said with a smile.

It was Mark's mom that noticed us first. "You two look gorgeous!" she said. I took the first step down as Alexis followed me. The two boys waited. I walked over to James.

"Had to make your grand entrance, huh?" my mother whispered in my ear as she glided past me.

James never took his eyes off me. "You look soft," he said.

I started laughing. "Well, I've never been told that before," I said, as I noticed him start to touch my neckline. "Oh, the dress. Yeah, it's soft," I said.

We lined up for pictures and then walked outside to the limo that was waiting for us. Alexis climbed inside first, looking around in amazement.

"See you guys later, and have a good time!" the parents yelled as the driver shut the door.

We arrived at the club to see many people there. "Do we get out now?" Alexis asked as she looked out the window with excitement. I had to admit the look on her face was so cute, as if she couldn't contain the excitement that dwelled in her.

"No, we wait until the limo gets to the front and the doorman opens the door," I said, my arm interlocked with James's.

"You look really pretty," Mark said to Alexis.

Alexis blushed. "Thank you," she replied as she looked at me. The smile on her face screamed that she was in bliss at that moment. Nothing was taking her off the cloud she had been on all day.

The door opened and the doorman's hand reached inside. I grabbed it and he helped me out of the car. "Good evening, Miss Kartone," he said.

"Good evening," I said.

"Your friend's last name, Miss Kartone?" he asked in a whisper.

"Miss Santiago," I replied with a smile.

"Good evening, Miss Santiago," he said as he helped Alexis out of the car.

"Hello," she said as Mark followed her.

James stepped out, looked around, and he put his arm out for me. We walked in the entrance and were greeted by the hostess.

"Follow the snowflakes to the ballroom," she said with smile as she pointed to her left. We walked down the hallway looking at the beautiful decorations and heard the sound of the music that was coming out of the ballroom. We came to the huge double doors and walked in. The decorations made it look like there was snow in the room and snowflakes hung from the ceiling. There was an ice sculpture of a swan at the hors d'oeuvres table and a fountain that was probably filled with punch that you could get drinks from.

"Serina!"

I looked over to see Mandi waving from the table. I pulled James and we walked over to it. The boys pulled out our chairs as we sat down. Holly and Heath were already there.

"Where are Anna and Adam?" I asked.

"They're running late," Mandi said.

"They did a good job with the decorations," Holly said, looking around the room. "Did you see the nice swan sculpture over there? I wonder whose idea that was?"

"Yeah…it might have been better if it were a snowflake or something wintery," Mandi replied with a snicker.

"There they are. Adam, over here!" Heath yelled.

"Hey, guys, my mom was acting all nice to me when I got home, and made sure that everything was all set up for me to get ready," Anna said as she rolled her eyes. "Nice to see you again, James," she said.

"Hi, I'm Adam," he said, holding his hand out to James. They shook.

"Hi," James said.

"So tell us, James, where are you from? And what made you move out here, besides Serina?" Adam asked. "Do you play any sports?"

"Well, there is not much to tell." As James started, Crystal's voice could be heard through the sound system.

"Good evening, everyone," she said from the stage. She waited for the music to be lowered and the crowd to stop talking before she continued. "Welcome to the annual winter ball," she exclaimed with a smile of a snake. "We will be serving chicken or beef, whichever you prefer, and then we will have a dance. There are also a couple of contests going on tonight. So everyone relax and enjoy yourselves. And, some of our parents are here, so we still have to be on our best behavior. Have a good night."

"I don't like her dress. It makes her look like a streetwalker. It's too tight," Anna said.

"Yeah, she thinks that just because her mom is head of events at the club she has free rein," Holly chimed in.

"You do know that Crystal was the reason Serina never got that close to Steven," Matthew said, leaning toward James.

"Why? Did Steven break up with Crystal or something?" Alexis asked, trying to get the story.

"Well, it looks like Serina brought some new friends," Crystal said as she put her hand on James's shoulder. "Hi, I'm Crystal," she said with a smile, and held out her hand.

"I wouldn't touch that. I don't know where her hand might have been before she came over here," Anna snapped.

"Yeah, why don't you go and bug someone else," Holly joined in.

"I'm supposed to greet everyone," Crystal said with an evil grin, as she turned her attention toward James. "So, you must be the new guy here...James, is it?"

I started to feel a headache coming on and lowered my head. "Serina, are you OK?" James asked as he put his hand on my back, ignoring Crystal's question. I shook my head and quickly regretted it. It just made it worse.

"So, Serina, where is Steven?" Crystal asked, pulling up a seat next to James and smiling at him. "You know, Serina, it's very rude not to introduce people."

As My headache started to worsen, James lifted my chin and looked at me. "Excuse us, we need to get some air," James said. He shoved Crystal out of the way, as we rushed into one of the deserted hallways, and pressed me up against the wall.

"Ow! That hurts," I said. *Great, now my back and my head hurt*, I thought. *Good going, James!*

"I'm going to do it again if you don't calm down. Your eyes are as black as night!" he informed me.

I fumbled through my purse to find a mirror and looked at myself. "Oh my gosh! How do I get them to return to normal?" I panicked.

"Tell me your problem with her," he said.

I looked at him with confusion. I wasn't sure who or what he was talking about, when it suddenly hit me.

"With who? Crystal?" I asked as my anger grew a little more.

"Yeah, but keep it under control!" James said as he put his finger in my face.

"At one time I did like Steven. But, then he started to want something more from me and I was just not like that. I mean, I want to go to college, and what if… Anyway, Anna was having a party at her parents' cabin and Crystal showed up. I was talking to Mandi when I noticed Steven and her down at the lake talking. I didn't think anything of it and continued to talk with Mandi. She and I walked outside and noticed Steven's car door was open slightly. I went over to close it and there she was with him. Ever since then, it's been…I don't know…not good between the two of us."

"But, you continued to hang around Steven," James said.

"He tried to make it up to me, and told me he was sorry and that it would never happen again. But, I just knew we would never be anything more than friends," I said. "He made me feel like I wasn't special, like I was just an object to him. Not like you—you make me feel special and loved," I said as I wrapped my arms around him.

He held my mirror up and I saw my brown eyes again. "It made you angry, huh?" he asked.

"Yeah, but it doesn't matter now," I said as we started walking back to the ballroom.

I saw that Crystal had taken my seat. "Have a seat, James," she said with a smile.

"You know, I think I would like to dance with my girlfriend," he said. All the eyes at the table got wide. "Would you like to dance?" he asked, as he bowed in front of me.

"It would be a pleasure," I said with a smile.

I took his hand and we went to the dance floor. The rest of the table got up and followed us, wanting to know the story. I didn't notice anything as James and I danced that night. Looking into his eyes, which were crystal blue, made everything go right.

"Have we danced like this before?" I asked.

"Yeah, a long time ago," he said with a smile. "Do you remember where? And when?" I closed my eyes, trying to remember. I saw a picture in my mind. I was wearing a little blue dress and he was wearing khakis and a nice white shirt. It was in the same ballroom and everyone was there. from family and friends to some people I didn't recognize. I looked toward the stage where a banner was hung and it read: *Congratulations James and Serina*. "I love you," I heard him whisper in my ear as I opened my eyes.

"It was the night before our wedding," I said.

James smiled at me. "You're starting to remember," he said as he kissed me.

There was nothing that could ruin this night. Not Crystal, not Steven, nobody could ruin it.

XXII

Happy Birthday to Me!

I woke up the next morning to hearing things being banged around in the backyard. I heard my dad yelling instructions to people and my mom yelling at him. I looked out my window to see people setting up tables and cooks setting up grills and a smoker. I shook my head. *I wonder if this party is for me or for my parents and their friends.*

"Happy birthday, Miss Serina," Nan said, poking her head in.

"Thank you, Nan," I said as I went over to hug her.

"This for you," she said, and she handed me a little box with a bow on it.

"You didn't have to get me anything." I smiled as we sat on my bed. I slowly undid the bow and opened the box. It was a pair of turquoise beaded earrings that had the number eighteen in white beads.

"I made them for you," she said.

I looked at her and hugged her. "This is going to be my favorite present I get today." I put them in my ears. "How do I look?" I asked.

"Pretty," Nan grinned.

"I guess I have to get ready for the day. People are going to be coming in and out all day." I rolled my eyes as I got up, took out the earrings and put them on my dresser. I took a shower, did my hair and I went downstairs to be greeted by my mother.

"Happy birthday, honey!" she said as she hugged me. "How are you feeling?"

"Feeling OK, why?" I asked.

"You don't look eighteen," she said with a laugh. "Who gave you those earrings?"

"Nan made them for me," I said, as I put my hand underneath them to show them off.

"That was nice of her." My mother smiled. "They are very pretty. Come out and see what your dad and I have been doing all morning long." She guided me to the outdoor patio. I looked at the backyard with all the flowers, balloons, and tables.

"Happy birthday, princess!" my father yelled from the far end of the yard.

"Thank you, Daddy!" I yelled as I blew a kiss at him.

I saw Alexis start running toward me. "Happy birthday," she said as she hugged me. "So, guess what?"

"What?" I asked with a smile.

"I hope you don't mind, but Mark is going to be here this afternoon," she said, smiling.

I looked at her with a serious face. "You mean you invited Mark to my birthday party?" I asked with my hand on my hip.

"I can always call him and tell him he can't," she said quietly. "I'm sorry. It is your party," she said with her head down.

"You know, Alexis, it is my birthday and I can pick on you all day if I want to." I laughed. I don't care if he comes over. So, did he call you or did you call him?"

Alexis lifted her head and smiled. "He called me, and that's when I told him he should come over."

"I invited his parents last night," my mom said. "Not too sure if they are going to fit into our group."

"It just means the group has to behave," Nan said, as she went by my mom with a vase full of flowers.

"Mom, it's my birthday, and to tell you the truth, we have all these people setting things up and cleaning things up. Why can't you let Nan have the day off?" I asked. "Let her go home and get ready for the party," I pleaded.

"Is that what you want?" she asked.

"Yes, and pay her for the day," I added with a grin.

"Her heart is just as big as her mother's sometimes," my dad said, coming up behind me. "Nan, the birthday princess has spoken. You are to go home and get ready for the party, and you'll be paid for it."

Nan turned around. "Thank you, Mr. Kartone," she said with a smile. I watched as Nan thanked my dad again and turned to me. "You'll make a great guardian," she said, and left to get ready.

"How does she know?" I asked my mother.

"Who do you think showed me where you were when your dad had you?" my mother asked with a smile.

"Is she a guardian?" I asked.

"Used to be. She decided that she just wanted to be here for you. She fell in love with you when you were little and wanted to make sure that nothing happened to you. She has been watching over you since I was not able to," she explained. "She has no powers or anything because she decided to live her life as a human until her mission was done."

"So she was there for me when my dad had me?" I asked.

"Yep. You didn't know it, but she never left your side," she explained. "She kind of kept your good side strong. Well, as strong as she could. She is also here to make sure that I kept my end of the bargain."

"What bargain?" I asked as my curiosity heightened.

"The man that will visit you told me that I was not able to come back if I didn't make things right this time. I had to explain things to you and find James, because the two of you together are stronger than Christina and I would ever imagine being."

"When is he coming?" I asked as I watched my mom look at the sky.

"Not sure. He will be here, though. He never misses an appointment," she said as she turned to me. "Anyway, let's go in and see what else we have to do."

The rest of the day I watched people set things up and watched as cooks started preparing meals and hors d'oeuvres. I watched as the caterers started to set up my cake in the middle of the yard.

"Mom!" I yelled.

"What? What's wrong?" she asked, looking around the yard for the imperfection and then staring at me. "What happened?"

"How tall is my cake?" I looked at her.

"I told them two tiers this year," she said proudly as she watched them put it together. "Isn't it pretty?"

"Are that many people coming?" I asked.

"Oh, come on, honey, everyone is coming," she said, as she continued to watch them put the cake together.

I put my head in my hands. *Why did my mom order such a huge cake?* I thought.

"Excuse me. Serina?" one of the waiters asked.

"Yes?" I asked with a sigh.

"Someone is waiting for you in the front yard," he replied.

"OK," I said as I walked to the front yard. I opened the door to find a carriage with Midnight and Starr hooked to it.

"Would you like to accompany me while we pick up your friends?" James asked as he held out his arm.

"Come on, Serina! This is going to be fun!" Alexis screamed from the carriage.

"Who are we picking up?" I asked.

"Mandi, Holly, and Anna," he answered.

"Well, if we're not going out of the neighborhood with our horses, I guess that would be fine," I said as I took his arm. He helped me up into the carriage and the driver guided the horses around the corner.

"Whose idea is this?" I asked as James put his arm around me.

"Your father's. He said that you are his princess and he wanted you to be treated like one today," James said.

As we pulled up to Mandi's house, she was waiting outside. "Well, you said a horse-drawn carriage," Mandi said as she got into the carriage. "This is pretty nice."

"So, are Matthew, Heath, and Adam meeting us at my house?" I asked.

"Yeah, they are all meeting us there. I think it should have just been you and James," she said with a smile.

"Cool!" I heard Holly scream. "This is awesome. We can arrive at your party in style," she said as she climbed into the carriage.

"Well, I'm glad that we don't live that far away from each other." I giggled as James moved closer to me. I did feel like a princess, with all my friends around me and one of the most caring guys I had ever met with his arm around me.

"Anna lives one street over, though," Holly said, laughing. I watched as the carriage turned the corner.

"We're going to go on a carriage ride later tonight," James whispered in my ear. I squeezed his hand with excitement. The thought of riding in a horse-drawn carriage under the stars seemed like the perfect ending to a perfect day.

"Hi, Anna!" Holly screamed and waved at Anna, standing by the front of her house and waiting for us. She smiled as she saw us coming up with the carriage.

"Wow! I wish my mom would let me take my horses out of the stable like this," Anna said as she took her seat next to Holly.

"Your horse wouldn't let you ride her very far before she started whinnying, let alone pull a carriage," Mandi laughed.

"That's because she is spoiled, like me," Anna said. She eagerly looked around the inside of the carriage and watched as we slowly started back toward my house.

"OK, now that we're all here, I think it's time for a song!" Holly said with a smile.

"Holly, no, please don't," I pleaded.

"What kind of friends would we be if we didn't embarrass you all the way home? Not good friends," she said. She started singing "Happy Birthday." The rest of them started to sing along with her as James started laughing and joined them. I sat there with a smile, trying to hide my face as we pulled up to my house.

"OK!" Matthew shouted. "Do we get to pick our princesses as they come out of the carriage?"

My street looked like a parking lot. Everyone was there. All my mom and dad's friends and their kids came. I went into the back where everything was set up and the music was playing. I watched my mom talking to her friends and laughing. They had transformed the backyard into what looked like a reception. I watched as people put gifts on a table and thought, *Wow, that is a lot of thank-you cards I'm going to have to send.*

"Your cake is beautiful!" Anna said. "What's wrong with Alexis?"

Alexis sat at one of the tables looking around as if she had lost her best friend. I quickly walked over to her. "What's wrong?" I asked, taking a seat next to her.

"Mark said he was coming," she said, her eyes filled with concern. She looked around again and then back at me. "I know I told him the right time. Maybe he just didn't want to come. Maybe it's me," she said, putting her head down and staring at the ground.

"He'll be here," I said, looking through the crowd and trying to see if he was lost somewhere in the sea of people. "Don't worry, he's fashionably late." I tried to make light of the situation hoping to get her to smile, which didn't seem to work.

"He's been here," James said with Mark by his side. "We were just in the house for a minute. And no, I didn't threaten him."

"Did you think that I would not come?" Mark asked as Alexis looked up at him and smiled. "Happy birthday, Serina," he said as he hugged me.

"Thank you." I hugged him back.

"This is one big party," Mark commented as he looked around the yard. "It looks like your parents invited everyone in the neighborhood and then some. I think you have enough food to feed an army, and you have a DJ." Mark stopped and looked at Alexis. "Do you want to dance?" he asked, holding out his hand.

"I would love to," she said, taking his hand and smiling. She followed him out to the dance floor in the middle of the yard.

Just then, the music stopped and my dad got hold of the mic. "Well, I have just been told that my princess has arrived at her birthday party. Where is she?"

"I'm here, Dad," I said, waving at him with a smile on my face. I watched as everyone turned to face me and immediately regretted my actions.

"Come here," he said with a drink in his hand. I walked over to him on the patio. He put his arm around me and kissed me on the cheek. "We are here to celebrate my little girl turning eighteen." Everyone started clapping. "Happy birthday, princess! And now I need you to go into the garage 'cause I fixed your car." He handed me the keys. I grabbed them and walked over to the garage. "Tell her to pull it out," he instructed.

I shut the door and looked at my car. I hadn't forgotten that my mom had said he was getting it painted for my birthday. I looked inside and screamed. The light blue, with the gold Mercedes symbol, looked gorgeous. I opened the door to get in and saw that he had had *Princess* embroidered into the white leather seats. I turned the car on and backed out.

"Tell her to turn her radio on."

I looked down to see that the radio was nowhere to be found.

James ran over to me. "Your dad told me to let you know to push the button on the steering wheel and say 'radio,'" he instructed.

I looked down at it, pushed the power button, and said, "Radio." The top of the console unfolded and a small flat-screen TV emerged. On the TV screen, it read: *Happy Birthday Princess*. I jumped out of the car and ran to my dad, giving him a hug.

"Do you love it?" he asked.

"It's better than I ever could have imagined," I said.

"OK, princess, let's eat. We have steak, ribs, hot dogs, burgers, sausage, shrimp, and other stuff. Let's eat!" he said, as the music turned back on.

"Wow, Serina, you'll be riding in style come Monday," Matthew said.

"I absolutely love it," I said, as I stood back with my friends to admire it.

"I think it looks good," Adam said with a mouthful of food. He swallowed it and noticed the group starting at him. "What? These ribs are banging!"

"Come on, let's eat," I said, and we went over to the food.

The party went on into the night and the waiters started to take my gifts into the house. My mother told them to put them in the family room and that I would probably open them tomorrow. We danced and even had a karaoke session where my friends got up to sing songs. To be completely honest, it was the best party I had had in ages. People started leaving around eleven and I went into the house. The guys and girls left at ten thirty because we decided to get up early tomorrow to try out my car and to go shopping. We said good-bye to the last guest at eleven fifteen as my dad shut the door.

"Everyone will be here to clean up this mess tomorrow," he sighed. "Too tired to try and get it cleaned up tonight, and I think we're all ready to go to bed."

James, Alexis, and Mr. Santiago looked exhausted. "I'm going to bed," Alexis said as she started up the stairs.

"Are you guys spending the night?" I asked.

"No, they're spending the week with us 'cause your father and Mr. Santiago have business out of town," my mom said as she hugged me.

Suddenly, the doorbell rang. "I'll get it," my dad said, as he got up and slowly walked to the front door. He opened it. "Well, we were expecting you earlier," he said as he let the man in. "Serina, your visitor is here," he announced.

XXIII

The Decision

I watched as a tall young man with a long white cloak entered the house. He took his hood off and I saw he had shoulder-length blond hair, which was neatly tied into a ponytail. His crystal-blue eyes shone by the light of the room. "My Serina. You have grown into a very beautiful young lady. You look like your mother," he said in a very distinguished voice. "May I have a word with you alone?" he asked.

I looked at my mother. She walked over to me and hugged me. "It's OK, he won't hurt you." I walked past James as worry set into his eyes. This was it. James knew that once I walked out of the room I would either be with him or he would continue doing this work alone. I tried not to let it sway me one way or the other. I had thought about the decision I was about to make, and to be honest even with myself, there were still a lot of questions I wanted to ask. Things I wanted to know—no, that I needed to know before I decided.

"Sure," I said as I walked toward the family room. He followed behind me and shut the door. I sat down in the chair in front of the fireplace.

"Have you been expecting me?" he asked.

"Yes," I said, sitting up straighter in my chair.

"Happy birthday," he said with a smile. "Now, down to business." I watched as he took a seat on the couch in front of the window. "Do you understand why I'm here?"

"Because my mother is a guardian and I'm half," I answered nervously.

"So she has told you," he said as he folded his hands. "If you are half guardian, what is your other half?" he asked.

"Human," I answered him confidently.

"Well, your mother didn't explain that to you. So I'm going to have to," he said as he sat back.

"No, she did," I contradicted him. "She said that my father, who is human, made a deal with someone who was evil. From my dreams I learned that he was a vampire who turned my father into a vampire. My mother was burned for being a witch 'cause she helped someone, and then my father took me and raised me for a while. He wasn't a vampire when I was conceived, he was human, so that, sir, makes me human," I said proudly. That explained it, point one for me!

The man just looked at me calmly. "You have an evil side," he said. "How do your powers become evil?" he asked.

The image of the day Steven hit James popped into my head. The anger that I felt and the pain I wanted to inflict on him. He was right—I was half evil. How was that? "I'm not too sure," I answered, my voice almost dropping to a whisper. In fact, I never really thought about it. *My mother was pure good, how can I be half good and half evil?*

"How old are you?" he asked, as if the question before had no relevance.

I sighed. This was an easy one. "Eighteen. Duh," I said, pointing at the earrings Nan had given me.

The man just sat back and smiled. "If that were true, you, being half guardian and half human, would age like a human with extraordinary gifts. Which means you would be dead by now."

He sat back, looking at me and waiting for what he had just said to sink in. He waved his hand and a birth certificate appeared. He handed it to me. I looked at what it said. Serina Starr Anderson. Born on November 29, 1691.

"How old are you, Serina?" he asked me.

I looked at the paper. This wasn't me. He had me confused with someone else. Someone with my name, but the last name was different. I smiled at him. "I'm sorry to say, but you have the wrong person. This girl's name is Serina Starr Anderson. My name is Serina Starr Kartone," I said, pushing the paper toward him.

He sat there with his arms across his chest. "Serina… you were born Serina Starr Anderson. Your father's name was Brad Anderson and your mother's name was Hope Anderson. It wasn't until your mother married the man that you came to know as your father that your name was changed to Serina Starr Kartone. This would make you how old?" he asked with a smile.

I was shocked at this. "I'm three hundred and eighteen years old," I said in a whisper, never taking my eyes off the birth certificate. "So I would be dead by now if I was half human." There had to be an explanation for this. "But what if my mom took me through time?" I asked, grasping at any explanation I could think of.

"It is true that we can travel through time, but we don't because it can cause more harm than good. The only reason your mother was given that permission was to get you away from your father. You would have still aged as the years went by and she would not have been able to take you very far into the future," he explained.

That was it. I had no more answers and now was more confused than when I came in to speak with him. I shrugged my shoulders in defeat. "I don't know, then. Will you please explain it to me?" I asked.

"Your father killed you when you were four," he said.

"What do you mean, killed me?" I asked. I was still alive. *I'm sitting here now. I go to school and people see me. I have a heartbeat.* How could my father kill me and me still be here? This I had to hear.

"He killed the human side of you by turning you into what he was," he said. "He was unsuccessful in completely turning you, though. You still had half of your mother in you, which saved you from being completely evil. Now…you have a choice of either using your powers for good or for evil. Which is another reason why I am here. But, before I tell you any more, I need you to decide whether or not you want to continue down this path, or if you would like me to erase all this and let you lead a normal human life," he said.

I sat back in the chair. I had been thinking about it all day. It was nice to do things for people, but then I would have to watch as all my friends grew old and died. I would not age. I didn't know what to say. What would happen to James and my mother if I said no? "What's your name?" I asked, trying to stall for time.

The man gave me a questioning look. It was as if he was very surprised at my question. "Why do you ask?" I could tell he was intrigued by my question.

"Because everyone has told me this man was coming to see me, yet they cannot give me a name. I want to call you by your name and know how you are connected to all this," I answered him.

"I will tell you my name after you have given me your answer," he said as he sat up. I watched as he nervously looked at the clock. I turned around to see that it was eleven forty-five.

"I have to give you an answer before midnight, don't I?" I asked.

"You're catching on," he replied. "You must understand that you have been the exception to our rule due to everything has happened in your life. You are three hundred years behind." He smiled. "Your answer?"

I knew what I had to do. "Sir, I want to continue my mother's good work," I said confidently.

"Good," he said. "My name is Taurus and I watch over the guardians. There are many of you still out there, however, many of them have decided to take the easy way out and become human, because the world is becoming harder to deal with. You, my dear, are one of a hundred here in the states that have decided to stick it out. Let me finish explaining. Although your father turned you, you did something that no one could have anticipated. Your guardian side, or what we think must have been your guardian side, took over and allowed you to adapt to what he was, giving you the chance not to fully become evil. This is because your mother is one of the strongest guardians I have. When you become angry or have been around evil for so long your evil powers are heightened. You must learn to balance as James has learned to balance. Do you understand?" he asked.

"I must not let my evil side take over. Got it. I will learn with time." I tried to reassure him—as well as myself, for that matter.

"I'm sure you will. Your purpose here is much different from your mother's. You and James are very different from the guardians that I have, and with the two of you possessing both good and evil powers, you must use them wisely. The two of you must make sure that evil does not cross the line," he explained. "The single most important thing that you must know is that sometimes certain things will happen for a reason. People must die every day because that is how it all works in a plan. We cannot intervene in that plan, and if we do it can cause great harm, not only to us, but to them as well. Do you understand?" he asked.

"I will. Can I talk with you if I have questions?" I asked, still trying to fully understand my new responsibilities.

"I will be here if you and James need help," he said. "Now is the hard part, and that is understanding your powers and what you can and cannot do. James will teach you along the way, but for now, I have to go and check on some others. You and James are going to need each other for support and guidance. Remember, you are the only two that have this gift of being both good and evil, and can balance the two because you are mixed. The two of you are very special." He got up and held out his hand. I took it as he opened the door, and we walked out.

"It was good seeing you again," he said as he kissed my mother on her cheek. "James, you show her and teach her everything you know. Also watch over her." He placed my hand in James's hand. "Happy birthday, Serina. I will be seeing the two of you soon." He then turned to the door and disappeared.

I looked at James with a sheepish grin. "I guess you're stuck with me," I said.

James grabbed me by my waist and thrust me into the air. "I'm not alone anymore!" he lowered me back down and kissed me. "I've missed you."

"I still have to remember that, but then again, I still have to remember the other three-hundred-odd years that I've missed, too," I said with a smile.

"So he explained all that to you?" my mother asked.

"Some of it. The rest of it I will just have to figure out," I said. "But I have had a long day and am ready to go to bed. Good night," I said, as James and I walked up the stairs.

"I'll see you in the morning," James said with a smile, and kissed me good night.

"Yes, you will," I said as I turned and closed my door. My heart skipped a beat knowing that tomorrow was going to be a new day with new adventures. I finally felt as if I belonged somewhere. That I was needed. My whole being had a purpose. I smiled as I lay down in my bed. I looked up at my canopy and closed my eyes.

James felt a chill as he turned over in his bed. He looked at his clock and saw that it was three fifteen in the morning. He shut his eyes again hoping to find sleep. He took a deep breath and instantly sat up in bed. He breathed in again, smelling the foul stench of death in the air. He got out of bed and opened the door, only to see the dark hallway. He sniffed again, only to find the odor to get stronger. A chill ran down his spine as his powers ached to be used. Something was here, and whatever it was, it was strong. He needed to get to Serina. He started walking down the hallway toward her room when he heard her scream.

"LET ME OUT!" Serina screamed.

"SERINA!" James screamed, running to her door and grabbing the handle, only to find it locked. "Serina, open the door!" he yelled.

"LET ME OUT OF HERE! he heard her sob. "James, HELP ME!" He could hear her starting to cry.

"Serina!" her mother said as she ran down the hall. She grabbed the door handle and tried to open it. "Open the door," she said, pounding on it.

"MOM! I want out of here!" Serina screamed again.

James pushed her mother out of the way. "Serina, listen to me. Close your eyes and picture yourself outside the door. Like you did on the boat."

"I can't! I've already tried that!" she screamed. "Someone is in my room!"

James put his head against the door. "Serina, nothing is going to work if you are scared! You have to regain control of yourself!" he yelled. The room went quiet. "SERINA! SERINA!" James yelled as he pounded on the door.

"James, I'm scared! OPEN THE DOOR! OPEN THE—"

The room went quiet again and the door slowly opened. James turned the light on to find her room empty. Her bed was messed up and her room was cold. He looked around the room for anything that might have given him a clue to what was in the room with her. James looked at the back of the door.

"Good girl," he said aloud, reading what she wrote. Her mother looked at the name on the door, which Serina used her eyeliner to write.

"Luther," her mother gasped. She quickly turned to James with tears in her eyes. "James, you have to find her, and quick. Luther is too strong for her yet. He could…" She started to cry.

"I know," he said, holding her mother. James heard the cry of Midnight and Starr as they pulled themselves free from the tree they were tied to. Midnight had already changed and Starr was in the middle of changing.

James grabbed Serina's mother. "I will bring her back before anything happens to her. I promise." He then went outside to the horses. He felt the familiar weight on his back of his sword. He jumped onto Midnight and patted his head. "Looks like we won't be enjoying tomorrow. We need to get Serina back," he said. Midnight let out a loud whinny and Starr joined him.

"Bring Serina home!" her mother yelled at James.

"I will."

And with that, James, Midnight, and Starr vanished into the cold night air.

XXIV

Luther

I slowly opened my eyes as the throbbing in my head started to subside. I stretched my arms out, letting them move slowly along the bed. I noticed in an instant that I wasn't in my bed. I looked around to see the burgundy velvet blanket with the sheer burgundy curtains that enclosed the bed.

I immediately sat up and tried to remember what had happened. I went to bed and I woke up to a sound in my room. I remembered being afraid of what or who was in my room. That was it. Who was in my room? I closed my eyes to remember, seeing the man that was with Mrs. Stevenson and gave me the note at school that day. He was the one in my room. He told me that—what was his name? Larry? London? No, Luther—wanted to see me and not to be afraid. I remembered hitting him and hearing my door lock. I remembered hearing James and my mother banging on my door and then I recalled the man coming closer. I grabbed my eyeliner, threw the top off, and wrote the name on the back of my door. After that, I remembered nothing.

I slowly climbed out of bed, only to have my feet hit a cold stone floor. I looked down to see what looked like cobblestone and something you might see in a castle. I looked around to see a giant rug and quickly put my feet on it. The room seemed like something out of a dream.

"My dad always did call me a princess. I never thought I would wake up in a room like one," I said aloud.

"Why not?" the deep voice asked, and I jumped. I looked around to see where the voice came from. "Don't you think that you deserve it?" he asked. I saw a boy of medium build that seemed to be the same age I was. He had brown hair that was pulled neatly back in a ponytail. It was the guy that gave me the message. He was sitting on the ledge of the window in the room. He slowly rose and started to come toward me. I quickly backed up. He noticed this and stopped. "I'm sorry. I haven't properly introduced myself. My name is Tim," he said as he bowed.

"Nice to meet you," I said. "You do know that James will be here, and I don't think he will be happy," I said, trying to put fear into him.

Tim looked at me and laughed. "He can come here any-time he wants. I'm sure his father would love to see him."

I looked at him awkwardly. "James sees his father every day," I shot back.

Tim giggled this time. "Kind of like you see your father every day?" he asked.

"Yes," I said as the anger started to build up inside me. *Who does this guy think he is? He doesn't know me or my father. For that matter, he doesn't know James or his father, either.*

Tim's smile started to widen. "You're starting to get angry. You're cute when you're angry," he said as he looked behind me. I looked behind me to see a dresser with a mirror on it. I saw that my hair was so black it looked like midnight blue and my eyes were starting to turn black. *I have to control myself,* I thought. I closed my eyes, took a deep breath and calmed down. I opened them and saw that I had returned to normal. "Ah, so he did teach you something," Tim said. "Control your anger. Very good." He complimented me with a slow hand clap.

"Look," I said sternly. "Why don't you just show me the way out of here and I'll go home and James will come back to deal with you later."

"Spunk, too. I like spunk," he said smoothly. "I'll make a deal with you. Have breakfast and meet my friend, and if you decide to go home then you are free to leave."

I didn't like the choice I was given. I wanted to go home now. I didn't want to be here. "Look…Tim, was it?" Tim nodded his head. "Tim, I just want to go home," I said casually as I smiled at him.

Tim smiled back. "Get dressed, then, and meet me downstairs. I will give you directions out of here," he said. "Breakfast is still on the table, of course," he reminded me as he shut the door.

I glanced around the room to see that one of my outfits was laid out on the bed. I quickly put on my shorts and blue top and slipped on my shoes. I pulled my hair back into a ponytail and slowly opened the door. I looked down the stone hallway that was covered in long beautiful rugs. The rugs looked to be a Persian type and were deep red with gold designs around the borders. I bent down to take a closer look at the design. It looked as if it were vines with thorns. *That's an odd design*, I thought. I looked up to see a marble staircase a few feet to my left. I quickly walked down the stairs, only to see no one was there.

I looked behind me to see a set of double doors. The doors seemed to be made of some type of bronze-colored metal, with etchings that looked like vines with leaves at the end of each that intertwined. The door handles were a dull silver that looked like scales and gave the illusion that the other half of the snake was on the other side. It sent chills down my spine just thinking of touching them.

I suddenly felt a cold chill run through my body. I quickly rubbed my arms as I felt my goose bumps. I looked around at the two other doors that were on either side of me. All doors looked to be in the gothic style and seemed go well with the decor. I saw the big door in front of me, all wooden with no latch. I saw the long thick piece of wood that lay horizontally across it and giggled to myself.

"You have to be kidding me. Every door here has a handle, but the front door. The big piece of wood locks this door? Who does this guy think he is? A king?" I said under my breath.

"A leader, yes, but not a king," Tim said from behind me.

I jumped at the sound of his voice. I turned around to see that the double doors with the snake handles were open and Tim stood there in between them. The aroma of breakfast filled the air and made it a bit warmer.

"Can I have the directions, please?" I asked, holding my hand out in front of me.

Tim smiled as he slowly put his hands together as if he was planning something. "My leader, as you put it so coyly, is saddened that you will not join us for breakfast."

"Sorry. Not a big breakfast eater," I said. "The directions—or I can just walk out of here now."

"Well…if you insist," Tim said as he handed me a piece of paper.

I opened it to see what looked like an old map of a kingdom. I looked back at him. "Is this some type of joke?" I asked.

"What do you mean?" he asked innocently.

"Where did you get this?" I asked as I waved the map in the air. "At the Smithsonian? Fine! I'll find a way out myself," I said as I headed toward the door.

I watched as my hand waved as if it was going to remove the long piece of wood. *Maybe my instincts are coming back*, I thought. I waved my hand to remove the long piece of wood and nothing happened. I did it again and still nothing happened. I closed my eyes, took a deep breath, concentrated at the task, and waved my hand again. Still nothing. I turned to see Tim trying to cover a smile.

"A little help," I said, looking at the door.

Tim straightened up. "Sure thing," he said. As he waved his hand, the piece of wood slid to the right, opening the doors in front of me.

I turned to look at him suspiciously. "How did you do that?" I asked.

"Do what?" he taunted me, and admired his hands as if what he had just done was normal and nothing out of the ordinary.

"You know what. Don't play dumb with me," I said. "The door." I pointed to it, not taking my eyes off him.

"Oh, that," he said. "What? Didn't think that I knew who you were, Serina?" he asked with a smirk. "Come on. I wouldn't bring you here if I didn't have good intentions."

"How did you know my name? Is Brad in there?" I demanded. I didn't know Brad, but I was pretty sure he would do something like kidnapping me from my family in the middle of the night.

"Everyone here knows of you. Brad is not in there. In fact, he is not here. He's in another town. Well, two towns away, I guess," Tim explained. "Look, give my friend and me ten minutes to talk with you and explain ourselves, and if you don't like us then you are free to leave. Or you can leave now. The choice is up to you. There is a big bowl of fruit here for you and the latte that you like."

My stomach started to growl at the sound of the fruit, and I wasn't sure if it was hunger or just my curiosity about who was in the room behind Tim. I shrugged my shoulders and gave in to my curiosity and hunger as I followed Tim into the room, watching him cautiously. I looked to see a large oval table in the middle of the room with a beautiful red tablecloth and a breakfast spread that would outdo any buffet. At the head of the table sat a young man who looked like he was in his early twenties. He had short brown hair and hazel eyes. He almost looked like James. He stood up as he saw me walk in. Tim ushered me toward him and a headache started.

"They'll go away eventually," the man said in a strong voice. Not a voice that sounded like it belonged to someone his age. It was the voice of a man that had lived a long and enduring life.

I looked at him. "What will go away?" I asked, trying to play it off to see if he knew what was wrong with me.

"The headaches," he said. He pushed out a chair for me and I sat down. "Would you like Tim to get you a Tylenol or something?"

"No, thank you," I said as the headache became duller.

"My name is Luther," he said as he extended his hand. "And you must be Serina," he said, as he took my hand and kissed it.

I slowly took my hand back and felt the chills that started to run down my spine. "Yes, my name is Serina."

"Well, it's nice to finally meet you. I have heard so much about you, but to finally meet you is a pleasure," he said as he sat down at the head of the table.

Tim handed me a bowl full of fruit. Cut strawberries, blueberries, raspberries, and any other type of fruit you could think of. I bowed my head, closed my eyes and said a little prayer. I looked up to see Luther smiling at me. "Strong in your faith, I see," Luther said. "That's good. Everyone should be that way."

I looked at him, trying not to seem disappointed. I wanted to see if this was the evil thing that James and my mother had warned me about. It didn't even faze him. "So how do you know James?" I asked as I stuffed a strawberry in my mouth.

"James is my son," he said casually as he smiled at me.

I quickly started to choke on the strawberry that was in my mouth. Luther began to get up and I put my hand up to stop him. I grabbed the water that was in front of me and took a long gulp. When I finally was able to compose myself, I looked at him. "Your son?" I managed to get out.

"I'm sure he has told you about me," he said. I looked at him blankly. The only person James had ever told me about as a father was Mr. Santiago. "Well, it doesn't surprise me. He has never liked me because of his mother." Luther stopped and looked up at the wall in front of him.

I looked over to see a huge painting of him and a woman with long brown hair and hazel eyes looking lovingly at a baby she was holding. "Is that…?" I started to ask.

"Yes, that was James when he was first born. Of course, I had to have myself put in there, because after she found out she was pregnant she wanted nothing to do with me," he said with a sigh.

"Why is that?" I asked. "Did she give you a reason?"

"She had her reasons," he said darkly. "But sadly, I lost the only family I knew. My son and my love." He sighed again.

"So, are you telling me that Mr. Santiago is not James's father?" I asked, taking another bite of fruit.

I watched Luther's eyes fill with hurt. "No, but he knows that as well. He knows that I'm his father, although he won't admit it. Do you know how bad that hurts?" he asked.

"I'm sorry," I said, not knowing what else to say. "Have you tried talking to him?"

"Yes, but he gives the same answer you gave when your father reached out to you," he answered.

I sat back in my chair. I noticed the door behind me. The evil side of James came from this man. This was not a good situation I was in. I had just found out who I was and now I was here, with no one to help me. Would I be able to make a run for the door and make it? Probably not. Nope, I would have to talk my way out of this. "So...I'm just taking an educated guess here, but you're the one that gave James his evil side," I said, hitting the problem head-on.

Luther looked at me and smiled. "Let's talk about evil," he said. "What would you call evil?"

The question surprised me. What would I call evil? That little thing I saw the day James and I were at the principal's office was evil. Killing was evil. So what was evil? "I guess people or things that do evil," I said, searching for an answer.

"So…you're not too sure," he said. "Would you say that someone who has stolen something is evil?"

"Look," I said, trying to avoid the conversation altogether, "James is probably looking for me and I need to meet him."

"James," he said, "is here. I know he's here. He just went to the wrong town. In fact, I know that he is headed this way, so if you would like, you can wait for him. He should be here in a day or so. Let's get back to defining evil," he said with a grin.

XXV

Sluos

J ames looked at the desolate place that surrounded him. He saw the long dirt road ahead of him as Midnight let out a low sigh. "I know," James said, patting the horse on the side of the neck. "Never thought we would come back here." Starr looked down and gave a sad look as they walked toward the nearest town.

Not much had changed. The trees were black as if a fire had consumed them. No leaves, no grass, even the sky looked dim and dreary, with a hint of red in it. Nope, it looked like a total wasteland. He watched as a group of nuisances passed by him and snarled, baring their rigged yellow teeth. He gave them no satisfaction by acknowledging them. He soon noticed the long cobblestone wall that surrounded the town and saw the small, insignificant sign that read *Sluos*. Midnight stopped at the big iron gate and James dismounted. James's eyes met another set of eyes as they stared back at him.

"Your business here?" the man asked through the black iron gate.

James laughed inside, thinking that with one swipe of his sword this gate would come down like a stack of cards.

He also knew to try not to draw attention to himself, so he decided to just answer the man. "Stay the night," James said. "Let me in."

The young man looked to be in his late twenties with blond hair that was streaked with dirt. His face was old and a scar ran down from his left eye to his chin. "We don't let in anyone we don't like, and I don't like you," he said, starting to walk away.

James smiled. "Then I guess you don't know who I am," he said with a snarl. It had been a long day, and James had no patience for the young man's games.

The boy turned around. "And what importance do you think you have?" the boy asked with a smirk.

James thought for a moment. He could use the evil that ached through his bones to get out, but it was more dangerous in this place than it was on Earth. He could lose the control that he had fought for so many years to attain in a matter of seconds. It wasn't worth the risk. Of course, mentioning one name could get him through that gate.

"What's your name?" James asked.

"None of your business," the boy answered with a snarl. The boy lunged at the gate to try and intimidate James, and saw to his dismay that James didn't even flinch. This seemed to make the boy even more angry and spiteful. He smiled and said, "You know, if you don't get in here…you could die out there. So many things out there ready to eat the flesh off your bones while you're still alive. We'll hear your screams all night long, but that won't stop them. They like to hear you scream."

James was getting tired of this game as he listened to the boy go on about the creatures that could be found out in the woods behind him. James tried not to laugh at the boy, knowing all the while that the screams the townspeople heard at night were not from someone being tortured—they were of someone new just getting here and scared. The boy was right on one account, though. The things here did enjoy the screams and the frightened souls that came to this place. James was growing more tired of the boy and his tales. "Tell me your name!" he shouted.

"James!" a girl shrieked ahead of him. James saw a young girl with straight brown hair and gray eyes running up behind the young man. "Anthony, you better let him in," she warned. Then she leaned close and whispered something in his ear as a smile grew across her face.

The young man's eyes grew wide. He quickly opened the gate and stared at the ground. "I'm sorry. I didn't know who were," he said as James passed by him with a confused look on his face.

"It's all right," James said as the young girl hugged him. James looked down at the girl, trying to remember exactly who she was. She certainly seemed to know him.

"Don't remember me?" she asked, looking up at him.

James thought for a moment as she pointed down at a pocket on her dress, which was torn at the bottom. James saw the top of the little leather-bound book. "Emily?" he asked.

She smiled. "It's me!" she exclaimed. "I didn't think I would ever see you again," she said as she jumped up and down.

James smiled as her memory became clearer. "Didn't think I would ever be back," he said as he started walking. "How have you been?" he asked.

"Getting smarter every day, thanks to you," she said. "You do know that I have to read this thing in places that no one would dare go."

James smiled. "I'm glad you're reading it."

"So…what are you doing here?" she asked. "You've come here to get her," she blurted out with excitement.

James stopped. "Get who?" he asked, trying to see if word had spread that fast.

"The key," she said. "I don't know her name, but we've all been told that it will be a couple of days before Luther takes her to the gate and she can open it," Emily said with a smile. "That means I can go back and live life the way I was supposed to."

No. Serina couldn't possibly be able to open a gate. She wasn't a key. Was she? If she was, that meant he had to get to her soon. He couldn't waste spending a night here to get her out of there. "Who told you that?" James asked.

"Tim," Emily said innocently. "You know, he is like the person under—"

"Tim?" James asked. "Tim is—"

Emily laughed. "If you would let me finish. Tim is the person under Luther. He's kind of like his errand boy. He has the position—"

"OK," James said, cutting Emily's short. He had to find out exactly what was happening. This could not be true. "How does Tim know about this key, or why does he think that she is the key?"

Emily shrugged. "Don't know. You know, I've looked through this book for that answer and found nothing," she said. "Although I don't exactly understand the last book in here," she said. "Maybe you can help me find the answer?"

James sighed. "If it's not in there, then it's not true." But why tell these people that. Why get their hopes up of escaping this place?

Emily's smile faded. "I know, but I was hoping that's why you were here."

James looked ahead to see the tavern that he was going to stay in. It had been a long night and day riding to get here. The horses were tired and so was he. He wasn't going to be any good to anyone if he didn't get some rest. He also knew that it was a full day's ride to the next town. He started to pick up his pace to reach the tavern.

"Is this where you'll be spending the night?" she asked.

"I'm only spending the night," he told her as an older man approached.

"Can I take your horses?" the man asked.

Midnight eyed him cautiously. Starr started to back away slowly. James took notice and grabbed both their reins. "Where are the stables?" he asked. The man pointed in front of him at a set of stables that sat right next to the tavern. "Can I take them myself?" James asked. The man shrugged and went off to fetch some water as James walked the horses to the stables.

"Is this her horse?" Emily asked as she stroked Starr.

"Yep," James said. He put the reins down and the two horses started to nibble on the hay bale that was placed inside the stalls of the stable.

"She's pretty. I like her horse," she said as she admired Starr. Starr seemed to take no notice as she slowly chewed on the hay. It was as if Starr was like James, not wanting to give in just yet. To just get Serina and get out of here.

James smiled as he saw the man return with the water and put it in the trough for them to drink. "The owner is waiting for you inside," he said to James. James nodded and turned to Emily.

"I can make you something to eat. I'll be back, and maybe you can help me understand a little more about the book!" she shrieked with excitement.

"Sure," James said as he watched her dart out the stables. James walked toward the tavern and watched as people slowly went about their day here. The nuisances were chained to them. They were never allowed to go without them. Emily was different. She had her chains broken once she started to understand. James wondered how long it would take before they actually got to her. The book was not allowed here, although everyone had free will. Nothing here was supposed to help them get to where they should go. Nope, this was a choice they had to make, and in this place it was a hard choice. James opened the big wooden door and chuckled to himself. This place never changed. It was like he was living back in history. Dirt roads, old wooden doors, and no electricity.

"James!" the tavern owner shouted from behind the counter.

"Hello, Leonard," James said as he hugged him. Leonard hadn't changed since the first time he met him. The big burly man with dark red hair and a full beard to match looked like he should have been there when Daniel was in the lion's den.

"How have you been?" Leonard asked, as he looked at James and smiled.

"Good," James replied. "I'm going to need a room for the night."

"I knew you wouldn't be too far behind knowing that your love was here. How come you didn't just go there?" he asked.

"I know he knows I'm here. Just buying some time," James replied as Leonard handed him a set of keys.

"Time isn't on your side, my boy," Leonard replied. "He already has Tim setting things in motion."

"So I've heard," James replied. "She isn't a key, though."

Leonard shrugged. "She must be able to do something. Otherwise he wouldn't have taken her."

James smiled. "She can do a lot when she remembers."

Leonard shook his head. "It was a shame what her mother did all those years ago. How long has it been?"

"Twenty long years, and as soon as I get her back she's gone again," James said with a sigh.

"Well, get some rest. You have a long road ahead of you," Leonard said as he watched James climb the wooden steps.

"Thank you," James said.

He reached the top of the stairs and looked to his left. He looked down at the key. Room seven. The room at the end of the hall. He slowly pushed the key in and opened the door. He walked into the darkened room, snapped his fingers, and the candles came to life to give the room light. He shut the doors behind him and took his boots off, then plopped himself on the bed and let the blanket engulf him. He was almost asleep when he heard a soft knock at the door.

"Room service," a small, timid voice sang lightly from the other side.

James lay there with his eyes closed and smiled. "Hold on." He slowly opened his eyes, lifted himself up, walked over to the door and opened it.

Emily stood there with a smile on her face and a basket hanging off her arm. "Told you I would make you something good to eat," she said with a smile. "Can I come in?"

James opened the door wider and welcomed her in. "After you," he said.

Emily sat on the ground and started to lay out a tattered blanket as she set up the meal. She had bread, meat, and some water. "We can have a picnic," she said innocently.

James sat down. "Thank you."

———※———

I watched as the scene in front of me started to fade away. I could feel the hurt, betrayal, and anger start to grow inside me. It was like a cancer that was crawling through every inch of my body. "Who is she?" I asked, trying to control my emotions.

"Her name is Emily," Luther said as he put his hand on my shoulder. "Looks like more than a friend to me," he said with a sympathetic face.

"How does she know him?" I asked, still trying to control myself as the tears started behind my eyes.

Luther looked at me. "You know he gave her something he shouldn't have," he continued. "Something she holds near and dear to her heart."

I turned to face him. "Like what?" I asked.

"A book. A book about love," he said, smiling.

I felt my legs give out from underneath me and my hands felt the soft rug. The tears started to stream down my face and a mixed emotion ran through my head. He wouldn't. He said he loved me. He said he waited for me and looked for me. He said that he would be there for me. Was it all a lie? Was he no better than Steven? "I want to go home," I said in a whisper.

"My friend," Luther said, taking my hand and helping me up. He wiped my tears away. "You can run from this, or I can help you get him back."

"I don't want him back if this is what he is," I said. "I deserve better than this." I wasn't sure who I was trying to convince, myself or him. Either way, it wasn't working. My heart was breaking in two, and by the look on Luther's face, he wasn't being fooled my act.

Luther looked at me and hugged me to him. "Then I can help you hurt him the way he has hurt you. Or do you think that is evil?"

I looked up at him. "You mean revenge?" I asked. I stepped away from him. Revenge was something that was wrong. Would that make me evil? I thought for a moment. "I'm not sure," I slowly replied, thinking about this new revelation.

"It's only one person. Then after that you can be good again," Luther encouraged. "I'm sure one time wouldn't hurt."

I thought about it. "I guess one time wouldn't hurt," I said. He hurt me deeply, and frankly I was tired of being hurt. Steven treated me like a trophy and James…well, he had secrets. "You're right. One time wouldn't hurt. Then I could go back home and be good again."

Luther clapped his hands. "Good. Let me teach you other things you can do," he said with a smile.

A thought occurred to me. "Can I ask you something before we get started?"

Luther smiled. "Anything. I will answer any question you have."

I hesitated. "Where am I?"

Luther stepped back for a moment and searched for an answer. "You're in a place where you're free to make any choice you want. No one is here to judge you or hold you back from doing something you want to do." He smiled.

I shook my head. "OK," I said. "One more," I urged.

Luther waved his hand. "Anything."

"James can usually know what I'm thinking or feeling. How is it that here he doesn't? I mean, he doesn't even know how much he has hurt me," I said.

Luther grinned. "Is it that he doesn't know or he refuses to come straight here?"

"You mean he could have just shown up here?" I asked, shocked.

Luther nodded his head. "Yep, and he chose to go to the town of Sluos first. Maybe to visit Emily."

The vision appeared again. I watched as she handed him another glass of water and laughed. James smiled at her as he took a sip and started to help her clean up the picnic in his room. My anger boiled over.

Luther watched as my hair turned black and my eyes followed, and smiled. "Are we ready for our first lesson?"

"Definitely," I said without hesitation, as the vision disappeared again.

—⁓—

James looked at Emily and helped her clean up the mess. "So, if I have questions about the book…would you help me understand?" Emily asked, looking up at James.

"Sure," he said. "Ask and I will do my best," he answered her.

"This book has a lot of stories, but I don't understand what it all means," she said.

James sat down and took his small book out of his pouch as Emily sat down next to him. James opened it and turned to one of the books within it. "Read this whole chapter," he said, pointing.

Emily sat there like a child as she read with an eagerness to learn more. When she was finished she looked at James. "It's about love," she said.

"That's because he loves us unconditionally, in everything that happens and everything that goes on. It's his love that keeps us safe and secure." James smiled.

"Does he still love me after what I've done?" she asked.

James smiled and flipped through the book again. "Read this."

Emily read. This time her face was cautious. James knew that she wanted to know the answer and at the same time didn't. He watched as her face showed signs of confusion. "Into the sea? Even after what I've done he has compassion for my mistakes?" she asked with wide eyes. "All I have to do is ask?"

James smiled and nodded. "All you have to do is ask."

"Will you help me?" she asked in a childlike way.

"I can only listen. You have to do the rest," he explained. He watched as she bowed her head and closed her eyes. James did the same, and listened as she asked for forgiveness and expressed how sorry she was. He listened as she asked for him to come into her heart and make her new. James peeked at her and smiled.

"Did I do well?" she asked.

"Perfect," he said. "You better get home. I need to get some rest."

"Thank you," she said, hugging him.

"For what?" he asked. "You did everything."

"For teaching me what I needed to do. Have a good night," she said as she closed the door.

James looked at the room and once again went to the bed and lay down. He blew out the candle and lay in the dark. He knew that tonight was a good night. She would be going home soon. Tomorrow he would make his trip toward the next town and give himself more time to think. He knew that he couldn't act too quickly. Luther knew he was there, and James, after all, had not been back in a long time. Things that once were easy to him had become hard—not to mention that he was a little nervous. James closed his eyes and concentrated on Serina. Her beautiful eyes and smile. How he longed for her to be here with him. How he wished that this would have never happened. Sorrow started to turn to anger at the thought of how he had lost her for all those years, only to have her back with him for a few short days before she was gone again. He rolled over and looked at his sword that glimmered in the corner. James sighed as he closed his eyes. Sleep finally found him as he lay peacefully in his bed.

XXVI

Christina

I let my head hit the pillow and it felt so soft and inviting. The rigorous workout that Luther had put me through to-day seemed as if it would never end. At first I got tired and he helped me fight through it. The things I could do now were incredible—from changing forms to being able to make things and people do what I want. It was something I would never forget.

Besides, it wasn't my fault that James had lied to me, and I was very angry over it. It was all in how people dealt with it. I was going to deal with it in my own way. I heard a small tinkling of laughter in my head. I opened my eyes to see the dark room around me. I snapped my fingers; the candles quickly came to life and lit up the room. I looked around to see noth-ing. I waved my hand and the lights went out as I lay my head down again. I stared into the darkness for a while and drifted off to sleep.

The tinkling of laughter returned and I tried to figure out where it had come from. In my dream I sat up in bed and looked around. Someone was here; the candles burned softly, but the light only touched some corners of the room. I slowly climbed out of bed. I looked around the room to see that there was nothing and nobody there. The laugh came again and it sounded as if it were behind me. I slowly turned around to see a beautiful woman with long brown hair and hazel eyes standing there giggling. Her skin seemed to give off an iridescent glow that made her hazel eyes look like pools of water. I could feel the peace that surrounded me and embraced it.

"Well, I finally get to meet you after all these years. My, have you grown," the woman said as she pushed my dark hair behind my ear. I could feel the warmth and love that radiated off her.

"Who are you?" I asked.

The woman giggled again. "My name is Christina," she said in her melodic voice. "You know my son, James."

"James!" I exclaimed. "James is your son?"

Christina smiled proudly. "Yep," she said, still playing with my hair. "I remember when the two of you were little, and seeing you guys play. It was just relaxing."

"I...I don't remember," I admitted shyly.

"Don't worry. You will. James will help you remember," she said, as she stepped back to look at what she had done.

I looked in the mirror to see that she had braided my hair. It was beautiful the way she had done it, with a small flower on the side. "James...well, I think he's more into someone else at the moment."

Christina looked at me with amusement. "Is that what Luther showed you today?" she asked. "You know, it's funny how he can show you what is going on, but you can't hear anything. So it's kind of like watching a movie with no sound. You can make your own assumptions on what is being said between two people." She giggled as she sat on the edge of the bed. I followed her over and sat next to her.

"How do you know Luther?" I asked.

"Well," I would like to think that I know the father of my son," she answered.

"Luther is—"

"James's father, yes. I know, I know, not a good mixture, but while I was on Earth I lost some of my senses," she said, still smiling.

"What do you mean?" I asked. "Lost your senses?"

"Well, if you haven't figured it out yet, Luther is not really someone we should be asking for advice or taking it from. Good and evil...well, they really don't mix well. I was just lucky that Luther—not saying he didn't try—for the most part stayed away from us," she explained. "I was able to teach James right from wrong and it's stuck with him. He has had his trials, and on some occasions he went in the wrong directions, but quickly gathered himself up and got back on the right path."

"So lying to someone must mean that he's on the wrong path again," I said cynically.

"He's not perfect, my dear, but know that as long as he's known you he has never lied to you. He tells you everything that is true." Christina smiled.

"So, the girl he was talking to today was an old friend of his. He could be here right now and chose to go to her first. Right?" I asked with sharpness in my tone.

"Again, I say you watched a movie with no sound. Besides, he has his reasons for why he is not here right now. But, not being in love with you is not one of them," she answered.

I looked at her with confusion. "In love with me?" I repeated.

Christina took my hand and held it tight. "Yes, in love with you. Ever since your mother was allowed to come back and get you and then caught up with us, he has watched over you. It was a long time ago, but we had gone to an island where it was warm and sunny, and your mother knew your father probably would not follow us there. The two of you were starting to grow up. Your mother and I watched as the two of you became closer. Your mom didn't like that James was showing you some of the powers he had discovered and teaching you, but I watched over your mother and told her that things were going to change. We eventually just let the two of you figure things out."

I listened like a child hearing a bedtime story, but she was telling me the story of my life and how I grew up. I wanted to know every little detail that I could. I wanted to know about my past and how things were before...

"Before your mother erased your memory. If you listen I will tell you." Christina laughed. "And yes, that power he learned from me."

"The one where you can listen to other people's thoughts?" I smiled.

"Yes, let me continue," she said. "The two of us fell in love, once again, and we moved to where you live now. James couldn't be very far from you knowing that he wanted to protect you. So we moved next door to you and your mother. The two of you were getting ready to graduate and the night before your ceremony he proposed to you. You said yes and your mother gritted her teeth. The two of you moved quickly and, knowing that you were going away for college, you guys decided to get married the month before you moved. There was a lot of excitement in the air and James made the wedding bands. The morning of your wedding your mother could not bear it anymore. Things were getting to her and she knew the trouble that brewed around the two of you. Evil danced around awaiting the new challenges that it was going to face with the team that was about to be formed. She worried, like any other mother, that you weren't ready for it, and she didn't want you to face it. She also knew that she still had not explained anything to you and that Taurus was to show up that night. So she did the only thing she could think of, and that was taking you back to an age she could watch over you."

"Why didn't she teach me or tell me anything?" I asked in amazement.

Christina lovingly took my hand in hers. "What mother would not shield her child if she could? We would all probably encase our children in bubbles to make sure no harm would come to them. We very rarely think of the consequences that follow. But, your mother learned the hard way. James left that day, but not without leaving you something. He left it behind knowing that your mother could not take it, could not destroy it, and could not keep it from you," she said as she released my hand.

I felt something in my hand. I slowly opened it and saw a ring. The small ring was platinum on the outside rim with a gold band in the middle. On it were words raised up against the ring itself. I studied the words to find that I didn't understand them. "What does it say?" I asked.

Christina looked at me and read it to me. I heard her speak each word, but it was an ancient language I did not understand. "Need a translation?" she asked. I nodded my head. "Here's my heart. Guard it well."

Tears immediately started to form in my eyes. The words hit my heart in such a way that it took my breath away. He truly loved me. "He made this?" I asked.

Christina smiled. "Well…James is pretty advanced in the things he knows, but yeah, he made it. He wanted you to know that no matter how far apart you guys were, you always had his heart and he always had yours. He would guard yours and he hoped that you would guard his."

I placed the ring on my finger and looked at it. It was beautiful in the light. Christina smiled as she removed it. "You're not married yet, but you can wear it like he wears his," she said, as she put it on a thin chain and placed it around my neck. "There now, guard this well. It's what will keep the two of you in touch."

The foul stench of death filled the room. My eyes wandered around as Christina hugged me. "I have to go, but know that I am not far and neither is he. He will be here for you soon," she said as she disappeared.

"Wait…don't go. I have so many questions. Don't leave me," I said as darkness started to surround me.

"It's OK," I heard a man's voice say. I opened my eyes to see Luther over me and stroking my hair. I looked around to see if Christina was still there and saw nothing.

"I'm all right. I just had a dream," I said, slowly lifting my body and sitting up in bed.

"I know," Luther said. "We have a lot to do today. Let's try out some of these new powers."

I hesitated. "I'd like to see James's first," I said.

"That's who we're going to see," he said as he opened the door to my room. "Oh yeah, by the way, next time Christina comes to visit, you tell her I said hi." He smiled and closed the door behind him, leaving me in the room alone.

I quickly touched my neck for the chain and felt that it was still there. I picked it up to see the ring still attached as it dangled in front of me. I sighed and relaxed a little. *James will clear all this up*, I thought, as I sighed again and looked out the window. I looked around the room to see some light in the dismal-looking sky; I sighed once more as the thought of James entered my head again. I wondered where he was and how long it would take for him to reach me. A ping of jealousy hit me again as the picture of him and the girl sitting in the room reading a book appeared in my head. I quickly shook my head to release the image, but it just came back to me. I could feel my anger starting to get the best of me and fought it, but the thought kept my anger strong. I finally gave in and got out of bed to get ready; Luther said that we were to see James today, and today I was going to get my answers and confront him about it. I looked at myself in the mirror and didn't even recognize my own reflection. I smiled. Good, I thought, now I was ready to confront him. Let's see how he would explain himself and what lies he could conjure up—just like Steven.

XXVII

Emily

James awoke the next morning refreshed and ready to head out. He put his boots back on, grabbed his sword and closed the door. He slowly walked down the stairs to see Leonard at the door of the tavern. James walked up behind him as quietly as he could and struck the man on the back. "Good morning," he said, laughing. Leonard turned around frightened half to death. James could tell that it was not just the way he greeted him. Something else was bothering the man. "What's wrong?"

"She tried to make it here, but didn't," Leonard answered. "If she could have, she would have been safe."

James looked at him, confused. "Who?"

"Emily," Leonard answered. "They saw that she had the book and came to get her. She ran here knowing that she would be safe, but didn't even make it to the door before Tim caught her," he said, hanging his head. "I tried to reach her, but those pesky nuisances, they were everywhere and—"

"I'll help her," James said, cutting him off. He followed the crowd through the city. James watched as the crowd seemed to know exactly where to go. He tried not to look like an outsider. He watched as the crowd gathered around a town square with a wooden platform in the middle of it. James began to step closer when he felt a hand on his shoulder. He quickly turned around to see a friend.

"Not too close," he warned James.

"Luke. What are you doing here?" James asked in amazement. Luke never came here unless...unless someone might be able to go home. That meant the person was about to be put on trial and tortured. Most people didn't make it through the torture; they gave in to the idea of just giving up. James's heart sank. This meant maybe Emily would be strong enough to withstand it.

"Hopefully leaving with someone," Luke answered him.

"Emily?" he asked.

Luke nodded his head. "Yep. She asked and she was received, but she is still doubtful. She still leaning on her own understanding. I have to wait for the word. The only thing we can do is watch."

"I got her into this mess," James said with his head down.

"Is that what we're calling this now, a mess? As far as I knew we fought for good." Luke smiled.

"You know what I mean," James answered him. "I don't want to see her suffer."

"You know I won't let it go on." Luke tried to soothe the situation. "She still has a lot of doubt, and she still has not forgiven herself."

James looked at him. "We are harder on ourselves than he is on us."

"This is true, but you have to learn that once he has forgiven you, all is forgiven. That's why he died for you." Luke looked up at the platform.

James saw that Tim was standing there. "Who is that?" he asked.

Luke smiled. "That is Tim, Luther's new errand boy. He tells everyone that Tim's the closest person he has to a son."

"Is that supposed to hurt?" James asked cynically.

Luke shrugged. "Does it?"

"Not at all," James replied quickly.

"We are gathered here today to lay down the law! We don't ask much from you, but what we do ask we expect you to follow," Tim said loudly as a hush fell over the crowd. "The one thing we ask is that this book stays out!" he said, as he held up the little leather-bound book over his head. The same book that James had read with her last night. "This book was brought in here and hidden from us. We discovered it with the owner and she ran. Why did she run? Because she knew that it wasn't supposed to be here!" Tim shouted again.

"Let me go!" Emily shrieked as two big men brought her out and shoved her onto the wooden platform. James watched with a heavy heart. The people in the crowd stared at the platform. Some shook their heads in dismay while others stood there waiting for the show.

Emily lay on the floor of the platform and looked out at the crowd. Tim pulled on her hair as her face showed pain. "Who gave this book to you?" he asked.

"A friend," she answered.

Tim let go of her hair and softly touched her head. "If you give me the name of this friend, we'll get him instead of you," he bargained. "After all, this friend deserves this punishment more than you do. This friend should stand trial, not you. You're innocent in all this."

Emily smiled. "The blood that runs through his veins is the same blood that you wish ran through yours!" she shot back.

This enraged Tim and he shoved her face into the platform. Emily covered her face and winced in pain as blood flowed from her nose. She tried wiping it away, but more just seemed to keep coming. "I want the name of this person, NOW! Or you, my dear, will be the one that pays for this crime," Tim said with a smile.

James looked over at Luke. Luke watched the whole thing not budging. He looked calm and collected. "You can stop this at any time," James said to him.

Luke did not look at him as he answered. "Still waiting."

"I've committed no crime!" Emily shouted. "What's in there that you guys don't want us to read? What is in there that you guys are so afraid of? Maybe it's the truth!" she screamed. "Maybe it's because you know that what's in this book will set me free and could set everyone here free!" Emily said as she looked out into the crowd. Her eyes met James's for a split second and he saw a small smile flit across her face.

Tim took his sword out, raised it above his head, dug it deep into one of her legs and twisted it. Emily screamed in pain. "The truth, my dear, is that you brought yourself here. YOU made this decision. It's YOUR fault that this is happening!" he said, and he quickly removed the sword as blood gushed from the wound.

Emily slowly moved her hand toward her leg to try and stop the bleeding. James could see in her eyes she had no strength left. In an instant a man stood behind her with a chain in his hand. He bent down close to her. "My dear, I hate to see you suffer like this. My boss is impressed with the way you have handled this situation, but what are you trying to prove?" he asked calmly.

Emily looked at him with tears in her eyes. She smiled a little. "I…I've been forgiven and you don't own me," she said.

Luke looked pleased at this answer. Then his eyes looked at what was at the end of the chain. "Looks like Luther has a new pet," Luke said to James.

James looked to see a black panther that paced back and forth behind Emily, looking for a chance to strike at the poor girl. "When did he get that?" James asked.

"Not sure. But it doesn't look good," Luke frowned.

James studied the big cat as it looked out into the crowd. James noticed that it was staring at him. The eyes. They looked familiar. That's when James heard bones breaking and the cat snarling. Emily screamed in pain again.

"Listen!" she shouted to the crowd. "It's easy! Just ask and know that he will never leave you. He forgives you all. All you have to do is ask!"

James watched in horror as Luther dropped the chain and the cat leapt for its victim. James turned one more time to try and persuade Luke to do something, only to find that he wasn't there. James searched frantically in the crowd to see if he could find him. It was Luke's voice that boomed from the front where James saw him standing. "That's enough!" Luke said as he made his way toward the platform. He waved his hand and the big cat fell on its side, but quickly got to its feet again. It looked up at Luke with its ears down and bared its teeth with a low growl.

Luke reached down and picked Emily up. "Are you ready to go home?" he asked as Tim went toward him. Luke reached to his side, pulled his sword out and pointed it at Tim. "Ashes to ashes and dust to dust. I don't want to have to do that. Or do I?" he asked with a threatening smile. Tim stepped back, his eyes wide with fear.

"I want to go home," Emily whispered.

Luke looked down at the broken body of the girl and smiled. "Let's go," he said, and with a flash of bright light they were gone.

James stood there with a smile, knowing that she was safe, and then he made his way to the back of the crowd. He listened to some of the people as he passed by them. Most of them wondered where she had gone and who the man was that took her away. Some of them wondered where she had gotten the book and why she would not have turned her friend in. James passed two women discussing the events that had just happened.

"I know I would have turned my friend in as soon as he had me on that platform," the younger one said.

"I know!" the older one answered. "She sure was brave. I'm not sure how much I could have taken when he shoved his sword through my leg." Her face twisted with pain at the thought.

"You know," the younger one said as she looked down at the ground, "these things aren't half bad once you get used to them." She pulled on the chain with her nuisance staring up at her.

The older one laughed. "You don't have to feed them, water them, or clean up after them. It's not that bad."

James kept walking until he reached the tavern. Leonard greeted him. "How is she?" he asked.

James smiled. "She went home today. She went through a lot at the end, but she is now safe and sound at home. No more pain and no more hiding. She's free."

Leonard followed James toward the stables. "How much pain did she go through?" he asked sadly.

"Luke stepped in and rescued her. She was in pain, but know that she is now in a better place." James tried to make his friend feel better. He walked the horses out to the road and mounted Midnight.

"Be careful, my friend, and bring her back," Leonard said.

James said good-bye and started out of the town.

—⚊—

We returned to the castle in which I was staying. The door slammed behind us as I looked around the room. Tim was confused as he sat down his head in his hands, but Luther looked very calm and collected. It was as if the events that just happened didn't seem to bother him. How could that be? She wasn't supposed to be able to leave! Why was she so special? What was different about her that she got a free pass? I could feel the anger building up inside me just waiting for me to release it. "Who was that?" I demanded as I paced the floor, searching for answers.

Tim looked at me cautiously. "I...I don't know," he said, still in shock from the events that had just happened.

"His name is Luke, and there was no way to stop him from taking her," Luther said calmly as he sat down.

"So you're just going to sit there?" I asked in anger. "You promised me revenge, and I got nothing!" I shouted as I stomped my way toward him.

Luther shook his head. "I promised revenge on James, not on the girl that was with him," he corrected me. "Remember, once wouldn't hurt. She would have just been a bonus."

Luther smiled at me. "Serina, remember that all in due time will things happen. So…we lost one. You don't have to answer for that. I might, but you, my dear, won't. She was someone who was and still is insignificant." Luther got up and walked toward me. He put his hands up to my face and he pushed my hair to the side. "We have you. We don't need them. You are strong and can take them down. No one promised that you would win every battle, but you will help us defeat the people who have wronged others."

I could feel the anger start to subside inside me. I felt weak and sat down. "I don't understand. What is so special about her? Why was he with her, and how does she get a free pass?" I asked.

Luther smiled. "Because not all are as strong as you. As strong as I can help you become. Some need a free pass, but not you! You can fight, you can win, you don't need someone to help you when you're in trouble. You can do it all on your own."

Tim smiled as he approached me. "Yes, Serina…think about it. Do you really need James?" he asked. "Or does James really need you?"

I sat back and thought about it. What had James taught me thus far? He taught me to disappear and reappear. That was about it. Tim was right! I didn't need him. All I needed was to learn more, to become stronger. It was Luther and Tim who were teaching me to all these new quick ways to fight. It was they who taught me how to change forms and how to make people know and feel some of the things I wanted them to. I was in charge. James couldn't do that, and if he could he wasn't teaching it to me, and why not? Maybe because he was afraid of how much more powerful I was than him. That was the explanation. It was because he didn't want me to be better than him. He wanted to hold me back from my full potential.

"Did you see the way he looked at you today?" Tim asked as he saw me smile at him. "He didn't even recognize you! Did you see that while all that was happening to that girl, he just stood there? He did nothing to help and didn't come forward. He was going to let her take the blame. He just stood there as we did justice to the wrong person. He's a coward and a liar! What a man!" Tim snickered. "What if that was you? Do you think he would have helped you, or even make an attempt to stand up for you? Besides, like Luther said before, she wasn't your target—he is."

I looked at him with hate in my eyes. He was right. She wasn't my target. It wasn't her fault, it was his. He even stood there like a coward watching her go through all that. Was he not man enough to save her? This just taught me that if the same thing happened to me, then he might just stand back and watch as well. He was no better than Steven!

"You know what? You're right! She wasn't my target and he stood there and watched. He's afraid of me and he just wants to keep me from doing better than him."

"A typical man." Tim laughed. "Do you see the difference between Luther and myself and him? We want to see you succeed. We want you to be better and teach you all you need to know."

"Are you ready for another lesson?" Luther asked. I looked at him and smiled. "Good," he said. "I still have a lot more to teach you if you are ready to put this nasty loss to the side." Luther paused for a moment and smiled. "I wouldn't even consider this a loss. I would say this was more of a learning experience. What's that old saying…we learn from our mistakes. Let's take this mistake and not make it again."

I nodded my head in agreement. "No more mistakes. I will not allow it! I will not stand for it! It won't happen again."

Luther smiled at me as we started down a hallway. "You're right. It won't happen again. You know why?" I shook my head, eagerly awaiting his answer. "Because next time you'll beat him at his own game. Next time you will be more prepared and ready for anything he has to throw at you." I smiled as Luther shut the door behind us and waited for his next lesson.

XXVIII

Nomed

James had ridden half the day and knew that he had made good time, but the horses needed a rest. He stopped at a stream to see if they would drink. He stepped near the river to see that the water was black. Midnight looked at him with sad eyes.

"I know, boy," he said gently to the horse. He looked around to see if there was anything he could use as a bowl for them and decided that he would have to just make one.

He found large stone sitting near the water's edge and walked toward it. It just needed an opening to pour the water in. He put his hands on the stone and closed his eyes. *Please, I need the horses to drink*, he thought. He opened his eyes to see a hole large enough for him to put water in. He poured his canteen out, the horses noticed and walked eagerly over to it, and James watched as the two horses began to drink. He took his other canteen out and drank from it. The next town shouldn't be that far from here, from what he remembered about it. Just a few more miles and he should be there.

He felt in his pouch and his finger found around something. James took it out and looked at it. The wedding band he had made for them. He looked at the words written in an ancient language. "Here's my heart, guard it well," he said in a whisper. He felt a nudge at his arm.

Starr looked almost too sick to carry on. James rubbed her head. "I know. She's listening to him." He noticed that her coat was no longer the bright white; it had turned a dull gray, as if she had played in ashes and needed a bath. The star shape on her head had started to turn black, and with each move she made he could tell that it hurt her. "We'll get her back," he promised. He put the ring with the chain around his neck and under his armor.

He quickly mounted Midnight and they started on the long dirt trail. He decided that it might be best if they trotted rather than ran. Starr looked as if she were going to collapse at any moment.

They rounded a bend and James watched as some ogres passed by him. They were a grotesque sight; James noticed their warty green skin with patches of hair growing on the warts and their long tusklike teeth that shoved out of their bottom lip. Not to mention the piglike snout that oozed a clear liquid out of it that ran down their faces and over their lips. James shuddered as he passed by them but they seemed to take no notice of him.

James saw a small sign that read *Nomed* on it. The town was made up of all things that many people feared, and it fed off those people's fear; that's how the town thrived. Midnight seemed to sense something up ahead and jerked his head up and down. James patted him on the side of his head. "It's OK," he tried to reassure him. James looked up to see a man leaning on a tree as if he were waiting for him. James tried to focus in on him. Starr reared up and James grabbed for her reins while he was still on Midnight. He waved his hand through the air trying to grab them when he noticed that someone already had.

"I haven't seen her in a while. I do remember her being white, though. What happened to her?" the man asked. The same man that had been leaning on the tree.

James jumped down from Midnight and looked around to see Brad stroking Starr on the side of her head. "Give me those!" James said, snatching her reins from him.

"A little uneasy, are we?" Brad asked with a smile. "Haven't seen you in a while, either. How are you?"

"What are you doing here?" James asked. He decided to walk both the horses into town. "Don't you have to find some poor defenseless rat to torture?"

Brad half laughed at the statement. "Aren't you supposed to be protecting my daughter?" he shot back.

James released the horses in an instant and drew his sword. He held it up to Brad's throat. "Dare you to say it again," he said through his gritted teeth. "Besides, if it wasn't for you, they wouldn't be able to find her!"

"Well, I see the two of you have finally crossed paths again," Taurus said as he looked down on them from Starr. "Starr is sick and needs to rest. Let's get her to the stable and you guys to the inn. We can talk there. By the way, James, you need to put your sword away and not kill him. It's not in your best interest right now," he instructed as Starr slowly walked toward the town entrance.

James huffed as he put his sword away and grabbed Midnight's reins. Brad slowly followed behind them. James could not stand his presence. The awful smell of death followed Brad wherever he walked. James walked Midnight to the stable and put him beside Starr. Starr was up near the trough and gently lowered her head. It was breaking James's heart to see her that way.

"She'll be OK," Taurus said. He and James walked back toward the gate where Brad was waiting for them.

They entered the inn and James got a room. They walked upstairs and James sat on the bed. Brad took a seat by the small wooden table and Taurus looked at them both. Fire started to flicker behind his eyes and James quickly stood up.

"Sit down!" Taurus commanded. James sat back down on the bed. "How did he get to her?" Taurus asked.

"He found her, thanks to Brad," James said as he shot him a look.

"Thanks to me! What did I do?" Brad asked. He quickly stood up and looked at James. Brad was going to defend himself one way or the other.

James leapt up and met Brad's cold, dead eyes. "You told Serina's mom that you had found her and that you were going to tell her everything! That's what started this whole thing!" James said.

Taurus looked at James in disgust. "Have we forgotten? Or are we just trying to place blame?" he asked. James looked at him with confusion in his eyes and then worry. James had no idea what Taurus was getting at. Taurus immediately understood. "He found her because her mother is now human and Serina has taken her place," Taurus explained.

"Yeah, but she's not a guardian," James went on to say.

"You're right," Taurus said. "But she still carries the traits of one, and although I don't know what his plans are for the both of you, it would seem to me that someone wasn't watching over her very well," Taurus said, eyeing James.

James sat back down on the bed as his heart sank into his stomach. Was this his fault because he wasn't paying attention? He should have known that night was going to be difficult. He should have known that she would have been in trouble because of her decision. How could he have avoided it, though?

Taurus looked at James, understanding that he was questioning himself. He walked over to James and tapped him on the head. "It's been a while since you and she have leaned on each other," he explained.

James looked up at him. The thought had never occurred to him. Taurus was right! Where Serina was, he could be. All he had to do was connect to her. But he had no connection. There was nothing that both of them had that was theirs together. Taurus tapped James on the chest and James felt his ring against his skin. "But she doesn't have hers," James said.

Taurus smiled. "Get some rest while I talk to the undead," Taurus said, motioning toward Brad. "Try your little trick out."

James leaned his head against the pillow and heard Taurus and Brad leave the room. He closed his eyes and gripped his ring. He slowly drifted off to sleep.

James could smell the scent of death as he looked around in the middle of a large foyer. He smiled. *She's here*, he thought. *It worked.* He quickly scanned his surroundings, noticing a large stairwell to his right. He slowly walked up the marble steps and saw a light coming from down the hall. He looked to his left to see if there was anything there and noticed nothing. He crept down the hallway ever so quietly and every so often looking over his shoulder. A sweet scent started to linger in the air. It was her! She was here and he was getting close. He noticed the light that was shining was coming from underneath the door and moved closer. He opened the door to see a burgundy room, and on the bed was the black panther from earlier that day. This was where she was. James knew it. He could sense her again. The cat growled as it slowly jumped down off the bed.

"Here, kitty-kitty," James said as he backed his way out of the room. He thought if he could get the cat out that she would come out. Maybe it was what was holding her there.

The cat slowly made its way toward him with its ears down and its teeth showing. It was stalking him and trying to figure out its next move. James noticed that the cat shifted its weight to its hind legs and was going to jump. This was the opportunity James needed. He watched as the cat leapt toward him and slid under the cat as he kicked the door shut. James listened as the cat growled and slashed at the door outside. "Stop clawing the door or no catnip for you," he taunted.

James looked around the room to see that it was empty. He opened the closet door and looked under the bed. "Serina," he said. "Serina, it's me, James. Come out, come out, wherever you are," he said. His heart skipped a beat to think that she would come out and jump into his arms. But he was met with only silence. "Serina!" he shouted. Maybe she couldn't hear him. "Serina, come out. It's safe now," he said again. He was met with silence once again.

James slowly walked toward the bed and sat down. He could feel his heart break in two. He was so close, but where? That cat wouldn't let him go too far into this place, and it probably wouldn't fall for the same trick twice. James ran his fingers over the bed and felt something. He quickly turned the covers back to see her ring. She had it and she was here!

All of a sudden, the black cat busted down the door and stood there, teeth glaring and eyes full of hatred. This time it didn't give James a chance to move, it just leapt toward him.

When James sat straight up in bed, Taurus looked up from his book. "Did you find her?" he asked.

Out of breath, James answered, "Yep, she's there, and that new cat of his is going to be a problem!"

Taurus raised his eyebrows at James. "Luther has a cat?"

James nodded his head. "Yeah, a black panther. That cat is a pain!"

Taurus shrugged. "Never thought of you as someone to be afraid of an animal. Especially a cat," he laughed.

"Not afraid of it. It just gets in my way!" James said as he threw his head against his pillow in frustration.

"Get some rest. You still have a journey ahead of you," Taurus encouraged, and he turned his attention back to the book he was reading.

James lay on the bed and shut his eyes. *I promise to come and get you*, he thought. *I promise.*

———m———

I quickly sat up in bed and my dark hair surrounded my face. Was it all a dream? Did I dream that he was here? His words still ran through my head. *I promise to come and get you.* I quickly felt for my chain, found it, and let the ring dangle in front of me.

"Did you have another bad dream?" Luther asked as he leaned against the door frame.

"I…I'm not sure," I said.

I let the chain fall. Luther came over and sat beside me.

"You do know that if you like it here, you're more than welcome to stay," he said quietly. "You could rule with me."

I looked at him. For a man his age he was cute. Again, how old was I? I didn't like who I was becoming. It felt wrong and uncomfortable. "I…I don't know about that," I answered. "I'd like to finish school and—"

"It was just a suggestion," Luther said. "The offer is still on the table. Take some time to think about it," he encouraged. As he made his way to the door, all the candles went out slowly. I watched as the door shut behind him.

I lay back down and stared into the darkness. What was happening to me? Why would I even consider doing what he offered? I wasn't supposed to. Was I? James's words rang through my head. *We're not demons! We're guardians!* I turned over in bed to try and escape the words and found that I couldn't. I slowly got up and walked over to my window. I looked out over the dark wasteland these people called a home. Torches shone very little light around the castle walls. In the distance I could see a tall figure of a man. I squinted my eyes to see if I could see him better, and that's when I noticed that he was staring at me.

His eyes were full of sadness and disappointment. I quickly ducked behind the wall, took a deep breath, and let it out slowly. *Wait a minute*, I thought. *Why am I afraid?* He couldn't get to me from way out there. It had to be a good mile or so to the castle gate in which he stood. Besides, Luther and Tim would have known he was there and if he meant harm to me. I looked out the window to see the man still standing there, staring up at me.

"What do you want from me?" I asked very quietly. "Who are you?"

I heard a voice in my head answer. *Don't ever forget who you are and what you were meant to do. You can run and hide, but your purpose here and there will never change. Only you can make the right the choice, and only you can decide which path you will take.*

I shook my head as the man stood there, still watching me. How could he have heard me from way out there? It would have taken someone with very good hearing to know what I said. Then I noticed that I wasn't afraid; in fact, I felt a peace that surrounded me. I watched as other things darted around him as if they couldn't see him at all. It was as if I was the only person seeing him and able to hear him. "What is my purpose? What should I do?" I asked.

I noticed a small smile form on the man's face. His eyes seemed to brighten at the question. *Seek guidance from the right person. In your heart you know the right decision, yet you choose to ignore it. Remember that I will also help you and never leave you. All you have to do is ask.*

I felt a tear roll down my cheek. "Ask what? What do I need to do? Tell me, please," I pleaded.

The man smiled at me again. *In your heart you already know the answer to that question. Know that I am with you always, even if you can't see me. Know that I stand by your side and will always be there. I've never left you, and in many instances have even carried you through the roughest times in your life.*

"Ask him where he was when Steven did what he did to you." I turned to see Luther standing behind me with his arms crossed and a smile on his face. "In fact, ask him where he was when James was there breaking your heart, or when Emily was in pain. Where was he then?"

I turned back to see the man still standing there with a solemn look on his face. "Where were you when I was hurting?"

I asked as more tears rolled down my face. "Where were you when that girl was being put through pain like she was?" I felt the anger start to build back up inside me. "Where were you then?" I shouted.

The man's eyes turned sorrowful again. *Remember that I will never leave you. Remember that I will always love you. Don't ever forget these words.* I watched as the man slowly faded away and I felt a hand on my shoulder.

"Stand up for yourself," Luther said as he turned me to face him. "I would hate to see you hurt again, and as you can see, I've never left your side since you've been here. You can always see me and I will always help you."

I hugged him. "I know," I said as I closed my eyes. "You've never left me behind."

XXIX

Replaced

James lifted his head to see some light in his room. He knew there was no sun here; it just looked as if it was going to rain all the time. James could feel his body ache from riding Midnight for the past two days. It had been a while since he did that. He stretched, quickly got dressed and walked down stairs. He saw Taurus and Brad sitting at a table talking, and Taurus noticed him and got up.

"Sleep well?" Taurus asked.

"Ready. I should be able to reach his castle today. It would be late today, but I can reach it," he answered proudly.

"Take the undead with you," Taurus said, nodding his head toward Brad. "He's gonna come in handy in the future."

James rolled his eyes. "Fine," he huffed as he mounted Midnight. "Where's Starr?" James asked.

"She'll stay here with me," Taurus said. "Now go. Get Serina back here as soon as possible."

James looked at Brad. "Guess you're walking. Midnight won't let you ride," he said with a smirk.

"I can keep up." Brad returned the smirk.

"Fine," James replied, as he and Midnight took off.

Taurus shook his head as he watched James and Brad quickly leave the town. Taurus looked at Starr. She was in her stall; he went over to her and stroked her head. "You'd think that at some point they would act their age," he said. Starr looked at him with sad eyes and Taurus felt her pain. "I know. I know. We'll get her back. I promise," he said as he watched her put her head down.

It was a good hour before James and Brad decided they were going to race each other. James looked over to see Brad keeping pace with Midnight with no trouble. It didn't look like he was even out of breath. James pushed Midnight harder, yet Brad kept up with him. He watched with agitation as Brad sometimes moved just a little ahead of him and then pulled back. Brad was toying with him and that made him even madder.

Midnight finally slowed to a trot and James sat up, noticing that he was slowing down. "Come on, boy. Don't let this old man beat you," James encouraged him. Midnight came to a complete halt. When James saw that Midnight was going down, he quickly jumped off and looked at the horse. Midnight got right back up and stared at James, out of breath.

James quickly recognized the look in Midnight's eyes. "I'm sorry, boy. Do you need a rest?" he asked as he searched for his canteen. James quickly scanned for a large rock nearby and found one near a half-burnt tree. He walked over to it and imagined a large hole. He opened his eyes to see that the rock was just as he had envisioned, and he poured water into it.

"Horse gave up on ya," Brad said with a smile, breathing evenly, as if he had not run for the past hour.

This enraged James, who shot him a look. "Give him a minute. He'll be back to his old self." Midnight's fire started to burn brighter as he huffed and continued to drink.

"Look," Brad said as he stepped near James, "we're both here to accomplish the same goal. To get Serina back home."

"I still don't know why I need your help," James huffed.

"I'm not sure either. I just know that I was told to meet Taurus at Nomed," he answered.

James looked at him, confused. "You mean you just didn't show up?"

Brad shook his head. "Nope. I was summoned," he said as he plopped himself down next to the tree. He pulled a piece of dead bark off the tree and watched as it turned to ash and fell to the ground.

"What do you mean, summoned?" James asked, and he gulped down some water from his canteen.

Brad looked up at James. "A couple days ago Serina's mom got in touch with me and asked me to come see her. So I did, and when I did, she told me that Taurus had asked me to meet him in Nomed. I was there since yesterday morning and Taurus told me that Serina was here and she was in danger. Why her mother couldn't tell me that I don't know, but anyway, I was going to leave and he told me that I had to wait for you. He said I wasn't strong enough to go up against her."

James looked at Brad. "Go up against her? What do you mean? Fight her?" he asked.

"Apparently," Brad answered. "Taurus said that Luther has gotten to her in more ways than we know, and it's not going to be easy to take her out of here."

James looked at the harsh red sky. If that was true, then it was James who was going to have to face her. He didn't want it to come to that. He couldn't imagine a battle against her. He could never harm her. Not now! Not ever! He loved her, and it would break his heart to see her in pain.

"I know it's not going to be easy," Brad said with his head hung low. "But, that's why I'm here. To try and make it a bit easier."

"Easier?" James said as he rolled his eyes. "How is you being here going to make it easier?"

Brad shrugged his shoulders. "Don't know yet, but I'll help get my little girl out of here and back to where she belongs."

James quickly grabbed Brad by the collar and lifted him up to look into his eyes. "No harm is to come to her. Understand?"

Brad threw his arms up. "I understand," he said quietly. "She still is my daughter, although she won't admit to it. I still love her and would protect her from anything. Don't you ever forget that," he warned.

"I won't," James said. He let go of Brad and watched him hit the ground. "We're wasting time here," he said. He grabbed Midnight's reins, mounted him again and started off, not waiting for Brad. James watched the road ahead of him and could see Luther's castle start to emerge from beyond the desolate hills. His heart sank, knowing what was to come.

I sat up straight in my bed, out of breath. I clasped the ring that hung from my neck and looked around the quiet room. Somehow I knew James was close. It was almost like I could hear Midnight running along a dry dirt path. I slowly lifted the covers, let my feet hit the cold stone floor, and walked over to the window. I saw the dark red sky and the burnt trees of the landscape as I clutched the ring harder.

"Everything all right, my dear?" I heard Luther say behind me.

I gasped as I put the ring down my shirt. "Everything is all right," I said as I turned to face him. "He's close…James is close."

Luther looked at me and smiled. He put his arm around me. "I know. Are you scared?" he asked.

I looked at him, puzzled. "Why would I be scared?"

Luther turned me to face him. "Because you finally get the chance to confront him. To ask him why he chose not to come straight here. To ask him why he wanted to visit that girl. Are you not special? I mean, are you not as special as she?" he asked with a smile.

I could start to feel that warmth of anger again flow through my veins. Was I not special? Why did he start there? Why did he lie to me? He told me that he loved me, that he would not let harm come to me, and that he would watch over me—and he left me here.

"I think that he almost sounds like Steven," Luther began as he stared out the window. "You remember that night. He kissed you and told you that he loved you and said he'd never do anything to hurt you. Then he told you that he needed some air, you know, so he went down to the lake. That's when you noticed—" Luther snapped his fingers. "What is her name? Cindy, no…Crystal," he said. "He and Crystal were by the lake, and then you and Mandi went for a walk, and by the time you got back…well, it seemed like you were replaced by her."

The thought sickened me. Steven told me the same thing that James did. I was special and he loved me. Now I was being replaced! Replaced right in front of my eyes.

"That's my girl!" Luther said as he clapped his hands. "You're not going to get replaced again. Don't give him that opportunity!" he said as he pushed me in front of the mirror.

I didn't even recognize myself. My hair had turned so black it had a dark blue tint. My eyes were as black as night with fire that burned in them. No, I wasn't going to give him that chance. He wasn't going to do this to me. "I'm ready," I said as I looked at Luther. "Teach me some more."

"With pleasure," Luther said as he ushered me toward the door.

—⁂—

James looked up the big castle from behind the half-burnt tree. "So how do we get in?" he asked.

"From the back," Brad said. "There's an escape tunnel back there. All these old castles have them."

James smirked. "Really? An escape tunnel. Lead the way." James followed Brad for what seemed like hours to the other side of the big castle. He could see that it was starting to turn dark and wondered if an attack now would be wise. He knew that Luther knew he was here. He just didn't want Luther to know when he was coming in. James felt his stomach growl.

"Getting hungry?" Brad asked.

James looked at him. "Yep, that's what humans sound like when they get hungry, their stomachs growl. You've been undead for so long I thought you might have forgotten."

Brad smirked. "I'll never forget that. Oh, to eat a nice steak again with a side of mashed potatoes and some broccoli." Brad looked over at James, who was sitting on the ground with the plate he had just described.

"You know, boy, for being a type of guardian, I think you let your evil side win a lot," Brad said with harshness.

James smiled as he cut into the thick juicy steak. Brad watched the juice slide down the nice piece of meat. "I don't know what you mean," James said as he slowly chewed his food.

Brad shot him a look, and with lighting speed vanished behind some bushes. James was glad for the silence as he looked up at the castle. He could see some light coming through some of the windows. She was in there and he knew it; he could feel it. He ate some more of his steak as he thought of the things he would do. How could he get in there undetected? What was Luther saying or making her believe that she would want to fight him? His heart started to hurt and his appetite vanished. He made the plate disappear and he lay back on a nearby rock.

Midnight sat down next to him. James stroked Midnight's mane as he watched the blue flames around his hooves glow in the coming of the night. He was going to try once more tonight to connect with her. Maybe he could get her out of there without going in and without a battle that Taurus was expecting. James heard the rustling of dead leaves as Brad reappeared behind the bush in front of him.

"You know, for as ugly as they are, they sure are good," Brad said as he wiped his mouth.

"What are?" James asked.

"Ogres," Brad said as he sat down next to James. "I did what I did to be with the two of them forever, you know."

James looked over at Brad with a disgusted look on his face. "You thought that if you made a deal with the devil they would be all right with it?"

"First off, I didn't make a deal with the devil. I made a deal with Luther. Second, I didn't think that she would leave me for it and take my child with her," Brad said. He started to draw something in the ground.

"First off, she didn't leave you. She was burned to death for being a witch, or they thought she was a witch. Second, when she was burning, you did nothing but take Serina and run. I don't think you'd win any father of the year awards with that," James huffed.

Brad looked angry, but sighed and kept drawing. "I love her. Her mother. She was my first and only love. I thought…I thought that if I had Serina I would have a piece of her with me all the time. I didn't want to go in there and have them get to my daughter as well. She's all I had left," Brad said as a blood tear started to run down his face.

James watched as it hit the ground. "There were other ways to keep your family together besides making a deal with someone as deviant as Luther."

"Don't you think I know that!" Brad shot back. "I wish I would have known it at that time. You know, living for as long as I have, I've learned a lot about what I could have done. Every day I wish I could have taken it back. Every day I wish I could walk into the church and ask for forgiveness and have it all taken away."

James watched as more blood tears streamed down his face. James set his hand on Brad's shoulder. He was starting to feel bad for him. "Have you tried asking for forgiveness?" James asked quietly.

Brad nodded his head. "Yeah, but I haven't changed back. I don't know what else to do. I've tried speaking to her mother, but she won't even give me the time of day. I don't think she even has the answer."

James felt a lump in his throat. "It's because she doesn't have the answer. There is only one person who has that answer."

"And he isn't listening!" Brad looked up at James with anger in his eyes.

James saw his bloodstained face and the hurt and anguish in his eyes. "He listens, but it's up to us to hear," James said as tears started to form. He was actually starting to feel sorry for the guy. Brad had lived for so long in this form that he had forgotten that sometimes he just had to sit back and listen.

"There's no hope for me. I made my decision a long time ago, and now I have to live with that decision," Brad said, as he sat back and looked at the drawing on the ground. "You know, I see this picture in my head every day. The way we were. The happy family." Brad sniffed. "Then, in an instant, it was all taken away from me." He got up and walked off.

James looked at the ground and saw a portrait of Brad, Serina, and her mother. He saw that they were all smiling and happy. James noticed how old the clothing looked and realized that it was the last happy memory that Brad had of them. He kept that picture of them in his head to remind him of the happy times with his family. James's heart sank. How can someone with no heart still have a heart? Most of the things here didn't even remember their past lives, or what they did remember was all the bad things. That's what kept them trapped here. Maybe in some small way this was a type of torture for him.

"James, I think it would be best to get them in the morning," Brad said as he came back from around the bush. "If you follow this passage it will take you to the holding cells. Follow the hallway and up the stairs to the kitchen, which will lead you to the foyer. From there you're going to have to follow your senses."

James looked at Brad with concern. "I thought you were going to show me the way. I mean, you know this castle better than I do."

"You're going to have to search your memory. You'll remember this castle in time. It will be like riding a bike. As soon as you enter you should remember where everything is. I will be out front trying to keep as many of the others as occupied as I can. Go in there and get my daughter out," Brad said, as he leaned down and looked at the picture once more. He rubbed his hand against the picture and left again.

James looked down to see that the person that was missing in the picture was Brad. All that remained was Serina and her mother. James sat back and shut his eyes. *One more time*, he thought. *One more time to try and find her*, he thought, and allowed himself to fall into a dream state.

James opened his eyes to find himself in the room again. He quickly looked around to see it very neat and tidy. No one was in there. He slowly made his way around the room to see if there was any sign that she was there. He stepped carefully, making sure there was no sound.

Nothing. James huffed and slowly started for the door when he heard the low growl behind him. He turned around to see the black panther stalking him from the closet. "Sorry, kitty. I have no treats for you tonight," James said as the panther kept its eyes on him. "Where is your master?" he asked it.

The panther growled, leapt on the bed and lay down. James watched curiously, as the cat seemed to have no intention of getting to him tonight. He saw that the panther seemed tired and had no energy. "Has he fed you already?" James asked, and the panther once again growled and sighed.

"You know…Luther knows you're here, and how dare you not come in," the all-too-familiar voice said.

James heard the door shut. "So he sends you to do his bidding," James said, as he turned to see Tim.

"You know he still loves you, and would still love to get to know you," Tim said with a snarl.

"Oh, you know better than that. I would never want to take your place," James said with a smile. "Besides, you know the end to this story. You lose and then you die."

"I'm sorry. Is that what your book says? 'Cause as far as I know, there is no ending to that. I mean, everyone speculates. I guess it's all in who you ask," Tim shot back.

"Then I guess someone should teach you how to read!" James growled. "Where is she?"

"She's safe. Luther has taken very good care of her and taught her so much. It's almost like she's a natural. How great for it to be the day after her birthday and you leave her so unattended. She should feel so safe knowing that you are watching over her. What was it…two…four hours tops and you already lost her?" Tim half laughed.

James could feel his anger start to build up inside him. He knew he was in too dangerous a place to let it go. He slowly closed his eyes and took a deep breath. He thought of Serina and her beautiful smile that day on the boat.

"Oh, come on," Tim taunted as he slowly walked a circle around James. "Let it out. Let's see how much of that is truly you. We would like to see the real you! The you that you were meant to be, instead of this shell of a…whatever you are now," Tim said.

James could take it no longer. He balled his hands into fists and then stretched his fingers, letting his energy drain out. For the moment it was working. He just didn't know for how long it would work.

"You know you want to release all the pent-up energy," Tim said, getting in his face. James could hear each breath Tim took and tried to ignore it. "You really are something. Nothing gets to you. But like so many other things, I guess if you keep poking at it, it eventually fights back. So, let's see…let's talk about your mother and the lies she has filled your head with. How about the day she died, and why your stepsister can't move on. How about that?"

James could feel the anger turn to rage inside him. He had to get out of there. Taurus was right. They had gotten to Serina. They were getting to him. James slowly opened his eyes, looked at Tim and smiled.

"I don't have time for this. If you don't tell me where she is, then I guess I'll just have to find her. I'm going to go now," James said, fighting his rage.

Tim quickly and harshly backed James into the wall. "Well, look at that. Sometimes I don't even know my own strength. I guess we'll have to fix that crack in the wall after you're gone."

James watched as the panther slowly jumped off the bed and made its way over toward them. James noticed something about the big cat that made him shiver. The cat was the same color as Midnight. It was so black it looked like midnight blue, and the eyes were a deep emerald green—no, wait, they changed colors.

"What are you looking at?" Tim asked as he turned around. He noticed the panther had come off the bed. "She's a beauty, isn't she?" He let go of James and casually walked over to the big cat and stroked its head.

"When did Luther get a pet?" James asked.

Tim put his finger on the side of his face and acted like he was thinking. "About a couple of days ago," he said with a smile. Tim bent down toward the cat's ear and whispered something.

James watched as the cat crouched in an attack position. Its ears went back and the cat snarled, showing it dangerous teeth.

Tim slowly stood up. "So here's the deal. You don't belong here and you should return from whence you came. Leave her here because you know we'll find her again, and next time might not be as comfy as this time. Or stay here with us and you can finally do us all a favor and make him happy."

James smiled as he looked at Tim. "What if I don't like either of those choices and decide to make my own?"

"You won't have time to make your own!" Tim said as he stepped to the side.

James had no time to react before the big cat lunged at him and sank its teeth into his arm. He tried to fight off the cat as it took a swing at his other arm. James felt the cat's powerful claws rip his flesh. He winced in pain as its strong jaws ripped at his other arm.

"James! James!" he heard Brad's voice. That's when James felt another stab of pain in his shoulder.

James opened his eyes to see Brad by his side. He quickly noticed the two perfect bite marks on his shoulder. He got up and grabbed Brad by his throat. "Bite me again and I'll rip your fangs out! Do you understand?" James threatened.

Brad's eyes were wide with fear as he nodded his head and was released from James's grip. "Have you taken a look at yourself? Where did you get all those wounds? My bite was nothing compared to what you have there."

James looked down at his arms; both were covered in blood. One had puncture wounds from teeth; two sets of teeth and one with claw marks. James watched as the wounds slowly started to close up and the pain began to subside. He closed his eyes again and leaned back as his breathing turned normal.

"Did you find her?" Brad asked.

James opened his eyes. "No, but I found Tim and that cat in her room. We are going to have to do something—and fast." He stood up and looked out. He could see the sky start to turn light and he knew that the day was coming. He felt as if he had no energy and needed to rest now. James shook his head to try and compose himself. No, he needed to go, and go now. If there was a time to attack it was going to be now. James looked over at Brad. "Are you ready?" he asked.

Brad looked at him and sighed. "If you're ready, I'm ready," he answered.

"I follow this tunnel into the holding cell area and then feel my way around, right?" James asked, to make sure he understood the directions Brad had given him earlier. Time was of the essence, and the sooner he got Serina out of there, the better.

"Well, you should come to a kitchen area, like I said before, out to the dining area, and then to the foyer," Brad answered him. "Be careful and get her out of there…please," Brad pleaded to James.

"I will," James said. He felt something in his pocket and patted it, and knew that it was his book. It was something that was going to keep him safe. "Let's go," he said with a smile, as he started his way through the tunnel. He turned back to see Brad watching him, and then he too turned to make his way to the front. James looked ahead and sighed. "Serina," he said in a low whisper, "I'm coming. Hold on."

XXX

Mine

J ames looked at the stone walls around him as he walked
through the tunnel. He could smell the mildew and stale
air that was starting to linger. *Must be getting close to the cells*,
James thought as he kept walking. He didn't want to tip off
anyone or anything that might be around. He made sure that
his steps were precise and quiet as he moved through the tunnel. Once he was out of the tunnel he might be able to move
more freely; there were things that would muffle the sounds
around him.

James could see a light at the end of the tunnel. The stench
of mildew and stale air filled in around him as he entered the
cell room. He looked around to see that six cells all lined each
wall. He quietly stepped toward one and looked at the thick
wooden door with a small window with bars on it. He looked
in to see nothing. He quickly went to the next door and looked
in. Nothing was in that one, either. So far so good.

"Hey! Hey, you!" James heard a gruff voice come from a
cell further up. He saw a dirty arm waving to him.

James crouched down and moved quickly toward it. He
looked in to see a small frail man that looked as if he hadn't

eaten in months. His dirty hair was matted to his head and his short beard was full of what looked like pieces of dirt stuck in it. "Are you here to get her?" the man asked in a whisper.

"Get who?" James asked, trying to get more information out of the man.

"The girl that will set us all free. I knew that you guys wouldn't let him have her for very long," the man said.

James looked at him suspiciously. "I don't know what you're talking about," he answered him.

"Don't play with me, boy! I know exactly what and who you are. Look, I'm down here awaiting my punishment. I've been here for over a hundred years. My crime? Carrying a book that wasn't supposed to be here," the man said as he reached into one of the holes in the wall. He quickly showed James a small leather-bound book with gold writing on the front of it. As he did a spider crawled across his hands. The man gently brushed it away and it scurried into a dark corner of the cell.

"How'd you get that?" James asked.

"You have to know someone who knows someone. If you get what I'm sayin'," the man said. "Look, they think she is some sort of key which can open a gate. They're half right. She is a key, just not that key. You have to get her out of here," he urged.

"How do you know all this?" James asked.

The man gave a grimy smile. "Some of us didn't start out bad, and some of us lost our way, but then made the decision to start over again. We're not perfect, just forgiven. Look, the guards were called to a disturbance outside. All part of your plan, I'm guessing. So, if you follow this hall you should come to some stairs, and at the top of them is the kitchen. The kitchen shouldn't be busy, since the only time Luther eats is when he has company. He's mostly a drinking kind of person, if you get my drift. Anyway, there are three doors. One leads to the backyard of the castle, one leads to the dining room, and the third is the one you'll come out of."

James looked at the man. "Thank you. Is there anything I can do for you?" he asked.

The man smiled. "Get her out of here, and this time watch over her," he demanded. James nodded his head. He looked at the door, took the small knife out of his pocket, and picked the lock. The door opened and the man smiled. "Thank you, my boy, but I prefer to stay in here. It's a lot worse out there than it is in here. I get quiet and enough time to read. Much time to meditate, and every so often I get a meal. This is their torture for me," he said as he closed the door again. "Get her and go home, and I will be judged accordingly one day," he said as he slowly backed into the darkness of his cell.

"Thank you again," James said. He was met with silence. James looked ahead of him to see the stone stairway that would lead him up to the kitchen. He quickly made his way up the stairs and slowly opened the door.

James peeked around the door to see that the kitchen was deserted, just like the man said. He looked around to see the three brick ovens that sat on the farthest wall from him. He saw one large stove that lined the wall adjacent to it and saw a door. He quickly made his way over there and opened the door. He peered outside to see the yard full of what looked like red clay on the ground. A few patches of dead grass sprouted up in a scattered pattern. James closed the door and looked behind him, and he saw another door, a large dark mahogany door with a small window. James made his way toward the door and peeked out the small window, where he saw a large table with a red tablecloth on it and a black candelabra that sat in the middle of it.

James quietly pushed the door open and walked through the dining room. He made his way to the door and opened it slowly, looking around to make sure there was no one there. When he saw that it was empty, he stepped into the foyer to see the massive portrait of the Colosseum with people screaming for help as lions tore at them that was etched into the floor. Some of this place was coming back to him. He looked to his left to see the staircase that led upstairs to where he saw Serina. She wasn't up there, though. He closed his eyes and took a deep breath. *Where are you?* he thought.

"Oh, so nice to actually see you in the flesh," Tim said as he leaned against a column. "Follow me, I'll take you to see her." He started walking toward the double doors in front of James.

James looked up to see the hideous gargoyles whose eyes followed him until he entered the door. "I see you guys still have them. How long have they been here?" James asked with a snicker.

"Longer than you've been here," Tim said with a smile. "You didn't notice that those are the older ones, of course. We moved the younger ones outside. You know how young ones make such a mess."

"Well, look who we have here!" Luther smiled from his seat in front of James. "Has my son decided to grace me with his presence?"

"Don't call me that," James growled under his breath.

"What?" Luther asked innocently. "I should have known most kids are ashamed of their parents. But still, even they come home every so often to say hello."

James watched as the black panther came out of the shadows and sat next to Luther. He patted the big cat on the head. "Look, son, I bought you a pet."

"I don't want a cat," James snapped. "Where is she?" he demanded. He could feel her presence here but he didn't see her.

"Let's have a father-son talk," Luther said. "You know, I never did get a chance to talk to you about girls. Here is my chance."

"I don't have time for this. Just tell me where she is and I'll leave," James snapped back.

Luther stood up. "You will listen to me! Don't anger me again!" he said as he slowly sat back down.

"Or what?" James asked. "You gonna put me in the corner? I'm too old for that. Tell me where she is."

"Your mother was someone I thought I could convince to stay with me. Especially since she had my son. Little did I know that she was connected to Hope and her daughter! Then it hit me. I could have both of them." Luther's evil grin sent chills through James's body. "You see, my son," he said, as he waved his hand at James, "you could be with Hope's daughter, and then I would have Taurus's two main guardians at my disposal. Unfortunately, they could not be persuaded. So what does your mother do? What most harlots do. Take something and run."

James smiled. "I'm glad she took me away from you."

"Are you, my boy? Think about it. You could have all this. You could sit next to me and rule all this," Luther said as Tim looked at him in disbelief.

"You don't rule this. You just watch over this and torture people for fun. Besides, I already told Tim he could take my spot," James said through his gritted teeth.

"Tim does not possess the powers that you do. I need someone strong, like you," Luther said.

"No, thank you," James said. "Now, if you would kindly let me have Serina, I will be on my way."

"I don't think you know just how much she means to me. She is a key and I need her to open something for me," Luther said quietly, petting the big black cat.

"She can't open that and you know it," James snapped back.

"She opens something, and with your help I know that the two of you can open a lot more," he accused. "You know it and I know it."

"I know none of which you speak. All I know is that she doesn't belong here," James said. "I've had enough. WHERE IS SHE?"

Luther smiled. "Maybe she doesn't want to go home with you. Maybe she wants to stay here with me. Someone who doesn't lie to her. Someone who can offer her more than you can," he said as he looked the panther in the eyes.

James watched as the panther rubbed up against Luther. Something glittered from the cat's neck. James tried to concentrate on it to see what it was. It was a chain with something round dangling from it.

"How is Emily?" Luther asked.

"Emily?" James asked. "Oh, Emily. Well, I guess that's one soul you lost." He snickered as he pulled his book from his pocket and waved it in the air.

Luther became enraged. "You're the ONE! You're the one that gave her the book! All I ask is that that book stays away from here, and you go and bring it here! How dare you!"

"Why not?" James asked as he put it back in his pocket. "Why can't they have any reading material?"

"I give them all kinds of books to read," Luther shot back. "They can read whatever they want—except that book!"

"Well, I would hate to upset your boss, but that book should count as reading material." James laughed. "I mean, it is a book. The pages are filled with words which make sentences. I would count it as reading material," he mocked.

"How do you feel, James? How do you feel that because of you she went through more pain than most do in their lifetime? We give these people everything here and we ask for one thing in return. Not to have that book!" Luther took a deep breath and sat back down. "You know Emily had a crush on you ever since the day the two of you met. Do you remember how you met?"

James grew angry. "I don't want to go through this again. I want to know where Serina is!"

"Let's see," Luther said, ignoring James. "It would seem that even when you met Emily you were with Serina. It seems that with everyone you meet, they all seem to go through a lot of pain. Tell me why Serina would even want to go with you. You lied to her like Steven lied to her. Isn't that right, my precious?" Luther said, stroking the cat.

James watched as the panther put its ears back. It made a low growl as it turned to face him and slowly walked toward him. James smiled. "So you send your pet after me," he said as he took notice of the chain again. James looked harder to see that the cat had Serina's ring hooked to the chain.

A wave of fear hit James instantly. What had Luther done! Did he let that big cat get to her? "If you let that cat hurt her, I'm going to kill you!" James threatened. James crouched down to prepare for the cat's attack. He watched as the cat started to run toward him in slow motion and leapt into the air.

James quickly moved and grabbed the chain, breaking it from the panther's neck as it gracefully landed behind him. James looked in his hand to see nothing but the chain and quickly looked around him to see where the ring was. He noticed it as it rolled toward one of the columns. James ran over to get it as the panther took a bite of his leg and ran ahead. "That doesn't belong to you!" James screamed as he started to limp toward the cat. The pain seared up his leg as he touched the wound to heal it. James grabbed the back leg of the panther and noticed as it began to change. James looked up to the black eyes of Serina.

"It does belong to me," I said coldly, looking down at him. James watched as I picked up the ring and placed it on my finger. "It's mine," I said as I stared at it.

James quickly jumped to his feet and tried to hug me, but I pushed against him with all my might and watched as he hit the wall on the other side of the room. My anger grew inside me. James recovered and looked at me in disbelief. "What's wrong?" he asked lovingly, and in an instant his lips curled and his voice became deep. "What lies has he told you?"

"Lies?" I said with an evil laugh, not recognizing my own voice. It had changed with the anger and hatred I had at this moment. "What lies have you told me?" I asked, crouching down and awaiting his next move.

James stood his ground and looked at me. "I have told you nothing but the truth," he insisted. "Serina, please don't do this. I don't want to fight you," he said, as he put his sword down on the ground and held his hands up. "See, no weapons."

I smiled an evil grin. "Too bad for you." I taunted. "Let's see…you could have been here sooner. You could have come to see me first, but you didn't. You went to see her!" I shouted.

James looked confused. "See who?" he asked. "Serina, I don't know who you're—"

"Don't lie to me!" I cut him off. "You're just as bad as Steven. I guess it is true what they say about boys. They're nothing but a bunch of dogs!" My breathing had become labored; the adrenaline was rushing through my body and I could feel an aching that wanted to be released.

James quickly looked at Luther. "What did you show her?" he demanded. "What lies have you told her?" he accused.

Luther sat back and put his hands together to hide his content. "Nothing, my boy. I only showed her what has happened since your arrival."

James looked back at me and thought for a moment. Then his eyes widened with fear. Luther was right when he trained me. I could smell his fear and I could hear his heart beat faster. *Probably going to tell me another lie*, I thought. "Go ahead. I'll give you time to think up another story," I said as I folded my arms across my chest.

"Emily. We're talking about Emily," James said. "Serina, she was someone I was trying to help. Let me take a guess…

you could see everything, just not hear a word of what was going on. He probably even shut his little mirror off when I was reading to her from the book," he said as he looked over at Luther with disgust.

My heart fluttered with hope; maybe he hadn't lied to me. He was right about me not being able to hear anything. Had I not seen everything? Tears welled up in my eyes. I shook my head. *No! No! I want to be mad! I want to be angry!* Steven had told me something along the same lines. Now James was doing it, too! "Not this time," I said with a smile, as I waved my finger in the air like a mother scolding her child. I felt my body change as the panther emerged and I slowly walked toward James.

James looked at me. "Serina, this isn't who we are. This isn't what it supposed to be like. I have told you no lies. It's true that I could have been here before this, but I didn't want Luther to hurt you and that's why I made the journey here. I just wanted to make sure you were safe. I wanted to make sure that I had some sort of plan."

The anger inside me drove me crazy. I felt my razor-sharp claws as they tapped against the stone floor. James sat still in front of me, watching me. He slowly put his hand out toward me as I pulled my ears back and growled. "Serina, please don't do this. Let's talk," he said, trying to touch my head.

I quickly dug my paw into his arm and thrust myself against him, pinning him to the ground. Without thinking, an instinct took over as I bit down on his arm and thrust my head from side to side. I could taste his blood from the wound I was creating. His blood didn't taste anything like what I expected. It had a sweet taste, like candy. I heard him cry in pain as I bit again. I then felt a surge of energy go through my body as I hit a column. I watched helplessly as the column came tumbling down around me. I turned quickly back to my human form and I put my hands up to protect my head. I heard James scream my name as I pushed the heavy parts of the column off me as if they weighed nothing. I rose up and looked at James, who was holding his arm, the blood running down and starting to make a small pool of blood beneath his fingers.

I smiled as I wiped his blood from my mouth. "Guess I'm not just another girl, huh?" I asked.

James picked up his sword and looked at me with hurt in his eyes. "Serina, please. Let's go home," he pleaded. "We can talk this out there."

"I'll go home, just not with you," I said as I lunged forward again.

James grabbed my arm and swung me into another wall. I watched as more rock surrounded me.

"Serina, I don't want to do this anymore!" he yelled.

I got back up. "Too late," I said with a smile.

I felt the anger inside me release and watched as James was picked up and hit another standing column. I watched the column come tumbling down around him. He put his arm up to shield his head just like I had before. His arm had healed by the time he got back up and looked at me. He was angry now, too. *Good, now he knows how I feel.* I waved my hand as another column came straight for him. I watched as he put his hand up and the column stopped.

"So, he's taught you some things, has he?" James grinned evilly at me.

I started to walk toward him and he disappeared in front of me. I crossed my arms. "That tired old trick," I said with a laugh. "Come out, come out, wherever you are," I said, looking around the room. "He must have gotten stuck some-where." I laughed.

All of a sudden I felt my arms pinned to my sides, and with every breath I took I felt his grasp on me get tighter. "Serina," he whispered into my ear. "Stop this. Remember how much energy it takes to do this," he warned.

"Let…me…go!" I said, as I twisted my body against his to try and loosen his grip on me. It didn't work. Each time I twisted, his grip on me got tighter. I finally stood still, breath-ing hard from the fight he was giving me.

"Calm down," he said. "Listen to reason. I can explain Emily and explain what you saw, if you can just take a minute to listen."

Luther laughed and shook his head. "Wrong thing to say, my boy," he said. "There's nothing like a woman scorned."

The anger of just hearing her name come out of his mouth threw my hatred toward him even more. I felt a rush of energy come through my body as I felt James's grip on me disappear. I turned around and watched as a man helped James up off the floor. I focused to see who it was. I saw them talking as I tried to listen in on their conversation. Who was that?

James looked up to see Brad with his hand extended. "She's stronger than you remember," he said.

James took his hand and Brad lifted him up. "Yeah, but she's been taught a lot, too. That panther is her!" James said in anger. "He taught her how to change."

Brad looked at him in disbelief. "She's the panther?"

James shook his head as he watched as I stared at him. "I don't think she recognizes you," he said.

Brad looked over. "She looks just as beautiful as her mother," he quickly noticed. "I think I can help. If I can get close enough she'll adapt to me."

James looked at Brad. "Great, turn her into a vampire. They move quickly and are even more lethal." James sighed between breaths.

"Yes, but we have our weaknesses," Brad said as he inched his way toward me. "Hi, Serina," he said.

I watched carefully as this young man inched his way toward me. He was just a bit shorter than James, with long brown hair neatly tied back with a ribbon. Who was he? He smiled at me and I quickly felt a pain in my mouth. I covered my mouth.

"Something hurt?" he asked.

"You have no business here!" Luther's voice boomed. "You will surely be punished for interrupting my business," he threatened.

Brad smiled as I looked at him. I noticed his teeth—no, his fangs—and instantly realized who he was. "Brad," I said with a smile. "Nice to finally meet you."

Brad stopped in his tracks. "Do you remember me?" he asked, shocked and hopeful. A light behind his eyes started to shine as if for that split second he was happy that I remembered him.

"How can I forget the man that broke my mother's heart and then tried to turn me into something I'm not?" I shot back as the pain in my mouth subsided. I ran my tongue against my teeth to feel the two fangs that now hung in my mouth and smiled. "He taught me about you, too," I said. "You're in trouble," I snickered. I ran at him with lighting speed, but felt him grip my arms and throw me against the wall just as fast. I felt some of the stone give way behind my head as I looked at him.

"I'm older and faster than you," he taunted. I watched as his two fangs gleamed from the light of the torches around the room.

"You may be older than me, but not better," I said. Letting my fangs show, I quickly moved behind him and shoved him up against the wall. I watched as he planted his two feet on the wall and took a leap over me. I watched in slow motion as he smiled upside down at me, landing behind me and shoving me face-first into the wall in front of me. I could feel his grip on my arm, which was twisted behind my back.

"Now, you need to listen and go home with James," he said with authority.

Who did this guy think he was? He hadn't been a father to me in many years, and now he thought that just because he was here I was going to listen to him. Wait a minute—he longed so much to be my father. I decided to tell him what he wanted to hear as I smiled inside.

"Daddy," I said in my best little-girl voice, "you're hurting me. Please stop." I felt his grip on me let go and turned to see him walking back. It worked. He hadn't seen me in so long and would never hurt his own flesh and blood. I seized this chance and jumped on him, pinning him to the ground. "Old and stupid," I said with a smile.

Brad looked up at me with a smile. "Old…maybe. Stupid, never," he said, and he plunged something wooden into my chest. I looked down to see half of it sticking out of my body and I felt myself go limp. I slowly rolled off him, looking up at the ceiling. I could hear James running toward me. He slid next to me and lifted me to him. The wooden thing moved, which made me wince from the pain.

"Serina!" he gasped. "Hold on! What did you do?" James yelled at Brad. I felt my anger subside as I looked up at James's hazel eyes. The look of worry was there as tears started to flow down his face. I felt my life slipping away from me as he held me tight. I could feel him stroking my hair to the side as he rocked back and forth.

"James." I coughed and tasted the blood that entered my mouth and started to run down my cheek. It was in that instant that the feeling of anger left me and a new feeling replaced it—the feeling of helplessness and emptiness. I looked up at James with tears in his eyes and immediately my heart started to hurt. I had hurt him deeply and now I lay dying in his arms. I then felt something else...something I remembered feeling not too long ago...it was love. No, it was his love...the love he had for me, and now pain. I felt my life start to inch away and wanted James to know how I felt before I went. "I'm... sorry," I said, as I let the last bit of energy drain out of me and shut my eyes.

XXXI

Regret

James looked over at Brad with hatred in his eyes. "What did you do?" he screamed again.

Brad lifted himself up and moved to touch Serina. "I... don't...know. I mean, I didn't know what else to do," he said.

James quickly struck his hand. "Don't touch her!" he commanded.

Luther strolled over to them and looked down. He saw her face without color. He shrugged his shoulders and looked at James. "She's no good to me dead. Take her back to her mother and have a nice funeral," he said as he slowly exited the room.

James watched as Luther left without a second glance. What else did he expect from the man that was born with hatred in his heart? Did he really expect Luther to care and be a normal human being? James listened as the heavy door slammed, and his head went down as tears streamed down his face and hit hers.

Brad sat down on the floor next to them. He watched as James held her tight and tears formed in his eyes. What had he done? She was going to kill him and he had to defend himself.

Her eyes were black as night and her thirst for blood was overwhelming. It was either him or her. The thought stopped him. She reminded him of someone—she reminded him of himself. The black soulless eyes and the lack of fear. When he looked into her eyes he was looking at himself. He had helped her become this way. Brad sat there with James and cried with him. He killed his daughter—his own flesh and blood—and didn't think twice of doing so. What kind of monster does that?

"Excuse me." A familiar voice entered the room. James and Brad noticed Tim standing at the door. "The door is open and I think it's best that you take the body back to her mother," he said coldly. "We have no use for her now. Pity," Tim said, shaking his head in disappointment. "We had such plans for her, and now…well, I guess she wasn't as strong as she could have been. Oh, well. Of course, James, the offer still stands, and your father—"

James looked up at Tim. "He's not my FATHER!" James shot back.

Tim smiled at him. "Then I guess it would be time for you to make your exit," he said as he opened the door wider.

James sighed and picked Serina up. He carried her out the doors with Brad following behind him. James heard the heavy front doors shut and carried her out the front gates. He whistled and Midnight came from around the corner. James watched as his blue flames started to die out and he let out a whinny at the sight of Serina. James climbed onto Midnight, being very careful of Serina's body, and nudged the horse to go. Midnight slowly started walking away from the castle as James hung his head.

"Wait!" Brad yelled. "Where will you take her?" he asked.

James looked over at Brad with a deadly stare. "Away from here and away from you," he answered. "You've done enough damage. Go away!" Brad watched as James left with his daughter's body. In that instant, Brad felt the sting of his heart breaking in two again, seeing his daughter's lifeless body. There was only one other time he had felt this alone—the day his wife left with their daughter.

James looked down at Serina. She looked so serene, like she was sleeping. He lifted her lip to see that she no longer had fangs, but her body was still very cold. He watched in vain hoping to see her chest rise and fall, but nothing. His heart broke in two and the tears started to flow again. How had it come to this? Why didn't he just keep fighting her? She would have gotten worn out eventually. "I'm sorry I failed you again," James said as he stroked her cheek with the back of his finger. Images of her smiling at him that day on the boat emerged from his mind. Her laugh and excitement of learning things she already knew all over again. The way her eyes turned to a soft brown when he kissed her for the first time in many years. Her smile that could light up a room, and the way she bent her head and blushed when he hugged her. He had lost it all again in a matter of minutes. All because he trusted Brad not to hurt her! How could he? How could Brad do something like this to her? This was his daughter! He really had no heart. He stabbed her like he would stab any other enemy, and without hesitation.

James stroked her long dark hair. It was soft and shiny. He loved it when she put it up in a ponytail and it cascaded down her back. He especially loved the way it had looked at the winter ball. The light blue dress with the embroidery of silver sparkled snowflakes had seemed to make her tanned skin glow, accented by her dark hair that flowed behind her when she walked. Her smile that night had been especially bright as he watched her descend the stairs toward him.

James looked ahead to see the sky start to turn dark. He hadn't been traveling very long and knew that he still had a long road ahead of him. He didn't care. Nothing seemed to matter much now that Serina was gone. He would go on alone again. The thought struck his heart hard, and again more tears slowly ran down his face. He felt that a piece of him died when she shut her eyes.

James watched the road for what seemed like hours and it disappeared around him as night started to settle in. He then saw in the distance two lanterns that seemed to float in midair come in sight. He was close to the town. He tightened his grip on Serina's body and urged Midnight to go faster. Midnight picked up his pace as James watched the approaching town. Midnight needed no direction; he slowly walked through the opening in the town wall and started heading toward the inn.

The owner was outside waiting with a lantern in hand. "James?" he asked. "Is that you?"

James nodded his head as he slowly got off Midnight. He held Serina's body very tightly to him and cleared his throat. "Is Taurus still here?" he asked as the stable hand took Midnight to the stable.

"No, he left a couple of hours ago," the innkeeper said, not taking his eyes off Serina. "Is that...is that her?" he asked.

James ignored the innkeeper's question. "What do you mean, he left?" James asked as he entered the inn.

"He told me to tell you to meet him at Sluos. The other horse...well, she disappeared a couple of hours ago," the innkeeper said. "That's when Taurus left," the innkeeper explained, as he opened the door to the room and let James in.

James almost dropped Serina on the bed as he tried to find his balance. If Starr had disappeared that meant she was gone. Starr would no longer be needed, and would go on living life as a regular horse. For the first time in a long time he felt completely alone. He had felt alone before, but Serina was alive, and that was what kept him going. Knowing that one day—one glorious day—she would remember him and things could go back to what they were before. All this died the moment her father stabbed her.

"Is that the girl?" the innkeeper tried to pry again.

James solemnly looked at the innkeeper, trying to keep his anger in check. "Yes," he finally choked out.

"Will she be all right?" he asked.

"If I can get her to Taurus," James said. "Get my horse. I will ride through the night to get to Sluos," he said, as he moved to grab Serina's lifeless body.

"No," the innkeeper quickly replied. "Taurus said to get some sleep and to leave in the morning. He said that he knows it will be hard, but to try and rest up for the long trip tomorrow." And with that, the innkeeper shut the door.

James looked at Serina and saw her wedding band on her finger. He knelt beside the bed and put his hands together. "Please don't take her from me. Not after all we've been through to get us back together. Maybe it's your plan not to have her here, and I will not interfere with that." A tear started to roll down his cheek. "Please take extra care of her until I get there," he said and he opened his eyes.

He lay on the floor next to the bed and clung to his band. The thought of their love for each other ran through his mind again as he started to drift off to sleep. James knew that the energy he used today had started to take its toll. He hadn't fought with someone his equal and more in a long time.

—✺—

I slowly opened my eyes and waited for them to adjust to the brightness that surrounded me. I rubbed my eyes and looked around. I put my hands down to lift myself up and found what I was on to be very soft. I quickly rubbed my fingers around me. This was unlike anything I had ever touched. I tried to figure out what it was that surrounded me. It had the texture of cotton, but was ten times softer than it. I waved my hands through it and saw how it engulfed them. I quickly pulled it back to see that my hand was safe.

"It's perfect, isn't it?" a soft voice said behind me.

I quickly turned to see the long radiant brown hair and hazel eyes staring at me again. "Christina?" I choked out.

"Yes," she said. She offered me her hand and helped me stand up. I quickly shifted my weight, afraid that the ground under me would not hold me. Christina laughed again. "It's not a cloud."

I looked down to see the white fluffy stuff as it swirled around my feet. "What is it?" I asked.

"I could explain it, but it won't make sense. Besides, we have more urgent things to talk about right now," she said as she put her arm around my shoulders.

I looked around me again. "Yeah, wait a minute. Am I dead?" I asked.

Christina shook her head with a smile. "No," she said. "However, you sure did give James a scare and a workout. I don't think I can remember the last time he had to fight so hard. I think it was harder for him to try not to hurt you."

I put my head down. "He's already hurt me," I said quietly.

Christina gave me a confused look. "Has he? What did he say or do?" she asked.

"He told me he loved me, and then he went to see Emily first. I knew things were too good to be true," I said angrily.

"I didn't know that talking to someone meant that he doesn't love you," she said with her arms crossed. "You talk to Mandi, Holly, and Anna, and that doesn't mean he has the right to get mad at you."

"That's because they are all my friends and he knows them. Besides, they're all girls," I said with a huff.

"Ohhh," Christina said with a smile. "So because Emily was a girl that makes a difference. So you're not mad, but jealous. Luther really did a good job." She rolled her eyes.

"What do you mean?" I asked, still feeling angry.

"Well, jealousy turns to envy and that is one sin that can really break someone. So let's look at this: you basically watched him from a distance and listened to their conversation. Did he say that he loved her?" she asked.

I thought back to the room where Luther showed me the whole thing. "I couldn't hear anything," I answered her.

Christina snapped her fingers. "You couldn't hear anything, but maybe you could have read their lips, or even tapped into their thoughts," she said.

I shook my head. "I didn't do any of that," I replied with a heavy heart.

"So let me get this straight," Christina said. She slowly walked a circle around me, like a lawyer getting to her point. "You couldn't hear them, you didn't read their lips or see anything that looked like he said he loved her, and you didn't ask," she said, staring directly into my eyes.

The realization of the situation hit me like a ton of bricks. I got mad over nothing; I had no idea about what was going on. I felt ashamed and angry at myself. I had taken all my anger out on him—and for what? Something that I thought might be happening?

I felt Christina put her arms around me and I rested my head on her chest. "You know, you told him you were sorry before you closed your eyes," she said.

I lifted my head and looked into her soft hazel eyes. "I did? I don't remember that," I said.

"Of course not," she said. "It's because for that one moment, in your conscience you knew that you were wrong, and your good side took over."

"I want to ask him," I quietly replied. "I should have let him explain everything to me before I lost my cool."

"About the conversation?" she asked.

"Yeah," I replied with a heavy heart.

"You'll get to soon enough," she said as she hugged me closer. "Soon enough."

XXXII

Peter

James woke up early the next morning not feeling the slightest bit rested. He had tossed and turned all night long wondering what would become of Serina. His one and only mission today was to get to the town of Sluos and find Taurus. He hurried around the room grabbing his stuff and then he looked at Serina, her eyes still shut and no movement of breathing. What did he expect? That overnight she would wake up and be all right? James gently lifted her body off the bed and headed downstairs.

"Morning," the innkeeper greeted him.

James nodded at him. "Is my horse ready?" he asked with urgency. James wanted to waste no time getting to the next town. He wanted to reach there by night; hopefully, Taurus would be able to fix this. Knowing in his heart that he might not be able to, James shook his head, trying to rid his mind of the thought and keep moving forward.

"Ready and waiting," the innkeeper announced proudly. There was a moment of silence between the two and James knew he wanted to know more. "Is she…?" he asked, almost afraid of the answer.

James looked at him. "I don't know," James said, but knowing in his heart of hearts that it was a strong possibility. "Have to get to Taurus, and quickly," he said.

"Then go, my boy, and do it fast. We need the two of you back together," the innkeeper said, as he slapped James on his back and ushered him out the door.

James found Midnight impatiently waiting at the gate, and the sight of James and Serina seemed to give his some hope that James did not see. Midnight's fire started to burn brighter as James walked over toward him and got on. "Do you know something I don't?" James said as he patted Midnight on the head.

Midnight nodded his head up and down as if to answer and started to take off out of town. James held on to Serina tighter, not ready for the fast pace that Midnight was ready to go. He watched the road ahead of him and the burnt trees that lined the road seemed to blur. James looked down at Serina. "Well, obviously he knows more than I do. Hopefully, once we get there you'll be with me again."

Midnight had started to slow his pace. James took notice and looked around him. He saw a man sitting in the middle of the road who looked confused and scared. Midnight slowed to a trot as the man got closer.

"I wouldn't go in there, mister," the man said. Then he noticed Serina's lifeless body and started to back up.

James looked at him and then back at Serina. "I'm taking her to get help," he said. The man started to run toward the town of Nomed as James huffed and rolled his eyes. "I wouldn't go that way, either. It's worse there than it is here!" James yelled.

"Worse than there?" the man said as he slowly came to a halt.

"I just came from that way, and yes, it's worse there than here," James replied.

"How do I know you're telling me the truth?" the man asked.

James took a deep breath and closed his eyes. "What does your heart tell you?"

The man studied James for a moment and started back slowly. "What happened to the girl?" he asked.

"She was attacked," James said. He knew that talking with this man was something that probably needed to be done, but all he wanted to do was go and see Taurus.

"How do you know about what's around here? How'd I get here, and where exactly is here?" the man asked.

James looked down to see the man standing next to him, still sensing that the man was afraid of him. *Why shouldn't he be? He sees me riding a black horse with blue flames that burn at his hooves and me carrying a dead girl*, James thought. "You are in a place that will give you a chance to make the right decision this time," James answered. "What is the last thing you remember?" he asked.

"I was on my way to the store, and then nothing but darkness," the man replied.

James looked down at the man and saw the nuisance that had made its way around him. The man must have taken notice and sat still. "What is that?" the man asked.

"Why don't you try telling me the truth," James asked wearily. James wanted to get this conversation over with quickly and move on to more important things—like getting Serina to Taurus.

"What?" the man asked, as if what James had asked him was insulting.

"The truth. On how you got here," James repeated himself.

"Are you calling me a liar?" the man snapped back.

James gave him a wary look. "If you tell me the truth then it might go away," James said, nodding his head toward the nuisance, which seemed to be making itself comfortable with its newfound friend. The man watched as the nuisance stared up at him with an evil grin, its long pointed fingers waving at him. The man shivered as he watched drool from the nuisance's mouth run down as if it were going to eat him.

"I was…I was selling drugs and the police caught me, so I stole a car and it turned into a chase. I didn't realize how fast I was going and I hit something. I knew it was wrong, but I'm young and I could clean up my act later." The man shrugged. James watched as the nuisance started to back away. The man took notice of it, too. "What's it doing?" he asked.

"You're telling the truth and it doesn't like that," James explained. "How old are you?"

"Twenty-three," the man replied with confidence.

"What's your name?" James asked.

"Smoke," the man answered. James watched as the nuisance's head perked up and smiled. "What?" the man exclaimed. "It's the truth." James looked at him doubtfully. The man sighed and then answered. "Fine, my real name is Peter. My mom named me after some guy in some book."

James raised his eyebrow at the man. "Do you know from what book?" James asked.

"The one they use in church. You know, my mom's a Bible-thumper," Peter said as he gave a quick grin. The nuisance seemed to like that comment; it jumped up and down, moved closer to Peter, and hugged his leg.

"What's it doing?" Peter asked.

"Making a new friend," James said. The whole thing came together. Peter was here not because of what he did, but because of his mother. His mother knew deep down that her prayers would keep him safe, and he had knowledge but he refused to see it. James reached into his pocket, pulled out his book, and showed it to the nuisance. It bared its yellow rigged teeth and hissed as it backed away. He showed it to Peter. "This is the book you were referring to?"

Peter eyed it. "Yeah. My mom's is bigger and she carries it with her everywhere," he said.

James leaned down toward Peter. "You want to know something?" he asked. Peter nodded his head. "You're in a place and a position to make a decision. This book is forbidden here, so you'll have to keep it hidden. Read it and study it, and it will give you all the answers that you seek."

"Will it tell me how to get back home?" Peter asked, his eyes wide.

"Yes, it will tell you how to get back home. When you get back home, make sure that you thank your mom for everything she has done. The thing that is here with you will slowly disappear as you learn more from this book. At night you can keep it away from you with this book. Remember, it doesn't like the truth. You might even learn the meaning of your true name in that book, Peter," James said. "Would you like mine?" James asked as he urged the book toward Peter.

"Why? Have you found the way home? Can't I just follow you?" he asked.

James looked at him. "I'm not going home. I'm here for another purpose," he said as Peter looked at Serina.

Peter nodded his head. "Oh, that's right. Yeah, man, you might want to get her a lot of help," he said as he took the book from James.

"Remember, you need to go back the way you came. It's safer there than it is out here or behind me," James said as Midnight started to slowly walk away.

"Thanks!" Peter said. "By the way, you never told me your name."

"My name is James, and I was named after someone in that book, too," he said with a smile. "Good luck, Peter." Midnight started to walk faster and broke into a run as James looked behind him. He watched as the man held the book in front of him and the nuisance kept backing away. "It's not a toy," James said under his breath as the wind rushed by him.

He knew that he had lost time, but not how much. James looked up to see the sky turning dark and knew that it would be night soon. Midnight must have sensed James's worry and started to run harder. "Sorry about that, but our work is never done," James said as he looked at Serina lovingly. "Taurus will be in the town and he will know what to do."

After what seemed like hours James finally arrived in the town of Sluos. Midnight, needing no direction, again headed toward the tavern where Leonard was waiting for him. Leonard's smile turned to a look of death when he saw that James was carrying Serina's body. James quickly jumped down and started walking toward Leonard. "What happened?" Leonard asked.

"A battle and it's her father's fault," James answered him with a snarl as he looked down at Serina.

Leonard shook his head in disbelief. "What are we going to do?" he asked.

"Is Taurus here?" James asked.

Leonard shook his head. "Not yet. Is he meeting you here?"

"Yeah. I need to get her into a room. I don't want people or things knowing she's like this. Have you heard rumors or anything like that today?" James asked.

"Nothing yet. The room upstairs is ready for you," Leonard said.

"Thanks," James said, as he entered the tavern and made his way upstairs. He gently put Serina's body on the bed and stretched his arms. His muscles ached from the position that he carried her in all the way here. James impatiently went to the window and looked out. "Taurus, where are you?" he said, watching the things move around through the town.

Brad stood near the fence at the tavern. He looked up to see the light shining through the window and saw the curtain move. *James must be looking for Taurus*, he thought.

Brad could feel a tear start to come down his face and quickly wiped it away. He looked at his hand as the thin blood stained his already pale hand. What had he done? He hadn't seen Serina since she was little and this was what happened when he saw her for the first time in many years. What could he have done differently? She had him pinned down, and by the looks of things she was getting ready to kill him herself. He felt another tear roll down his face. He slowly closed his eyes and thought of the time her mother showed her the light. The memory flooded his mind.

Brad could hear her mother and Serina talking. As he peeked through the door, he could see her mother on her bed and

Serina safely tucked in. She was arguing with her mother about falling asleep. Nowadays, at the age of seven, she was always arguing with her mother to see how far she could get. It was a game to her, and it made him smile every time she would try to convince her mother that her idea was the right idea.

"Mom…I'm afraid of the dark. I want to sleep with you and Dad," Serina whined.

Her mother brushed Serina's dark hair to the side. "Honey, there's nothing in the dark to get you. Besides, your dad and I are next door," she said gently.

Serina smiled a cute little smile and it made Brad smile. "You know…I'll fall asleep now, and in just a little while I'll climb in bed with you guys anyway," she said, proud of herself.

Brad laughed and quickly put his hand over his mouth. Her mother looked at the door and saw that he was watching. She smiled and then looked back at Serina. "How about if I teach you something that will protect you from the dark and everything that's in it?" she said.

Serina sat up. "Really? OK," she said, her smile bright and full of life.

Her mother lay her back down, took one of Serina's hands and held it up. "Make a fist," she said. Brad watched as the little hand balled up quickly in front of her mom as her mom laughed. "Now, do as I do. OK?" Serina quickly nodded her head.

Brad watched as her mother started to sing a tune as she put her index finger up. Serina watched with anticipation and followed her motions. Serina's little finger stood up. "This little light of mine, I'm gonna let it shine. This little light of mine, I'm gonna let it shine. This little light of mine, I'm gonna let it shine. Let it shine, let is shine, let it shine." Brad watched

Serina's eyes get wider as the tip of her mother's finger lit up and cast a small glow around the room.

"OK," her mother said. "I'm going to blow out the candle and you sing with me, OK?"

"OK," Serina answered in her little voice. Brad watched as her mother blew out the candle and started singing. Serina followed as the tip of her finger started to glow. Serina lay on her side, mesmerized by her talent. "Let it shine, let it shine, let it shine," Serina sang as she yawned.

"Now," her mother said gravely, "we don't let anyone know about this talent. OK?"

Serina nodded her head as she closed her eyes. "James said that it's a secret. It's our secret," she said.

Her mother gently kissed her head. "That's right. It's our secret." Brad watched as her mother lifted herself off the bed and walked toward the door very quietly. "Hey," she said, and kissed him.

Brad pulled her into his arms. "Will it stay like that all night?" he asked.

"Nope, only until she falls completely asleep," she said. Brad watched the light start to fade, until there was no light at all. "She's asleep," her mother said with a smile.

Brad was still standing near the fence as he hummed the tune.

"Thinking of happier times, are we?" Taurus asked.

Brad immediately recognized the voice and opened his eyes quickly. "Tell me she'll be all right! Tell me I didn't hurt my little girl," Brad said, and he grabbed Taurus by the arm.

"First, let go of me," Taurus said. Brad quickly let go of his arm. "Second, I'm not sure. I have to assess the damage. So it was you who did this to her."

"I didn't mean to. I'm sorry. If you have to trade my life for hers, then do it," Brad said.

Taurus smiled. "Now, you know I can't do that. Is he up there with her?"

"Yes," Brad answered. "Oh, please check on my little girl," he pleaded.

"All right. All right. Stay here. I'll be right back," Taurus instructed.

Brad watched as Taurus entered the tavern, and waited to find out what was to become of his one and only little girl.

Taurus knocked on the door and it swung open immediately. James looked back at him with worry. "Where is she?" Taurus asked.

"On the bed," James answered, as he moved to the side to let him in.

Taurus walked in and saw Serina lying on the bed with a wooden stake in the middle of her chest. For the first time, fear ran through his body. He didn't know how she was hurt, just that she was hurt. This was not good. "Tell me she didn't adapt," Taurus said with his eyes closed, although he already knew the answer.

"She did," James said with his head down. "Brad thought it would help. I tried to tell him it was a bad idea. This whole thing is my fault! I should've watched over her that night. I should've just kept on fighting her. She would have eventually worn herself out. Instead, I listened to someone I shouldn't have. Now this mess. Taurus, please tell me there is something you can do. Tell me I haven't lost her forever now."

Taurus gazed at James knowing that his heart was heavy. He looked back at Serina, who seemed to be asleep yet was not breathing. No, she would have to go back to her mother. Hope would be able to give James the answer he was looking for. James was smart, but still needed to learn not to give up or give in. Taurus took a deep breath and opened his eyes. "Let's take her to her mother," Taurus said. He turned around and vanished outside the door.

James gently picked Serina up and walked downstairs with her. He saw Taurus holding the door open as the Leonard waved good-bye to him. James nodded. "Thank you for everything," he said.

"No problem, my boy. Anytime. Take care of her," he said with sorrow in his voice. "Take her away from here."

James continued to walk out and could see the flames from Midnight lighting up the front of the tavern. Then he saw Brad and anger grew inside him. "What are you doing here?" James snapped.

"I…I just wanted to see her one last time," Brad said.

James quickly turned to see Taurus standing directly behind him. "You know the right thing to do," Taurus instructed.

James huffed. "That doesn't mean I have to like it," he said under his breath.

Taurus gently put his hand on James's shoulder. "You're right. That doesn't mean you have to like it, but you know the right thing to do."

James turned back around as Brad looked at him. "Say your good-byes and then we're out of here."

Brad slowly approached Serina and placed his hand on her head. "I'm…I'm so sorry. I didn't mean for any of this to happen. I love you. Your daddy loves you!" he cried.

James rolled his eyes. "We're wasting time. I have to get her to her mother."

Brad nodded his head. "I understand," he said as he backed away.

"Brad, you know how to get back. Make sure that you talk to her mother a couple days from now. OK?" Taurus said.

Brad just nodded his head as he watched James, Taurus, and Midnight slowly fade away from him. His heart felt empty and hollow. He felt his legs give out from underneath him; he sank to the ground and tears started to flow. He took no notice of the things watching him from the darkness that surrounded him, nor did he care. Whispers could be heard throughout the background, but nothing mattered to Brad. His little girl was dead because of something he did. He knew that word traveled fast in this world, and by morning everyone would know that Serina was dead and it was her father who killed her.

James looked around him to see that the party was all cleaned up. He couldn't remember how time differed from this world to one he was just in. He looked over at Taurus. "How long has it been?" he asked.

"About a week," Taurus said. "You moved quickly. I'm proud of you."

James looked down at Serina. "I don't feel like I did anything to help. I feel like I made it worse," he said, fighting back the tears.

"Don't blame yourself," Taurus said. "Let's see what her mother can do first."

"James!" her mother yelled, as she ran out of the back door and practically jumped off the porch. James could feel his strength starting to leave. Her mother hadn't seen the damage and his heart felt broken again. He watched as her mother's smile started to fade and her running slowed. She noticed Serina lying in his arms and a look of terror was in her eyes. "Serina!" her mother yelled, as her once light run turned into one of urgency. James felt his legs give out, and he knelt to the ground and placed Serina's body in the grass. Serina's mother was at her side in a matter of seconds and looked in terror of the way her daughter's body was.

"I'm...sorry," James choked out. "Her father..." He couldn't finish the sentence.

Serina's mother gasped. "Her father was there? Did she adapt?" she asked. James nodded as he wiped tears from his face. He watched as Serina's mother's eyes lit up and she smiled again. She even began to giggle. James gave her a puzzled look. How could she smile? Her daughter was in front of her, dead. She wasn't breathing, and everyone knows if you drive a stake into the heart of a vampire, it will die. Serina's mom waved her finger at James.

"I can tell what you're thinking," she said. She reached down, grabbed the stake and dislodged it from her chest. It made a *squish* sound as she pulled it from Serina's body. James winced just from the noise as he watched her throw it to the side. It hit the ground with a soft thud. "What usually happens to vampires when they are staked?" her mother asked with a smile.

James, still not understanding, went through the stories he had heard. "They die...they burn up...they turn to ashes," he said, feeling around for answers.

"OK. And Serina didn't do any of those things. Her body is still intact, and look, her blood is still flowing," she said, pointing to the gaping hole.

James watched as new blood started to pour out. He quickly put his hand over it to stop it. "She still isn't breathing," he said.

Serina's mother looked at her. "Yeah, that could be a slight problem."

"A slight problem?" James gasped. "I think it's a big problem."

"Remember who you are. Remember who she is…who we are," her mother answered him. She gently placed her hands over his. "Close your eyes. Remember the last time you saw her alive. Her smile, her laugh, her being."

James saw it. James saw her again the night they went to the ball. Her long dark hair flowing down her back. Her smile that could light up a room. Her laugh that day on the boat when she learned her new trick. She was his one true love.

—⟋⟍—

"Tell me more," I said, looking at Christina. "I want to know more and hear more about my life."

Christina laughed. "You still have to figure some of this out on your own," she said. "I can't give you all the answers."

My heart sank. I felt an overwhelming sense of sadness start to well up.

Christina must have taken notice, as she looked at me with concern. "Is everything all right?" she asked.

"I thought you said that we don't get sad here," I said, fighting back tears. Why was I sad? I had been happy the whole time I was here. What was happening to me?

Christina smiled. "We don't. Do you feel sad?" she asked.

I nodded my head. "Yeah, really sad. Like it's starting to hurt. My heart feels like someone has ripped it in two."

"Then it's time for you to go home," she said. "I've told you enough stories for tonight, and now you have to go," she said, standing up.

"I don't want to go," I said. "I want to stay here in this perfect place. I don't want to feel sad and I don't want to feel angry and—"

Christina pressed her finger to my lips. "Shh. It will be OK. You'll be here soon enough, but your work isn't done yet. You and James and all your friends have so much more to do. Besides, James is waiting for you." I sighed. The thought of James made me feel worse. I had to go back and tell him how sorry I was for all that I accused him of and all that I did. Christina smiled. "Saying you're sorry is probably the hardest thing to do. Admitting you're wrong is something to be proud of, not ashamed. It means that we all make mistakes. Remember there is only one person who is perfect."

"You know him better than I do. What do I say?" I asked. "I mean, how do I start?"

Christina smiled as she hugged me. "Just tell him that you're sorry. He'll forgive you and all will be well," she said, and gently let go of me. "It's time for you to go home. It was nice talking with you, and keep in touch. Watch over my boy. He can get a little…careless sometimes. Send them all my love," she said as I watched her slowly disappear.

I felt my body start to feel tired as I lay back down on the softness below me. I would be seeing James soon. The thought made me smile as I closed my eyes and drifted off to sleep.

XXXIII

Sorry

My mom watched as the hole slowly closed up and the blood faded away. She watched as my chest started to move up and down lightly, and she knew that I was breathing. She waited in anticipation for me to open my eyes. I opened my eyes to see my mother looking down at me with a smile. "Mom?" I said hoarsely.

"Hi, honey," she said gently, tears starting to form in the corners of her eyes. I watched as she looked over to the side of me.

I looked up to see James with his eyes shut and tears running down his face. "James, what's wrong?"

He opened his eyes and a look of shock spread across his face. I felt myself being lifted and my head hit his chest as his arms wrapped around me. "OK…losing feeling here," I said as he let me go.

"I'm sorry," he said. "Did I do that?" He looked over to my mother.

My mother shook her head. "If it's not time, the two of you have the ability to heal. James, you thought she was dead. She wasn't. If she was completely evil, she might have burnt up or turned to ashes. Her guardian side wasn't going to let that happen."

I looked up at my mother. "I was dead? No, I wasn't. I was talking with Christina. Who, by the way, told me to tell everyone hi and that she loves you guys."

James and my mother looked at me. It was James who asked what they both must have been wondering. "You talked to my mother?"

"Yeah, she told me a lot," I said.

"Like what?" my mother asked with a smile, as she sat on her knees to listen.

"Well, for starters, it seems like our fathers are more than they appear," I said as my mother smiled. "I mean, Mom, just how old is Dad?" I asked.

"He's forty-two," she answered with confidence. "He looks good for forty-two, too. I mean, I might be a little biased, but he does." She smiled.

"This year, or like fifty years ago? After you erased my memory you went back to Dad. He knew all about you. No, he was sent here to watch over you," I said.

My mother looked at me, embarrassed. "Yes, he was sent here to watch over me. To make sure that I kept my end of the bargain."

"So he and James's dad are in on this, too. I'm just not sure exactly how," I said.

James looked at me, baffled. "Did my mom tell you all this?"

I shook my head. "No, she talked to me—a lot. I started to remember—a lot," I said with a smile. "Anyway, I'm still not sure exactly what our dads do, but they have a purpose here, too."

She shrugged. "Guess that's just something the two of you will have to find out on your own," she said. "Keep going. I like hearing about our past."

"OK. So after James leaves, you guys stay here. Why? Because my dad wants James to know where I am—at all times. Little do we know that Alexis is fighting her own battles. She's fighting depression, and after seeing my mother's little fiasco it's like living her own mother's death all over again, although she was just a baby when her mother died. That night she was going to commit suicide. She had the gun and she was going to end her life. Christina, sensing something wrong, went into her room to grab the gun, but it went off. Not at the person it was meant to, but Christina. James and his father ran in, but it didn't look good." I looked over at James as tears started to flow again.

"I asked her to heal herself and she kept saying no. She said it was her time. She wanted to go home. We took her to the hospital, and that's when Taurus came to see me. Alexis kept telling my mom she was sorry and that it wasn't supposed to be this way. We had to make her leave. Before she left, my mother grabbed her hand and kissed it, saying that I was going to watch over her, and when the time was right she would be able to move on. She grabbed my dad's hand and kissed it as well, telling him that he would be able to watch over his daughter for as long as this took, and to watch over me. They both left, and Taurus asked me the same thing he asked you," James said. "I accepted, and that next morning we watched the sunrise as a family for the last time."

My mother looked at him with tears in her eyes. "I'm sorry," she said. "I didn't know that I would cause so much trouble."

I grabbed my mother's hand. "Mom, if there was one thing I learned from Christina, it was that everything happens for a reason. If it wasn't meant to be, then it wouldn't have happened. We don't go by our plans, we go by his," I said.

"Well, by gosh, I think that's the smartest thing I've heard you say since I've been here," Taurus said.

I looked up and practically jumped into his arms. "How are you?" I asked.

"Not expecting that," he admitted with a smile.

"I've learned a lot about you, too," I said with a bigger smile.

"I can only imagine. However, I'd like to know more about you," he said. "I'd like to know if you remember Emily."

I put my head down, knowing that I was wrong. I had made a mistake and I needed to make things right. I had fought him over this. Taurus looked at me and turned me around to face James. James looked at me through his understanding eyes as a smile crept across his face.

"Did my mother explain that to you, too?" he asked.

I shook my head. "I'm sorry," I said. "It's...I mean, what happened to her was all my fault."

James took my hand. "You were young and didn't quite understand."

"But you did," I said as I looked at him. "Why didn't you stop me?" I asked.

"Because, like you said, if it wasn't meant to be, then it would have never happened," he answered.

"But, she was so young," I started.

"A young mother," my mom said. "You did only what you thought was right."

"Didn't I break some kind of rule of free will?" I asked.

James looked at me. "Tell me the story."

"We were at dinner. We saw her sitting at a table with the new baby—she had to be only seventeen. She was depressed and sad and the nuisances that surrounded her were nasty. They told her everything—she was a failure, a shame to her family, she didn't deserve to live," I said. "I felt bad and went to the bathroom and cleaned up. I passed by her on my way back to the table. I couldn't help but to stop and play with the baby, so I did. I told her how beautiful he was and how beautiful she was. I gave them the same mark your mom gave Alexis and her dad. Is that why she was there?" I asked.

James nodded his head. "Yep, keep going."

"She went home that night and killed her baby and herself. She didn't want to live anymore with the guilt and the shame that she felt. She had asked for forgiveness, but she still had not forgiven herself," I said. "Is that why you were talking to her?" I asked.

"I gave her a book and told her that she needed to learn on her own. She did, and she still had questions. I just answered," James replied.

I felt like the weakest link. I had blamed him for lying to me and gotten angry at him for cleaning up my mess. "I'm sorry," I said as I threw my arms around him.

"You're forgiven," he said as he stroked my back. He pulled me away and I looked up at him. "On one condition," he said with a smile.

"What?" I asked.

"Don't ever turn into the big cat again or fight for that side," he said.

I held up my hand. "I promise."

"She can only keep that promise if someone can keep an eye on her," Taurus said. "Now, about your dads. I'll tell you the answer. Your fathers are seekers. They look for things you guys need. They have the ability to know where the artifacts are, things you guys will need on your journey here. I also have a feeling that, well, they too will get to rest since the two of you are back together."

"Really?" my mother asked.

"Yeah," Taurus said with a smile.

James hugged me. "I'm just glad you're back," he said.

"Me—" I stopped as I looked into my backyard and pushed away from him. I could see the dozen sets of little yellow eyes peering at me through the darkness.

"Serina?" James said as he looked at me. "What's wrong?" I pointed to the dark as he turned around to see the same thing.

"Are they out there?" my mother asked. "I can't see them anymore."

"Yeah, but these seem different. Did they follow us out here? Because that could be a problem," James said.

"They can't follow us here. They would have to be brought here," Taurus said, as James quickly took his stance and looked around.

My mother's eyes darted around the yard, trying to see what we saw. I could feel James grab my hand as we stood back-to-back. "Listen to me," he said softly. "They know you can see them now. They know you are here. One thing we forgot to mention on why your mother was so quick to hide you from all this is that now that you know, you've basically become a GPS for trouble. They can locate you now."

"I don't understand," I said, as I watched one jump into the tree above us. It glared down at me with its catlike eyes and snarled. I watched as it slowly stretched its leather-like wings and start to move like a cat in a tree. I could feel a scream moving up my throat but quickly exhaled, trying not to make a sound.

"James and you are different. The two of you are a product of both good and evil. Like humans, you have the choice to choose which side to be on. Remember, you cannot do both. Ever hear the term 'sitting on the fence'? You cannot sit on the fence," Taurus said. "Serina, you were a product of good and human at one time. It was only after your father did what he did and took you away that you adapted to evil. The guardian side of you refused to give in, thus making you the same as James," Taurus explained.

I watched as another medium-sized nuisance appeared in front of me and scurry back into the shadows. "Are they multiplying?" I asked.

"No, once you learn more, you're able to see more," James answered from behind me.

"So I am a walking GPS for trouble. Great!" I huffed. "So tell me about my friends. Do they have the same choice?" I asked.

James snickered. "They should be here any moment. We work as a team. We all have a job, and if they decided to stick it out this long, then we should see them."

"So you're telling me that everyone knew, but me," I said.

"No, everyone forgot. It's just waking them back up again. You see, Serina, once you remember, then everyone follows. You follow the leader," Taurus said as he backed up toward the porch, leaving James and I surrounded.

"Where are you going?" I asked, watching him.

"I don't fight. You guys fight," he said.

"With what? I haven't learned enough," I said. I felt James shift his weight behind me and in an instant he was right in front of me. I had to look again because I almost didn't recognize him. He wore a black chest plate with a two swords that crossed down the middle of it. I looked down to see his arms were covered with black leather arm bracers with a red design that etched its way up each. He looked like a modern-day knight.

"Take a look at yourself. Not too long, we have company. Serina, you've already changed," he said, as he lifted my hands up to my face. I looked at my arms with the white bracers that touched to the tip of my middle finger. I saw a gold vines with gold leaves etched in the white leather that surrounded the cross that started at the base of my middle finger and stretched out to my elbow. I looked down to see the white outfit, which was not much different from my cheerleading outfit. Gold outlined the bottom of the skirt and a gold leather strap went across my body. I felt something hit my shoulder and quickly turned to see nothing there. I put my hand behind my head and felt a handle. I brought out a gold double-edged sword with writing that went down each side of the blade.

"I haven't seen that in ages!" James said as I looked on in amazement.

"What is it?" I asked. "Besides the obvious."

"It's a warrior's sword," James said. "I'm a little surprised to see the warrior outfit, because I thought they were only for the warrior angels, but stranger things have happened."

I felt the weight of the sword in my hands as the tip of it slowly sank to the ground.

James snickered. "Forgot how heavy it was, huh?"

"Still remembering," I said as I raised it up again. I watched as the darkness that surrounded us started to grow more pairs of yellow and red eyes. "So, do you think I remembered enough? I mean, I really don't want them multiplying any more than they have to."

"We can do something about them if you would like," James said.

It was at that moment I heard the heart-stopping scream of my mother. I turned around to see her suspended in the air, gasping for breath. James took his place beside me and waved his hands in front of my face. In an instant, I saw the tall figure of a man with his arm stretched out to the side of him as my mother's helpless body dangled from his grip.

"You know the worst thing about what your mother did when she passed this on to you, Serina?" Luther smiled as I stared at him coldly. "It was that she turned human, and unlike her state before she can break like humans, too," he said, as he slowly started to twist my mother's neck.

"NOOO!" I screamed as something whizzed by my ear. I watched as a golden arrow struck Luther in the shoulder and he released his grip on my mother. Taurus quickly helped my mother to the porch as Luther tried to get the arrow out. He touched it and it burned his hand.

I looked behind me to see Mandi jumping down off from tree and Matthew with what looked like a machete killing the nuisances behind us.

"Sorry. We're a little late," Mandi said, out of breath.

"Yeah, man. Why'd you start the party without us?" Matthew asked as he came up beside James.

James smiled. "The party is just starting."

XXXIV

The Team

Luther stared intently at the four of us as we stood waiting for him to make a move—Mandi to my left, James to my right, and Matthew to the side of James. "So there are four of you now. Where are the rest?" Luther laughed, still trying to get hold of the arrow.

"You'll never take it out," Mandi said with a smile. "Don't you know the truth hurts?" she asked.

Luther laughed. "I'm not sure how much the truth hurts. Let's ask my son. James, you seem to be the only one to stand out in this crowd of do-gooders. Everyone else is in white and light. You seem to be the only one in dark. Do you know why?"

James smiled. "'Cause I like to be different. It's OK. It'll be funny when you see your own armor coming after you, won't it?" he taunted.

"You don't deserve those colors!" Luther said with a snarl.

"Then take them back!" James yelled.

Luther stepped toward us as another arrow hit his other shoulder. "I wouldn't take another step," Mandi threatened. "I have an endless supply." She smiled.

Luther looked at me and extended his arm toward me. "After all I've taught you, child. After everything I did for you. I gave you a nice bed, your own castle, and this is how you repay me?"

"You lied to me! You stole me from my room. I owe you nothing!" I said with hate in my voice. "Not to mention you just tried to kill my mother. You think I want anything to do with you? You're sadly mistaken."

Luther's eyes turned hard and flames seemed to dance behind them. "I will ask one more time and then I'm taking you back. Serina, come back with me."

"You threw her away when you thought she was dead!" James yelled at him. "Why do you want her now?"

"She's a key and I need her to open something for me," he said with an evil grin.

Everyone stopped and looked. Taurus seemed to be taken aback by this new revelation.

"James, what is he talking about?" Mandi asked, not taking her eyes off Luther.

James stood there for a moment and smiled. "A key for what? Why don't you open it yourself? I mean, I know you're old, but I'm sure Tim can find you a key."

Luther stood straight up. He knew that not one of us understood what he needed. He clasped his hands together. "Not one of you knows," he said, looking around. "Taurus... you know, right?"

Taurus looked at him with fear in his eyes. "You're the father of all lies. She's not a key! She can't help you in any way."

Luther threw his head back and laughed as he waved his long slender finger back and forth. "Taurus, you of all people should know that she can get into things that others can't, and with the help of my son they can both get into other places. I want what's in that room and behind that door! Why do you think I came to Christina in her time of need, when her husband was always away? I needed good to mix with evil. Now look, I have two of them."

I looked at James as he looked at me. "I think he's crazy," I said in a whisper.

"Crazy? You think I'm crazy?" Luther asked. "My dear girl. if there is one thing that you need to learn is that everything happens for a reason. There are no mistakes. Look at the world around you. You think the sky is blue on accident? You think what your mother did to you was an accident? Nothing happens without cause! You think your father met me by accident? No…I waited for that. I waited for him to be so desperate to live forever with your mom and you. You see, when Christina took James from me I needed to replace him. That poor unsuspecting girl that happened to walk by just as your mother healed that solider was there because I put her there. The townspeople were afraid of witches. I was the one, along with my pets, that made them afraid. I was there telling your father to drain the life out of you. It wasn't until a few minutes of watching behind your little eyes that I knew he would never be able to. I saw the light behind your eyes, the light that was so bright I was afraid it was going to burn me to death. Then I watched as your little arm lay helpless at your side. Your father cried, thinking that he had killed you. I saw the little fangs in your mouth and watched as they slowly disappeared and you took your first breath. You hadn't died. The guardian side wouldn't let you. Why?" Luther asked me.

I stood there in disbelief as he went through my life. I thought about it. Why? Why didn't I die? I shrugged my shoulders. "Obviously you know the answer. Why?" I asked.

Luther smiled because he knew that he had beaten me at this game. He turned his attention to Taurus. "Taurus, why didn't Serina die that night? Hmm?" he asked.

Taurus looked at him with wide eyes. "He's stalling for time. Get rid of him!" he shouted.

Luther's smile grew even wider. "Either you don't know or you don't want them to know," he said. "What a shame. And you call me the father of all lies. Tsk, tsk, tsk."

James was growing tired of this game. "It was knowledge that doomed us all from the beginning. So when I do meet my maker, I'll make a note to ask him myself about all this," he said as he leapt forward.

I watched as James was thrown back into a tree and Luther laughed. "Still have a lot to learn, son. Still have a lot to learn."

"Serina, listen to me," Mandi said. "Choke the life out of him."

"What?" I asked. "Did you see what he just did to James? I wouldn't be able to even reach him before I'm thrown that way, let alone wrap my hands around his throat."

"You don't have to get close to him. Throw your energy toward him and lift him off the ground. Act like you're choking him from here. Try and feel your hands wrapped around his neck," Mandi said.

I extended my arm in front of me and cupped my hand. I watched as Luther's body was lifted off the ground and he struggled to catch his breath. His long fingers tried in vain to loosen the hands that weren't there. I could hear his heartbeat in my head.

"Remembering…some…things," he said between breaths. I could feel my fingers tighten as he breathed in. The anger that raged inside me was being taken out on him.

I could feel my energy start to drain and my fingers start to slip.

"Not out of anger!" James said as he walked up behind me. He put his hand on my shoulder, and I felt another surge of energy run through my body and my grip get stronger. "If you do this because of revenge, because of something evil, it will only last so long. We do this to protect ourselves and others. He's not meant to die yet," James said.

I moved my arm slightly and saw that he moved with it. I cocked my head to the side and quickly found the large oak tree in the back of the house. I swung my arm around, opened my hand, and everyone watched him being tossed through the air and hitting the tree. I turned around and looked at James. "Sorry. I slipped," I said with a smile.

James rolled his eyes at me. "Really? You slipped?" he said as a grin started to form at the side of his mouth.

"That slip is going to cost you, my dear!" Luther said as he slowly stood up. I felt my feet leave the ground and my body being thrown back. I closed my eyes and waited for an impact but I hit something soft.

I opened my eyes to see the white coat in front of me. I stepped back as Starr looked at me. "Starr!" I shouted. I threw my arms around her neck as Midnight jumped over us. I watched in awe as the blue flames lit the area around us.

James quickly mounted Midnight as Matthew and Mandi joined us. "I can distract him from above," he said.

"I can send some more arrows his way," Mandi chimed in.

"I can try and distract him from down here," Matthew said.

James looked at me. "Serina, your sword is the thing that's going to send him back. We need you to get close enough to him and get him out of here," he said.

I nodded my head as I mounted Starr. Midnight started to run toward Luther. I watched blue fiery wings emerged from each side of his body and he lifted into the sky. James circled above Luther.

Luther laughed. "You do know that I want that horse, my boy!" he said. He was quickly cut off as an arrow hit him in his neck, and I watched as Luther fell to his knees with his hands clutching his throat.

"Serina! Now!" James yelled.

As Starr took off running toward Luther, I took the sword out. I watched as we got closer to Luther and I stuck my sword down to strike him. Then I felt sharp claws dig into my shoulders, and before I knew it, I was being lifted into the air. I looked above me as one of the winged nuisances looked down at me with a grin. "Let me go!" I shouted as I felt its claws dig deeper into my shoulder. It sent a wave of pain as we climbed higher into the sky.

"James! Get her!" Mandi shouted.

James looked up to see that the nuisance was taking off with me and Midnight started toward it. I could see Midnight catching up and kept a good grip on my sword. "Serina! Your sword, swing it!" he yelled.

I lifted it up and pain seared through my arms and shoulders. I saw that the words on my sword had lit up, and I watched as the blood started to run down my arm as I raised it. The nuisance made a screech and dust settled in around me. I felt my body start to descend, and terror filled my being as I realized that there was nothing underneath me. "Help me!" I screamed.

"You don't have to yell. I'm right here," James said, as I opened my eyes to see him smiling down at me. "What? You don't think I'd just let you fall. Do you?"

I threw my arms around him. "Thank you!" I said. "I have a confession. I don't like heights."

He looked at me quizzically. "Something else you'll have to remember. I do think that it was you that taught me how to land on my feet from that high up," he said as Midnight landed on the ground. He helped me down as the nuisances started toward us. Mandi looked around and shot arrows at some of them. James put his hand on my shoulders and I felt the warmth as my wounds from where the thing had me at my shoulders closed up.

"Another plan?" Matthew said, out of breath.

"All of you will pay for this!" Luther said.

We watched him pull the arrow from his throat. Smoke rose from his hands as he touched the golden arrow, pulled it out and threw it at the ground.

I extended my arm in front of me, grabbed him by the neck, and pulled him closer to me. The others watched as his body was dragged across the ground toward us. He looked up at me with a smile. "What are you smiling at?" I asked.

"When…you get strong enough…it will be fun…to watch you…die," he said.

I lifted the sword above my head and watched as the words on it glowed against the gold. With all my might I swung it down, only to watch Luther disappear and the sword dig into the earth in front of me. "Where'd he go?" I asked.

"Back to where he belongs," Mandi said with a smile.

"Like I said," James said, "we will fight him later. It's not his time yet."

"Yeah, but when it is his time, I think you should get the first crack at him, James," Matthew chimed in.

I looked over at Mandi and she smiled at me. I was excited to see her. She was part of the team that would help us out on our journey. I smiled as I threw my arms around her. "Hi!" I said.

Mandi stepped back. "Hi. We've missed you," she said, looking at me.

"I've missed you, too!" I exclaimed.

"Hey there, bro," Matthew said as he hugged James. "Took you long enough to come back. Hey, here's an idea. Next time you decide to leave, at least leave a number," he said, laughing.

James looked at him. "I'll have to remember that. Of course, I'm hoping there won't be a next time."

"So, where are the rest of us?" Mandi asked, looking at me.

"I dunno," I said. "Are Holly and Anna one of us?" I asked.

Mandi smiled. "You know she has a bad memory," she said, looking at James.

James smiled. "She has her mother to thank for that." James hugged me. "Of course, this time I think we can handle it—so there won't be a next time for us having to jog her memory."

Mandi turned back to me. "Yes, they are both with us, along with Adam," she informed me with a smile.

"What about Heath?" I asked.

"That's just Holly's boyfriend for the moment. He won't be around too long, though," Matthew said. "She won't be happy about that. I mean, I think she was starting to enjoy just living the human life for a while, so she may not be too pleased about our team anymore."

"Why not?" I asked.

Matthew sighed. "Because Heath refuses to remember. Holly has to because of what she is. She was made for a different reason," he explained.

I took a step back from James. "Holly was made for a different reason? She isn't like us?" I asked. Matthew shook his head. "Then what was she made for, and how does she fit into all this?" I asked.

"You'll find out when she gets here, and then you can ask her yourself," James said. He took the sword out of the ground and looked at it. "Have you taken a real look at this?" he asked.

I took the sword from him and looked at it. The gold shone even in the dark of the night, and there were words inscribed on the blade. I took a closer look to see what they said. *In the beginning,* I read. "It's the whole—"

"Yes, and that's what keeps you safe," Taurus said as he came up behind us.

"Serina!" my mother shouted as she hugged me. "Let me look at you," she said as she stepped back. "Taurus, I don't understand. That's a warrior's outfit. Why does she have that? She's not a warrior. Is she?" she asked.

Taurus looked at me and studied me for a moment. "I'm not sure myself, but I will make a note of it to ask," he said. "It doesn't make sense. You, her mother, are a guardian, and her father was something evil. I'm not sure why she would have a warrior's outfit. However, I would say that she has earned it."

"It's so beautiful," my mother said, still admiring the outfit. "I love the gold trim that goes around the bottom of the skirt. I love the crosses on the arm bracers and the white boots with gold crosses with wings behind them! This outfit is gorgeous. I don't think I've ever seen a white so bright!"

Taurus laughed. "That's because here on Earth there isn't a white that bright," he said. "There are a lot of colors that don't exist here on Earth that will surprise you once you get to see them."

"James!" I heard Alexis scream. We turned to see her running toward us. "James, I've missed you!" she said, running into his arms.

James smiled as he hugged her. "Missed you, too," he said as he ruffled her hair.

"Ugh! I hate this thing. Change into something normal," she said, pounding at his chest plate.

James smiled and backed up. "It doesn't make me look dashing?" he asked.

Alexis crossed her arms with a smirk. "No, it makes you look dark. That's not who you are," she huffed.

James smiled, and in a blink he was in his jeans and T-shirt. He held out his arms. "Better?" he asked.

"Yes!" she said, hugging him again. She looked at me and gasped. "I love your hair!" she said, quickly letting James go and coming toward me. She lifted some of my hair up and let it fall. "I love the sparkle."

"What are you talking about?" I asked as I pulled some of my hair to the front. It was then that I noticed the gold that intertwined through my black hair. It did sparkle. It looked like Starr's tail and mane.

"OK," Mandi said as she put my hair back. "We need to get in touch with Anna and Holly."

"One step ahead of you," Taurus said, and ushered us back toward the house.

"Hey, Mandi," I said, looking at her. "Are your arrows like my sword?" I asked.

Mandi looked at me. "You mean with the writing and everything?" she asked. "Yep, that's why I said the truth hurts." She smiled.

I looked down to see myself back in my jeans and T-shirt as we walked into the house. "So what did you mean, you were one step ahead of us?" I asked Taurus. He just smiled as the doorbell rang.

"We have company." James smiled as he ran toward the door.

XXXV

Anna's Choice

My mother moved ahead of James and answered the door. There were Anna and her mother. Anna's mom hugged my mom with tears in her eyes. "Is it true?" she asked between sobs. "Serina remembers?"

My mother nodded her head and pointed to me. I waved at Anna's mom. "Hi," was all I could think to say. I could sense that the tears were not tears of joy. They were tears of sadness and worry.

Anna came up and hugged me. "I thought something happened to you. I had a dream—a terrible dream. You were in a room and there was a panther, and I thought it was going to attack you and you would die, and it was horrible," she said, hugging me tighter.

"It wasn't a dream, Anna," Taurus said, coming out of my parents' study. "It was a vision."

Anna looked up and saw Taurus. She studied him for a moment. "I know you," she said. She slowly let go of me and made her way cautiously toward him. "I think I know you. I mean, you seem familiar."

"Hello, Edana," Taurus said. "Haven't seen you in a long time."

Anna's mom rushed over to him. "Please don't take my one and only," she pleaded. "She's all I have."

Taurus's eyes became stern. "Are you starting to play the same game Serina's mom played? I have to remind you that she lost," he said.

"We never in a million years thought Serina would remember," she said. "This life is all these kids know and nothing has happened to them since. We've taken very good care of them. They have all they need to live and survive. We even have funds set up for their futures. They're fine. They don't need this life," she pleaded to Taurus.

"Hi," Mandi said as Matthew came up behind her.

"Hi," Matthew chimed in.

Anna's mom's eyes became wide. "They're all here? Mandi, where is your mom?" she asked.

"Yes, Mandi. How is Faith? I haven't seen her in a long while," Taurus asked.

"She's fine," Mandi said. "She's at home. She actually told me to get up and go, that I would remember on the way."

"Did you remember?" Taurus asked with a smile.

"Yep, nothing much to it. There's a lot to do. A lot that we need to do as a team," she said. "I'm glad we're back."

"Matthew?" Anna's mom looked at him for an explanation. Something she might be able to use against all that was happening around her. She wasn't about to let her one and only go so easily.

"My parents basically told me the same thing," he said. "I agree with Mandi. We need to get the team back together.

We have a very important mission here and have to make up for lost time."

Anna's mom looked back at Taurus. "She's happy with who she is. She is fine." She faced Taurus eye to eye as she grabbed Anna by the hand. Anna quickly yanked her hand back. "Honey." Her mom smiled sweetly at her. "We need to get home. Let them deal with this. They have Serina, James, Mandi, and Matthew. Those four can do all the work that is needed. You can come home with me and not have to worry about a thing."

Taurus crossed his arms as he looked at Anna's mom with a deadly stare.

Anna looked at me. "What is going on?" she asked. "What team? The cheerleading team? What is happening?" she asked as she crossed her arms.

The room looked at me. What was I to say? I didn't completely know the whole story. I remembered a lot, but I didn't know Anna's story. "See that man over there?" I said, pointing to Taurus. "He's really nice, and he can tell you everything you need to know," I said.

"Did he tell you everything?" she asked with a smirk, as if to question his integrity.

"Yep…well, I learned a lot from James," I said. "Taurus knows a lot about us. A lot of what we were put here to do. You know, I always felt as if I was meant to do more and felt like something was missing in my life. Taurus talked with me and explained what my mother wouldn't and what your mother won't, either. All you have to do is listen and from there make a decision," I explained.

Anna's mother turned her attention to James. She slowly walked over to him. "Oh my goodness," she said. "It is you. I mean I've seen you, but never really paid attention."

"Edana," my mother said. "I told you all this at Serina's birthday. Why is this such a surprise to you?" she asked.

Anna's mom's face turned to anger. "I never thought that you would let her remember. I went to bed that night knowing that she had looked at Taurus confused and he'd just walk away."

Anna looked at me. "What is happening?" she asked. "Why do I feel like I should remember all this?"

"Because you should," Mandi said. "We are special. We have many talents."

James stepped in between them. "Listen to me, Anna. You'll have a choice to make tonight. Everyone here you will remember in time for exactly who and what they are. It's your choice and your choice alone. If you decide to remember, then I promise we will work as a team to help you remember."

The doorbell rang again as we all jumped. My mom answered it. "So am I late for the party?" Adam shouted as he walked in. "Hey there, guys," he said as he walked over to us. He hugged Anna and looked at her. "Isn't this great? All of us back together."

Anna looked at him, confused. "I…don't remember," she admitted.

Adam looked at her as he slowly let go of her. "I… thought…Taurus is here and everyone's around," he said as his smile slowly faded.

"Her mother stands in her way," James said.

"It's not your concern and it's none of your business!" Anna's mom shot back.

I'd had enough. "It is our business. We work as a team! Anna, look, go talk to Taurus and everything will be cleared up," I said as I moved her toward him.

Anna looked back at us with concern in her eyes. "Anna..." Her mother went over to her. She took Anna's face in her hands with tears in her eyes. "Answer his questions truthfully. Don't ask any, just answer his," she said with a grin.

Anna stepped back from her mother. "What?" she asked. "I answer all his questions and I don't ask him any? Why not?"

Anna's mom smiled. "Because it's what's best for you. Trust me," she pleaded. I felt the ping of anger hit me. James grabbed my arm and shook his head as I stood there with my arms crossed. Anna looked back at us one more time as she entered the study and Taurus closed the doors behind him. Anna's mom looked at me with hate in her eyes. "Why now?" she asked. "Why would you want to change your life?"

"I felt out of place. I felt cheated not knowing about my life. I don't want Anna to feel that way and neither should you," I shot back at her.

"Yeah, but at least we had a chance at a normal life," Holly said as she appeared beside my mom.

"Holly," I said as I walked toward her. She shied away from me. "What's wrong?" I asked.

"Some of us don't have the luxury of a choice," she said with an attitude.

"What do you mean?" I asked.

"Some of us weren't born into this life. We were made for this life. We were assigned a team and then we got a taste of the life here on Earth and actually enjoyed it. But then, out of nowhere, someone shows up and helps to jog someone else's memory, and now I have to go back to feeling like a failure," she said, her eyes never leaving James.

"Are you blaming me?" James asked. "If you are, just say it."

"Of course I'm blaming you!" Holly shot back. "Why couldn't you just leave well enough alone? We were happy and having a good time."

"I wasn't happy," I said. "I felt like something was missing in my life. Like I didn't belong."

Holly looked at me. "Are you kidding me? You had it all. The good-looking boyfriend. Captain of the cheerleading squad—which, by the way, I made sure you got because I didn't want you to even think about not fitting in. I wanted you to enjoy the life around you. The popularity. All of it. You had it all, and then you go back to this."

Holly's rant had struck my heart. I had always wondered why she had not made cheer captain. It was because she made sure that I was the one who was constantly busy, and tried to keep my mind off what I was supposed to be doing. This whole life that I'd lived was nothing but a lie. My mother lied to me and my friend helped her. This wasn't a life—this was the perfect-life syndrome that everyone helped create for me. I wasn't going to stand for it anymore. I drew in a deep breath, keeping my anger under control, and confronted Holly about the life that, along with my mother, she helped to create.

"I had someone who treated me like a trophy instead of a person. I'm still the captain of the cheerleading squad, and who cares about popularity. Where does it get you?" I asked. "I now have someone who cares about me. I have my friends and now I feel like I'm actually making a difference," I said. "Why do you feel like you're a failure?"

Holly looked at me. "You don't remember what I do? Of course," she said with a smile. "Figure out what I do." She sat down on the floor with her knees up to her face. I started to sit next to her, but she put up her hand to stop me. "Don't. I'm just here to see what Anna decides," she said.

Adam looked over at James. "She'll blame you until the end of time," he said. "You'll be the reason she goes back to living this life and putting her back to doing what she was meant to do all these years. I don't think you'll be friends for a long time, not until she gets over this."

"I don't expect anything less," James said as he watched Holly sit on the floor with a deadly stare.

I walked up to him. "So you want to tell me her story?" I asked with my arms folded.

"It's her story to tell. Just give her some time," Mandi said. "Look, she throws a fit and then in a matter of days it's over."

James grabbed me by my waist and pulled me to him. "Would it matter if I told you her story?" he asked with a grin. "You're her friend and you'd side with her anyway."

I was taken aback by this. I would side with her anyway? No, she just told me about her help in all this and he expected me to side with her. "Does she not like you? Or is it just the situation now?" I asked, still not unfolding my arms.

"It's the situation now," Adam said as he looked over at Holly.

I looked at Adam. "So what's your story?" I asked.

"Me?" Adam asked. "I find things. My family has done it for years," he said. "I just happened to find this team and a cute girl," he smiled.

I rolled my eyes. "So, are you here for the team or for the cute girl?" I asked.

"Oh. Now she sounds like a leader." Matthew laughed. "It's good to hear Serina finally sound the way she was! It gives me goose bumps. We finally get to fight and have a good time again. Fight for what's right and protect people. So, yeah, Adam, are you here for the team or the cute girl?"

Adam shrugged his shoulders. "Ultimately the team. The cute girl is definitely a bonus," he answered with a sheepish grin.

"What could be taking them so long?" Mandi asked as she eyed the door and her watch. "James, did it take Serina this long to answer Taurus?"

James shook his head and looked at the door.

"She's probably in there asking him, like, a million and one questions," Adam said. "She's like that. Why is this and what is that."

"It wouldn't be happening if we all decided to stay in the same place as we were. We could all be home right now, relaxing and getting ready for the weekend," Anna's mom said coldly.

"Now, Edana," my mom said. "It took me years to figure out that what I was doing was wrong. You'll see this team has potential."

"They're kids. Look at them!" she pointed toward us. "Not just that, Hope, they're our kids. Our flesh and blood. We're supposed to be protecting them like any normal parent would."

"They look like kids," my mom corrected her. "They are just like us. How old are we?" she asked with a smile. "Because they look like kids, we have to remind ourselves that we ourselves still look like kids to some people."

"They're our kids," Anna's mom said. "I don't want to see them hurt. I want Anna to grow up and go to college, find a man that she will marry, and have grandkids for me. I want to see her safe, and not have to worry about whether or not she'll be fighting something that she may not come home from."

"Have faith. He will protect them. Guide them. And keep them safe. I had to learn the hard way that we were given the opportunity to raise them and that they have always belonged to him. He will make sure that they will always have what they need, when they need it," my mom said. "I mean, look at us. For centuries it was just Christina and me, and then later we found you guys. The two of us worked alone, but our children have the opportunity to work together and with each other. Anna will never be alone. She'll always have them to help her."

Anna's mom sighed. "That makes sense. Being a mother here is a lot harder than just working from home," she said.

My mom hugged her. "I know it is. Look at them," she said, as they watched us talk and laugh. "They will be fine."

Anna's mom shrugged. "I guess they do have it easier than we did. They have each other from the beginning. Their children will get to grow up together as well. We didn't have that until just recently."

I noticed Alexis walk around us and toward Holly. She sat down next to her and started talking. Holly seemed to be entranced by the floor, never moving. Alexis put her arm around Holly and she leaned over. As I walked over James grabbed my arm. "Let her be. She needs time to get over this," he said. "It's a big shock. She has to go back to doing what she does."

"What does she do?" I asked. "I mean, we help people. What is the worst thing in anything that we do?"

Everyone looked at me. It was James who answered me. "Serina, we have the easy job of fighting. We protect and try to keep everyone safe—"

"That's the easy part?" I asked sarcastically.

"Compared to what she does," James said, "yes. Our battles only try to help hers. At the end of the day, it's her battle that makes the difference."

"I don't understand," I said.

"You will in time," Mandi said as the door to the study finally opened.

We all turned to look as Anna stood there with Taurus behind her. She seemed confused and a little scared. We sat still to watch what happened next. Holly slowly rose and looked at her. Anna smiled at her. "Go see them," Taurus said.

Anna looked at me and started to run. "Serina!" she said, throwing her arms around me. "Why would our parents keep things like that from us? Why?" she asked.

"Because they think that they are protecting us," I answered. "Did he answer all your questions?" I asked.

"Yeah, but I still feel like we're divided," she said, as she turned to see Holly with her arms crossed.

"Holly," Mandi asked, "are we divided?"

Holly looked at us. Her icy stare chilled me to the bone as she shook her head. "Not divided, but not happy, either," she said, and slammed the front door behind her.

Anna's mom slowly walked toward her. "Anna," she said softly as Anna turned to face her.

"Mom," she said. "Why? Why keep this from me? Do you understand how dangerous that is?" she asked.

"I guess I wanted the same thing Serina's mom wanted for her. I didn't want to see you hurt. I wanted to protect you from all this," she said.

"From what? Things that I would be able to see later? I would rather see what I'm dealing with now, rather than later. Later, it might be too late," Anna said.

Anna's mom wiped the tear that ran down her face. "I know," she admitted. "It's harder to live here. The emotions of everything. Anna, when you're at home it's always happy.

Always light. I never felt like I needed protection because I was protected. Then I get here and it's like…a whole other world. I felt like I needed to protect you to keep you safe. It's so…just so hard being here."

Anna hugged her mom. "I know, and I grew up here," she said with a little laugh. "I have my friends and I'm sure they wouldn't let anything happen to me."

Anna's mom looked at her. "You look older now…well, more mature."

Anna rolled her eyes. "Yeah, Mom, how old am I, anyway?"

"Not as old as James and Serina," she laughed.

"James is older than me," I said with a smile.

"Not by much," he shot back.

"We are all old, and if we had to live that way they would encase us in a museum and put 'oldest living people' on our plaque," Mandi said. "So, I take it you're here to stay with us."

Anna looked at her and shrugged her shoulders. "Guess you're stuck with me," she said. "I still don't know what I do to help."

"That's easy!" Matthew shouted. "Your homework. Your mom's name means something. Look it up and it will give you a clue."

Anna looked over at Taurus. "I thought you said they would help me, not give me homework!" she grunted at the thought. "I do enough homework for school!"

Taurus threw his hands up. "If it makes you feel any better, they aren't making it any easier on Serina, and she needs to know more—fast."

Adam pushed his way toward Anna and picked her up. "I am so glad you decided to stay," he said, kissing her.

Anna smiled. "I have a bone to pick with you, too," she said, half laughing. "Why didn't you say anything?"

"I had to wait to hear from Serina," he said. "I never heard from her, but once James came back I knew that was it. We were going to be back."

"What do we do now?" Anna asked.

"Now the battles begin," Taurus said. He opened the door and motioned for us to follow him outside.

We stood on the front porch and looked. Anna watched in amazement as she started to see the little yellow eyes that peered at her from the darkness. "What are those?" she asked.

"They're a nuisance," Mandi said, as she watched one back further into the shadows.

"Is that what we fight?" Anna asked.

Adam put his arms around her waist. "Yep, but not tonight."

"Yeah, not tonight. We already had a battle tonight. I'm not sure if I can handle another one just yet," Matthew said. "A little out of practice and all," he said, stretching his arms over his head with a smile.

Adam slugged him in the arm. "Come on! You know if you had to you could."

Another nuisance came up to the porch and studied us for a moment. I could see out of the corner of my eye that Anna was holding her breath as it put its hand on the porch to lift itself up.

I bent down to get in its face as it cocked its head at me. "If you know what's good for you, you'll leave," I said. It looked at me again and hissed, baring its teeth at me. I shrugged my shoulders. "I warned you," I said. I waved my hand and watched as it was flung back into the darkness. The little yellow eyes watched in terror as the nuisance disappeared from sight and I listened as twigs started to break. They were moving away from the house. They would be back. Just not tonight. Tonight they were going to spread the word that the team was back together. Tonight they were going to warn the others of things to come. I looked up at James. "No more fighting tonight. I'm ready for bed." James looked at me with concern. "What?" I asked.

He pulled me close to him. "I dunno. I guess from what happened last time. I don't know what to do," he said.

I looked at him, confused, and behind his eyes I could see him reliving the night I was taken. My door shut. I could hear my screams and the pain of him knowing he couldn't get to me. "Oh," I said. "Do you really think they'll try again?"

James sighed. "Luther will send Tim back, but I'm not sure if Tim will come knowing that I'm still around. Still, I don't know how to make you safe." It was in that moment that I saw James's eyes light up as he snapped his fingers. He quickly let me go and whistled. Everyone watched as Midnight and Starr appeared in the sky, running toward the house. Midnight landed in the yard as James greeted them.

"No!" my mother protested. "Horses belong in the stable. They are not staying here," she said.

James turned around. "Yes, horses belong in a stable." He turned back to face Midnight. We watched as he talked to Midnight, and both Midnight and Starr seemed to disappear. Then, James was being pulled by something back toward the house. "Dogs can come into a house, right?" he asked as two big dogs pulled him along. The first dog had Midnight's color and red eyes. It was a Rottweiler. The second was a white American Eskimo dog.

I looked on in shock. "Starr?" I asked, as the white dog came up and licked my hand. I put my hands through the soft coat and buried my face in it. "What did he do to you?"

"What?" James said. "She still has her star."

I looked to see a small brown star that covered her right eye as she looked up at me. "So, what are you thinking?" I asked.

"Well," James said, "the two dogs could sleep with you in your room…if your mom says it's OK." He smiled.

Anna bent down. "I want a dog!" she said.

My mother came over and looked at the two dogs. "Change Midnight's eye color. I mean, if Serina wakes up in the middle of the night it would scare her half to death," she said.

James bent down and looked. "Yeah, I guess brown may be better," he said, as Midnight looked up at him with a smile. "There you go. All better?"

My mom looked. "That's better," she sighed. "They can come in, I guess."

And with that, the dogs ran into the house and up to my room.

"They better not pee in my house!" my mother yelled up to them.

They both looked out my door, and then quickly ran back downstairs and into the yard. We all laughed as we watched them run around the yard sniffing at the trees.

My mom walked over to James and handed him a bag. "Your dogs, you clean up the mess," she said.

James rolled his eyes and smiled. "Promise," he said.

Anna looked at me. "Will those things come back? You know, the nuisances."

James smiled. "Not tonight, but soon. Right now all they need to know is that we are here and back together. Let them sleep tonight in fear."

Epilogue

I lay down in my bed and let the covers engulf me. I felt something jump up on it and quickly got up to see Starr in her dog form. She came over and licked my face. "Hi," I said, petting her. "So, I guess you and Midnight will be watching over me tonight," I said, as Midnight lay down on the floor next to my bed.

Starr turned in circles until she got comfortable and lay next to me as I snuggled deeper into my covers. I shut my eyes, wondering where the next adventure would lead us. I had my friends and now we were a team. My life had gone from nothingness to something. I felt like I was going to help make a difference.

"SSSerina," the raspy voice called out from the darkness. I bolted up and looked around the room.

Starr lifted her head. I looked at my window and it was shut. The door to my room was still open. That was a battle in itself. James insisted that my door stay open. He won because the light of the hallway shone a little into my room. He even put a hinge on my door to keep it open. I looked down to see Midnight was still there and obviously did not hear the voice. "Still getting used to this, girl," I said, petting her. I lay back down and shut my eyes. I waited to hear the voice again—still nothing. I relaxed a little and cuddled next to Starr.

It was in that instant I heard my door trying to shut again. I watched as it tried to swing forward. I rolled my eyes. "Not again!" I said as I heard a low growl at my side.

I looked down to see Midnight was standing up. The hair on his back stood straight up as if he was waiting for something. Starr stood at the end of my bed growling. I threw the covers back to get out when Midnight jumped at me. He barked.

"What?" I said, putting his massive head between my hands. "What is it? What's in here now?" I asked.

Midnight cocked his head and whined, then jumped back down and growled. I watched as he slowly moved toward my door that was still trying to close. Before I could follow him, I felt something tug at my shirt. I turned to see Starr looking at me with sad eyes.

"Do you want me to stay up here?" I asked, as my door slammed shut and Midnight barked and growled. I couldn't see anything. I snapped my fingers and the lights came on, and I looked around the room. There was nothing there.

Midnight paced the room. He walked from my window to the door, barking.

"SSStupid dogssss," the voice hissed.

I watched as Starr put her ears down and growled. Midnight looked frantically around my room, climbing under my bed and back out. He suddenly stopped, put his ears down, and growled at the door. I slipped off my bed and headed toward the door. I reached to turn the knob when the door bowed in. I screamed.

"Serina!" James yelled. "Are you OK?"

"I'm fine. Don't break my door!" I said, as I turned the knob and opened it.

James pushed by me. "I told you I want this door open!" he said, walking toward my window.

"I didn't close it," I snapped back. Midnight, now by his side, looked up at him.

"Where is it?" he asked, leaning down toward Midnight. Midnight whined and panted. He looked over at me. "Where is it?" he asked.

"I don't know. All I know is that I heard it," I said.

"What is going on?" my mother asked with a yawn, as she appeared at my door with her robe on and her hair pulled back. "What is happening now?"

"I'll never be able to sleep in my bed again." I pouted with my arms crossed.

James quickly left and Midnight followed him. My mom came in and hugged me. "It will be all right. As soon as you learn more, you'll be able to do much more and protect yourself." James came back in with pillow and blanket in hand. He waved his hand and a single mattress was placed in front of my vanity. He put the pillow down and spread out the blanket. He went back over to the door and fixed it again.

"Does my door still have my eyeliner on it?" I asked, remembering that I had written Luther's name on it. I really needed to clean it off—or maybe James could clean it off for me. I smiled at the thought.

"What?" James asked, still trying to fix the hinge.

"Does my door still have my eyeliner on it?" I asked again.

James looked at the back of the door. He waved his hand and looked at me. "All clean," he said with a smirk.

"Thank you," I said as I climbed back in bed. Starr lay down next to me.

"The door stays open," my mother said, "if this is what the sleeping arrangements will be."

"Not a problem," James said, still looking out the window.

"James," my mother said, "try and get some sleep. If they know you're here I'm sure they won't come back around." James ignored her and continued to look out the window. This infuriated my mother. "Go to BED!" she said as James turned to look at her with her arms crossed. "NOW!" she said.

James knew he was defeated at that point and lay down. As she began to turn off the lights, she noticed the light switch was in the off position. She sighed. "Serina, turn off the lights," she said. I snapped my fingers and the lights went out. "Now, both of you get some sleep," she said, and went back to her room.

I sat there in silence as Midnight snuggled close to James. "So…what happens when our fathers come home? You can't stay here sleeping on my floor forever," I said.

"Watch me," James said. "I lost you twice now. Third time is not a charm." He sighed. "Besides, one day I won't be sleeping on the floor. One day I hope to be sleeping next to you."

I smiled at the thought. One day he might be sleeping next to me, with his strong arms wrapped around me, keeping me safe. I sighed lightly and closed my eyes. "Good night," I said.

"Good night." He smiled as Midnight sighed and closed his eyes.